The shotgun blast echoed in the steel and concrete stair-well like a dynamite explosion, rocking Cody back against the wall. Before the sound faded she felt Creed propelling her forward again, his fist once more closed around her coat, lifting her to her feet, keeping her going.

Who was this guy? she asked herself. And how in the world was she going to get away from him—if, by some chance, they got away from Bruno?

At the next landing, he slammed into a door leading to the outside, and in the next second the two of them were stumbling out onto the roof.

"Come on," he insisted, urging her into a run.

A flash of light and the sound of the door banging open again had him making a sudden, lightning-quick change of direction. In her leather-soled shoes, she had no traction, and she slipped, landing against him with enough force to send them both tumbling.

"Geezus," he ground out between his teeth, falling into a slide and taking her with him, his arm coming around her.

Cody went down on top of him, and the two of them careened across the roof, heading for the edge. A low wall kept them from going over, but he couldn't stop their slide, and they ended up jammed behind a ventilation unit in a tangled heap of arms and legs.

In the middle of scrambling to his feet, he suddenly froze, still on his knees, and pulled her tight against him with his gun hand, his other hand going over her mouth.

She heard it, too, the sound of someone approaching, their footsteps crunching through the snow and slip-sliding every few steps on the ice.

He caught her gaze, his warning clear—don't move, not a muscle.

CRAZY
WILD

Tara
Janzen

A DELL BOOK

CRAZY WILD
A Dell Book / February 2006

Published by Bantam Dell
A Division of Random House, Inc.
New York, New York

Dell is a registered trademark of Random House, Inc., and
the colophon is a trademark of Random House, Inc.

ISBN-10: 0-440-24260-6
ISBN-13: 978-0-440-24260-4

Printed in the United States of America
Published simultaneously in Canada

www.bantamdell.com

OPM 10 9 8 7 6 5 4 3 2 1

THIS ONE IS FOR THE
REAL "WILD BOYS," C. ROYCE AND KARL,
WITH RESPECT, APPRECIATION, AND MY MANY THANKS.

AUTHOR'S NOTE

Anyone familiar with the beautiful city of Denver, Colorado, will notice that I changed a few parts of downtown to suit the story. Most notably, I took Steele Street and turned it onto an alley in lower downtown, a restored historic neighborhood in the heart of Denver known as LoDo.

CRAZY
WILD

$\mathscr{P}$ROLOGUE

Washington, D.C.—Thursday evening

IF HE'D HAD a window in his office, General Buck Grant would have been staring out of it, watching the snow fall on the nation's capital while contemplating the possibility of retirement, the somewhat remoter possibility of saving his ass one more time, and the truly remote possibility of reining in the unruly crew of hotshot Special Defense Force operators under his command.

But in the L-wing of the lower basement in a World War II-era bunker complex east of the city, there wasn't a window or a snowflake to be had. He was hell-and-gone out of the loop at the Pentagon, and the reasons why had been very neatly spelled out for him—again—in the letter in his hand.

UNITED STATES DEPARTMENT OF DEFENSE
Office of the Honorable William J. Davies
*Assistant Secretary of Defense for Special Operations
and Low-Intensity Conflict*

To: General Richard "Buck" Grant
Re: Special Defense Force (SDF)
Mission: Containment/Crisis

Buck,

Put a leash on your boys, now. I know we all signed off on the Colombian job, targeting the rebel forces that killed J.T. Chronopolous, but rumors are leaking out of South America faster than spin hits the fan in an election year. Your guys are running wild all the way down to Peru. *Los asesinos fantasmas?* What the hell is that? The ghost killers? Don't bother to tell me *who* it is. I narrowed it down on my own, and I want both of their butts back stateside ASAP. I've got a job for your team—top priority.

- **Creed Rivera**—a ghost killer if I ever heard of one. Jesus, Buck, your jungle boy isn't even cleared for active duty, and with his psych evaluations, he might not be for a long time. Pull him out, and the next time the boiler starts up in the room next to your office, remember this.

- **Peter "Kid Chaos" Chronopolous**—ghost killer, and obviously damned good at it, but he's running on guts, vengeance, and nothing else, which is a good way to get killed, which we can't afford. I need him in Denver.

- **Christian Hawkins**—okay, I know Superman was in South America: Kid didn't take out all those murdering rebel bastards I've been hearing about on his own. But I suspect Hawkins had enough sense to come home when

Rivera replaced him. If I'm wrong, make it so. I need him in Denver.

- **Dylan Hart**—he's the ramrod of this wild bunch. Call him in Manila or Jakarta or wherever the hell he is, and tell him to lay down the law to these guys, get his ass on a plane, and call me on a secure line, immediately. I need him in Washington. His mission is on hold. The Colombian mission is over. I know two of the rebels are still on the loose, but tracking them down is just going to have to wait. We have a crisis on our hands.

A nuclear warhead crisis, Buck. Somebody's got one, and they're selling it on the black market. This morning's intelligence reports point toward the deal going down in either Houston or Denver, or hell, maybe even Wichita. God only knows why this has landed in the U.S. heartland, but that's where the spooks say it's headed, and your boys have been tagged. The bomb is Soviet. The woman selling it is Czech. And the crisis is international. Everyone from Israeli Mossad to MI6 to the CIA is after the seller, and the secretary of defense wants your SDF team to deliver her, in chains if necessary. He wants Hart, Hawkins, and Chronopolous on this thing yesterday. The orders are black, off the books, and straight from the top—the *very* top. I don't need to say more.

I'm counting on you, Buck, and I know you're counting on your pension. Hell, you can't afford not to, so let's not make any mistakes.

Buck stared at the letter and swore under his breath. He had a problem. Three of them. Hawkins had disappeared on the world's longest honeymoon, somewhere in the South Pacific. It could take weeks to track him down, and that was if he wanted to be found, which Buck highly doubted. He could find Hart, but the guy was working so deep undercover, it would take a couple of days to even make contact with his contact. Chronopolous was a done deal. As soon as his current mission was over, he was on official loan to the U.S. Drug Enforcement Agency's office in Bogotá, Colombia.

Which could have left Buck and his pension in kind of a bind. Davies wanted Hawkins, Hart, and Chronopolous, and the best Buck could deliver on short notice was the psycho jungle boy and a clairvoyant street rat named Skeeter Bang who ran the office at SDF's headquarters in Denver. Somehow, he didn't think that was going to go over very well in the hallowed halls of the Pentagon—at least not until Creed hit the streets.

Then all bets were double-downed, hard.

Buck didn't have any trouble wagering his pension on SDF's jungle boy. Even half broken, Creed Rivera was twice the warrior of any honcho cruising the Pentagon's E-ring. He always got the job done, whatever it took. He had the warrior's code in his heart. It was embedded in his bones—and that's where it counted, by God.

Two days, that's what it would take to get Rivera out of the mountains of Peru and back to the States. Buck knew exactly where Creed was and what he was doing. All he had to do was pull Creed off the chase and order him to leave—to leave Kid, to leave the mission half undone, and to leave while Pablo Castano and Manuel Garcia, the last two murdering rebel bastards, were still alive.

Davies had been right. A leash would have come in damned handy.

CHAPTER

Peru, South America—Thursday evening

TIMING IS GOING to be everything," Creed said, watching the two-and-a-half-ton truck grind its way up the switchbacks on the steep mountain road below them.

Next to him, Kid Chaos Chronopolous let out a short, humorless laugh.

Creed lowered the binoculars and wiped the back of his hand across his mouth. Behind them, the sun was setting on the high peaks of the Peruvian Andes. A light mist of rain turning to snow filled the air.

That was fine with Creed. He preferred his revenge cold.

They'd been in Peru for three weeks, traveling the desolate backcountry of the Cordillera range, roughing it out of an old army Jeep with no windshield, no doors, and no roof—waiting for Castano and Garcia to make a run for Puerto Blanco, the rebels' last refuge.

They weren't going to make it.

Kid reached for the binoculars and set them to his eyes. "Two guys in the cab."

"Castano riding shotgun," Creed said, pulling his black stocking cap lower on his head, then reaching around and tying his hair back at the base of his neck.

"Garcia at the wheel," Kid confirmed. He was unshaven, his skin burned brown by the sun, his dark hair long and shaggy from his months on the trail. He and Creed had chased Castano and Garcia from the jungles of Colombia and across the fetid swamps of the Amazon, like hounds on the scent, down the length of Peru.

But this is where it ended, here in the wild mountains in the wind and the snow.

"This remind you of something?" Creed asked, gesturing at the weather, before reaching for his pistol, a Glock 10mm. His knife was in a sheath on the right side of his tactical vest. He checked the load on his pistol and returned it to its holster. The action was automatic, rote. The actual weapon of choice for the night was on the ground at his feet, locked and loaded: an RPG-7, a Soviet special Rocket Propelled Grenade launcher.

"The Shah-i-Kot mountains, Afghanistan," Kid said. "That night it started to snow, just like this, just as we were ready to move out." They'd both been doing recon out of Kabul for a major offensive against the Taliban and al-Qaeda, Creed with another group of operatives from Fort Bragg, and Kid with the Marines.

"Yeah, that's what I was thinking, too." They'd gotten exactly what they'd gone after that night. Tonight would be the same, or Creed would die trying. He didn't have any compromise left in him, not for this mission.

"Wait a minute . . ." Kid hesitated and adjusted the focus on the binoculars, then swore under his breath. "We've got a problem."

"What?" Creed looked up.

"There's a third guy in the middle—but . . . it's not a guy."

"They're taking a woman to Puerto Blanco?" *Fuck.* That changed everything.

"She's gagged."

And that *really* changed everything. Creed's jaw hardened. He knew what Castano and Garcia had done to Kid's brother before they'd killed him. The nightmare was etched into every breath he took. He knew their demented brand of brutality—and he could imagine what they would do to a woman, what they'd probably done to a lot of women.

"Okay. So we can't just blow the truck." That had been the plan. Blow the friggin' truck right off the side of the mountain and send Castano and Garcia straight to hell.

"No, *mi hermano,*" Kid said after a long, silent moment, still looking through the binoculars. "We're going to have to do this the hard way."

Creed could tell Kid was trying not to sound too

satisfied, but he did—damned satisfied, as if the woman's abduction had played right into his hands. Without wanting to, Creed knew exactly where Kid's satisfaction came from. He understood it—and he wished to hell he didn't. There was a world of difference between wanting someone dead and wanting to kill someone. Kid wanted to kill Castano and Garcia—face-to-face, hand-to-hand, take their lives from them the way they'd taken his brother's.

So did Creed. The need drove him—had been driving him ever since he and J.T. Chronopolous had been ambushed in Colombia six months ago. Their mission for Special Defense Force, SDF, a clandestine group of special forces operators who worked out of the underbelly of the U.S. Department of Defense, had been compromised beyond all repair. Worse, he'd lost J.T., his partner.

Creed had nearly died himself, been beaten to within an inch of his life. He still had places on him that hurt, places that were never going to work right again. He didn't know why the National Revolutionary Forces, the NRF, a rebel group fighting the Colombian government, had killed J.T. and let him live. He probably never would—but he couldn't forget it. The fact haunted his days, made him break out in a sweat every night while he slept, even in the frigid highlands of the Andes.

"We're going to have to take them in Puerto Blanco," Kid continued.

"Well, that ought to get real damned interesting." *Shit*. Puerto Blanco was a hellhole, a magnet for every thief and murderer in Peru. There was no law in Puerto Blanco, not that he and Kid were counting on anybody else to save them if things went bad. On the contrary, they were the guys who *guaranteed* that things went bad, real damn bad, real damn quick. Kid Chaos hadn't come by his name by accident.

Three governments had sanctioned them to take these men out, and not one of them expected two SDF operators to need any help doing it. The Defense Department wanted to send a message to the NRF: "Kill our guys, and you'll pay the price." The Colombian government just wanted Castano, Garcia, and every other rebel in their whole damn country to disappear, and Peru didn't like Colombia's bad boys crossing the border and stirring up trouble. So all the diplomatic gloves had come off. Creed and Kid both knew nobody was going to save their asses if they failed, but neither was anybody going to get in their way—which suited them both just fine.

The snow thickened, driven by a rising wind. In about ten minutes the sun would be completely behind the mountains, and they'd be driving to Puerto Blanco through a blizzard, in the dark, on a road whose winding curves barely clung to terra firma.

Or maybe they wouldn't.

Two turns below them on the mountain, Garcia shifted the deuce-and-a-half into a lower gear and the truck slowly ground to a halt.

"Looks like we've got another change in plans," Kid

said, handing the binoculars back to Creed and picking up his bolt-action M40 rifle. He set his eye to the scope.

Creed looked down the mountain. Sure enough, the bad guys were getting out of the truck and hauling the woman with them. One side of her face was bloody, and her blouse had been ripped. Creed let out a long, slow breath, glanced at Kid, then went back to the binoculars. No one else was on the road for as far as he could see, which didn't surprise him. In the three days they'd been waiting, no more than five vehicles had passed in either direction.

Garcia rounded the truck, a big grin on his face, a slouch hat pulled low on his forehead—and that's the way he died, his grin frozen on his lips for a split second as Kid's 7.62mm match-grade round hit him dead between the eyes, right through his hat, a sniper's cold zero. The man was crumpling toward the ground before the crack of the rifle sounded in the cold mountain air.

Castano quickly jerked the woman in front of him and pulled a pistol out of the holster on his belt. Crouching, with his back up against the truck, he peered over the woman's shoulder, his gun pointing up the mountain.

Creed was already on the move, heading toward the road, swiftly, silently, using what cover there was to keep himself out of Castano's sight. Kid's second shot went through the windshield, shattering it into thousands of pieces and spooking Castano into pushing the woman away from him. The Colombian dove underneath the truck. Creed saw him scramble across the road on the other side and take off running down the mountain.

Kid's third shot caught Castano in the shoulder, and the guy fell, tumbling and rolling down the steep slope.

Creed cleared the first stretch of road and kept running, ignoring the pain shooting up into his hip.

Leaping off the next embankment, he landed on his weak leg and stumbled, but righted himself and kept going.

Castano had barely made it to his feet when Creed caught him and brought him down hard. The two of them slid a dozen yards, grappling, before they came to a halt.

With lightning-quick skill, Creed cut the Colombian twice, trapping his wrist and slicing through tendons, then reaching down and severing the bastard's femoral artery at the groin. Each cut took less than a second to make. Both of them were executed with a razor-sharp, seven-inch blade. The man's gun fell from his disabled grip, and Creed picked it up and threw it farther away.

Breathing heavily, his heart racing, Creed set the tip of his knife above Castano's heart and watched terror flood into the other man's eyes.

He knew this man—his flattened, broken nose, the scar that ran from the corner of his mouth—knew his pockmarked face from endless nights of beatings and torture. Pablo Castano had been his and J.T.'s jailer. He'd been one of the men who had taken his knife to J.T.— and for that, he would die by the knife, slowly, with all the skill and ferocity at Creed's command.

He pressed the blade down and felt the thin layer of Castano's skin give way.

The man's breath caught on a muffled groan and

with a surge of strength, he pushed Creed back and rolled out from under him. Creed was on him again in an instant, holding him down, putting his knife to the rebel's throat.

Darkness moved farther up the slope with every passing second, sliding over them like a veil, taking the last of the light from the sky. Above them, up on the road, Creed could hear the woman praying for mercy, and he knew her prayers would be answered. But there would be no mercy down here on the side of the mountain— and no cold revenge. Everything inside him was hot, burning through him, setting his heart on fire.

From somewhere deep in his memories, a terrible sound came to him: a keening death cry, the scream of a man in agony beyond what he could bear. It echoed in Creed's mind, over and over again, making his hands shake.

He tightened his grip on the knife, tightened his fist in Castano's hair, and pulled the man's head back. The Colombian tried to struggle, but was weakening beneath him. Creed had cut him deep, making a river out of his blood—still, it wasn't enough.

Slowly, carefully, he increased the pressure of his blade on Castano's throat and just as slowly, lowered his mouth to the Colombian's ear. An awful pain lodged in his chest, making his words hard to speak, making his voice harsh— yet no harsher than the deed he was about to commit.

"*Dile al diablo . . .*" he whispered, "*que fue Creed Rivera quien te quitó tu vida.*" Tell the devil it was Creed Rivera who took your life.

CHAPTER

2

Denver, Colorado—Two weeks later

SHE DIDN'T LOOK like bait.

From where he sat in a comfortably upholstered chair, reading the newspaper, Creed watched the woman limping across the third floor of the Denver Public Library. It was her fourth trip from the reference section over to the copy machine. Each time, she made a couple of copies and returned to the reference desk. Each time, her mousy brown hair had come a little more undone from the scraggly bun at the top of her head, until the whole thing had completely given up and reverted back to a raggedy-edged ponytail—except the pencils that had been holding the bun were still stuck in the pony band.

And so he repeated to himself: She did not look like bait.

What she looked like was a scatterbrained librarian with pencils coming out of her head.

Carefully stretching out his left leg, Creed eased the pain in his hip, then rolled his shoulder. Sitting for long periods stiffened him up, and the library didn't close for another hour. Hell, he'd probably be half paralyzed by then, and that was about the way things had been going for him lately. He didn't know which was harder on him, the running around he'd done in South America or the sitting around he'd been doing since he'd come home, sifting through a lot of intelligence reports that never seemed to pan out and waiting for a Czech national with a Soviet missile to stick her nose out somewhere.

Well, if today's intel from the Defense Intelligence Agency, DIA, was good, she'd finally done it—here, in Denver, in the public library.

Kee-rist. He stretched again when a sharp pain cramped his calf. His body was a friggin' train wreck.

Reaching into one of the pockets on his cargo pants, he pulled out a couple packages of ibuprofen tablets and figured four ought to take the edge off.

The pencil lady was a little wrecked, too. She was wearing an ankle brace, and the strings were loose and trailing behind her, and her socks didn't match. One was definitely black; the other was a different shade altogether. The rest of her matched perfectly—painfully perfectly. Not only was her hair brown, but her eyes were brown. Her shoes were brown. The frames on her Coke-bottle-thick glasses were brown. Her big ugly sweater, though a lighter shade, was brown; so was her thick wool skirt. It had also been rolled at her waist, giving it an uneven hemline. The combination of her uneven hairdo, uneven hem, and uneven gait gave her the appearance of a floundering ship, a small, sort of skinny ship with a cargo of books in her arms—a ship lost at sea, being beaten by the waves, and no doubt about to be sunk by the force of the storm heading its way.

Bait, by its very definition, meant an allurement, an enticement.

Cordelia Kaplan was neither alluring nor enticing.

But then, neither was she Cordelia Kaplan.

According to today's intel, the Denver Public Library's newest reference librarian was actually an illegal immigrant from the Czech Republic by the name of Dominika Starkova, the supposed moll of a former Soviet KGB colonel. She'd been the current *belle du jour* of the Prague club scene up until she'd skipped town and ended up in the good old U.S. of A., in Denver, Colorado, working at the library and looking like a fishwife.

Through his work with SDF, Creed had known a few Eastern bloc colonels and their very expensive girlfriends, and Cordelia Kaplan didn't fit the bill, not even close.

Dominika Starkova did, though, in spades. The photo Dylan had sent from Washington, D.C., the one he had in his coat pocket, had been taken in Prague six weeks ago, and the girl had rocked—all legs and breasts and silky blond hair, her ass barely covered by a little silver dress, her mouth lush and made for blowing a guy's mind, if a guy went for bad girls . . . very bad girls.

The little librarian didn't seem to have much going for her in the legs, breasts, and lush mouth category. What she had going was the brown category.

He returned his attention to the newspaper he wasn't quite reading. If there'd been a mistake, then the quicker Creed found it out, the better off the scatterbrained young woman would be, because the storm heading her way was real. It was Creed's job to keep Dominika Starkova from sinking like a stone when it hit, to make sure she didn't complete her mission or slip through the government's net and run back to the Czech Republic. The fate of the free world depended on it—which unnerved the hell out of him, because he really wasn't up to the job. His track record on saving people's asses, let alone the whole freakin' free world, was pretty grim this year.

He lifted his gaze back up over the edge of the newspaper to the librarian. If she was Dominika Starkova, she'd come a helluva long way to sell a Soviet nuclear warhead. Of course, there wasn't a terrorist leader from Fallujah to Islamabad who wouldn't be happy to make the trip halfway around the world to Denver to buy it. As best as the alphabet soup of U.S. government intelligence agencies had yet determined, the missile had disappeared from a military base near Tbilisi in the Republic of Georgia during the dissolution of the U.S.S.R. and had never been accounted for by the Russians. Rumors had placed the warhead somewhere in the "Stans," a collective group of third-world countries carved out of the Russian frontier, but that was a helluva lot of territory. They needed better intel if they were going to find it. They needed the woman.

Blonde Bimbo with the Bomb—that's how she'd been described in one of the reports, the bait sent out by Sergei Patrushev, her ex-KGB colonel boyfriend, to soften up the clientele and keep them happy until all the players were in place and it was time to make the deal of the century. And it was the deal of the century that had gotten the attention of the United States government and its allies. They wanted the provocative Ms. Starkova stopped cold.

In the circles she usually traveled in, jetting from Moscow to Prague to Berlin, Denver was no more than a backwater, no less than an aberration, the last place on earth anyone would have expected her to pop up, which, of course, made it perfect.

Because the odds were that it was Dominika Starkova making another trip to the copy machine, except she wasn't a blonde, and the reference desk of the public library was not the usual haunt of bimbos—none that Creed had ever known, anyway, and it was a sad but true fact that he'd gotten tangled up with a few over the years.

Cordelia Kaplan—he watched as she made her copies

and headed back toward the reference desk, limping along, the strings on her ankle brace trailing on the floor. Behind the hair hanging in her face and her big glasses, she had a small, unremarkable nose and a mouth to match, a somewhat narrow chin, and cheekbones high enough to qualify as almost interesting, if not exactly classic; all the parts seemed to work together into a blandly acceptable whole. What she lacked was any spark. Stand her in front of a shelf of books, and she'd blend in to the point of disappearing, pencils and all— which made her damned suspicious looking as far as he was concerned. Camouflage of that caliber was an art, not an accident.

Halfway back to the desk, she stopped, her already colorless face paling even more before she suddenly changed direction and made a beeline into the nonfiction stacks.

Her hesitation lasted no more than a second, but it was enough to bring Creed awkwardly to his feet. Yeah, he was a real smooth operator all right. Ignoring the twinge in his hip, he casually folded his newspaper and cast a sideways glance toward the reference section. A man stood at the desk, one who hadn't been there a few seconds ago. Tall and barrel-chested, he was built like a bull, a bald-headed bull in a black suit and a Fu Manchu, his long mustache flowing past his chin. He was leaning on the counter, showing the librarian a photograph.

Hell, Creed thought, as the librarian nodded at the picture and peeked around the big man, pointing toward the copy machines. The man pocketed the photo, checked his watch, and turned toward the copiers.

Creed grabbed his coat and moved toward the stacks. Glancing down one of the long aisles, he saw Cordelia Kaplan dart to the left, and he picked up his pace to cut her off. If the bull with the Fu Manchu wanted the skinny librarian, he was going to have to get through Creed first—and it took more than one guy to get through Creed Rivera, even a busted-up Creed Rivera.

In that respect, he knew his looks were damned deceiving—which suited him just fine.

Slipping into his long, dark coat, he made the left turn just in time to see a blur of brown make a sharp right into the 900s, heading toward the stairwell door. Ms. Kaplan was running like a rabbit and seemed to have left her limp back in the 800s.

She left her sweater in the 920s.

He found her skirt balled up and shoved on top of the books in the 940s with the ankle brace. Her glasses and her raggedy ponytail were in the 955s.

Shit.

He broke into an out-and-out run.

There weren't many people in the nonfiction stacks late on a frigid January night with a blizzard blowing outside, but he came across five—exactly five, only five: a tall, thin man in a gray coat reaching toward a top shelf, a dark-haired kid sitting on the floor while his grandmother searched the 975s, a librarian he'd seen reshelving books earlier, and someone he hadn't seen before—a woman with short spiky red hair in a slinky black sweater dress and black boots walking past the stairwell door.

Geezus. She was good.

She passed the stairwell door and headed back toward the escalators in the middle of the library, probably feeling pretty secure in her new disguise, all of which could easily have been hidden under her other outfit and the brown ponytail wig. She could have stashed the boots in the library anytime. Still, she was one of the quickest quick-change artists he'd ever seen. Real quick, he thought, following her at a more sedate pace.

Maybe too damn quick.

He stopped when the woman did and watched her slide a book off the shelf. As if feeling his gaze, she turned and lifted her eyes to meet his—and he knew he'd been screwed.

It wasn't Cordelia Kaplan, or Dominika Starkova, or whatever she wanted to call herself. The face was all wrong, too long, the skin tone too olive, her eyes too far apart. Everything about the woman's face was the wrong shape.

Damn. He turned back around and quickly retraced his route. The librarian was still reshelving books in the 980s, but the grandmother was alone in her aisle. The "boy" was gone, the damned dark-haired boy, and so was the brown sweater that had been stashed in the 920s.

Son of a bitch, she was good.

He started cross-sectioning the nonfiction section, trying to catch sight of her, but the only other person he ran into was the bald man with the Fu Manchu, and he did it deliberately.

" 'Scuse me," he mumbled, brushing by the man in the stacks.

Five fruitless minutes of searching later, he got in the elevator going down and pulled the photograph he'd lifted off the man out of his pocket.

It looked like a school picture, and compared to the one General Grant had sent him, it was definitely more Cordelia Kaplan than platinum-haired Dominika Starkova. She was about seventeen in the photo, dressed in a school uniform, her long dark hair pulled back on one side and clipped up. She looked ridiculously young, oddly sweet, and too innocent to have ever ended up with a man old enough to be her father, or in the middle of an illegal international arms deal of world altering proportions.

Baldy was a different story. Creed quickly looked through the guy's wallet. Bruno Walmann was his name, computer parts were his game, with offices in Berlin, Moscow, and New York City. At least that's what his business card said—in German. He had fifteen hundred dollars in cash, half a dozen platinum and gold credit cards, a driver's license, a couple of restaurant receipts, and a few scraps of paper with phone numbers and addresses written on them—all good stuff, but not what Creed had come for tonight. He shoved the wallet into his coat pocket. It would all go to SDF, the organization that wrote his paychecks and assigned him jobs like the one he'd just screwed up.

Damn. He'd lost Dominika Starkova, which frankly unnerved the hell out of him. He'd never lost anyone he was tailing, not ever.

Shit. He'd promised himself a break, that all he had to do was get Castano and Garcia and his part would be over for a while. Someone else could handle making the world safe for freedom, democracy, and a latte stand on every corner. Cars, that's all he wanted now—to work on his cars and forget how fucking brutal real life could be, to forget how fucking brutal he could be.

Geezus, with the fate of the free world hanging in the balance, he couldn't even stick a tail. But at least he could report that the spooks and the pencil pushers in Washington had finally gotten something right. Cordelia Kaplan was no librarian.

Turning away from the information desk, he glanced at the exits on either end of the atrium that spanned the library. There was a pumped-up, flat-faced, gorilla-looking guy in a leather bomber jacket loitering in front of the west doors, looking very much like a hired gun. On the eastern end, another man stood in the center of the hall, out-and-out commandeering the exit onto Broadway Avenue, checking his watch and looking like he was hell-and-gone out of time and none too happy about it. His other hand was stuffed into the pocket of a very expensive, gray wool topcoat, his black hair combed back off a hard, carved face, everything about him speaking of money and power.

Creed swore under his breath. Dylan had sent him this guy's picture, too: Reinhard Klein, one of the nuclear warhead buyers identified by the CIA and the DIA. If Bruno was working for Klein, he was working pretty high up the ladder. Reinhard Klein owned and ran an international conglomerate that included everything from the controlling interest in an oil refinery in Azerbaijan to a fashion house in Milan, a string of hotels from Bern to Berlin, a lot of pricey real estate in the Czech Republic, and not a damned thing in Denver, Colorado.

Suddenly, things were getting complicated. Why would Dominika Starkova be hiding from one of her buyers, a guy she was supposed to be bringing in on the big deal? And why was Reinhard out in a blizzard, instead of holed up in a plush downtown hotel, waiting for Bruno to buck the cold and bring him the girl?

The whole setup smacked a little too much of desperation to do anything but put Creed even more on edge.

Shit. The frickin' fate of the free world was *always* hanging in the balance. Always, and God knew he'd done his part to save it at least twenty times in the last ten years. But the price for saving the free world had gotten too damn high, costing him more than he was willing to pay ever again.

Ever.

He'd left his blood and sweat on all seven continents for Uncle Sam, and unknown to anyone but himself, he'd left a bucketful of gut-wrenched tears on one—for all the good it had done him or his partner, J.T.

His best friend, J.T., who was dead.

Well, hell—he dragged in a deep breath—*that* was a place he definitely wasn't going to go tonight.

He scanned the library again, wondering whether or not Dominika Starkova had already gotten out, when she suddenly came into view—a dark-haired "boy" wearing an ugly brown sweater and a nondescript gray coat, riding down the escalator with her nose stuck in a book.

Hell, the escalator was going to dump her right at Reinhard's feet. He started across the lobby, determined to get to her first.

CASTING a quick glance up from underneath her lashes, Cordelia "Cody" Kaplan saw and instantly recognized Reinhard Klein. She swore under her breath, her already racing heart taking a quantum leap into overdrive.

Relax. Relax. Relax, damn it, she told herself, trying to ignore the sudden sick feeling churning to life in her stomach. *Stay cool. Don't give in to panic.* The moment she'd seen Bruno the Bull, she'd known Reinhard would be somewhere in the library, waiting for her. Bruno was Reinhard's favorite dog, and the two were never very far apart.

So suck it up and tough it out. All she had to do was act natural, make no odd movements or show any interest in anything other than her book, and slip into the fiction stacks as quickly as possible. She could make her escape through the service entrance on the north side of the building. Chances were Reinhard wouldn't recognize the scruffy kid on the escalator as Sergei Patrushev's club princess from Prague.

It would be a helluva stretch for anyone. Really. She knew what she looked like, and she did not look anything like Dominika Starkova. Not tonight.

Not ever again—so help her God.

Chances were she'd get out of this mess alive.

She swore again, silently, not inclined to self-delusion. She was in up to her neck, and the chances of her getting out of her current mess in one piece were slim and getting frighteningly slimmer. How in the world had they found her? Denver, Colorado, was nowhere, and she was clean as Cordelia Kaplan, perfectly clean, an all-American girl living an all-American life on a set of perfectly forged papers.

An all-American girl who was running out of places to hide.

A little cover might have helped, but the snowstorm outside had kept people away from the library. The place was practically deserted, which left her alone to run the Reinhard gauntlet.

Her stomach clenched at the thought.

They'd danced together one night in Prague, at a club

called Radost FX, and she'd turned down his offer of a more intimate association. But Reinhard Klein was used to getting what he wanted.

The warehouse in Karlovy Vary. A trickle of fear ran down her spine. Out of the corner of her eye, she saw his gaze shift. Suddenly, he was looking right at her . . . but he wasn't seeing who he was looking for, not yet.

She considered running back up the escalator, but discarded the idea as too risky. It would only draw attention to her, and she figured she had a better than fifty-fifty chance of cruising by Reinhard as an ill-kempt boy.

God, even one other person in the main hall would have been helpful. Someone, anyone, to draw attention away from her, even if only for a couple of seconds.

In the next moment, she got her wish, but in the worst possible way. A noisy commotion above her drew her head around and made her blanch. Bruno had boarded the escalator and was pounding his way down the moving stairs behind her.

The natural reaction would be to get out of the big man's way, but for the space of a heartbeat she was frozen, the last of the stairs slipping out from under her and Bruno bearing down on her.

"Hey, kid," someone said at the bottom of the escalator, the voice casual and friendly, low-pitched.

She jerked her head around, the stairs came to an end, and a large hand came down on her shoulder, making sure she didn't fall.

Oh, God. Her breath stopped. She'd been caught

by—of all people—the angel-faced surfer god from the third floor, the one who'd been reading newspapers all evening.

"Hey, watch it, buddy," he said as Bruno pushed by them, heading toward the main doors where Reinhard was waiting, his face a mask of cold anger.

"Geez." The surfer guy turned back to her, meeting her gaze. Then he smiled, a blindingly white grin that flashed across his face and lit up the whole atrium. "Where've you been, huh? I've been looking all over for you," he said, guiding her away from the escalator, his body loose and angled between her and Reinhard, every move he made as smooth as silk, so natural that for a micro-instant even she believed she knew him. "Come on. I just need one more book, and then we can get out of here."

Damn, damn, damn. Her mind was spinning. Who was this guy? No one from Eastern Europe. She wouldn't have forgotten him. She wouldn't have forgotten anyone who looked like him. He sounded American. He looked American, pure California beach boy, and when she'd seen him in the reading room she hadn't for a moment considered him a player. He'd been too noticeable with his sun-streaked hair falling to his shoulders, his face pretty enough for magazine fashion ads, and wearing clothes that looked like they came straight out of those ads: casual but very expensive cargo pants and hiking boots, and a fisherman's sweater, all in black. He'd been impossible to miss, and because of it, she'd dismissed him completely, and now he'd caught her—whoever the hell he was.

Cursing herself as a fool, she fell in beside him, because with Bruno the Bull and Reinhard Klein not twenty feet away, there wasn't a damned thing else she could do, not for the next few seconds. Her only consolation was that out of all the men, the California surf angel had to be the least dangerous of the three.

She knew what Bruno and Reinhard were capable of doing. She knew how coldly brutal they could be.

Oh, yeah. The pretty slacker dude saggin' in the designer clothes was easily the least dangerous of the three.

Easily.

CHAPTER
3

WELL, THIS WAS GOING pretty good, Creed thought, walking Cordelia Kaplan right past Reinhard Klein and into the fiction stacks. She was stiff as a board beside him, her face perfectly sullen, which he supposed wasn't such a bad thing for the teenaged boy she was pretending to be. Up close, though, the disguise was ridiculous, and he was disappointed in himself for buying it even for a second. True, she'd been sitting cross-legged on the floor at the older woman's feet up in nonfiction, which hadn't given him a very good look at her. He'd seen the dark hair falling over her face, cut short in back like a boy's, and a wrinkled plaid shirt she must have had on under the sweater, and in his eyes he'd seen a boy with his grandmother instead of a female tango—terrorist—dealing in deadly contraband.

But up close, she was no more a boy than he was the King of Siam. Delicate, that's what she was. He could feel it in the shoulder beneath his hand despite the bulky sweater and old coat. Without the big glasses overwhelming her face, what had looked like a small, unremarkable nose was actually a delicate curve, a very refined curve, and her cheekbones went way beyond classic into exotic. She was Dominika Starkova, all right, and her eyes weren't brown. Up close, they were a dark mossy green.

His gaze dropped down the length of her body, remembering the picture Dylan had sent, but there wasn't a curve in sight, not a one that he could see with her bundled up in her homeless-boy gear. Given time, she probably could have perfected her transition, looking as much a boy as she'd looked a mousy librarian, but she'd had no more than seconds.

Damn, she'd moved fast.

And if he wasn't mistaken, she was getting ready to move fast again. Another level of tension had stiffened her up even more, the old fight-or-flight reaction.

"Don't," he said, losing the friendly tone and tightening his hold on her a fraction of a degree. They had just passed out of Reinhard's line of sight. There was a service entrance on the north end of the building, and the two of them were going out of it—ASAP.

"You've got the wrong kid, mister," she said belligerently, trying to shrug him off.

He wasn't having any of it. "I haven't got a kid at all, Ms. Starkova. So let's just keep a low profile until we're out of here."

"I don't know what you're talking about." She started to struggle, trying to break away, but Creed just held on tighter and moved her along faster.

Then she kicked him, got him right in his bad leg, and a little bit of his self-control snapped.

Coming to a sudden, tight-jawed halt, he took big fistfuls of old coat and baggy sweater in his hands and hauled her up to meet his glare. Nothing but her tiptoes touched the floor.

"Don't," he repeated in his best I'll-eat-your-balls-for-breakfast voice. "Not if you want to get out of here alive."

It was a tone and an expression guaranteed to put the fear of God in whoever was on the receiving end of it—except, it seemed, Dominika Starkova.

Rather than quail and capitulate, she wasn't even looking at him. Her gaze had slid over his shoulder.

"*Oh, God,*" she whispered.

It was the only clue he needed. He whipped his head around, saw what she saw, and wondered how in the hell the flat-faced hired gun on the west side of the hall had beaten them to the service entrance. It didn't make sense, but there he was, still looking every inch the gorilla, guarding their escape route.

"Ernst Braun," she continued under her breath. "Or maybe it's Edmund. I . . . I can never tell them apart."

Oh, shit, was more like it. "Twins?" he asked, realizing it meant there were four bad guys in the building, not just three.

"Identical," she said, her attention coming back to him, and for a second, as their gazes met, it occurred to him that her eyes were like a forest, a dark, richly verdant, mysterious forest, the mossy green centers flecked with the gray of mountain granite and streaked with the colors of the earth and sky.

Sweet Jesus.

"I can't believe he's here," she said, and his momentary lapse came to a halt, leaving him even more unnerved—as if he needed that.

Well, hell. There was another option, and without a word, he turned her around and headed back down the stacks, toward the far east side of the building, to the stairs. From the stairwell, it was possible to get out onto the roof, and from the roof . . . well, it was a helluva drop from the roof.

But he'd think of something before it got to that. He always thought of something. At least he'd always thought of something up until the Colombian mission had gone bad.

There hadn't been just one guy waiting for him and J.T. on that godforsaken jungle trail. They'd been ambushed and captured by a platoon's worth of NRF narco-guerillas, and he hadn't been able to think of anything, not once J.T. had started screaming.

Nothing.

There had been nothing but horror and pain—black pain, terrifying, blind horror, and a failure he would never be able to face.

Never.

He squeezed his free hand into a fist to stop its sudden trembling, and tightened his hold on the woman. *Damn.* He'd known he wasn't ready for this, ready to save anyone, let alone a woman who'd sold her soul for money and endangered everything he believed in—not when he hadn't been able to save J.T.

It wasn't far to the stairwell from the service entrance, but only single-minded determination got him there—for all the good it did him.

Jerking her back behind him, he swore under his breath, then glanced back around the corner to the stairwell door. Gorilla number one from the main hall had moved to cover the last base.

"Edmund," she whispered, looking around him.

Edmund and Ernst—one of them had to go if he and the woman were going to get out of the library.

A voice raised in anger with a German accent came from the direction of the service entrance, suddenly making it the least effective line of escape. Fine. Edmund's number had just come up. Creed would be damned if he got caught between a rock and a hard place because of Dominika Starkova.

"Come on." He grabbed her by the arm and started forward. He had his Glock 10mm in a holster at the small of his back and Kid Chaos's pistol-gripped shotgun secured in a long pocket inside his coat. He wasn't planning on using either of them to get by Edmund Braun, any more than he was planning on using the garrote in his pants pocket or the razor-edged Randall fighting knife strapped to his ankle.

Yeah, he was a paranoid son of a bitch, psychologically unsound. All the head-shrinkers had said so. Posttraumatic stress disorder, the last one had written in his file.

Yeah, right, Creed had thought, not doubting the doc's diagnosis. He'd found watching the Colombians work over J.T.—fucking massacring him—yeah, well, he'd found that pretty fucking traumatically stressful.

The Colombians had paid. They'd paid with their lives. The last one had died under Creed's knife in a lake of his own blood in the mountains of Peru, but killing him hadn't been enough.

Nothing was ever going to be enough.

But all Creed was going to do to old Edmund was put him down hard, and get him out of the way fast.

Hard and fast, that's the way he and J.T. had always worked.

A cold sweat broke out on his brow. *Geezus.* They'd been invincible for ten years. What in the hell had gone wrong?

Real life. That's what had gone wrong, and he wasn't

ready for it again. All he wanted was to be back at SDF's Steele Street headquarters with Skeeter, with his head under the hood of her Mustang, a sweet little pony car she'd named Babycakes—as if that was any kind of a name for a car, especially a badass GT 350.

But ready or not, real life was waiting for him less than twenty yards away, and its name was Edmund Braun.

CODY had made a mistake, a big one, possibly a fatal one. The surfer dude hadn't been her wisest choice. He wasn't safe. He was nuts. Six feet of crazy wild with a look in his eyes that sent a chill down her spine.

And it had all happened so fast—the change from easygoing guy to whacko boy who was getting ready to take on Edmund Braun of the notorious Braun twins. Their reputation was the stuff of nightmares all over Eastern Europe—with good reason. She knew the stories and had made a second career of staying out of their way, out of their sight, out of any place they might be. Most of the time she'd been pretty successful, but running with Sergei Patrushev's *reketiry* meant running in a pretty tight circle, and their paths had crossed more than once.

"Th-this guy, Edmund—" she began, breathless from their hell-bent march toward disaster. "I don't know what you're thinking you're going to do, but Edmund is a . . . a killer." She couldn't say it any plainer.

The man with the death grip on her coat, the one dragging her along faster than she could keep up with, slanted her a brief, piercing glance, and with sudden clarity, she understood exactly how much trouble she was in.

The angel-faced surfer dude was a killer, too.

Oh, God—just when she'd thought she was safe, she was going to die, and in the library of all places. The irony of it would have been laughable, if she'd had a laugh in her.

She didn't, not one, and the last thing she needed in her life was more irony. She was drowning in the stuff, had been drowning in it ever since she'd defied her mother's wishes and gone looking for the father she'd never known.

Well, she'd found him all right. Dimitri Starkova, before his recent demise, had been a professor in Prague— charming, urbane, and highly educated. In short, some of what she'd hoped her father would be. Unfortunately, he'd also turned out to be a former general in the Soviet army with a mountain of debt, close ties to the Russian Mafia, and damn little conscience. Over the planned weeks of her visit, her journey to see him had slowly turned from the trip of a lifetime into the vacation from hell, and then it had taken a turn for the worse and gone downhill from there.

Since the night he'd died, she'd been lost, trying to juggle the realities of her father's past, the dangerous legacy he'd left her, and the very harsh realities of trying to stay alive—and it was all coming down to this: Edmund Braun was huge. The beach boy was not.

They were eating up the distance to the stairwell door. Any second Edmund was bound to notice.

And sure enough he did, his beady-eyed gaze turning on them, zeroing in on them, his simian features clouding up.

It was said he'd once torn a man in half with his bare hands. Impossible, she'd thought, but three separate accounts of the deadly brawl had surfaced in Prague, with people from all sides claiming to have seen the body.

Her gaze went to Edmund's hands, big, coarse hands, and she stumbled—but she didn't fall. The crazy man hauling her to her doom didn't let her fall.

"Wh-what's your name?" she asked. If she was going to die with him, or die because of him, she should know his name.

"Creed," he said without slowing down.

The strangeness of the name barely registered. Cody was too busy recalling another story about Edmund killing a girl with a single blow to the head. She knew that one was true. She'd known the girl.

Ernst wasn't quite so impulsive, quite so psychotic—but it was Edmund starting toward them, his mouth set, his hands clenching into fists, ready to take on the challenge her captor was telegraphing like an air raid siren. There was absolutely no hesitation in Creed's long, forceful strides, no hesitation in the way he was dragging her with him. Except for that one brief glance, his gaze hadn't wavered from Braun's for an instant, and every inch of him was sending out one signal, loud and clear: "I'm coming down your throat, *zhopa*."

It was insane, and she was caught in the middle of it with no good end in sight. Edmund sometimes forgot himself, sometimes lost track of the big picture—in this case, it being that his boss, Reinhard, would want her alive, at least to begin with.

God save her. The voices behind them were getting closer, and one for certain was Bruno. He wouldn't let Edmund kill her, not on the spot. Even more than Reinhard, Sergei Patrushev wanted her alive, and Bruno knew why. Sergei needed the map that would lead him into the mountains of Tajikistan, where her father had hidden one of Mother Russia's nuclear warheads.

And so help her God, she had the map.

She didn't want it, could barely read it, and wished to hell she'd never seen it, but she knew deep in her heart that the last thing her father had given her, a slim volume of self-published poetry titled *Tajikistan Discontent*, was a coded map to the warhead, and she was pretty damn sure Sergei had figured it out the same time she had. But by then, she'd slipped his noose.

At least she'd thought she'd slipped his noose. Tonight had proven her wrong.

"My name is Dominique Cordelia Stark. Cody Stark," she said to the stranger, wanting him to know. If bad came to worse, he should know her real name, the one her mother would recognize in the newspapers, and it wasn't Kaplan.

"Well, Cody Stark," he said, not sounding like he believed her for a minute, "when I let go of you, I suggest you run like hell for the stairs. Klein has this floor covered."

A spark of hope ignited in her breast. He was going to let go of her. Thank God. The one thing she could do was run like hell. She just hoped the beach boy put up enough of a fight to give her a chance to escape.

She no sooner had the thought than she felt a twinge of guilt. Edmund was going to hurt him, badly, maybe even kill him. She shot her captor a quick look and had the unbelievable thought of "what a waste." He truly did have the face of an angel, his eyes a pale bluish gray, his brown hair streaked with gold, his face artfully carved and too pretty by half, and he was about to be mangled by a psychopathic brute.

It was his choice, though. She'd warned him, and she had no intention of sticking around and watching Edmund beat him to a pulp.

With less than twenty feet left between them and the German giant, Creed released her from his hold with a hissed command to run, and she obeyed, skirting a pair of study carrels and heading fast for the stairwell door.

A gasp and a grunt, both sounding like they came from a cold-cocked bull elephant, preceded a crash behind her. Against every ounce of common sense and good judgment she had, she turned at the door and looked back.

She'd expected blood and mayhem. What she hadn't expected was to see the surfer boy rising from the wreckage unharmed, and for Edmund to be sprawled across the floor, out cold.

The California surf angel looked up and caught her gaze, and her breath stopped short. Without looking away, he reached inside his coat and withdrew a wicked looking shotgun. Then he glanced back at Edmund and, using the gun, struck him hard at the base of his skull.

When his gaze returned to hers, a ton and a half of adrenaline drop-loaded into her system, igniting a panic so pure it damn near paralyzed her.

He *was* wild. Crazy, crazy wild. It was all over his face, deep in his eyes. With a gasped breath, she wrenched the door open and took off up the stairs like the hounds of hell were after her.

CHAPTER
4

HE CAUGHT HER at the second landing, his fist closing on the back of her coat and hauling her upright. *Oh, God.* She damn near had a heart attack.

"Keep running," he growled, half lifting her off her feet as he ran beside her, taking the stairs two and three at a time, making sure she kept up with him.

Below them, the door opened with a commotion. The pack had arrived. The sound of men moving, talking, swearing, of feet pounding, filled the stairwell and spurred her on, caught between the devils behind her and the devil beside her.

"Did . . . did you kill him?" Edmund had looked dead, lying there on the library floor.

"Not this time," he said, racing her across the third landing and hauling her up the next flight of stairs.

As she ran beside him, growing more breathless and wondering how long she could keep up with him—and what he'd do when she couldn't—it occurred to her, ridiculously, that she'd probably lost her job, damn it. Of course, if she died tonight, her whole library career was going to be a moot point, which was a damned disconcerting thought.

Lungs burning, heart pounding, she grabbed the rail and rounded the next landing with Creed's hand still buried in her coat. He wasn't even breathing hard, and she could hardly breathe at all. He still had the shortened shotgun in his other hand, and she didn't doubt for an instant that he would use it—maybe on her.

So help her God, who was he? The name Creed meant nothing to her, and she wouldn't have forgotten it any more than she would have forgotten him.

He had to want the nuclear warhead. That's what everybody wanted from her, a chance to get in on Sergei's big deal. But Sergei didn't have a deal without her, and the minute she'd figured that out, she'd known that simply escaping the Russian and running back home wasn't going to work.

Oh, hell, no. She was in way more trouble than that.

Damn! She tripped on a stair, stumbling, and only Creed's hold kept her from falling flat on her face.

Behind them on the stairs she could hear someone struggling to keep up, probably Ernst. He was big and brawny, but out of shape. Bruno was big, too, but he was all muscle and horrendous strength, and he had to be the one gaining on them, his footsteps sounding closer and closer as he climbed, hot on their tails.

"*Faster*," Creed commanded, doing his best to single-handedly carry her up each succeeding flight.

It wasn't going to work. Her feet were sliding, slipping out from under her. She was at the end, exhausted from weeks on the run. He was pushing her beyond her limit, and she didn't have an ounce of "go" left in her.

Or so she thought.

A shot fired from below had them both leaping up the next few stairs. A second shot sounded, and Creed shoved her ahead of him, toward the outside wall, then leaned against the rail and returned fire.

The shotgun blast echoed in the steel-and-concrete stairwell like a dynamite explosion, rocking her back against the wall, hurting her ears, but she had enough sense to keep scrambling. Before the sound faded she felt him propelling her forward again, his fist once more closed around her coat, lifting her to her feet, keeping her going.

Who *was* this guy? she asked herself. And how in the world was she going to get away from him—if, by some chance, they got away from Bruno?

At the next landing, he slammed into a door leading to the outside while using the butt end of the shotgun to release the lock, and in the next second the two of them were stumbling out onto the roof.

The cold hit her like a runaway train, knocking her back on her feet. She gulped in a great lungful of frozen air, and the pain of it almost put her on her knees.

"*Come on,*" he insisted, urging her into a run.

The roof was slick with ice and drifted in snow, and she felt almost sick with the sudden, awful cold, but he wouldn't let her slow down for an instant to catch her breath. Surefooted, he raced across the roof, through a maze of air conditioners, ventilation equipment, stacks of all sizes, and a blinding, swirling blizzard of snow, keeping her firmly in tow.

A flash of light and the sound of the door banging open again had him making a sudden, lightning-quick change of direction. In her leather-soled shoes, she had no traction, and she slipped, landing against him with enough force to send them both tumbling.

"*Geezus,*" he ground out between his teeth, falling into a slide and taking her with him, his arm coming around her.

Cody went down on top of him, and the two of them careened across the roof, heading for the edge. A low wall kept them from going over, but he couldn't stop their slide, and they ended up jammed behind a ventilation unit in a tangled heap of arms and legs.

In the middle of scrambling to his feet, he suddenly froze, still on his knees, and pulled her tight against him with his gun hand, his other hand going over her mouth.

She heard it, too, the sound of someone approaching,

footsteps crunching through the snow and slip-sliding every few steps on the ice.

He caught her gaze, his warning clear: *Don't move, not a muscle.*

She gave a short nod and had to wonder why. She didn't know him. It was entirely possible he was even more of a danger to her than Bruno the Bull.

But she stayed where she was, kneeling with him, facing him as he slowly and silently lifted his arm from around her waist and angled the shotgun toward the opening they'd slid through. If anyone rounded the ventilation unit, they were going to be looking straight down the gun's barrel—but probably not for long.

She shivered with the awful thought of seeing someone get shot at very close quarters, and she shivered with the aching cold. It had to be below zero, the snow falling in endless, white waves from the sky, and it had to be Bruno getting closer, because the next sound she heard was another guy coming out of the door, cursing the cold: Ernst.

Reinhard wouldn't have run up the stairs, not even for her. Given that Edmund was hurt and out cold on the library floor, Reinhard had probably gotten in his car and left. Cleaning up messes wasn't what he did. Bruno was his cleanup man, and he would undoubtedly pay for letting this night's job turn into a mess in the first place.

"Why are we out here, Bruno?" Ernst grouched in German. "Why don't we just get the book and go?"

"Get the book? You idiot. We need the girl," she heard

Bruno reply. "We don't even know if the book is here, and there are forty-seven miles, *miles, you idiot*, of bookcases in the Denver Public Library."

"You don't know that, Bruno."

"It's in the fucking brochure," Bruno said. "Now keep looking for her."

Another shiver racked her. Her feet felt frozen in her thin leather shoes, and she didn't even want to think about her knees. Her ears were so cold they burned. Her teeth started to chatter.

Without a word, the man holding her removed his hand from her mouth and reached down to open his coat. In seconds, she was wrapped inside, her head against his chest, his body heat seeping through her sweater.

God, he was actually warm—so warm. It was all she could do to keep from wrapping herself around him. She did wrap her arm partway around his waist.

And that's when she discovered his other gun—at the small of his back, underneath his sweater. A pistol.

Off in the distance, the low wail of sirens coming from different directions, converging on the library, told her someone must have found Edmund or heard the shots, or both, and called the police.

It wasn't good news.

She no sooner wanted the authorities to find her than she'd wanted Reinhard or the psycho-surfer to find her. All she wanted was to be left alone, to go back to her old life, the one that had been so predictably safe until she'd gone looking for her father. But that wasn't going to happen, not as long as she had the book and Sergei didn't. Even so, giving it to him was impossible. She'd seen the people he was lining up as buyers, and they were terrorists, every one of them, from every corner of the world.

There was only one way out for her—to disappear. She'd tried turning herself and the book over to the U.S. authorities in the Czech Republic, and that had gone terribly, horribly wrong. Her contact had been executed. It was her nightmare, what had happened in the warehouse in Karlovy Vary.

"Ernst! *Idi slanu yaytsa kachat'!*" Bruno yelled, sounding a crude retreat as the sirens drew closer. Blue and red lights flashed below on the street—the police cars arriving. The last thing the big German would want would be to get picked up by the police. He might have legitimate papers, but the Braun boys were definitely personae non grata in the West, having been linked to the death of a United States embassy attaché in Prague. CIA agent, not attaché, had been the word on the street— and the rumor had been true. She'd known the attaché, known he was an agent, and she'd been living for weeks with the awful knowledge that she was the reason he'd been taken to Karlovy Vary and killed.

She looked up at the man holding her so close, watching him, seeing his breath blow white in the frigid air. He was more death, an angel of death. She felt it in his heartbeat. She saw it in his eyes, in the utter commitment he'd made with the shotgun in his hand.

There wasn't a doubt in her mind about what would happen if Bruno or Ernst crossed into his space. They would die—blown to hell, straight to hell, by a sawed-off shotgun.

Creed—such a strange name.

Slowly, carefully, she slid her hand under his sweater and over the pistol's grip, until she felt it cold and solid in her hand.

The door into the library opened again, sending another slice of light across the rooftop, and the last of the voices faded away. Bruno and Ernst were making their escape.

It was time for her to do the same.

With an ease she was sure had been designed for his convenience, not hers, the gun slipped smoothly out of the holster into her hand. She didn't hesitate to shove the end of the barrel against the front of his sweater.

One breath passed, then two, before he cut his gaze to her.

"Have you ever killed a man?" he asked, his words as cold as the vapor surrounding them.

She said nothing, but neither did she move the gun.

"You won't like it," he assured her, his gaze sliding away to look out over the night. Hundreds, thousands of snowflakes drifted onto his shoulders, into his hair, onto his face, some vestige of warmth melting them when they touched his skin.

More long seconds of silence passed. She had demands, they were on the tip of her tongue, but she was too cold to get the words out—or maybe she was just too damned scared.

"The first thing," he said, returning his attention to her, "is to get serious."

He had dark lashes, as dark as his eyebrows, a fascinating contrast with his sun-streaked hair.

"If you gut-shoot me, I might still get a shot off myself." He lifted the shotgun slightly, making sure she noticed it, giving her fair warning. "But if you *get serious*"—he wrapped his other hand around hers and lifted both it and the pistol until he'd positioned the gun's barrel under his chin—"you can kill me without risking yourself."

Her hand started to shake, which didn't seem to bother him nearly as much as it terrified her.

He was crazy.

AND SO IT COMES *to this*, Creed thought, looking down at the woman looking up at him. It always seemed to come to this: a standoff, a gun in the dark, and one person just a shade more determined than the other. Before Colombia, that had been him, the more determined one, every single fucking time.

A sigh of frustration or weariness, or both, left him in a white puff of breath. Of course, if she shot him, it would solve a lot of his problems.

Hell, it would solve all of them—except for one. He and the Lord hadn't been on speaking terms for a while, and that was a helluva way for a good Catholic boy to meet his maker—pissed off.

Not that he was really too worried about dying on the roof. In about ten more seconds, Dominika Starkova was going to be too cold to squeeze a trigger, no matter how much encouragement he gave her.

Cody Stark, she'd called herself. He didn't know whether to believe her or not, but it was an easy enough fact to check. He did know she was pretty, much prettier without all the makeup she'd been wearing in the photo taken in Prague. With her dark hair really short in back and too long in front, hanging in her eyes, and that delicate nose, her eyes wide with a slight tilt, thickly lashed, she looked familiar in a way he couldn't quite place.

It had been a long time since he'd kissed a woman, a very long time, and he certainly had no business kissing this one—but there it was suddenly, in his mind, his gaze drifting to her lips, a hot longing curling deep in his gut.

It had definitely been a long time since he'd felt that. But then it had been a long time since he'd had a woman pressed up against him, turning him on, let alone one offering him oblivion with a gun jammed up under his chin.

He was a sick bastard. No doubt about it. But suddenly . . . suddenly she looked like bait, alluring, her mouth sweetly cold, enticing him to bend his head.

"No," she whispered, staring up at him, snowflakes drifting onto her hair, her eyelashes—melting on her lips.

In her position, he would have said no, too, but he didn't give a damn what she said. She had the upper hand here. She had it all. She was running for her life. She had a reason to live, and he had nothing.

Nothing except her kiss, if he took it.

For so long, the only thing he'd wanted was death, simple, straightforward, kill-the-pain death, but with Dominika Starkova wrapped in his arms, holding his gaze, the faint scent of her teasing his senses, the feel of her body reminding him of all he'd lost, of all he'd missed, his list of simple desires had suddenly, inexplicably doubled.

Now he wanted death . . . and sex.

CHAPTER 5

CODY KNEW HE was going to kiss her. With the two of them freezing to death on the roof of the library, the psycho-surfer was going to kiss her. The thought, even more than all the fear that had gone before, absolutely paralyzed her. She couldn't move, not an inch, not away, not a breath's worth of distance. All she could do was watch and wait as he lowered his head, his eyes drifting closed, his lips parting. All she could do was wait, her breath held in a painful knot in her throat, the gun freezing to her hand as his movement pushed it lower and lower.

Then his mouth touched hers, so softly all she felt was the warmth—sweet, alluring warmth, his arm tightening around her, pulling her closer to his body, closer to his heat. His breath was so warm, the faint touch of his lips. It was seduction on a primal level, the warmth of a kiss for a moment's respite from the cold, for a moment's comfort.

He brushed her lips again, lingering longer, and all she could think was that they were both crazy. She still had the gun under his chin. She had the power. But she was the one trembling in fear—and he was pushing her too far.

If he didn't stop this tender little assault of his, she was going to . . . going to . . . oh, God, she was going to cry.

She felt the first tear slip free and knew deep in her heart she should shoot him just for that, but he was right. She wouldn't like killing him, couldn't kill him— not because of all the kisses he was so gently pressing to her lips, her cold cheek, the corner of her mouth, soft kisses mixing with her tears.

What was he thinking? Was he completely insane?

Or was she.

"*Lo siento,*" he whispered, lifting his mouth from hers.

And what did that mean? she wondered. Then she knew.

Damn! She'd lost the gun. He'd disarmed her, the bastard, first with his kisses, then by taking the gun.

"I'm sorry," he said, though he didn't sound it, and she knew that's what he'd said in Spanish—*Lo siento. I'm sorry.* "I can't let you shoot me tonight."

Of course not.

"It's not you I feel like shooting right now," she said, unable to keep the bitterness out of her voice. She couldn't believe she'd been so stupid. And what the hell did he mean by not being able to let her shoot him tonight? Like maybe tomorrow night he'd be okay with it?

Biting off a silent curse, she pushed herself painfully to her feet, away from him and his warmth. He let her rise, but kept a strong grip on her coat, stopping her from what she really needed to do—run like hell.

Maybe to Los Angeles. Keep going west, if she could get away from him and stay out of Bruno's clutches. Denver was no good for her now. Reinhard wouldn't give up, not because of one small setback, not when he'd gotten this close. He was Sergei's right-hand man on the warhead deal, and he was going to want his cut of the take. Bruno and Ernst would be down on the street somewhere, waiting for her. She knew it as surely as she knew she wouldn't last much longer if they didn't get off the roof.

This must be what it's like on Mount Everest, she thought: frigidly cold, the wind blowing, cutting through your clothes, snow everywhere—but without the surf angel to share his heat and scramble a person's brain.

How could she have let him kiss her? Even if they had only been barely-there kisses. And how could she have been so cross-eyed stupid as to let him get the gun?

It didn't make sense. She'd spent the last three months living by her wits and doing everything in her power to keep Sergei and half his goons from kissing her, or worse, with varying amounts of success and one gut-awful failure, and she'd just let this total stranger get close enough to touch his mouth to hers? This very dangerous stranger?

Brain freeze, that had to be it, a total brain freeze. Disorientation. The onset of hypothermia. She did feel frozen clear through to her bones. She hurt with the cold, and it *was* hard to think. Her teeth were chattering again. Her breath was difficult to catch. God, they were going to freeze to death, if they didn't get off the roof.

She stomped her feet, trying to warm them, while her captor tried to stand up, and failed. He cursed and grabbed his leg, and the instant he let go of her coat, pure instinct flooded her body. She took off like a flash, but didn't get farther than a few racing strides before a shot rang out.

A bolt of fear sent her diving, and she crashed back onto the roof, her heart in her throat, her pulse pounding. *Good God!* He was shooting at her.

CREED lowered his arm from where he'd shot into the air. Hell, he hadn't hit her. No way. But she'd dropped like a stone, and it gave him kind of a sick feeling. He'd wanted to stop her, not hurt her.

Think on your feet—yeah, that was him. The trouble was he couldn't get to his frickin' feet, and he wasn't thinking at all. *Geezus*. He'd kissed her. Dominika

Starkova, international criminal, Russian Mafia moll, and the world's most dangerous woman according to Interpol and the DIA. Maybe he needed his head examined— again. Pushing himself up against the ventilation unit for support, he finally made it to standing and started a limping run across the frozen rooftop to where she'd fallen.

She didn't move, not so much as an inch, and his fear grew sharper with every awkward stride he took.

More sirens sounded below on the streets, coming from a couple of directions. They needed to get off the roof and away from the library now, before the cops found them. The last damn thing he wanted to do tonight was explain himself to Denver's finest, especially about Edmund Braun and the discharging of firearms in a public place. He was already into Lieutenant Loretta Bradley for a couple of traffic violations she'd taken care of for him—okay, a couple of dozen— and he doubted if she wanted to see him again any more than he wanted to see her.

And he sure as hell didn't want the cops to see Dominika Starkova. When Dylan said clandestine, he meant clandestine, and this op was as black as they came. That meant Ms. Starkova was his. He'd found her; he'd tailed her; and he'd saved her from Reinhard Klein. By jungle law, even the urban jungle, that made her his.

She still hadn't moved when he finally got to her, and he swore under his breath. He reached down, and in the next second found himself flat on his back, scrabbling to keep a hold on her, any kind of hold on any part of her, to keep her from getting away.

Kee-rist. She'd kicked him. In his bad leg. Again. His frigging bad leg, and it hurt like hell with pain shooting through his knee up to his hip, not to mention how badly it hurt to fall flat on your back on a frozen slab of icy roof—for the second frigging time.

He grabbed for her, and she rolled. He lunged, and she dodged, but with the roof slick, and her flailing on the ice, and him *de-term-ined*, it was a done deal, and in another couple of seconds he had her firmly under him, a squirming, Czech-swearing, very angry woman.

And that was his problem. She was a woman. He would have done whatever it took to put a man down, but he didn't have it in him to hit her. He didn't. No matter how many nuclear warheads she was selling. Not after he'd kissed her.

And if he was going to get any stupider tonight, he didn't want to know it. Not right now.

Using his weight to hold her down, he reached in his coat pocket and pulled out a flex cuff. In one smooth move, he had her wrists bound, which pushed her over the edge of angry into ballistic. He didn't know what language she was chewing him up in, but it sounded like she'd gone beyond just Czech, maybe into Russian with a little German on the side. He was reaching for another cuff to do her ankles when the stairwell door slammed open.

Time was up.

With a superhuman effort, he hauled both of them to their feet and slung her over his shoulder, capturing her legs with his arm and completely ignoring the searing pain that shot up into his hip. Behind him, he heard men coming out onto the roof.

Taking off at a limping run, he headed for the north side of the building and the ladder rail he'd seen curving up over the edge. There was no way to the street from the new library roof except down the stairwell and through the building, but the old library was a warren inside and out, including the roof, and it butted up against the new library. All he had to do was climb down two floors on the outside of the building, clinging like a limpet to a frozen ladder—without dropping her.

Piece of cake.

CHAPTER 6

WHO IS THIS GUY? The question tore around Cody's brain as she hung upside down over his shoulder, staring death in its cold, dark, ugly face. Two stories of sheer emptiness gaped below her, a swirling vortex of wind-driven snow spiraling down into a visually fathomless abyss.

An abyss—and he wasn't holding on to her. Not at all.

He was holding on to the ladder, leaving her balanced—*balanced*—on his shoulder like a bag of feed.

She had a hold on him, though. Oh, God, did she have a hold on him. Her frozen fingers gripped his coat with every ounce of strength she had left—which wasn't much. She couldn't see the old library below them, but she knew it was there, and despite her desperate desire to reach it in one piece, it was the last place she wanted to go with anybody involved with the warhead.

How long had he been following her? Days? Ever since she'd arrived in Denver?

Long enough to know what she'd done?

No, she told herself. She would have seen him if he'd been following her around while she worked, especially in the old library. He was impossible to miss. Every librarian and research assistant on the third floor had noticed him the moment he'd gotten off the escalator. The newspapers had been straightened so many times tonight, there wasn't a page left out of place, not even in *The New York Times*. There was no way he could have been following her without her knowing. In Prague, by necessity, she'd become an expert at watching her back, because there had always been somebody there, watching her, guarding her, keeping her from escaping—except once, and once had been enough.

He slipped on a rung, and her heart, which was already lodged in her throat, stopped for a long, painful second until he steadied himself.

So help her God, it was a long way down. Even squinting against the snow, she couldn't see the roof of the old library, and suddenly she was filled with an unreasonable panic that the building had disappeared. That it simply wasn't there anymore, and they would climb forever—or until she fell, whichever came first.

She started to tremble deep down inside, her body

shaking, and a strong arm immediately went around her legs—which meant he had only one hand left on the ladder, which didn't really help.

"I'm not going to let you fall," he said, his voice rough-edged, but calm. She didn't feel calm. She felt scraped and frozen and raw. Fifteen minutes ago she'd been calm, and warm, and gratefully going about her job. Fifteen minutes ago she'd thought she was safe.

Unexpectedly, he stepped down off the ladder to solid footing, and relief flooded through her. She hadn't died . . . yet.

But nothing else was right. Nothing. The night had spiraled out of control—and the only thing that could keep her alive was being in control. Helplessness meant death, and the psycho-surfer had handcuffed her.

A soft curse escaped her lips. She couldn't even control her body. She was shaking like a leaf, and the tips of her fingers were going numb.

"Y-you, you . . . we h-have to . . ." she ground out between chattering teeth, then gave up on a long explanation and cut to the chase. "I'm f-freezing."

CREED heard her and knew exactly what he had to do—get them off the roof and inside. He was cold, too, freezing, and his leg hurt like a bitch. *Geezus*—she'd practically crippled him.

Above them, a light cut down through the wind-driven snow and strafed the roof, crisscrossing the darkness. He glanced up; sure enough, a couple of cops were coming down the ladder, with a few more lined up along the roof ready to follow.

Okay, it was official now. Things were going to hell. The cops were taking the situation damn seriously, and he'd bet his Chevelle's pink slip that Reinhard, Bruno, and Ernst would be waiting for them on the street, if they'd gotten out of the library.

Something told him they had. They didn't seem like the kind of bad boys to get cornered by a few cops.

Neither was he.

Limping across the roof he headed into an alley of ventilation units, knowing there were a number of doors and windows that led inside. He'd been on a lot of downtown Denver roofs as a kid, messing around with his friends, hiding from the cops, and the roof of the old public library, overlooking Civic Center Park and the gold-domed capitol building, had been a favorite.

Halfway across the roof, he found what he was looking for, a skylight with a broken latch that led into an attic, but when he opened it and looked down inside, he got a bad feeling—real bad.

"What's going on in the old library?" he asked her. All he could feel was emptiness gaping below them in the dark.

"R-remodel," she chattered. "B-building an atrium, like in the n-new library."

As his eyes adjusted, he began to make out scaffolding along the edges, and what remained of the floor running along the walls. But it was the big hole in the middle, plunging four floors down, that kept snagging his attention. If they jumped and didn't land on what was left of the attic floor, they were looking at a thirty-foot-plus drop.

It was a chance he was willing to take. He could handle the heat of getting busted. Even if Lieutenant Bradley wanted to lock him up and throw away the key, she wouldn't. But the Prague princess was something else. It wouldn't take the Denver Police Department long to figure out she was a case for the feds, and once the CIA got ahold of her, or the FBI got involved, her life was going to take a very bad turn—and that was a chance he *wasn't* willing to take, not yet.

The woman calling herself Dominique Cordelia Stark had a really convincing American accent, and her school uniform in the photo he'd lifted off Bruno just happened to have the words Wichita Day School embroidered on the insignia—a little bit of information he'd been realizing, and assimilating, and shuffling around in his brain over the last few minutes. If she was Cody Stark of Wichita, Kansas, her whole Blonde-Bimbo-with-a-Bomb profile got shot right into the high-treason category, which, as he recalled, still carried a death penalty.

Before he let the feds have her, he'd like to get the facts. He knew for sure that Dylan would want them, even before they handed her over to General Grant—and Dylan was on his way home tonight. All he had to do was hold onto her and hold everybody else off for a couple more hours.

So it was going to be the drop into the attic. It wasn't that far, not really. With the extra flex cuffs in his pocket, he could make a rope and put her exactly where he wanted her. If it had just been him, he wouldn't have second-guessed it for a minute.

"Okay. You're going in first, and I'll follow," he said, lowering her off his shoulder and standing her on her feet.

"Wh-what?" she gasped, staring at him.

He took hold of her hands and began methodically looping one flex cuff after another together, starting with the one securing her wrists. Her skin was ice-cold, her body trembling. Cops or no cops, he had to get her off the roof.

"I'm going to lower you over the edge and swing you toward the wall. Once I get you over the floor, I'll let go of the rope and be right behind you."

"N-no," she said, giving her head a hard shake, her eyes wild. "N-no. You c-can't—"

But he could.

"Stay loose. Bend your knees," he advised, then lifted her up and put her over the side.

OH, SWEET *Mary, Mother of God.* Cody couldn't believe this was happening to her. She was dangling—*dangling!*—in the dark over an open construction site in an old building with nothing to stop her fall except a whole lot of thin air and the *lunatic* who was holding on to the other end of a rope he'd made out of plastic handcuffs.

And oh, so help her God, he was starting to swing the rope. She held on tighter and gritted her teeth, because her jaw was simply locked up in anger and fear. She couldn't see anything except the faintest grid of the scaffolding, but that was because she was right on top of it. She didn't know how he could see anything. As a matter of fact, she doubted if he *could* see anything, which meant he was swinging her blind, and he was going to drop her blind, and she was going to die—die like a homeless dog.

At the apex of her arc, her stomach flipped, and she thought *Oh, God, I'm going to be sick*, which was going to be the absolute worst thing.

But then the real absolute worst thing happened, and she realized being sick was way off base.

He let go of her.

Just let go and sent her flying through the air.

CHAPTER

7

THIS IS BAD, Skeeter thought. As a matter of fact, from where she was sitting in the elegantly appointed office on the seventh floor of SDF headquarters on Steele Street in Denver's lower downtown, the situation was worse than bad. It was skirting on disaster.

Three CIA agents were milling around the Scandinavian-designed furniture and a million dollars' worth of SDF's high-tech office equipment, and the one thing they were looking for wasn't anywhere in sight: Creed Rivera.

They wanted his ass, and if Dylan Hart, SDF's head honcho, didn't show up pretty damn quick, she was afraid they might just get it. She'd tried to call Creed and warn him not to come home, but—typically—his phone was turned off, and he hadn't bothered to check in. In truth, he hadn't really checked in since his partner, J.T. Chronopolous, had been killed in Colombia last summer. He was checked out, way out, and in Skeeter's opinion, Dylan had been crazy to put him on tonight's stakeout of Dominika Starkova.

She'd offered to go herself. Hell, she could do a stakeout or track somebody as well as the SDF operators, and she was a helluva lot more stable than Creed right now, which was a pretty scary turn of events as far as she was concerned. The guys were supposed to be rock-solid, and she was supposed to be the loose cannon, the spooky little wallbanger Hawkins had dragged in off the street. But she wasn't the one who woke up in a cold sweat every night, and she wasn't the one rebuilding a 1969 Chevy Nova into a 427-cubic-inch quarter-mile death machine.

She shifted her gaze out the window overlooking the seventh-floor garage. The damn Nova was parked in the first bay, taking up a piece of prime real estate. The paint on her was so black it looked blue. Her Rally wheels gleamed in the low light. She was wicked, absolutely lethal with a zero-to-sixty mph in under four seconds— and her name was Mercy, of which she had none.

Skeeter swore under her breath and forced herself to focus on what the head CIA agent, a man named Tony Royce, was saying.

"If you know where he is, Ms. Bang, it would be to your advantage to quit wasting our time and just tell us."

Royce had short brown hair, pale blue eyes, and a serious personality deficit, and by her count, that was his
fourth not-so-veiled threat, each and every one of them
delivered in a flat monotone voice that was really starting to grate on her nerves. Of the three agents, Royce
was the one playing "bad cop," but she didn't doubt for a
second that the other two had it in them. "Believe me
when I tell you I am *not* in a mood to be screwed with
tonight."

Yeah, she believed him all right.

"Creed Rivera is a danger to himself and to others,"
Royce gritted the words out between his teeth, standing
not two feet from where she was sitting, looming over
her in what she was sure he thought was an intimidating
posture.

Well, she wasn't intimidated, not in the least, but he
didn't have to know that.

She tugged on her ball cap, pulling the bill down a little lower, until it almost rested on the rims of her sunglasses. Yeah, it was dark outside, but she never went
without her shades, a fact which seemed to bug the hell
out of Royce. He'd asked her to remove them—twice.
She shifted in her chair, crossed her legs, and noticed
that while Royce didn't bat an eyelash, the youngest
agent, a dark-haired, dark-eyed rookie named Mathers,
quickly dropped his gaze down the length of her body,
taking in her black muscle shirt with the silver lightning
bolt streaking across her breasts, her waist-length platinum ponytail, her skintight black leather pants, and her

sturdy pair of black lace-up work boots. She'd been about to go out and look for Creed herself when the CIA had shown up—unexpected, unannounced, and unwelcome.

"That's his job," she said, keeping her voice as flat as any trained CIA agent. "To be dangerous."

"I know he's been highly trained to be a danger to others, to our country's enemies," Royce agreed. "But there are limits even in that arena. We all operate under certain rules of engagement, even in extreme situations, and Creed Rivera has overstepped those rules. We feel certain he'll do it again. He's not to be trusted, Ms. Bang, not by anyone. To put it bluntly, he's a danger even to you."

And that's where Agent Royce was wrong. No matter how many evaluations he'd read on Creed Rivera, he didn't know SDF's jungle boy the way she did. The only person Skeeter worried about Creed hurting was himself.

"I've seen your file . . . Skeeter, isn't it? Trying to protect him is just another bad choice in a life full of bad choices," Royce said, his voice losing its monotone in favor of a thick dose of condescension. "Do yourself a favor and help us out here."

God, she hated the CIA. If Dylan hadn't told her to let them in, she wouldn't have, not on a bet. And if Royce had seen her file, he knew she was a helluva lot older than she looked, twenty as of last summer, but he was still treating her like she was twelve. It was her face. Despite her five feet eight inches of height, she had one of those too-cute button noses and the kind of soft little cheeks that most people outgrew by the time they hit their teens. But not her. Oh, no. She was kicking twenty-one in the back and still had a baby face. Instead of the riot girl she was, she sometimes looked like a freakin' fairy princess, even in black leather.

"You saw the pictures," he said, and then, just to drive his point home, he picked a stack of photos up off the desk and dropped them into her lap.

She didn't need to look; she'd seen them. But her gaze dropped anyway—and there was Pablo Castano, looking pretty rough with his throat cut, the ground around him dark with his blood.

It was bad, but Castano's death had been deemed justice by three governments who had paid for him and Garcia to die. She'd read the reports. Neither Creed nor Kid had left anything out. Royce had to know the facts of the mission as well as she did, probably better. He was in the same business.

She picked the photos up and slowly flipped through them, one by one. They hadn't improved in the twenty minutes since Royce had first pulled them out. Kid and Creed had left a mess on that mountainside—and a message that had run the length of South America and gotten all the way back to the Department of Defense of *los asesinos fantasmas*, the ghost killers. Somehow, in the jungles of Colombia and in the mountains of Peru, in people's minds, Hawkins and Creed and Kid had become the vengeful reincarnations of Kid's brother, their sole purpose to bring death to everyone with the American soldier's blood on their hands.

And so it had come to pass. All the NRF rebels who had tortured J.T. to his death had been killed. None was left alive. The U.S. Department of Defense had ordered the deaths, and the CIA hadn't been too bothered by any of them—not until tonight, when Creed had suddenly gotten orders to stake out Dominika Starkova and pick her up. He hadn't been gone two hours before the CIA had shown up.

Skeeter could add well enough to put two and two together and come up with twenty-eight reasons why the CIA would want the Blonde Czech Bimbo who was selling a nuclear warhead on the black market.

"The way I heard it," she said, "Castano and the rest of the NRF were your responsibility, and your guys couldn't get the job done. So you called us in, and your screwups got our guy killed. You sent Creed and J.T. into an ambush."

"Us, Ms. Bang? Are you running ops with SDF now? Is this something else I need to write up in my report?" Royce asked.

"Probably not," another voice interjected, cutting the agent off.

Skeeter slanted her gaze toward the door. *Finally*.

She no sooner laid eyes on the man walking into the office than a soft flush of awareness washed into her cheeks—*damn it*.

That was one thing she *had* to get under control. This

ridiculous crush she'd allowed herself to get on Dylan Hart had absolutely no future in it. Worse, she had a terrible suspicion that he knew, and that her ridiculous crush was the reason he'd been pretty much avoiding the SDF headquarters on Steele Street ever since last summer. He'd been coming in, doing his work, and leaving—usually in the dead of night. She hadn't seen him in weeks.

He looked tired—tired and beautiful, and at least as dangerous as Creed.

Royce knew it, too. She could tell by the way he stepped away from her. Dylan and the CIA went way back, and none of their history was good.

"Hart," Royce said, acknowledging Dylan's arrival.

"Royce." The barest hint of a smile curved Dylan's lips as he met the agent's gaze and walked on by. He stopped next to her, and Skeeter felt her blush deepen.

Damn it.

"What's this?" he asked, pulling the photographs out of her hand.

"Castano and Garcia," she said.

He went through the pictures, slipping each one to the bottom of the stack after he'd seen it. He had silky dark hair and refined features, elegantly carved, but the underlying lines of his face were too hard for him to ever qualify as pretty. Dylan Hart, like all the SDF guys, had been one of the city's most notorious juvenile delinquents before he'd grown up and come into his own, and those years had left their mark inside and out.

"Where'd you get these?" he asked Royce, effortlessly achieving a perfectly bland tone of voice. He wasn't giving anything away, but Skeeter could tell he was furious. There was a stillness about Dylan when he was angry, and he was suddenly very still.

"We had a paid asset in Puerto Blanco. As for finding Castano and Garcia, your boys didn't do much to cover their tracks. Everyone north to the Colombian border knows what happened in the Cordillera mountains."

Dylan nodded once, glanced at the top photo again, then lifted his gaze to meet Royce's. "I think that was the point."

"They've gone rogue on you, Hart," Royce said. "Chronopolous and Rivera both. You know it, and I know it. Hell, you can't even get Chronopolous to come home."

"He's on temporary assignment with the DEA in Colombia, which I'm sure you know more about than I do," Dylan said.

"Then what in the hell is he doing going in and out of Peru? He's been in Cuzco four times in the last three months."

One of Dylan's eyebrows arched upward. "He won't like you following him."

"My boys don't care what he likes or doesn't like. They want him out of their territory. All he has to do is show up in a town and everybody gets spooked. What is it you all call him? Chaos? Kid Chaos? Well, you've got it right, and I want him out of there. And I want Creed Rivera now. I want to know what he's working on."

"And I'd like you to think twice before you ever show anything like these photographs to my personal secretary again." Dylan lifted the pictures, his tone absolutely even, his message more than clear. To Skeeter's surprise, Tony Royce actually clenched his jaw.

"You're in way over your head, Hart—especially if you've got Dominika Starkova. The case is ours. We've been on it for months, and I don't care if it was General Grant or the secretary of defense himself who sicced you on her tail. I want SDF to back off. I've got signed orders from Director Alden himself that says she's ours."

Well, the truth finally comes out, Skeeter thought. Things were definitely moving now. General Grant was the two-star who had created SDF nine years ago to conduct clandestine operations—a bone that stuck in everybody else's craw, especially the CIA's, especially since Alden had taken over.

"You had your chance in Eastern Europe," Dylan said coldly, "and you lost her."

To Skeeter's surprise, Royce let out a short laugh. "If you think you can hold onto her any better than we did, you're only fooling yourself," the agent said. "She's smart, dangerously smart, and if Rivera has her, he needs to turn her over now—before this thing gets any more out of control."

Dylan shifted his gaze to meet Skeeter's, and she shook her head.

"We don't know what he's got," Dylan said, returning his attention to Royce. "But I can guarantee you, if Creed has her, she's not going anywhere."

CODY'S solo flight through the old library's new construction lasted all of two seconds, but it felt like forever, and even after she landed on the floor and crumpled into a shivering heap, the spike in her adrenaline kept her emotions at full throttle.

He'd dropped her, the bastard, thrown her over the edge and dropped her, and her heart was never going to be the same. Her right cheek was pressed against the floor, her bound hands stretched out in front of her, clinging to the wood parquet.

"Are you okay?"

Damn! She jerked her head around and found him crouched over her. He must have landed like a cat. She hadn't heard a thing.

"N-no," she managed to croak out. She wasn't okay. She was half frozen, and half scared out of her mind, and half sick, and handcuffed for crying out loud.

"Who in the h-hell are y-you?" she demanded. With Bruno and Reinhard momentarily out of the way, she felt pretty safe venting her anger and frustration out on wild boy. Discretion be damned. The guy had been manhandling her from the instant they'd met.

But she hadn't really been hurt, something she knew she wouldn't be able to say if she'd fallen into Reinhard's hands. One of the Germans would have done something to her, just to make a point, just to put her in her place.

"Creed Rivera," he said, kneeling down and pulling her up to a sitting position. "Come on. Give me your hands."

"R-Rivera?" Yeah, right, she thought, a blond-haired Chicano. No way did he look Hispanic, but she wouldn't forget the name, not if she lived to be a hundred, which was looking damned unlikely tonight. Trembling and shaking, the cold aching all the way down to her bones, all she could do was sit there and shiver—even when he pulled a big knife out of a sheath on his ankle.

"Cesar Raoul Eduardo Rivera," he said, lifting the knife to her wrists.

She blanched, but didn't have the energy to pull away. If he'd wanted to kill her, he could have dropped her when they'd been on the ladder, or just now down into the old library. Or he could have shot her on the roof—or fed her to Edmund Braun. She still hadn't figured out what in the world he'd done to deck the beast, or how he'd done it so quickly. It was a wicked-looking knife, though, the blade long and gleaming in the low light, the tip sharpened on both edges, the handle wrapped in strips of leather. It looked like a knife that got used, a lot, for God only knew what.

"But everyone calls me Creed," he continued, and with a single, deft move, he cut through her handcuffs.

"Who do you work f-for?"

He sheathed the knife and then took her hands in his. "The government," he said.

His hands were warm around hers, and she was grateful, but he hadn't answered her question. She could think of at least half a dozen governments that might be after her, half a dozen governments that probably *were* after her, including her own, along with another half a dozen terrorist groups from rebels in Chechnya to Islamic jihadists from all over the Middle East who wanted what she had.

"Which government?" she asked.

He glanced up again and met her gaze. The faint light of an exit sign above them cast just enough illumination to turn his eyes a fathomless shade of gray. "The United States government. Land of the free. Home of the brave. I get paid to track down people trying to sell dirty bombs on the black market."

There wasn't an ounce of condemnation in his voice—just the facts, cool and damning all on their own. Still, she felt a sick little knot of tension tighten up in her stomach. Another shiver racked her body, and she wondered if she was ever going to feel warm again. The temperature in the old library was damn near balmy compared to outside, but she was still freezing.

"I'm not selling anything." It was the god's truth.

"Is that why Reinhard Klein is trying to kill you? Because you won't sell him the bomb?" he asked. "Or did you jack the price up on him, thinking to cut yourself a bigger commission than Sergei had built in for you?"

The knot in her stomach grew even tighter. He'd called her Ms. Starkova, and he knew who Reinhard was, knew about Sergei and the warhead.

He knew a helluva lot—but his version was a twisted version of the truth.

"I don't know anybody named Sergei, and nobody's trying to kill me." They wanted her alive.

"Tell yourself what you want, Cody, but when somebody shoots at me, I pretty much figure that means they want me dead."

Cody. He'd used her name again, this time making it sound like he knew her, like they were friends and she should just spill her guts to him.

Not likely. She didn't care how American he looked, or how American he sounded, or who he said he worked for—she had to get away from him. Cordelia Kaplan, Dominika Starkova, or Creed Rivera—it was easy for a person to say they were anyone, to be anybody. All she really knew about him was that he was dangerous. If he'd wanted to, she didn't doubt for a second that he could have killed Edmund Braun with his bare hands.

"Are you with the CIA?" She had to ask. Him being with the CIA would certainly explain how he knew what he did. She'd told Keith O'Connell everything—and he'd died for it.

So she'd decided not to tell anybody anything, ever again, to just disappear, to make *Tajikistan Discontent* disappear. But disappearing was proving impossible. Bruno the Bull, Reinhard Klein, and a complete stranger named Cesar Raoul Eduardo Rivera had all found her in Denver.

"The question, Cody, is who are you with?" He held her gaze intently, and the knot in her stomach started to twist and turn. He had to be CIA.

"I'm not with anybody." And that was her problem. She was completely alone and in way over her head.

"Reinhard Klein, Bruno Walmann, and Ernst and Edmund Braun came a helluva long way to find you. Why, if it wasn't to close the deal on the Soviet nuclear warhead you're selling?"

To take her back to Sergei, so he could torture her.

"I'm not selling anything."

He didn't seem the least bit concerned by her lack of an answer, which didn't fool her for a second. This was an interrogation. He was calm and steady, because this kind of business, this prying out of information, was best done calmly, steadily. He was still wild. He was just biding his time, and she didn't have a doubt in the world that he was damn sure he was going to get everything he wanted before he was finished with her.

Even worse, she had a terrible feeling he might be right.

He pulled a photograph out of his pocket and showed it to her.

"Is this you?"

The terrible feeling she had intensified. It was an old school photograph. Her mother had one, a larger copy in a frame on her mantel, and she'd seen another in her father's house—one of the few signs that he and her mother had ever kept in touch, if only distantly.

"Where did you get that?" He shouldn't have her school picture, no matter who he was. It made her feel queasy, and trapped, and like no part of her life was safe.

It made her feel like getting as far away from him as she could get, even if it meant taking her chances up on the roof with the police.

"I'm asking the questions, Cody, and what I want is answers," he said, still so damn calmly. "Like why you changed your name from Dominique Cordelia Stark to Dominika Starkova, and why you came into the country under the name Cordelia Kaplan, and how a brunette from Wichita, Kansas, ends up in Prague, meeting with known terrorists, and looking like this." He took another photo from inside his coat pocket.

It was a picture of Dominika, and the answer to all that platinum-blond hair, movie-star makeup, and scandalous dress was really quite simple—but he wasn't going to get it from her. Not when she felt like she was falling apart.

How in the world had he found out about Wichita?

"Or we can cut through all this crap and get right to the point," he continued. "Tell me where the bomb is, the exact location, and maybe we can cut a deal on the rest of your problems. And you've got problems, Cody. Serious problems. Enough of them to put you away for life."

That was a threat, and she felt the impact of it right

in her gut, but she would never confess to Wichita, no matter what he pulled out of his coat, not the shortened shotgun, the semiautomatic pistol, or her freaking birth certificate. Wichita was the hill she'd die on. It was where her mother lived, and the only way to protect her mother was by never going there, ever again—not in word or deed, and it broke her heart.

"A deal," she said breathlessly, trying to pull herself together. She could make a deal. She'd made all kinds of deals in the last few weeks, dozens of deals to get from Prague to Denver, deals for forged papers and deals for silence, deals to start a new life and deals to leave an old life behind. Cordelia Kaplan hadn't come into existence cheaply or easily, but if she had to start over again, she could.

She didn't have a choice.

Even maximum-security penitentiary walls wouldn't protect her from Sergei. She'd be a sitting duck in prison, and he wouldn't just have her killed when he caught up with her. He'd want to make an example of her, like he had with Keith O'Connell.

And he'd get the location of the book out of her. She knew he would. She wouldn't hold up under torture, not to save the world. Her only chance was to never get caught.

God, she'd been so naive before her father's death— but no more. Reinhard had cured her of her last shred of naiveté in a warehouse on the outskirts of Karlovy Vary in northwestern Czech Republic.

And that was something she couldn't afford to dwell on, not without getting the shakes. What had happened to O'Connell, what had happened to her—that whole night had been surreally bizarre.

She tried to push the memory away, but it wasn't easy, and her next breath came a little harder. She silently swore at herself. She was going to blow it, if she gave in to panic. Panic was the enemy.

"I . . . uh . . . can't tell you the location of any bombs. I swear," she said. "But you're right. Reinhard is after me, and he's into some pretty bad stuff. I can tell you what I know, but I want some guarantees."

That was the deal, and for basically coming off the cuff, she didn't think it was too bad. Everything she'd said was mostly true—an important aspect of any deal. She knew enough about Reinhard to talk plenty without incriminating herself, and she didn't know where the warhead was located.

She did know where *Tajikistan Discontent* was located— about two floors below them, in the noncirculating stacks of the old library, shelved in the 500s—and if it was up to her, it would rot there. No one ever needed to find that damn bomb.

Her father obviously hadn't found it before he'd died, or Sergei wouldn't have sent Reinhard and his dogs after her.

"So what do you think?" she prompted, trying to hold her anxiety at bay.

"What have you got on Reinhard?" he asked point-blank.

"He's bad. Really bad. Trust me." Okay, that wasn't exactly cutting-edge news, but she had to be careful. "He's into . . . well, you obviously know the kind of deals he's into, but there was this *incident*, you see . . . about a month ago in, uh, Karlovy Vary, and there are a few things your government would like to know about it, some very specific things. All I want is a guarantee of safe passage and enough money to make my life a little easier than it's been lately. That's all. I swear it."

INCIDENT *in Karlovy Vary?* Well, that was a damned interesting turn, Creed thought, looking down at her, listening to her talk and spin and try to hook him without actually giving herself away. She was still shivering, but the color was coming back into her face, washing her cheeks in soft pink, and her gaze was focused again, all green and aquamarine with streaks of brown and gray.

Geezus, she was pretty.

"There might even be a reward in this for you," she continued, looking so incredibly sincere, he couldn't find it in himself to believe her for a second. She was lying through her teeth about not knowing the location of the bomb. She knew. If she wasn't so damn frozen, she'd be sweating with knowing it. "And you can have it all. I swear. I don't need any reward, just enough money to get around. That's all. And the information is good, probably worth a promotion or something. You can count on it. Names, dates, places—the works."

He wasn't going to tell her, poor thing, but she'd already given him a name, a date, and a place. An incident in Karlovy Vary a month ago could only mean Keith O'Connell, December 7, in a warehouse on the outskirts of town—that's where the CIA had found the body. If she was telling him that she could positively hang O'Connell's death on Reinhard Klein, she indeed had something to sell besides a nuclear bomb. Daniel Alden, the director of the CIA, and every agent in Eastern Europe had laid O'Connell's death at the feet of Sergei Patrushev and the Russian Mafia. If Reinhard had also been involved, then his ties to the Mafia and Patrushev were closer than anyone realized—which wasn't good news.

"Okay," he agreed, lying at least as much as she was. "We'll talk and see what you come up with. Maybe you do have something I want." His gaze dropped to her mouth, just a slight shift in his attention that lasted no more than a second, but it was enough to unnerve her. He saw it in her sudden stillness and silently swore at himself for giving so much away.

It had been crazy to kiss her up on the roof—and it would be even crazier to kiss her again, but he was thinking about it.

He must be out of his mind. None of the shrinks had come right out and said it, not yet anyway, but they had to be thinking it. Skeeter was definitely thinking it. He could tell by the way she watched him—like a buzzard on roadkill, every move he made.

He needed to call her. Skeeter worried the way other people breathed, and she'd probably tried to call him a couple of times since he'd left. He needed to tell her—again—that he could take care of himself. It was the people who counted on him that got screwed. No matter how much shit hit the fan, he kept coming out in one piece.

Slipping his phone out of his pocket, he flipped it on and checked the screen. Fifteen missed calls. He ran through the first few numbers, got the general idea, and turned off the phone.

Hell. Fifteen calls from Skeeter were about twelve more than he could handle.

"Are you hungry?" he asked the woman he'd all but kidnapped. When Dylan told him to keep somebody in one piece, he meant with a sustainable body temperature, not one frozen piece, and Cody Stark was still shivering uncontrollably. He needed to do something about that before he took her back outside to get to his car, or she wasn't going to make it.

She shook her head, but he already had his hand inside his coat. He hadn't left Steele Street once in the last two weeks without Skeeter putting something to eat in his pockets. He knew he'd hit the jackpot when he pulled out three gold-wrapped candy bars.

Count on Skeeter to go first-class.

"Sugar rush?" He offered up the chocolate, fanning out the bars to give her a choice.

She shook her head again, the action almost indistinguishable from all her regular shivering.

"This isn't one of those don't-take-candy-from-a-stranger things, is it?" he asked. "Because if it is, I gotta tell ya, you're in more danger of going into hypothermic shock right now than you are from me."

She considered his words for a few seconds before making her decision and reaching for a candy bar. Her hands were too cold for her to get the wrapper off, though, which worried him plenty.

Damn it. He wasn't going to lose her to the cold after he'd saved her from Reinhard Klein and Denver's finest—who, from the sound of it, were entering the library down on the main floor. Flashes of light were coming up through the scaffolding, and he could hear voices.

"Come on, get closer," he told her, softening his voice so as not to be heard. It was an order, not a request, and he didn't wait for an answer before pulling her into the circle of his body and wrapping his coat around her. From another pocket, he retrieved his black knit cap and pulled it down on her head. He didn't know how in the hell she'd gotten so cold, so fast, unless she was running on empty. "Put your hands under my sweater, and let's not do the gun thing again. Okay?"

When she hesitated, he did it for her and tried not to flinch when her icy fingers rested on his T-shirt. Then he tore the wrapper off one of the candy bars and offered it to her.

"Come on," he urged. "Either we get you warmed up, inside and out, or you can forget playing 'Let's Make a Deal,' because I'm going to have to haul you over to Denver General where they're going to start something intravenous and ask a whole lot of questions and—"

She took a bite.

Finally, he thought, he was starting to get this mess under control, and for a moment or two it was kind of peaceful: his breathing deep and even, hers shaky as hell, him fairly warm and getting warmer, her like an ice cube; it occurred to him that feeding Cody Stark chocolate while he was half wrapped around her was as close to sex as he'd been in a long, long time—but not close enough, not tonight, and not when it was her.

And wasn't that a hell of a thing.

CHAPTER

8

I'M NOT SAYING your boys don't have plenty of reason to be wild," Tony Royce said, backing off from his last few rounds of demanding to know Creed's whereabouts. "Especially Rivera. *Jesus*, what he went through." Without looking back, he stretched his hand out to young Agent Mathers, who handed him a folder sealed with orange tape, which he in turn handed over to Dylan. "These were sent to us a few weeks ago. They were found in an abandoned NRF camp in northern Colombia."

Dylan took the folder, stacking it on top of the Castano photos, and broke the tape. Then he flipped the folder open.

For a long, silent moment he didn't move, not so

much as a muscle. He barely kept breathing. The top photograph was of Creed and J.T., and it explained a lot of things—like why Creed was so fucked up.

"He's got to still be thinking about it," Royce said, managing not to sound like a complete asshole.

Yeah, Creed was thinking about it. Dylan knew it for a fact. He'd come home late one night a couple of weeks ago and gone up to Creed's loft on the ninth floor. Creed had been asleep, curled up on the floor next to the kitchen, gasping for breath, sweating, his body twitching, fighting something in his dreams.

He'd started to wake him, but Skeeter had stopped him.

"Been there, done that," she'd said from the shadowed depths of the jungle Creed's apartment had become over the last two years. He hadn't seen her through all the vegetation and trees. "And it's better if you just let him work through it in his sleep."

Now he had a pretty good idea of what "it" was— *sweet Jesus*.

"Ms. Bang?" He looked up and gestured toward his private office. They needed to talk.

SKEETER rose to her feet even as her heart did a dipping flip to the bottom of her stomach. Ms. Bang? What the hell was up with that?

Dylan Hart *never* invited her into his private office, and despite what he'd said to Royce, she was no more his secretary than he was hers. At best they had what she would describe as a coolly cordial working relationship, no matter how heated her imagination. The other guys—Hawkins, Quinn, Kid, Creed—they all treated her like a kid sister. Dylan had always treated her like somebody else's kid cousin, a visitor, even though she'd lived at Steele Street for over two years.

But she'd seen the look on his face when he opened the folder; she'd felt a shift take place deep in his psyche, the closest she'd ever been to getting a real reading off of him, and she had a terrible, awful feeling that she knew what he'd seen.

He waited for her to precede him into his office before he closed the door behind them. The room was spartan, stripped down to the basics of a desk and chair in pale beech. Two black laptop computers sat in the middle of the desk, flanked by a black phone and a black-and-chrome lamp. A low bookcase, also in pale beech, ran along one wall. A bank of locked filing cabinets made out of the same pale beech took up another. There wasn't so much as a pencil or a piece of paper anywhere in evidence. Not so much as a paper clip. No stapler, no scissors, no handy-dandy glue stick. No coffee cup. No half-dead plant.

He worked in the office. She knew he did, sometimes all night long, but she didn't know how. There wasn't a picture on the walls, no calendar, nothing other than a clean expanse of elegantly expensive woven-grass wallpaper in pale green. Four tall double-hung windows overlooked the alley called Steele Street. There was a private entrance to the garage floor, but nothing else. Not so much as a single extra chair for visitors—for the plain and simple reason that nobody visited Dylan Hart in his private office, except now for her.

At first he said nothing, just stood by the door, his gaze angled toward the floor.

"I—" he started, hesitated, then cleared his throat and tried again. "I noticed you and Creed have been working on Mercy."

"Yes, sir," she said, then winced. She'd called him sir. There were a lot of things she wanted to call Dylan Hart, and "sir" was not one of them.

"How's it going?"

Well, she wasn't going to sugarcoat it for him.

"With high-octane gas and ten pounds of boost, we've got her up to over seven hundred ponies . . . way over." A lethal amount of horsepower.

Dylan nodded. "I see," he said, walking toward his desk and, after a second, laying the folder and the other photos on top. He left his hand on the pile, his eyes closing briefly before he lifted his gaze to hers. "I want you to blow the engine. I don't want Mercy leaving Steele Street."

"The drags won't even start until spring." Sure, Mercy was bad, but she was also a work of art.

"That won't keep him from going up there on a clear day and killing himself." Hart's voice was flat, matter-of-fact, but his whole body was tight with tension. The grace and elegance that usually defined his every move had been replaced with barely controlled anger—and pain. It didn't take any special insight to feel it coming off him in waves. Hell, she could almost see it, the emotion was so intense. It scared her a little bit, and it depressed the hell out of her.

Dylan had come home. They were finally in the same room together, actually talking, and everything was wrong—terribly, awfully wrong.

It broke her heart, the way looking at him broke her heart. The last few months had been so damn hard on everyone, and now this. Damn Royce. Dylan was tired. Lines of strain marred his features. His hair had grown longer since summer. Usually impeccably in place, tonight it fell on either side of his face, dark and silky straight, nearly to his cheekbones in front and brushing the collar of his white shirt in back. The carelessness of the style made him look younger than his thirty-two years, as did the leanness of his physique. Dylan was the brains of Special Defense Force, the geek extraordinaire, and the player when they needed one. She knew that, too. She'd seen him in action—an exquisitely elegant woman on his arm, an embassy invitation in his hand, a private jet waiting. Guys like Creed and Hawkins were the brawn. Not that they weren't all certifiable geniuses, given what she'd seen in their files, and she'd made a second job out of reading the guys' files, even the classified sections when she could break enough codes to access them. There was damn little she didn't know about any of the SDF operators, and nothing she didn't want to know.

She shifted her attention to the folder. Dylan still had his hand on it, keeping it closed . . . somehow, she thought, keeping it safe.

"Maybe you should let me see what's in the folder," she suggested.

She knew. In her heart she knew what was inside. Royce had given it away—*found them in an abandoned NRF camp in northern Colombia*—but that didn't keep her from needing to see it for herself.

"No," Dylan said, his voice losing its matter-of-fact tone and taking on a rough edge. "There's no reason for you to have this information."

"Is it J.T.?" she asked, undeterred. "Photographs?"

He didn't answer, but that was answer enough for her.

Royce was such a bastard for giving them to Dylan like that, without warning, without preamble. This wasn't like Castano and Garcia. J.T. had been one of their own.

"Creed never turned away," she said, telling Hart what she knew, what he needed to know. "Not once, no matter what they did to him or to J.T."

"He told you this?" Dylan looked up, his gaze sharp.

"Yes." She nodded. "He doesn't know he told me, but he did."

"What do you mean?"

She shrugged, knowing it wasn't easy to explain. "It was the second time I found him in the middle of a nightmare. I didn't wake him, because the first time, the night I did wake him up, he . . . well, he couldn't let go of the dream, and everything got a whole lot worse before it got better. So I just sat with him, tried to hold his hand when he'd let me, just so he'd know he wasn't alone."

"And?" he asked when she stopped.

"And he was putting out a pretty heavy vibe." Overwhelming, actually. Creed had almost drowned her with the intensity of the emotions running through him, tearing him apart; of the visions flooding his mind. She had hardly let him out of her sight since that night, except for tonight, when Dylan had sent him off into the storm to track an international criminal who had brought the CIA right to their freakin' doorstep—*damn*.

"A vibe?" Dylan asked, a note of skepticism in his voice. "What kind of vibe?"

She didn't blame him for doubting her, not really. He hadn't spent enough time around her to know what the other guys had long since started to take for granted— that she was hot-wired with extrasensory perception, ESP, the real deal, and it worked pretty damn well on the guys most of the time, but not on Dylan Hart. He was the shadow warrior in her mind, indecipherable, unbreachable, a fascinating mystery.

"He was handcuffed, chained to the back of a Jeep, on his knees in the mud," she said, describing the image she'd gotten of Creed's dream. It had been quick, a searing flash, but everything had been crystal clear. "He'd been beaten. He was bleeding. J.T. was someplace close. I couldn't see him, but Creed could, and he never took his eyes off him. Not once. He bore witness. It was what kept him conscious, the need to bear witness."

"You didn't see J.T.?"

She shook her head.

His gaze fell on the folder again, and a weary breath left him on a sigh. "You're a spooky girl, Skeeter."

Yeah, she knew it. She also knew "spooky girl" wasn't a compliment; far from it. Dylan went for sophistication, women who looked like fashion models and talked like college professors, women who had class—not weird little street rats with paint under their fingernails.

"What you described isn't what Creed wrote in his report, except in the most general terms," Dylan said. "It's not what he's been telling the doctors."

Yeah, she knew that, too. She'd made a whole sideline out of reading Creed's medical files.

"But it's exactly what's in the photographs inside this folder."

Sometimes she was wrong—not often, but often enough for her never to take too big of a risk based solely on something she'd "seen." It was just too damn bad she hadn't been wrong this time—too damn bad for Creed. She reached for the folder.

"No," Dylan said, holding it to the desk. "You've seen enough. Done enough."

"You're about five years too late to protect me from anything," she said, and tugged the folder free.

Hell, yeah, she was a spooky girl, from way back, and this wallbanger needed to know what the Colombians had done to J.T. She needed to know for Creed's sake, and for Kid's, and for her own. J.T. would never be dead to Steele Street. His spirit filled the place. She felt it all the time—J.T. Chronopolous, one of the original "chop-shop boys," guardian angel to all the other juvenile delinquents running wild on the streets of Denver with him. She knew the stories. He'd watched their backs, picked them up when they'd fallen, and kicked their butts when they'd made mistakes . . .

She opened the folder.

. . . and the Colombians had crucified him.

Crucified.

Oh, yeah, he'd been close to where Creed had been chained, barely ten feet away, nailed to a cross . . . his chest cut open.

For one blinding second, she flashed on the scene, the brutality of it, the viciousness, the smell of J.T.'s blood. She felt the strangling heat of the jungle, heard his last agonized scream, his last dying breath—and through it all, Creed, naked on his knees, screaming at their captors and crying out his name . . . *J.T. . . . John . . . John Thomas, I'm here. I'll never leave you . . . never . . . never . . . never . . .*

UNBELIEVABLE, Creed thought. Cody Stark had fallen asleep—like a rock. Warming her up had turned her sugar rush into a carbohydrate crash, putting her down for the count.

He checked his watch.

The cops had been crawling all over the library for the last ten minutes, and she hadn't moved so much as a muscle in the last five, just lain there against him, her head cradled in the curve of his shoulder, her body limp—which wasn't all bad. Someone had checked the skylight about eight minutes ago, giving it a good rattle and swinging their flashlight around through the glass before moving on. Given the number of nooks and crannies in the old building, he doubted if they'd be coming back to check this one again. Keeping quiet in the back-water corner of the attic where he and Cody had washed up was the smart move until the police left.

He'd had worse nights. That was for damn sure.

But few as interesting. His ops usually didn't include women, especially ones who had their hands inside his clothes. Dylan usually handled any women who showed up on Steele Street's radar. He was better than the rest of them with the sort of female who traded secrets for power and money on the world stage. Creed and J.T. had always been the down-and-dirty jungle boys, racking up more Boy Scout badges than the rest of the guys put together.

Yeah, him and J.T. That's the way it had been since he'd been fourteen. J.T. Chronopolous at his back— bigger, badder, faster, older, smarter. J.T. covering his ass every time they'd boosted a car, keeping him out of the kind of trouble that could have gotten him killed, giving him a place to stay on the nights when he'd had nowhere else to go. For years, the Chronopolous home had been like a frat house for the wild boys from the chop shop on Steele Street. Somehow all those wild boys had gone from stealing cars to serving their country, and for years everything had been going great—until it had all gone to hell in Colombia. Nothing had been the same for any of them since Colombia.

Ah, shit, J.T. He rubbed his hand across the sudden ache in his chest. *I'm so fucking sorry.*

The ache didn't ease. It never eased, and by his next breath, an awful heaviness had settled over him, making him even more miserable, a feeling he was getting so damn tired of fighting.

"Shit," he swore softly. He couldn't do this.

"What?" the woman in his arms whispered.

He glanced down and found her wide awake, her face tilted toward his, and his breath caught. *Geezus.*

A couple of candy bars and a little rest had gone a long way toward restoring her. Her skin had lost the icy paleness of Skeeter's manga paintings. She looked warm and alive.

Her mouth so soft.

The curve of her jaw so delicate. Her cheeks. The silky fall of dark hair across her brow, the long strands sliding across the tips of her eyelashes. So female.

His chest grew even tighter, but in a different way. She wasn't just pretty. She was beautiful, and he was insane. There was no other way to account for his slow, unstoppable slide into desire. It was impossible for any sane man to feel so awful and still get turned on. He had to have some kind of major glitch in his serotonin synapses or whatever the hell was supposed to keep this sort of thing from happening.

He wanted to kiss her again, really kiss her this time, his tongue in her mouth, her hands in his hair, and that was so crazy it worried him. She was an international criminal selling a nuclear warhead on the black market, for Christ's sake. He couldn't have her. Hell, he didn't even know her, and if she was half as smart as he thought she was, she sure as hell wouldn't want to know him—and he didn't blame her. He was no catch even on a good day, and even if she could overlook the fact that he was the guy who had captured her and was turning her in, Dylan was going to take her away as soon as he got back from Washington, D.C., tonight. The CIA was probably already at Steele Street, waiting for him to show up—which would explain Skeeter's record-breaking fifteen phone calls—and that would be the end of his whole involvement with Cody Stark. If he really worked at it, he might be able to follow the government's case against her, but more than likely it would all be so classified it would be as if she'd dropped off the edge of the earth. She would simply disappear into a maw of regulations and government double-speak, and he'd never know what happened to her, or whether or not she was actually Cody Stark.

And that was the way it was supposed to be. That's the way it always was when he brought somebody in. He wasn't supposed to care, and he sure as hell wasn't supposed to kiss anybody, or want to sleep with them. Dominika Starkova, Cody Stark, it didn't matter. He was on an op, not a date.

But something about holding her in the dark, feeling her hands on him and listening to her breathe, had crossed his signals. He wanted something from her—something he had a snowball's chance in hell of getting.

Loneliness, that was probably his problem, but he was lonely all the time, and being around Skeeter never gave him a jones.

Maybe he just needed to get laid. That was the simple answer—but nothing was simple any more.

She started to move away from him, but he gave her arm a light squeeze and shook his head. Then he pointed toward the scaffolding. Lights were still shining up from the lower floors. They weren't out of this yet.

In truth, she was never going to be out of it, not ever again, not in this life. The minute he'd grabbed her, she'd lost her last shred of freedom—and why in the hell that should bother him was just one more big damn mystery to him, like why he was having to work so hard to keep from reassuring her that everything was going to be all right.

For her, nothing was going to be all right—not if he did his job.

Down in the old library, Creed heard a few books

come off their shelves and land on the floor. He instantly froze, listening.

So did everyone on the main floor. Everything went silent.

After a second or two, a man spoke. "Sorry, guys. That was me."

Other voices chimed in, teasing the guy, and Creed relaxed from full-out ready-to-rumble.

"Smooth move."

"Way to go, Miller."

The police had to be about through.

Outside, the wind was howling, the storm picking up in force. His car was going to be a block of ice by the time they got to it. She'd still start; Angelina always started. But the ride to Steele Street was going to be a cold one . . . *if you take Cody Stark to Steele Street.*

Whoa, he thought. Slow down. Of course he was taking her to Steele Street—and he was handing her over to whoever was there, Dylan or the CIA. He hadn't completely lost his mind—despite the weeks he'd spent trying, before General Grant had let him go back to Colombia and relieve Hawkins. Apparently, soaking your brain in premium tequila, even for days on end, wasn't enough to make it pack its bags and go away.

Too bad, he'd thought at the time.

After a couple more minutes of holding her and trying not to think about it too much, the library was once again quiet, the lower floors dark.

"Okay. Let's move out," he said.

FINALLY, Cody thought, getting to her feet as quickly as she could, about ready to jump out of her skin. She'd had some incredibly bad nights since her father had died, but this one was heading toward the top of the crazy list. Not the top of her worst-ever list, just the crazy list. The all-time worst-ever top spot had been chiseled in granite in Karlovy Vary, and it was going to take more than a dangerous but oddly nice guy named Creed Rivera to change it.

Oddly nice? She stopped moving for a second, startled into stillness.

Well, that settled it. She *had* lost her mind. Nice men did not shoot at a person, handcuff her, drop her through skylights, or threaten her with lifetime imprisonment.

On the other hand, nice men did save a person from her worst enemies and the cops, and nice men did give you their hats and their candy bars and wrap you in their coats when you were freezing your butt off.

Of course, it wasn't very nice when that same guy turned you over to the United States government and your butt ended up in Leavenworth.

No. Her prime directive hadn't changed in the last few minutes. She had to get away from him, but even the briefest look around proved that getting away wasn't going to be easy. They had a sheer drop on one side, with some scaffolding holding up the floor; the other side was haphazardly blocked off with stored bookcases and a few pieces of piled-up furniture.

Her gaze went back to the sheer drop. She didn't really know him, but she knew him well enough to know that's the way he was going—heedlessly, without a thought. Over the edge. That was him.

Proving her right, he took hold of her hand and pulled her with him into the jungle gym of iron bars. "Watch your step."

It was only a couple of feet to the abyss, and when she looked down she could almost pinpoint the bank of bookcases where she'd hidden *Tajikistan Discontent*, the worst book of poetry she'd ever tried to read, which had been her second clue that poetry might not have been its reason for existing. That much dreck and drivel had to have another purpose, and when her father had keeled over in the mountains of Tajikistan, coerced there by Sergei's command to lead a group of Sergei's men to the nuclear warhead, she'd realized what her father had given her: the map he'd sworn he'd never made, and the absolute worst inheritance ever bequeathed. It was going to be the death of her, if she couldn't escape.

As soon as they got to the street, she was going to disappear into it. She'd been at a disadvantage with Mr. Creed Rivera so far, but her car was parked just a block away, and he had that weak left leg. One more good kick ought to put him down long enough for her to melt into the shadows, concealed by the blizzard. He wasn't going to shoot her, and she was betting that Bruno and Ernst weren't waiting right outside the front door, not with the cops all around.

She was betting her life on it.

"Here's the plan," he said, moving to the edge of the scaffolding and leaning into the darkness.

Out of pure instinct, she grabbed for him, her free hand closing around a fistful of his coat. Then she noticed the pair of ropes he'd pulled back.

"Thanks," he said, and she felt her cheeks burn. Damn him. She hadn't seen any ropes. And what was she doing grabbing for him? She sure as hell wouldn't have grabbed for Bruno Walmann. Pushed was more like it.

"We'll ride this down to the main floor," he said, looping a foothold into one of the ropes.

She had to admit that it was a hell of an idea, a hell of a *crazy* idea. She followed the ropes to where they wound themselves through a series of pulleys.

"Uh, what makes you think this is going to work?" She didn't even attempt to hide her skepticism. Right off the top of her head she could imagine a hundred real simple things that could go wrong—starting with them dropping three floors like a couple of stones and hitting the library floor at just under light speed.

No. She wasn't doing it.

"These are rigged for hauling supplies. They'll hold us."

"No." She shook her head. "No, I don't think so." She'd had enough of hanging off things.

"It wasn't a question, and I wasn't asking," he said,

scooping his arm around her waist. Before she could protest, he pushed them off into thin air.

Holy freaking Tarzan. She scrambled to hold onto him, clutching at him, her arms going around his neck, her feet bicycling in the air, trying to find the loop he'd tied in the rope.

"Stop moving your legs," he said.

"But I-I'm not on the rope." He should have warned her, damn him.

"I've got you."

"Yes, but . . . but—"

"I've got you." His voice was quiet, firm.

And he did, she realized. His arm was tight around her waist, holding her close—close enough for her to feel his breath against her cheek. They hadn't dropped like a couple of stones. They were actually swinging in a long graceful arc. At the end of it, they hung in the air for a second before swinging back toward the scaffolding—and all the while they were slowly descending toward the main floor, belayed by the rope he was holding at the small of her back. She looked up and saw his left arm stretched out above them, his hand wrapped around the other end of the rope.

He was strong.

Very strong, she realized—strong enough to hold the two of them in midair, strong enough to carry her around half the night without breaking a sweat, strong enough to take down Edmund Braun in five seconds flat.

Who in the holy hell was he? she wondered for about

the millionth time. And what were the chances that he would betray his country to make a deal with her?

Damn slim, she decided. He probably wasn't a traitor. That would have been too easy, and nothing had been easy for her lately. He was definitely a professional, highly trained. The truth of it had been in every move he'd made. She hadn't known it at the time, but he'd been in control of the situation from the minute he'd sat down in the reading room. Bruno showing up had just given him an opportunity to prove it. He was used to thinking fast on his feet, taking action, and coming out on top. He knew how to protect himself and others. He was skilled at evasion but not adverse to combat when evasion failed. He had weapons and knew how to use them.

In truth, he was a warrior, a warrior who won at any cost.

In fact, he was exactly what she needed.

The realization hit her hard, all of a sudden, like a thousand watts of halogen quartz snapping on at the end of a long dark tunnel. She needed help staying alive, help evading Sergei and the men like Reinhard Klein that Sergei would never stop sending after her until he'd recaptured her. She needed another new identity, and sanctuary if she could find it. She needed some breathing room, a place and the time to think—and she needed it all yesterday. She'd been on the run for weeks. She wasn't sharp anymore. She'd made a mistake somewhere, to have been found so quickly—but if she could win Creed Rivera over to her side, she'd have someone to watch her back. She could catch her breath.

All she had to do was get him to slow down, keep him from turning her in.

All she had to do was sweeten the deal.

She lowered her gaze, letting it drift over the tangled length of his sun-streaked hair, the short dark lines of his eyebrows, over the hard, wide curve of his jaw. He was the ultimate surfer boy all grown up, ocean blue eyes washed through with green and faded by the sun to a pale silvery sheen, his face tanned and carved in classic lines—which was, she admitted, all beside the point. But he was also rock-solid against her, which wasn't beside the point, all corded muscle-and-sinew-wrapped testosterone honed to a razor's edge. Despite the underlying prettiness of his rough-boy looks, everything about him said "switchblade" more than "surfboard."

He was more than a match for her nightmares. She was sure of it. The only remotely soft-looking thing about him was the slight fullness of his lower lip. It fascinated her, the one sensual touch in a face that could easily have been described as too hard by half.

And he'd kissed her on the roof. A smart girl would use that to her advantage.

She was a smart girl.

But maybe not that smart.

Hell. She'd spent too much of her time the last three months avoiding just that sort of complication, avoiding it at all costs, determined not to let herself be used like the bimbo she'd been pretending to be—and for the most part, she'd been successful.

So could she use him?

Of course she could, she told herself. Get a grip, take a breath, and grow up.

The deep shadows of the stacks suddenly rose up around them, signaling the end of their descent. It was now or never. She either ran and took her chances with Bruno and Ernst, or she took Creed Rivera for all she could get and let him be the one to make sure she got out of downtown Denver in one piece.

She didn't doubt that he could, and once he'd helped her escape downtown, she wouldn't have any trouble escaping him, especially if she could get him on her home ground.

He stepped off the rope onto the floor, and with all the enthusiasm she could muster on such short notice, she slowly slid down the front of him until her feet touched the ground.

Looking up, she let her arms gradually fall from around his neck. "I have something in my apartment you need to see," she said, adding just the slightest hint of breathlessness to her voice.

CREED looked down at her, wary as hell, with every cell in his body telling him she suddenly, for whatever reason, had just decided to set him up. She'd slid down him like hot on a Dreamsicle popsicle—and he'd liked it, a lot.

And that, he knew, was why Dylan always did any "girl work" that came SDF's way, because Dylan Hart was a cold-hearted, by-the-book, take-no-prisoners and give-no-ground kind of guy who would never fall for such a cheesy come-on, especially when it was delivered by a gamine-faced waif with boy-cut hair dressed in at least two layers of the baggiest clothes God had ever put on the planet.

I have something in my apartment you need to see. Of course she did, and it was probably a .357 magnum or a boyfriend the size of King Kong.

Dylan would never have taken such obvious bait.

But Creed remembered how soft her mouth had been beneath his, and even though he was absolutely positive this was one more sure step down the road to self-destruction, a real shit-for-brains idea, he was damned if he was going to say no. All she'd really done was give him the excuse he'd wanted. She had something in her apartment he needed to see, and if it bought him an extra hour of Cody Stark's company, he was going to take it. Maybe she'd show him the maps—or maybe she'd show him something else. And he'd be lying if he said a small, totally irresponsible, and undoubtedly crazy part of him wasn't hoping for something else.

"Okay," he said and hoped to hell his brain kicked in sometime soon, before he did any serious damage to the operation. "I'll take you home before I take you in."

On the other hand, it would save them all a few hours of detective work to have her show him where she lived. Dylan was going to want to go over the place with a fine-tooth comb, and he'd want to do it without the CIA on his ass. One of the basic truths of SDF was getting paid for getting results where other people failed. General Grant kept his office, next to the boiler room in the underbelly of a hell-and-gone annex, because his guys got the job done, every time, ahead of the pack. Without them, old Buck would have been put out to pasture a long time ago.

With his hand on her arm, he started toward the front door. Then it opened. The heavy handle rattled, the hinges squeaked, and a gust of frigid air blew inside.

He and Cody Stark froze in place. When the door closed, they heard two men whispering and the sound of footsteps crossing the foyer.

It didn't take Creed more than five seconds of listening to the voices to realize she'd been in danger from more than just the Braun boys blasting away in the stairwell tonight. *Damn*, she was starting to look like a friggin' magnet for trouble.

From the look on her face, she realized it, too. Without a word, they backed deeper into the stacks. The bookcases loomed up around them, deadening the sound of their retreat. After a few steps, he turned her around and they made a beeline away from the foyer. When he couldn't hear the men whispering any longer, Creed pulled her to a stop.

Making their escape through the front door was out of the question now. Bruno and Ernst were undoubtedly watching it, but he'd figured he could elude Reinhard's brigade. These new guys, though. Hell, they added a whole new dimension to the night. He didn't want to get caught on the Plaza with bad guys in front of them and bad guys behind them.

He looked around. They were at the south end of the building, which wasn't so bad. He'd parked Angelina on Bannock Street. All they needed was a way out. There had to be a back door somewhere.

In the end, he found a partially blocked fire exit behind the outdated encyclopedias onto Thirteenth Avenue. It took him all of thirty seconds to dismantle the alarm, and then they were squeezing out onto the street, right into the heart of the storm.

The wind had increased in velocity, blowing the snow sideways and causing the temperature to plummet. *Goddamn*, it was cold. Bruno and Ernst might be holding up in the wild weather, but the men inside the old library had to be desperate to have come out looking for her in a blizzard.

Of course, there was nothing like trying to pump up your country's nuclear capabilities to add a little incentive to your agenda. Having the Bomb was big on the world stage. Only eight countries could produce a mushroom cloud on demand—and every rogue state that had managed to pull themselves out of a Third World economy wanted to be number nine.

Add the nationless element of globe-trotting tangos to the mix and it was easy to see why Dominika Starkova was so popular. How they'd all traced her to Cody Stark,

Denver Public Library research librarian, was something he needed to figure out fast, before any more insurgent types showed up and started breathing down his neck.

He glanced up the street. Two police cars were still parked at the corner of Broadway and Thirteenth Avenue, covering the library's east entrance, and there were probably at least a couple of patrolmen on the Plaza and a couple more hunkered down in a cruiser on the Fourteenth Avenue Parkway, watching the main entrance. The Denver Police Department had been working hard tonight. It was time to give them a break.

Walking quickly away from the library, he held onto Cody with one hand and pulled his cell phone out of his pocket with his other. The 911 call was short and to the point, and after slipping his phone back in his pocket, he looked over his shoulder. The cops at Thirteenth and Broadway were piling out of their cars.

Perfect. The DPD wasn't going to go home completely empty-handed. They'd missed the Bimbo with the Bomb, but two Iranians trespassing in a closed section of the Denver Public Library after a reported shotgun blast ought to keep them busy the rest of the night.

CHAPTER 9

DYLAN WATCHED SKEETER put the folder back on the desk. With her ball cap low on her face and her mirrored sunglasses, he couldn't see her expression, but he'd seen the tremor that had gone through her when she'd opened the folder. He'd heard the catch in her breath.

Yeah, she'd had some idea of what she was going to see—they all knew J.T. had come home in pieces—but seeing it had still been a shock. He had to give her credit, though. Another kid might have buckled at the sight of J.T. being . . .

Jesus, J.T. A wave of heat washed through him, churning his stomach. *J.T., Christ.*

And Creed had been there, on his knees, chained in the mud at J.T.'s feet, helpless to stop it.

"Creed's been disappearing a lot lately, a few days at a time," Skeeter said, her voice low, her head still bowed.

"Disappearing?" he repeated. "You mean you don't know where he goes?"

She shook her head.

"I thought you tracked all of us when we were in town." Christian Hawkins, the SDF operator they all called Superman, had told him—or warned him was actually more like it.

"With Creed, it's only if he feels like letting me. He's disabled more of my tracking devices in the last two weeks than I've lost in the last two years," she said. "He's running so fast, I can't keep up with him."

But not fast enough, Dylan thought. There was no way in hell to outrun what had happened in that camp.

He dragged his hand back through his hair and took a breath.

"So you haven't just been putting Royce off? You really don't know where Creed is right now?"

"No," she admitted.

That was the last damn thing he'd wanted to hear. *Shit.*

"I should never have sent him." Hindsight was always so crystal-fucking-clear. *Jesus.*

"Creed can take care of himself," she said, her chin coming up. "He's like you. He doesn't need looking after, at least not for what you sent him to do tonight."

Intrigued, Dylan looked at her a little more closely—and wished for the hundred thousandth time that those damned mirrored sunglasses of hers would just disappear.

She was right, of course. Creed could take care of himself, if he wanted to, especially when he was up against a challenge.

As for her comment about him, she was right about that, too. He didn't need looking after, never had, not by anyone. What Dylan had never figured out was whether or not that was a blessing or a curse.

"What about you?" he asked, more curious than he let on—way more curious. How much looking after did she need these days, he wondered, and yeah, that was a whole separate part of his problem tonight: Skeeter Bang. He usually avoided her like the plague. But there just weren't enough people hanging around Steele Street lately for him to have his normal buffer zone. So he was stuck with her, and her platinum ponytail, and the Chinese tattoo running down her arm, and the black muscle shirt clinging to her amazing breasts.

And that, he reminded himself, was why he hadn't been coming home much since Hawkins had hired her to answer the phones, mess with the computers, and do race-quality tune-ups on the side. According to Hawkins, it had only made sense to also give her a loft up on the eleventh floor.

"I don't need looking after, either," she said, sounding damnably assured.

Right, he thought. That's why Hawkins had practically adopted her, because she'd been doing so well on the streets, only getting her butt kicked every other Saturday night and doing her best to hide the fact that she was older than she looked—which Dylan wasn't at all convinced had saved her from the more sordid aspects of street life. She'd been busted twice for stealing, eight times for graffiti, and had run away from four different foster homes before she'd turned eighteen and Social Services had simply cut her loose.

Skeeter Bang—honest to God, that was her real name. He'd checked. The hair was real, too. He and Hawkins had tracked down her parents once, and platinum blond was a Bang family trait along with poverty, squalor, and alcoholism. God only knew how many generations of Bangs had come and gone before the miracle had happened: a girl child whose IQ and psychic abilities were off the chart.

He knew why she wore her ball cap so low and never went without her sunglasses—to cover the scar on her forehead—and it was a testament to Hawkins's good sense that her father was still alive. Left to his own devices, Dylan would have taken the man out and never looked back. Dylan was, even by his own estimation, one coldhearted son of a bitch.

Except when it came to her, a girl who should have been way too young and way too edgy to even begin to catch his attention.

Hell, she'd been barely eighteen when Christian

Hawkins had dragged her in from the cold—disturbingly young and a street rat to boot. The women Dylan dated didn't know a wrench from a dipstick, and none of them had ever spent a night in anything less than a five-star hotel—let alone the flophouse on Wazee where Hawkins had finally tracked Skeeter down the night she'd been hurt.

So why had Dylan been riveted to every move she'd made for the last two years?

He swore again, silently to himself, refusing to answer his own question. He wasn't going there, period. She wasn't even old enough to drink.

"I've never found a tracker on Trina," he said.

"That's because I've never put one on the trailer queen."

The trailer queen, as Skeeter called her, was a silver 1965 289 Cobra roadster, the rarest piece of iron in the Steele Street stables, and she was Dylan's ride.

"Why not?"

Before she could reply, they were interrupted by a sharp knock on the door.

"Hart!"

Dylan crossed the room to open the door. Royce was waiting for him on the other side.

"I just got a call from my guy downtown, and there's been some sort of shoot-out at the Denver Public Library."

Oh, Christ.

"What's the CIA doing at the library?"

"The same damn thing you are," Royce said, clearly

not in the mood to play their usual game of cat and mouse. "My information has been running behind yours all day, but we finally got the name we'd been waiting for, the name I think you gave Creed Rivera: Cordelia Kaplan, newest employee of the Denver Public Library. Unfortunately, our guy didn't get there in time to do anything but mop up. The cops are swarming the place, and there's a man down."

"Rivera?" Dylan ignored the sudden clenching of his stomach. He was going to hate himself for a very long time if anything happened to Creed tonight.

"No," Royce said. "According to an eyewitness, another guy who looked just like the downed man came busting out of the stairwell with a third guy. They started for the man laid out in the study carrels, but the cops had about ten guns on him, so they hauled ass out of there. The witness thought she was hallucinating— two of the guys looking alike, all big and ugly, both of them with the same gorilla face."

Big ugly gorilla face was definitely not Creed, but Dylan had a damn good idea of who fit that description. "The witness saw twins?"

"Yeah, and another of the librarians remembers them coming in tonight," Royce said. "I'm thinking the Braun boys."

Who the hell else? Dylan thought. Nobody was bigger or uglier than the Brauns, and they were the only twins on Interpol's Most Wanted List.

"Somebody named Lieutenant Bradley commandeered the crime scene and is probably making a mess out of the place, but my man isn't leaving there without the Braun guy, or the two Iranian nationals they found sneaking around an abandoned part of the building."

That would be Lieutenant *Loretta* Bradley, which meant Dylan didn't have to worry about the library. It would take more than one rabid CIA agent to pull Loretta off her game. She'd have the place dusted and cordoned off before Royce could even get his butt down there, let alone win a jurisdiction standoff.

"Do you have names for the Iranians?"

"Not yet."

"Skeeter, run me a check on Ernst and Edmund Braun. B-R-A-U-N. Start in Berlin, then go to Prague. See if they show up in New York."

"Sure," she said, and slipped by him into the main office, heading toward the bank of computers spread out across the tables in the center of the room.

He couldn't help it. He watched as she walked by, all long legs, killer curves, and pure, unadulterated trouble laminated in black leather and silver studs. She was so incredibly sleek, the muscles in her arms smoothly defined, her hands strong yet elegant. And that platinum ponytail—it looked like watered silk. He didn't like to think about how many times he'd imagined it wrapped around his wrist and pooling in his lap.

And what a lie that was—he did like thinking about it. He liked it way too much.

Which brought him to her mouth. Skeeter Bang,

baby street rat, wallbanger, tagger, had a world-class mouth. Her lips always looked soft, barely pink, never covered with lipstick. Everything about her was so consummately feminine—soft skin, soft hair, softly curved face, wickedly curved body—everything except for the black leather and chain mail she wore exclusive to almost everything else. Her tattoos included a lightning bolt he'd seen parts of running down the left side of her body, and of course, there was always the switchblade she carried on her hip.

God help him.

"I'm hoping your guy is as good as you think he is," Royce continued, drawing his attention back to the real problem at hand—which was not Skeeter Bang's butt. "Or we're going to be picking him up off the street in pieces."

"What about Cordelia Kaplan?"

"Disappeared," Royce said. "One minute she was making copies up in Research, and the next she was gone, right after a big bald guy with a Fu Manchu was up there asking around for her."

"Bruno Walmann." Walmann took up a whole file in the Starkova/Patrushev case, as did a few other people—notably Reinhard Klein, and some shadowy characters calling themselves the Zurich 7, with everybody out to buy a multimegaton nuclear warhead. Dylan had crossed Walmann's path a few times in Moscow and Berlin. He knew what a dangerous son of a bitch Bruno could be.

"Look," Royce said, dialing his attitude down a couple of notches. "This thing is going down. With Walmann here, Reinhard Klein can't be too far away. We've got enough players to make one helluva bust, except we're missing the grand prize. You have to bring Creed Rivera in *now*."

"Yes," Dylan agreed. It was a damn good idea to get Creed off the streets tonight, Creed and Dominika Starkova—because every dime Dylan had said Rivera had her. No way in hell would Creed have let her get away.

He shifted his gaze to the windows overlooking Steele Street. There was a helluva blizzard tonight, but even with a snowstorm blinding the city, it wouldn't take Creed more than half an hour to travel the short distance between the downtown library and SDF head-quarters. Given that Royce had said his agent at the library was "mopping up," the action was over—which meant Creed and Ms. Starkova should be showing up any minute.

But Dylan didn't think his luck was running that good tonight.

Hell, no.

COME on, baby," Creed murmured. "Turn over. Come on."

Cody eyed the ignition on the steering column of Creed's car, then she eyed the man turning the key. This wasn't working, she thought, and even though she was trembling again, frozen right down to her knickers, she was starting to sweat. They weren't *that* far from the library, let alone safely out of downtown. All she had to do was glance through the rear window and she could see the lights on the police cruisers two blocks away. God only knew what she couldn't see—like Bruno the Bull or Ernst Braun sneaking up on them through the blizzard, or the two Iranians who'd slipped into the old library right there at the end.

She'd recognized one of the voices, Mohamad Jamal Khalesi, another buyer who'd come to Prague to get in on Sergei's big deal.

There had been ten buyers in the beginning—from extremist militant groups like Hamas in Palestine and the Indonesian Jemaah Islamiah, to the rebels in Chechnya and the remnants of the Taliban in Afghanistan, to shadowy men secretly representing the governments of North Korea, Libya, and Iran, countries who'd already been buying nuclear components and the instructions to use them from Pakistan. Reinhard, acting as Sergei's right-hand man for the deal, was looking to make the score of a lifetime, as was a certain Saudi prince. The other set of buyers had been nameless numbers on a computer screen who went by the code name of the Zurich 7.

Some of the buyers had fallen by the wayside over the last few weeks, coming up short of cash. Those who had set up the required bank accounts in Switzerland as per Sergei's instructions still had a chance at the prize, and there wasn't a one of them Cody would trust with ten grams of cesium-137, let alone a nuclear warhead. It would be Armageddon.

No wonder she never slept and could barely eat. She really was carrying the weight of the world on her shoulders.

"I know it's cold, baby, but you can *do* this. Come on."

He was talking to his car, possibly the coolest car she'd ever seen, a cherry red, double-black-striped Chevelle, but the car was not talking back. It was cold, stone cold, dead cold, ain't-gonna-start-in-this-century cold, and Cody didn't blame it. Despite the way it looked, the car was old, the type of car they'd made back in the sixties and seventies, a muscle car. She'd owned a few old cars herself, nothing fancy like this one, but they'd never started either, not once the temperature dropped.

"Angelina, baby. You can do this. You can start for me, baby."

Angelina? Cody thought. Now the car had a name? Well, name or not, he was wrong. This car was *not* going to—

Oh, sweet Jesus. The car started. No, that wasn't right. The car came alive, the whole thing, all at once, from the floorboards to the roof. It turned over, lifted its head, and roared. She could feel the rumble of the engine shimmying through the passenger seat and up her spine, and when Creed pumped the gas, the chassis rocked.

Good God. She grabbed the armrest and her seat and wondered if Angelina baby was even legal. She couldn't be. No one drove cars like this on the street. And Cody wasn't one to complain, but the cops were only two blocks away, and they could probably hear Angelina growling all the way to the interstate. The library windows were probably shaking. God knew she was.

"Buckle up," he said, and gunned the engine again, his voice back to all business now that Angelina baby was up and running.

And oh, God, the car was definitely running. Cody scrambled for her seatbelt. She could feel the Chevelle rocking beneath her, powering up, getting ready to do God only knew what when he shifted it into gear. What in the world had made her think she'd be safer with him? Her nice little Saturn was parked in the garage across from the library, all steady and reliable. She could have figured out a way to escape him and the Brauns and the Iranians and made it to the parking garage. She was so sure of it now that it was too late.

"What's your address?" he asked.

"I'm on P-Platte Street, just south of Fifteenth." She was so damn cold her teeth were chattering again, but she was still in charge, she assured herself, still in control. They were headed to her apartment, which was exactly what she wanted, and regardless of his car, and the big engine, and all the noise they were making, Creed Rivera was still a step up from Reinhard, Bruno, or Khalesi. She could manage him. He wasn't playing a blood game. The others would kill her once they got the information they wanted. He was only going to put her in jail for the rest of her life.

"South of Fifteenth?" He slanted her a sideways glance. "The old Morrison building?"

"Y-yes." Okay. She had a change in plan. She absolutely, positively needed to make her escape to someplace warm, really warm, like Mexico.

"I thought they condemned the place," he said, reaching over and pushing a button next to the glove compartment. Part of the dashboard retracted, revealing a small screen and keyboard. Good Lord, he had a computer built into his old car.

"Just the . . . uh . . . south building."

After he'd entered a four-digit numerical code—4167, which she wouldn't forget—his gaze came back to her. "I always thought it was the north building that looked like it was falling apart."

All right. So she lived in a dump. So what? And what was the computer for? she wondered. It looked very high-tech. The screen was dark except for a thin purple line tracking low across it in waves, and the keyboard was lit from underneath.

"They've been remodeling North Morrison," she said. "I've got one of the new apartments." Which still wasn't saying much. The best of North Morrison wasn't even close to the great lofts and condos just a stone's throw away on either side of her building. But she hadn't wanted great. She'd wanted cheap and low-profile, and as soon as she got back to her cheap, low-profile apartment in ratty old North Morrison, where paint qualified as a remodel and the elevators were always under repair, she was going to ditch Creed Rivera faster than he could say subsidized housing.

CHAPTER
10

SKEETER NO SOONER sat down and started typing in her access code for the check on Ernst and Edmund Braun than the screen next to her blipped on. She watched as a purple line snaked out of the lower left-hand corner and undulated across the black screen—*Hot damn. It was Creed.* A broad grin split her face.

By typing in his ID number she could pull up a map on the screen and track Angelina. She would know exactly where the Chevelle was and where she was going—but so would everybody else in the room, which probably wasn't what Dylan wanted, not just yet. *Hot damn. He's gotten out of the library and back to Angelina.* Getting back to SDF headquarters would be a piece of cake now. Angelina was heavy, with 454 cubic inches of raw power, a zillion upgrades on her suspension, and some big-ass snow tires to get her through the storm. She'd take Creed anyplace he wanted to go tonight. Skeeter just hoped to hell that was home—or maybe not.

Her glance skimmed over the CIA agent on the far side of the room. Hell, she didn't know what to think.

"I . . . uh—" She cleared her throat and turned around in her chair. "I'll be back in a minute."

She rose from her chair rather shakily, and slid a hand low across her stomach, giving a damn good imitation of someone in serious gastric distress. Like maybe somebody who was about to lose their lunch because of some really terrible pictures she'd seen.

The concerned look on Dylan's face lasted only as long as it took him to see the computer screen behind her. The sudden narrowing of his gaze and the glint in his eyes told her he saw the act for what it was.

In two steps, Dylan was by her side, his arm coming around her, and it was oh, so amazing, being that close to him. She leaned against his side, playing it up—soaking it up—knowing this was as good as it was ever going to get between them, a fake hug dramatized for the CIA.

Man, if her life was going to get any more pitiful, she didn't want to know about it. To her surprise, his arm tightened around her as they walked toward the elevator, pulling her in closer, as if he thought she really couldn't make it without his support, which was damned interesting, because he'd definitely seen the computer screen. He knew what scam she was running here.

"I'll be right back," he said over his shoulder to Royce, then added, "Don't touch anything."

Skeeter had to fight back another grin. Right, she thought. The minute she and Dylan got in the elevator, Royce and his goons were going to be touching everything in sight. She was counting on some truly cosmic odds of probability to keep them from punching 4167 into the tracking computer's keyboard before she could get to her loft and override the main office.

CODY Stark lived in a dump, but at least it was a dump with heat, and she'd fixed the place up so it had a homey kind of Arabian Nights feel, with scarves draped over her bed and a beaded curtain between the bedroom and the rest of the apartment.

Creed finished checking the room by looking in her closet, moving her clothes first to one side, then the other. When he didn't find anything, he reholstered his pistol.

She was watching him from the doorway, which he thought was a damn good idea. He was watching her, too. If she had a boyfriend, he wasn't home, and if she had a gun, she hadn't gone for it, but he wasn't taking anything for granted.

"Do you want some tea?" she asked.

"This isn't a social visit." He'd finally figured that out, and maybe he'd even convinced himself of the fact.

Walking back out into the living area, he scanned the combination living room/kitchen, looking for anything unusual, out of place, or incriminating. She had one window, and he walked over to it.

"You were going to tell me about an incident in Karlovy Vary," he reminded her, pushing the curtain aside. There was nothing outside but the blizzard and a couple of cars moving slowly down the street. "And you were going to show me something here in your apartment." He dropped the curtain and shifted his attention back to her.

She hesitated, then walked past him into the bedroom and pulled a cardboard box out from under the bed. After a few seconds of searching through some clothing and other items, including what looked like a few small jewelry boxes, she pulled out a notebook.

He followed her over and took it, and immediately wondered what was going on. The cover was made out of heavy purple paper with pressed flowers glued to the top—not exactly the type of document holder he was used to seeing. The first page explained it all. *To Prague and Back Again—The Travels of Cordelia Stark* was written across the top in bright purple letters.

He flipped to the second page, and then the third, and the fourth. It was a freaking photo album, a vacation photo album, with pictures stuck in special slots, and tourist attraction brochures stuffed into the binding, and looking at it, he had to wonder if he'd gone to a whole helluva lot of trouble for nothing. He should have taken her straight to SDF headquarters.

On page five he stopped and turned the album toward her. "Who is this?"

She glanced down at the photograph he was pointing at. "My father, Dr. Dimitri Starkova."

Well, there was a news flash.

"He's in Prague?"

She nodded. "That's why I went there, to see him."

I'll be damned, Creed thought. No one had mentioned a father. It wasn't in any of the intelligence reports. Starkova wasn't an unusual name, but the only Starkova anyone had connected to Sergei Patrushev was Dominika.

"Prague is a big city, though," she continued. "Lots of action, lots of trouble to get into, and I fell in with a bad crowd. When things got rough, I cut my visit short and headed home."

"Rough like the incident in Karlovy Vary?" The scene the CIA agents had discovered in the warehouse had been about as rough as it got.

"Yes." Cody turned her face aside and hoped he would interpret the move as a sign of distress and regret, and not anger. She couldn't think of her father without getting angry, and she couldn't afford to be angry right now. Cool, calm, collected, that was her, because in the next few minutes, she was going to escape. "My father, well, he'd be devastated if he knew what kind of people I'd gotten involved with."

But not nearly as devastated as she'd been to realize the kind of people *he* was involved with, people he'd practically sold her to in order to save his own hide. Her mother had tried to warn her, but Cody hadn't listened. In truth, her father was far worse than her mother knew.

"There are other pictures of him," she said, reaching over and flipping a page. "I left in kind of a hurry, and didn't say good-bye, and I was hoping you could contact him, let him know I'm okay."

"You're not okay," he said bluntly.

And her father was dead, which meant he was about as concerned for her welfare now as he'd been the night he'd taken her to Sergei's and signed her life away as collateral against the mountain of gambling debts he owed a whole consortium of the Russian Mafia.

Deliver the bomb, Sergei had told her father, *or she'll suffer the consequences*—which had been enough to put her in a cold sweat, because by then, it had become obvious that her father's problems far outweighed any parental sentiments he might have harbored.

For years, Dimitri Starkova had lived off the Mafia, untouchable because of the nuclear warhead he had been in charge of moving from a military base in the U.S.S.R. Their destination had been top secret, and Dimitri, as the commanding officer, had always held to the story that he was the only one with the exact coordinates of the missile's final location. Those security precautions had paid off, he'd often bragged. With the government in disarray and the army in transition during the dissolution of the Soviet Republic, he'd retired and taken his information with him.

Dimitri had never committed the location to paper or cyberspace. It was all in his head, he'd said, so his head had been safe—until his loans had begun to exceed his value with or without the rumored bomb to back him up.

With her father's growing debt, a heretofore unknown daughter in tow, and the world market desperate for a rogue nuclear weapon, Sergei had decided the time was ripe to force the issue.

"So your involvement with Reinhard Klein is purely social?"

She nodded. "A bad decision on my part, but I've learned my lesson. If I can give you information that will help put him away, my life will be a lot easier."

He didn't look like he believed a word she'd said, and she didn't blame him. She wasn't a very good liar.

"So tell me what happened in Karlovy Vary."

She took a deep breath, as if preparing to tell him a long, painful story, which it would have been, but then she paused.

"Do you mind?" she said, gesturing toward the bathroom. "I'll only be a minute."

CHAPTER

11

F OUR MINUTES LATER, after searching the rest of the apartment and half of her dresser, Creed got to her bottom drawer. He no sooner opened it up than a low whistle left his lips. The not-so-blonde bimbo had the days of the week embroidered on her underwear, and if Creed said so himself, Tuesday looked especially fine.

She also had some money tucked into the corner of the drawer. He picked up the small bundle and let it flip, bill by bill, off his thumb—five hundred dollars, five crisp one-hundred-dollar bills stacked in a neat pile and held together with a green paper clip.

He pocketed the money before picking up Tuesday's scrap of white lace and pink rosebuds and lifting it into the light. It was definitely some juvenile sexual fantasy he should have outgrown that made the pristine, virginal pair an instant favorite. Friday, he noticed, was black silk with a single, strategically placed red heart—pure Dominika. Sunday was baby blue with embroidered daisies—Cody Stark. Thursday got all bad-girl again: hot see-through red with a black lace trim and a matching push-up bra.

Her entire wardrobe was like that: half punk-rock raver and half pure Bible Belt librarian. He knew because he'd been through the whole thing, from her closet to her dresser, to the suitcase he'd found under the bed, and besides the five hundred dollars in the dresser, he'd found the equivalent of another five hundred dollars in Euros inside the suitcase. There hadn't been any cash in the cardboard box she'd pulled out, but he'd checked the mailing label and noticed she'd insured it, had it sent General Delivery to Denver from Dresden, and signed for it today.

A thousand dollars, all of it in his pocket, because where she was going, she was going to need it, probably sooner rather than later. Confiscating her cash before the CIA hauled her off was the least he could do. Money could grease a few wheels in Leavenworth just like it did everywhere else.

What he hadn't found was a map, or a computer disk, or jump drive, or any kind of electronic storage device, which didn't mean they weren't there.

The sound of the water being turned on again in the

bathroom made him pause. He lifted his head, listening. After a few more seconds he heard her rustling through her medicine cabinet—again. She'd flushed twice, which didn't surprise him. With all she'd been through tonight, her stomach was probably feeling a little weak.

He checked his watch. She'd been in the bathroom for almost six minutes now, a busy six minutes. He'd looked the bathroom over again before he'd let her go in alone, and the place was secure, a typical low-end bathroom in a low-end studio apartment: a single-piece shower/tub enclosure with a curtain, a commode, a sink with a cabinet underneath, a medicine cabinet above the sink, and a towel bar with some silky black fishnet stuff hanging off of it that had definitely caught his attention.

He went back to searching through her lingerie and enjoying it just a little too much. The woman had nice underwear, a nice stash of cash, and was living in a dump in a construction zone. When she'd said they were remodeling North Morrison, she'd meant daily, and from what he'd seen the job would last well into spring. They'd had to hike the four flights up and make their way around construction supplies on every floor.

Driving the few miles to her place had given him a chance to clear his head. He didn't know what he'd been thinking. He wasn't going to get laid tonight. Far from it. He was going to do his job and take her to headquarters. In his line of work, only an idiot would sleep with a black-market arms dealer—and there weren't any idiots in his line of work. Faulty judgment killed them off long before they got into Spec Ops.

So what was he doing with Tuesday's panties in his hand?

Nothing, he assured himself. Absolutely nothing. She was his wake-up call. That's all. He'd been hiding out under Mercy's hood for two weeks, but now he was back on the job, and it was time to come clean.

It was time to tell the truth.

Kid knew what had happened to J.T. Creed had told him everything—and Kid hadn't come home. Creed didn't know if he ever would. Apparently there was a girl, Nikki McKinney, an artist up in Boulder Kid had left behind. He'd talked about her damn near nonstop, but Creed didn't know if she was enough to pull Kid free of the bad places he'd been, of the bad things he'd done.

Ghost killers, *los asesinos fantasmas*, they'd all made names for themselves in South America, but especially Kid, and Creed felt guilty as hell about that, too.

The toilet flushed again—and every warning bell in his head instantly went off. *Shit!* He whirled on his feet and ran across the room. It was a fucking pattern—turn on the water, rustle through the medicine cabinet, flush the toilet. He didn't even bother to knock. He gave the door a roundhouse kick right next to the jamb at the lock plate. Everything splintered, and his foot almost went through the goddamned wall.

He jerked the door open on the tiny room—and it was empty. Totally fucking empty. Nobody there. *Nada*.

But she hadn't disappeared into thin air. He jerked the shower curtain off its rod. Nothing. Then he did a full 360. The silky fishnet stuff was missing from the towel bar, and there was about half a ton of makeup upended in the sink—bottles, tiny boxes, tubes, and a hundred, oh, hell, *two* hundred pencils of every color known to man, four or five kinds of hair spray and colored gel—all of it smelling overly sweet and flowery. There wasn't so much as a scuff mark anywhere, but she hadn't dematerialized and then rematerialized on the other side of one of these frickin' walls or through the ceiling.

That left the sink cabinet. Crouching down, he opened the small door. Nothing but three rolls of toilet paper and a box of tampons—he opened it up—with a tape player tucked inside.

Hell. She'd chumped him good, but she hadn't slid down any pipes or gone through the heat vent.

He ran his hand across the back wall of the cabinet, and sure enough, felt a tiny notch.

He was so fucked.

Using the tips of his fingers, he pried the panel loose.

Son of a bitch. There was a goddamned good reason she'd chosen an apartment on the fourth floor of a building where the elevators didn't work—because half of the fourth floor had been gutted. Behind the walls of her apartment was a no-man's-land—*and so it's down the fricking rabbit hole.*

Squeezing himself into the cabinet, he started inching his way around the pipes and through the too-damn-small-to-make-this-easy opening. It was pitch-dark on the other side of the wall, but he didn't give a damn. The scariest thing in the dark was *always* him.

RIGHT *along here somewhere*, Cody thought, shining her penlight on the floor, following a board. Then she saw it, a splotch of yellow paint.

Four boards south. She swept her light to the left and knelt on the floor. In seconds she had five hundred dollars in her coat pocket, getaway money to go with the two thousand in Euros she'd taken out of the cardboard box under the bed as she'd given him the photo album. She had another thousand in dollars and Euros squirreled away in her apartment, but if Creed Rivera was even only half as good as she thought he was, she could write that money off as lost, probably to Angelina's upkeep. Thank God she'd learned not to keep all her eggs in one basket. Twenty-five hundred wasn't much, but it was enough to get her out of town.

Sergei hadn't been a generous jailer, though he hadn't physically mistreated her either. But money had flowed like water at all of the bars and restaurants where he'd taken her to show her off, his little Dominika, his insurance policy, and the parties had always gotten out of hand—the booze, the drugs, the heat, the whores, the music. Sergei had wanted to make sure people saw her, and she'd made a point of picking up cash wherever she'd found it, off the tables and out of the pockets of men too drunk to notice. It had been Sergei's idea to dye her waist-length hair platinum blond. Turning her into a blond Russian bombshell, he'd said, but somehow, in Russian, the name had gotten twisted into the Blonde with the Bomb, which had suited Sergei just fine. He'd liked having her near him, like a pet.

She'd known her looks hadn't hurt, and she'd played them up to the max, seriously doubting that her father was going to come to her rescue. The minute he'd left Sergei's mansion, after making a touching good-bye with the slim volume of poetry, she'd known she was on her own. Sink or swim.

She hadn't figured her father was going to fare much better. After more than a decade of decadent living, however charming, urbane, and highly educated he was, she wouldn't have bet anything on his memory or him being able to even survive a trip into the wilds of the old Soviet frontier, let alone find anything there—and she'd been proven right.

Heart attack. Complete and total cardiac arrest had hit him in the mountains of Tajikistan.

God help her, she'd broken every law in the book since escaping Sergei's clutches—forged documents, illegal border crossings, out-and-out theft—and she'd known her freedom would be hard to hold.

But she was close again, so close she could almost hear it, almost feel it.

Staying very still, she switched off her penlight, and even in the dark, closed her eyes.

Yes . . . yes . . . yes. It was there, *thank God*, the distant pulse of freedom, the driving force of it, the chaos barely discernible beneath the beat.

South Morrison *had* been condemned—and like any condemned place, it attracted the wild restless creatures of the night in hordes. In those places, with those people, Dominika Starkova ruled. She'd "been there, done that" with the world's wildest party crowd—the Russian Mafia on the move across Europe, east and west.

Saturday nights at South Morrison meant crystal meth and skullcaps, ketamine and kamikazes, latex and leather, and industrial-strength garage bands blowing each other out of the basement. All she had to do was get there. Out of the six or seven hundred people who always showed up at the underground party, she wouldn't have any trouble talking one of them into giving her a ride back to her car—and then she was gone and Denver was just a mistake she'd survived.

Flicking her penlight back on, she quickly made her way to the back stairs and started down to the street.

CODY Stark's bathroom emptied out into the rubble and remains of another bathroom, and as soon as Creed left it, he lost the light from the hole. Wherever the hell he was now, he couldn't see his hand in front of his face, but he had it out there anyway, just in case the demolition crew had left another wall standing. In the Spec Ops community, they had a name for this kind of dark: *fucking* dark.

There had to be another door somewhere, or a window.

Since he couldn't see, he was following his nose. In her six and a half minutes of private bathroom time—a mistake he would *never* make again, a mistake Dylan never would have made in the first place, female prisoner or not—she must have put on enough makeup and hair spray to sink a battleship. He could smell it, the same overly sweet flowery scent from her bathroom. The question, of course, was why would a woman on the run take the time to fix her hair?

Did the King Kong boyfriend really exist? And was he scheduled to pick her up tonight? She'd still been dressed in her homeless-boy getup, unless . . . unless, *geezus*, that silky fishnet thing had been an outfit.

Now why in the hell would a person wear fishnet on the coldest freaking night of the year?

Then he heard it.

No. He felt it, the faint *thump, thump, thump-thump . . . thump, thump, thump-thump* of either the HVAC system getting damned creative—or of an electric bass running through an amp big enough to knock a couple hundred skinny kids on their asses. The hum of her refrigerator and the running of the building's furnace had been enough to drown it out in her apartment, but in no-man's-land, the sound was nearly tangible.

A shift in the rhythm and a crude riff put his money

solidly on the bass. There wasn't an HVAC system in the world capable of generating a backbeat.

Suddenly, her escape plan was clear. The Prague party princess was back in business on Platte Street. All he had to do was find the party and he'd find the girl, and he damn well better find the party fast, or the girl was going to be gone.

He couldn't allow that to happen, and yes, it was personal. Damn personal.

On his next step, his boot came up against something solid. He reached out with his hand and found a wall. *Thank you, Lord.*

Following it along, he was able to pick up his pace, and twenty steps farther on he came across a door. As soon as he opened it, he realized he'd been in a hallway for the last two minutes. Now he was home free, in a cavernous room with enough light coming through the windows to prove that she was long gone.

Damn it. He raced across the room, toward the steady rhythm of the bass. When he got to the windows, he was looking out across the courtyard at South Morrison and could hear the rest of the band and the low buzz of way too many people jammed into way too small a space.

Perfect. A freaking metal rave inside a condemned building was way down on his list of places to go on a frigid winter night. Then he saw her, a small form darting through the snow and weaving her way through the dozens of cars that had spilled off the street and were parked every which way in the courtyard.

He looked to either side of the room, and when he saw the back stairs, he took off again. He hoped to hell she was enjoying her last moments of freedom, because when he caught her—and he *was* going to catch her— her freedom was coming to a screeching, permanent halt.

He just had to make damn sure that he caught her before anybody else did.

CHAPTER

12

DYLAN STOOD IN the doorway of Skeeter's loft on the eleventh floor of Steele Street where she'd left him, taking his time, taking a breath, and taking a moment to try to figure out how in the hell to get inside. There was a trick to it, because the floor was missing. Not the whole floor, just a big piece right in front of the door, with a palm tree growing out of the hole. Now he did know where the tree came from. The tree was Creed's. Everything growing up from the ninth floor and through the exposed skeleton of the tenth floor belonged to the jungle boy's jungle. Dylan just hadn't known that the jungle had now reached and was slowly devouring the eleventh floor as well. It was a disturbing realization.

It was also all Skeeter Bang's doing. He didn't doubt it for a second. Up until she'd moved in, Creed's whole houseplant inventory had consisted of a philodendron, two scraggly ficus trees, and a couple of big ideas about someday doing something really cool with a whole bunch of plants.

"Someday" had come and gone. Hawkins had given the girl free rein and apparently an unlimited line of credit. With Creed out of the country most of the time, she'd taken over, and now Steele Street was being eaten alive from the inside out. The steel-reinforced building would never collapse, no matter what she decided to grow in Creed's loft, but the insides of the building could go. As a matter of fact, it looked like the insides of this floor had already packed its bags and left. What the ninth-floor jungle hadn't displaced, Skeeter had transformed beyond recognition.

J.T. and Kid's place up on twelve had always looked like a garage sale and a sporting goods store getting it on, with the sporting goods store on top. Hawkins's loft was an elegant, understated, but definitely uptown museum-quality art gallery with a kitchen and a bath. Quinn's place, on the other side of the tenth floor, looked deserted, because it was. Unlike Hawkins, when Quinn had gotten married, he'd gotten completely out of the spy vs. spy business.

Skeeter's place looked like a spaceship.

With a palm tree guarding the hatch.

What in the hell was she feeding everything down there on the ninth floor?

"Just step to your right." Her voice came from his left, sounding far away, like she'd dropped into a hole. "There's a weight-controlled extension ledge that will swing you around to the main gangway."

Main gangway? Since when had there been gangways on the eleventh floor? Or low curved walls with low curved ceilings covered in rivets and bathed in softly pulsing blue light?

He looked to his right, the direction she'd gone when she'd so neatly disappeared, and sure enough, there was an extended ledge hidden beneath the palm fronds, apparently weight-activated to swing him around and land him in her foyer—or maybe "deck" was a better way to describe the entrance to her loft with its three tubular gangways going off in different directions.

"Is this the *Enterprise*, or the . . . uh, *Nebuchadnezzar?*" The place had a definite high-tech, post-Apocalyptic look to it.

"*Millennium Falcon.*"

Of course, the *Millennium Falcon:* every galactic gear head's dream come true, a nuts-and-bolts hot rod with a hyperdrive. There was a reason this "thing" he had for Skeeter Bang was a nowhere deal, and it wasn't all age and edginess related.

Or maybe it was. Didn't people with Han Solo wannabe fixations eventually outgrow them? And what was with all the boxes piled everywhere? Was she moving, or just a pack rat?

He stepped on the ledge, and to his surprise, the extending action was incredibly smooth, almost undetectable. She had some nifty hydraulics back behind the wall somewhere; in seconds, he was connected to the *Falcon's* staging platform, entryway hatch, or whatever.

"Okay, I've got it." She popped out of the tubular hall to his left, slightly breathless, as if she'd been running. "I didn't mean to strand you there. I just needed to override the computers in the office. Didn't want Royce and his boys accidentally pulling up Creed's tracking device."

Yes. Of course. Good idea. All of those words rolled across the logical part of his brain without actually making it out of his mouth—because he was speechless, momentarily struck dumb.

She'd taken off her sunglasses and turned her hat around backward, and her eyes were more beautiful and the scar across her forehead worse than he'd ever imagined either. He'd heard about both from Hawkins, the same way he'd heard about her lightning-bolt tattoo, but he'd never seen them until now.

"Did you get Creed's location?" he asked, working real hard to maintain a normal tone of voice. He deserved an Academy Award. Her eyes weren't just blue, they were a pale, silvery blue, with eyelashes as blond as her hair, and even two years after the fact, the scar on her forehead was a jagged, dark pink line cutting into her creamy skin and across one pale blond eyebrow.

She was exquisite, her coloring otherworldly, and she'd damn near died in that flophouse up on Wazee. Hawkins had stayed by her side for a week and given her a pint of his blood that night in the ER. Dylan hadn't been around much during that time, but he knew she thought that's what had saved her, having Superman's blood pumping through her heart and running through her veins. It was her talisman, and it was always with her—always, with every breath she took ... *Superman* ... *Superman* ... *Superman*.

Dylan knew Christian Hawkins better than any man alive, and he didn't doubt her reasoning for a second. At one time or another, Superman had saved them all.

"I haven't pulled the map up yet, but give me two minutes, and I will." She grinned and ducked back inside the low curving hallway. "Come on."

Bingo. The Oscar was his. Nothing of what he was feeling and thinking must have shown, or she'd have been as horrified as he was. He knew from experience how hard a person had to swing a whiskey bottle to break it on somebody's head. Damn hard. What he didn't know was how a person swung a whiskey bottle that hard while aiming at a face like hers. It was incomprehensible.

"So what do you think of my place?" she asked. "Pretty cool, huh?"

"Uh, awesome," he said, and suddenly felt a hundred years old. She'd been so badly hurt, and was still so young, and he was a thirty-two-year-old guy who couldn't have lived in this rabbit warren to save his life. What in the hell was in all these boxes? They almost filled the tunnel. Half of them were open, spilling their junk onto the floor and into each other, and it all looked like stuff—not just car parts, though there were plenty of those, but bits and pieces of other things, like she spent her nights raiding the salvage lot, the junkyard, and the Salvation Army. It was enough to make him twitch. He wanted to straighten something, maybe close a lid—or three or four, after shoving a few things inside.

"Superman helped with the engineering and the hydraulics, not that we've got a lot in here, but there is some cool stuff, like the ledge. Kid helped with the welding, but it's just been me and Johnny for all the foam work. We've been carting the stuff in here by the bucketful and blowing it on, making the tunnels and things."

Foam, not riveted steel plates—well, that helped the weight problem, he thought, having to duck his head to follow her through the tunnel. Johnny Ramos was another of Hawkins's street kids. He worked up in their garage in Commerce City, but Dylan knew he spent a lot of time at Steele Street, too, tearing down engines with Skeeter and apparently blowing a whole lot of foam around in her loft.

Just when he was starting to get a little claustrophobic and was praying the tunnel didn't dead-end into something no bigger than an "escape pod," they came to "the bridge."

He straightened up, taking it all in, amazed. Logically, he knew they were still on the eleventh floor of Steele Street, not a thousand light-years from Earth, heading toward the Crab Nebula, but that's what it looked like—the illusion of deep space spread out before him, the safety of "the ship" behind him, with the city lights of Denver glowing soft and hazy through the snow, stretching to the dark horizon across a fifteen-foot-high wall of windows and looking very much like a quadrant of stars.

The space between "the bridge" and the windows was pitch-black, an abyss. Logically, again, he knew Creed's loft was below hers, the whole jungle of it, with a solid floor between them, but she'd created a visual chasm with only the most shadowy forms visible across its width. The lighting on the deck was still low, still blue, still pulsating, but it wasn't annoying. It was more like a heartbeat. It was also probably why she'd taken her sunglasses off here when she didn't do it anywhere else. It must have become habit, to keep from running into all the junk she had piled everywhere. He doubted if she even realized she'd exposed herself to him.

"Here we go," she said, dropping into a chair in front of a bank of computers and hitting a switch. Small, tubular lights hanging from the ceiling came on and cast a soft, steady glow over the computers. There were five screens lined up next to each other on a desk made out of a recycled dual exhaust system and a glass top. The desk was overflowing with crumpled wrapping paper and frazzled-looking bows, with yards of ribbon trailing off everywhere.

She pushed a pile of the paper trash away from around one of the middle screens and set her fingers to flying on the keyboard. A map of Denver immediately came up.

"Party?" he asked, lifting a metallic red ribbon off the desk, curious as hell. There were pop cans and coffee cups scattered around, a hubcap full of popcorn, an old set of rods welded into a sort of pencil cup, and a whole lot of candy bar wrappers. No ashtrays, though. He'd heard she'd quit smoking when Hawkins had quit—just one more thing he needed to thank Superman for doing.

"It was Hacker's birthday yesterday. Johnny and I threw her a bash." She tossed aside a few more crumpled balls of tissue paper until she found the mouse pad and her mouse. A couple of clicks enlarged the map, zooming it in on Denver proper and leaving out the suburbs.

Dylan knew Cherie Hacker. He'd almost asked her out once, then realized he wasn't quite that insane, not yet, so he'd hired her instead—to hack through other people's firewalls, keep the guys up-to-date with techno toys, and to turn Steele Street into one big hot spot. Then the feds had stolen her. The last he'd heard, she was still an off-site consultant for the FBI. Off-site, off the books, under the radar—that was Hacker's MO.

"She get anything good?"

"Doc Randall sent her a prototype of his newest wi-fi transmitter. She got pretty excited about that. Johnny and I gave her banana slippers. Get it? Banana? Slippers?" She glanced up from the screen, and he gave her a weak grin. Yeah. He got it—like he was starting to get a bad case of heartburn just looking at her place. She had a pile of pizza boxes stacked between two lime green beanbag chairs farther down on the main deck. There was a lamp sitting on top of the boxes along with a half-dead African violet, which officially made the boxes an end table—a pizza-box end table.

And the plant. Hell. She had the makings of a Third World economy growing two floors beneath her, and she kept a half-dead African violet in her apartment?

And why not? he thought, still looking around. She had a circular staircase made up entirely of headers and chrome wheels, a fish tank made out of windshields, and enough party trash to do the whole birthday thing over again tonight.

"Looks like a lot of people came," he said, glancing back at the screen. There seemed to be some kind of interference, probably the storm. It was really howling out there now—but Skeeter was working through it. After Hacker had left them, Kid had come on board, and between the two of them they'd gotten Skeeter up to speed, teaching her enough for her to more than earn her keep at Steele Street. Hawkins thought she was a bloody genius, and had made it clear to every gangster on the streets that they better not mess with Baby Bang.

She'd brought some freight with her, that was for sure, some unpaid debts and a few out-and-out threats, some incoming, some she was sending. Her crew hadn't wanted to lose her, either; they'd been stars tagging with SB303. But Hawkins had laid down the law. No more hanging with the crew, and no more hanging from the Fifteenth Street Bridge just to tag a girder. The spooky little wallbanger had brought out all of Superman's protective instincts.

That's the way he should feel about her, Dylan thought—protective, fatherly.

But that wasn't the way he felt, not even close, and he didn't like himself too much because of it.

And he really hated having to face that tonight.

"Not many. Not really. There's only a few people I even let up here—Johnny and Gabby, Cherie, Doc Randall, Doc Blake. We watched a movie," she said. "I stuck a note on your door in case you got home last night."

"Thanks." He hadn't been close to getting home last night. He'd been in Washington, D.C., at the British embassy with a woman named Deborah Layton, Dr. Deborah Layton from Georgetown University, whom no one ever called Debbie or Deb. It had been their fifth date in the last two months, and when he'd dropped her off at her brownstone and turned down her offer to come in, he knew she'd been both disappointed and confused—but that's the way things had been going for him for quite a while.

And just like the jungle down on the ninth floor, it was all Skeeter Bang's doing. He'd thought she was a cute, messed-up kid when Hawkins had first brought her home. Okay, a pretty damn cute kid, but still just a kid, with some major problems that he'd been sure Hawkins would help her figure out. That's what Superman did, helped people figure out their problems. Then Dylan had picked up on Skeeter's voodoo vibe, how she anticipated people's moves or what tool they needed, and how she'd sometimes look up at the elevator or a door a few seconds *before* it opened, or move toward the phone *before* it rang, and he'd started watching her a lot more closely. The more he'd watched, the more fascinated he'd become—until it had come to this.

A crazy bad case of . . . heartburn.

The map on the screen started to flash, drawing his attention back to the job at hand. It was moving faster now, each new map enlarging a smaller and smaller area, honing in on Creed's position.

"What the hell is he doing on the other side of the river?"

"I don't know," she said. She wasn't smiling now, and neither was he.

Creed needed to get his ass home.

"I'm going after him," Dylan said, making his decision. "Keep me updated on his position."

He started to turn and go.

"Wait . . . just a minute. I don't know for sure if that was him or not. I'm getting ghost images." She leaned over to the next screen and pulled up the map again. "Let me double-check what I've got. See if I can confirm that it's

Angelina. It'll just take a minute . . . or two, and save you a lot of time in the long run. Go ahead and make yourself a cup of coffee, if you want. I'll take one, too."

Actually, a cup of coffee sounded great.

"Please," she said, looking from one screen to the other, each hand working a different keyboard—which simply boggled his mind. "It's bad out there tonight. There's no sense in wandering around in a blizzard until we know exactly where we're going."

"We?"

"We," she said, leaning even farther over and firing up computer number three. "I'll take mine with cream and sugar. The galley is at the end of the deck. A lot of cream."

He wasn't an idiot. He knew how these things worked, and she was right. Taking off into the night before he was sure he was heading in the right direction was useless—and the galley was at the end of the deck. *Right.*

CHAPTER
13

CREED FOUND CODY'S baggy brown pants and her big gray coat just inside South Morrison's main door, neatly folded and placed in the shadows on a broken-down staircase leading to the upper floors.

Great. She wasn't wearing any pants, or her coat, which just left the fishnet thing, which meant she was practically naked. *Perfect.*

He set his jaw and grabbed her clothes and started down the dimly lit hallway, looking for a way into the basement. The music was so loud coming up from below, harsh and hard-driving, the floor was vibrating beneath his feet, a steady hum of energy.

The hall ended in a barricade of chain link attached

to the walls with scavenged two-by-fours. The opening was small and led to a flight of darkened stairs beyond. The music was almost deafening, rising out of the basement with an occasional strobelike flash of light.

Putting his back to the wall, he shoved two shells into the shotgun, replacing the ones he'd used in the library. Whatever Cody Stark was up to, Dominika Starkova was nothing but trouble, with more bad guys on her ass than he'd seen since Colombia.

Shit. He *wasn't* going to think about Colombia. Not now.

Reaching a hand to his waist, he loosened the tactical nylon holster looped under his belt and Velcro'd the barrel end around his thigh. He chambered a round before shoving the Mossberg home. He wanted the 12-gauge close to his body, not hidden inside the scabbard sewn into his coat lining. He checked the pistol at the small of his back, then pulled a pair of wraparound shooter glasses out of his breast pocket and slipped them on. The yellow lenses would give him an advantage in the basement, heightening the contrast of whatever light was there—which from what he could see wasn't damn much.

Suddenly, unexpectedly, a group of people spilled out of the stairwell and into the small opening in the fence, the noise of their ascent masked by the music. He tensed and flipped the edge of his coat over the shotgun. There were three men in their early twenties and two girls who looked a lot younger, one with pink hair, the other with blue—all of them stoned and reeking of alcohol.

"Hey, man," one of the boys drawled, his arm draped around the pink-haired girl's shoulders.

"Hey." Creed stepped back, letting them pass through the opening. The blue-haired girl's coat caught on a sharp end of chain link, and as one of the guys helped her get untangled, Creed noticed the tracks on her arms.

The next guy got caught on the same piece of fencing, and they all started to laugh.

"Oh, man, rough night," somebody in the group said.

Yeah, Creed thought, *and gonna get rougher if you don't get the fuck outta my way.*

But he didn't say a word. He did reach out and grab the next guy on his way through and made damn sure he didn't get caught up in anything.

"Hey, man. Thanks." Bleary eyes lifted to his.

"Yeah."

The last stoner slid by him, and Creed slipped sideways through the opening, entering the darkened stairwell, following the head-banging rhythm down into chaos.

PATIENCE, Dylan told himself, starting the coffee. Five minutes' worth of patience now could save him hours later. Just him. There wasn't going to be any "we" when he went after Creed, no matter what Skeeter thought.

The coffee started to drip, and he shifted his attention

to the rest of "the galley," looking for clean cups. Like the main deck, the galley's walls had been augmented in places with liberal doses of foam and make-believe rivets, but with better lighting—to better reveal the amazing amount of junk she had stored in the kitchen.

What *was* all this stuff?

He peered into the top of one box at a pile of broken ceramic tiles in blues and greens, and guessed they made a certain sense. The windshield fish tank was set into a wooden frame with a half-finished blue-and-green mermaid mosaic on it. The next box was purely unidentifiable junk, but the box next to that one held something of true interest.

More than intrigued, he picked up the small sketchbook on top, the one that said "Self-Portrait." He flipped it open, expecting to see her face, probably with the ball cap and sunglasses—and instead he saw the tail end of her ponytail and her butt. Her naked butt.

His heart slowed for a beat as his gaze slid down the piece of paper, taking it all in. The next page was more of the same. So was the one after that, an almost exact duplicate. Then he realized the angle on those amazing curves was slightly different.

Strange night, he thought, bending the sketchbook and letting his thumb hold back just the bare edge of each page before releasing it. One by one, in near-instant succession, each page followed the last, each one zipping by, the whole of them together making a brief animation of her butt swaying across the page, her ponytail flying, as she turned to one side.

He pressed his thumb down, stopping on an end page. More than once since Hawkins had first mentioned it, he'd wondered about her lightning-bolt tattoo—but his imagination had been lacking the necessary epic scale.

Wow.

He picked up another sketchbook, and then three more, before he found what he was looking for, a full side view. He tilted the book one way and his head the other, and he had to wonder how much of the tattoo Hawkins had seen. Not much, he hoped, because the only way to see the whole thing would be to see her stripped down to her birthday suit. The ink started at her ankle and streaked up her leg in all its zig-zag electrified glory, a racing stripe for her body. It curved over her amazing hip. Halfway up her rib cage it took a sharp turn onto her back and shot up over her shoulder.

The girl didn't have a mundane cell in her entire being, inside or out. She was *all* edge—and he'd just set some sort of a record. They hadn't been alone ten minutes, and he'd already seen her naked.

Not all of her, though. The drawings of herself were just bits and pieces, like her boxes of junk—her arm with the Chinese tattoo; her leg, hands, and feet; the curve of her hip; the muscles of her back; her belly button and her smooth abs but no full frontals, which was just as well. Even the side view stopped at her neck, and her arm was placed to conceal the curve of her breast. Her style was pure manga, but he didn't need the title of "Self-Portrait" to recognize her. She had an amazing body. She *owned* the words sleek and strong. There was no mistaking her.

And there wasn't a single drawing of her face in any of the sketchbooks. She had other people, especially Hawkins and Kid and Johnny. Hacker was in some of the drawings, and so were Quinn and Creed. In a couple of the sketchbooks, Skeeter had made them all into superheroes: Superman for Hawkins, of course, but an apocalyptic Superman, his hair wild and longer than it was in real life, his costume ripped, his expression one of stone-cold justice in the flesh—with Kid backing him up as Chaos, a fierce-looking dude in torn yellow spandex with a jazzed-up M40 in his hand. Cherie Hacker was a character named Metrogirl; she, too, had wild, flying hair and a rather menacing-looking utility belt strapped around her optimistically curvaceous hips. In real life, Hacker was no siren. Quinn was Captain America, wrapped in the flag and super clean-cut, which was stretching imagination to the breaking point, but compared to the rest of the chop-shop boys, Quinn was a bona fide all-American hero. Johnny was a squirrelly-looking, wiry little guy named Gearhead, and Creed was Tarzan, but he didn't look like any Tarzan Dylan had ever seen. Skeeter had turned Creed into some other kind of jungle boy—something more feral with a wild, primal edge and a catlike countenance. The jungle was part of him, the vines twining through his mane of hair, the trees making a fortress behind him. His fingernails, rough and horny claws, gripped the tree limbs, but it was definitely Creed snarling at him from out of the lianas and leaves, his teeth bared, his expression fierce.

The last few pages were all of J.T. as the Guardian, a dark angel with a sword and a ferocious scowl, short, spiky black hair, low-slung jeans, a torn black T-shirt, and powerful raven black wings. When Dylan flipped the pages, the wings beat and J.T. sliced the sword across the page.

It broke his heart.

God, J.T.

He closed the book and set it on top.

She hadn't drawn him, and he felt that as a hurt, too, and it irritated the hell out of him that he cared. It wasn't like him to be maudlin over some girl.

Except Skeeter Bang wasn't just some girl, not by anyone's standards. He knew that. He'd figured it out over a year ago, and that's when he'd started avoiding coming home.

He looked out toward the main deck and the huge expanse of windows beyond. The blizzard wasn't letting up. If anything, it was getting worse. He was going to have a helluva time getting to Creed, but his instincts were telling him to do it, and to do it now. Coffee time was up.

"Holy crap," her voice came from over by the computers.

"What?" he asked, stepping out of the kitchen.

"I've got a lock on Angelina." She looked over at him. "We better make that coffee to go."

"Where is he?"

"I've pegged him at Platte Street, just south of Fifteenth, which is the last place I'd expect Creed to be on Saturday night. It's just not his scene."

"What isn't?"

"The party." She gave her head a shake, her eyebrows drawing together into two white blond lines over her pale blue eyes. "The biggest freakin' party from the Front Range to the eastern 'burbs, every Saturday night in the basement of South Morrison. The place rocks hard, scary hard, even for me."

Well, that had to be pretty damn hard, Dylan thought. Like Skeeter, he'd done some time on the streets, and it took a lot to scare a kid who'd survived that kind of life.

"He could be at North Morrison," she continued. "There are a few floors of apartments in North, and there are a few shops around down by the river, but I bet they're closed tonight. So I'm guessing South Morrison is where we better start."

"I thought South Morrison was condemned."

"It is," she said. "The whole thing is coming down next month, if it doesn't fall down before then. The place is a disaster just waiting for the right time to happen."

"So what the hell is Creed doing there?" he asked.

"I don't know," she said, pushing out of her chair and heading for the kitchen. "But we need to find out, right now."

Dylan stepped aside for her to enter the galley and watched as she slammed through a couple of kitchen cabinets before she found a stash of commuter cups.

"Black?" she asked.

"Yes." He didn't know if she was conscious of it or not, but as she poured the coffee, she turned her hat around, so the bill shaded her face, and slipped her sunglasses back on. "You're not going with me."

She had to know that much. She'd been with Steele Street long enough to know the rules, especially since the only rules they had all pertained to her.

"Sure I am." She snapped the lid on one cup and handed it to him. Hers got loaded down with three tablespoons of sugar before she started pouring in the cream, which did nothing to ease the churning knot his stomach had been in since he'd seen the pictures of J.T.

"What are you making?" he asked, his gaze narrowing as she kept pouring in the cream . . . and pouring. It wasn't a cup of coffee anymore, no way, not after three tablespoons of sugar.

"Dinner," she said, finally snapping the lid on the cup.

Good god, she'd used over half a pint of cream, heavy cream, not half-and-half. Holding the tip of her finger over the drinking hole, she gave the cup a few good shakes.

"Or dessert. Take your pick."

He picked none of the above, thank you.

"I'm going alone." It was only reasonable, and she knew it as well as he did. After what Royce had said happened at the library, anything could go down at South Morrison, if that's where Creed had gone.

"You can't," she said matter-of-factly, opening one of the kitchen drawers.

"Can't?" That was a first. Nobody ever used the word "can't" in relation to what he could or could not do, not since he'd walked out of his mother's life at the tender age of fifteen and never looked back. Skeeter had no idea how similar their stories were—barring a rather staggering financial gap. She'd grown up in poverty, and he most certainly had not.

"You need me," she said, pulling out a holstered Heckler and Koch 9mm and strapping it around her hips.

"What for?" he asked. She sounded pretty damn sure of herself, and he knew she knew her way around the gun. In the months she'd been at Steele Street, Superman had all but turned her into the next Lara Croft, Tomb Raider. Dylan couldn't say he was all that pleased with that particular course of study. The car stuff was great, and she'd proven invaluable at meeting SDF's high-tech needs—but weapons training? He didn't like to think of her getting anywhere near a line of fire.

"South Morrison is a mess, a real labyrinth," she explained. "Half of it is already torn down inside. You could find the party without me, easy. There'll be six, seven hundred people there, maybe more, and a couple of bands loud enough to bring the building down on your head—but I can find Dominika Starkova."

He didn't say a word at first, just watched himself in the reflection of her sunglasses and wished to hell he could see her eyes again. In his gut, he believed her. He didn't want to believe her. He also didn't want her anywhere near Dominika Starkova. The woman was dangerous.

"And you don't think I can find her?"

"No." She shook her head. "Not like I can. I've been getting a vibe on her all night."

A vibe. Like the vibe she'd gotten on J.T.

Hell.

SDF had been given a mission, direct orders from General Grant, simple, straightforward orders: Find Dominika Starkova and bring her in—tonight.

And that meant tonight, not tomorrow, or the day after, or whenever the hell Creed got around to doing it—but tonight.

Despite what Skeeter thought, he knew he could find Dominika Starkova. But he had a feeling Skeeter could find her quicker, and in his business, that counted.

"Do you want me to fire up the Humvee?" she asked.

Humvee?

"What Humvee?" SDF didn't own a Humvee. They were rare-iron aficionados, muscle-car maniacs, chop-shop boys with a penchant for Porsches. They did not lunk around in seven-foot-wide four-wheel-drives.

"The one Johnny and I supercharged last week."

On the other hand, a supercharged Humvee could probably do zero to sixty in less than a minute and a half, even in the blizzard of the century.

CHAPTER 14

CREED KEPT CLOSE to the wall all the way down the stairs. On the landing, he strode past two kids trying to hold each other up and get it on at the same time and failing at both. *Geezus*.

At the top of the last flight of stairs, he found himself looking down onto a seething, whirling mass of humanity. Hundreds of neon glow sticks and the strobes going off everywhere made it damn near impossible to distinguish one person from the next—and freakin' black fishnet seemed to be the outfit du jour. It was everywhere he looked—a flash of stark light, a body frozen in midgyration, an upraised arm sporting a fishnet sleeve, but not her arm, not her sleeve.

Shit.

He checked the makeshift stage. There were people dancing with the band—but none of them was Cody Stark.

His gaze came back to the crowd, and he began systematically quartering the room, but everything in the room was moving, changing shape, shifting into the next quarter, creating chaos.

She could be right in front of him, and if a strobe didn't fire at the exact right time, and her face wasn't at the exact right angle, he'd never see her.

She could be anywhere . . . but the two dark-haired men flashing into view, flash after frozen flash of them plowing their way through the crowd, hell, they shouldn't be there at all. They were older; their body language quiet, serious, intent; their demeanor and their faces foreign, one tall and hawk-nosed, the other darker skinned and more rotund. They weren't dancing. They were searching for something—and his money said they were searching for Dominika Starkova.

As a matter of fact, his money said they'd found her. They were moving with unerring focus, and in the next flash of light, Creed saw the tracking device in the taller man's hand.

Fuck. He plunged into the crowd after them, and suddenly the chaos was on his side. They'd never see him coming.

———

CODY worked her way past the last group of dancers in front of the stage and slipped into the shadows at the back of the room. She had one hand wrapped around her middle. The other was clutching a glow stick somebody had shoved in her face.

Leaning against the makeshift platform, she closed her eyes for a second and took a deep breath. Everything was going to be okay, she told herself. She'd flashed a few smiles, made a few promises, and found a ride with a guy named Spence who'd been bragging about his new Escalade—just the kind of car she needed to get her where she wanted to go. All she had to do was give Spence a few minutes to close his deal and they'd be out of there.

Just a few minutes for Spence to unload the last of his disco biscuits.

Hell. She'd dealt with worse than drug dealers these last three months, a lot worse.

She wasn't worried about getting rid of Spence once he got her to the library garage. Spence was no Creed Rivera, not even close. She wouldn't have any trouble losing him.

She straightened up, taking another breath and looking around. The run across the courtyard had been unexpectedly icy, and unexpectedly painful. She'd fallen twice, scraping her knee on somebody's front bumper the first time and landing hard on something under the snow the second. She was going to have a bruise for sure, had ripped her fishnet, and even in the huge crowd of people she was still cold to the bone, her body trembling.

Glancing back over the crowd, she tightened her arm around her waist, trying to still her trembling. God, was she never going to be warm again? Forget Mexico. She needed something equatorial. She needed a jungle, a steaming sauna of overgrown vegetation and heat.

She'd gotten away from Creed Rivera, though, and Reinhard, and Khalesi hadn't even gotten close to catching her. By all rights she should be feeling a little more confident, a little less frantic. She was coming out ahead.

Sure, she thought, not buying her own bull for a minute. She had plenty of reason to feel uneasy, if not downright petrified with fear. How in the hell had the Iranians found her? By following Reinhard, was her best guess. She'd known he'd be the first dog Sergei would sic on her trail—but still, she was unnerved by the suddenness with which he and Bruno and the Brauns—and the Iranians, for crying out loud—had shown up, right in the library. They'd pinpointed her location, and that was no coincidence. She'd done something—or maybe left something undone, something she better damn well figure out and not do again.

Wiping the back of her hand across her mouth, she looked to the shadows behind the stage. There was a stairway back there somewhere, and a hallway off the third floor that circled around to the front of the building. It would be a lot less crowded than the dance floor. She was meeting Spence in South Morrison's lobby, where she'd left her clothes, and the last thing she wanted was to miss her ride because she couldn't make her way back through the crush of people.

Unbelievably, the blizzard had really brought out the party rats and ravers. She'd never seen the basement so crowded, literally packed like one huge can of slithering, glittery sardines. She'd come before a couple of times just to check things out, get the lay of the neighborhood, and she'd been fine. She knew how to stay out of trouble, how to work a party to her advantage if she needed something, but tonight the party and the music and the crowds were enough to turn her stomach—and all she needed was to get away.

Pushing off the stage, she glanced back over her shoulder, then turned into the shadows and headed toward the rear stairwell.

CREED spotted her just seconds before the two men tracking her came up behind her, a slender form in a body-hugging fishnet cat suit, her short hair falling over her face, her head bowed—and his heart sank.

The man with the tracking device did something he couldn't quite see through all the flickering strobes, but in rapid, stop-action motion he saw her go limp as a rag, falling into the other man's arms—and he was too fucking far away to do a damn thing about it.

She never had a chance.

He shoved his way forward, pulling the Mossberg

free—something, anything to get all these damn candy ravers out of his friggin' way, but shit, most of them were too high to notice that their wasted lives were in danger.

A few of the dancers noticed the mean-looking shortened shotgun and stumbled away from him, but he was still too damn late. When he finally reached the back of the room, Cody Stark and the two men were nowhere to be found.

They wouldn't kill her, not right off, he told himself. Information, that's what they wanted: maps, directions, coordinates—but he could guarantee they wouldn't be asking for any of it nicely.

Where in the hell had they taken her?

The thought no sooner formed than a flash of light revealed the shadowy risers of a stairwell. He took off running, taking the stairs two and three at a time. At the first landing, he found himself looking down a short hallway with half a dozen doors, most of them open, more than a couple of them hanging off their hinges. He discovered a gutted apartment with a kitchen and a bath behind the first door, five kids doing a group grope behind the second, and a cooking party behind the third, but what they were cooking was cocaine.

He swore under his breath, finished checking the other doors, and went back to the stairs—knowing he had seven more floors to go and that every minute she was out of his sight put her deeper in danger.

CODY drifted up into consciousness through an endless wave of pain. Her head was breaking, and she couldn't figure out where she was—except she was upside down, being carried over somebody's shoulder, and they had their hand flat on her ass. Something had happened.

She lifted a tentative hand to the back of her head, and her fingers came away smeared with something warm and sticky: blood.

She'd been hit. Hard. Most likely by the jerk carrying her. She wasn't that far from the floor, which meant he wasn't very tall, which meant he wasn't the badass, angel-faced Creed Rivera, who she was pretty sure wouldn't be feeling her up or have resorted to physical violence to subdue her. He wouldn't have needed to, and so far that hadn't been his style, not with her anyway. Edmund Braun would probably disagree.

The man carrying her walked through a circle of light, and she saw his pants, brown and baggy, and his shoes, soft, worn leather. Definitely not Creed Rivera. Out of the corner of her eye, she saw another man dressed the same way, at least from the waist down. She didn't have it in her to raise her head to see his face, not yet.

Then he spoke, his accent foreign, the language straight out of the Hindu Kush—Dari—and she didn't need to see his face. A memory flashed in her mind of a dark warehouse, the smell of cordite, and the scent of blood that wasn't her own. Panic, stark and razor sharp, skittered across every nerve ending she had. Nausea coursed through her, and she had to fight being sick.

Karlovy Vary—she would never forget the place, or the man who had died there. Keith O'Connell had died because of her, and she'd been captured by the same men who had killed him—Ahmad Hashemi and Qasim Akbar, the two Afghans negotiating with Sergei Patrushev for the Taliban. They were getting paid to get the bomb for their ousted leaders, and they weren't above cold-blooded, brutal murder to insure their success.

But they'd done more than murder O'Connell; it had been butchery by the time they'd finished. She'd lost count of the shots they'd fired into the agent as O'Connell had hung there in the warehouse, his hands tied above him, Reinhard and Sergei standing off to one side with the Brauns, all of them as culpable as the men pulling the triggers. Reinhard had kept an iron grip on her arm, making sure she learned her lesson. She hadn't watched. She'd turned away, but the German had held her, keeping her close, and she'd heard O'Connell die.

Now Hashemi and Akbar had her, and she was alone, terribly alone. She should never have left Creed in her apartment. The Afghans wouldn't have had a chance against wild boy, and anything, even a lifetime in prison, was better than what she was afraid she faced next.

Music, subdued but still raucous, coming up from below, made the building hum around her, telling her she was still in South Morrison. She hadn't been out that long, a few minutes at most, and she had to get away—now.

Staying perfectly limp, she started counting down in her head. When she got to three, she jammed her elbow into the middle of Akbar's back as hard as she could. The Afghan faltered, his hold loosening, and she twisted free, kicking at Hashemi. Her foot connected with the side of his head, stunning him for a second as she scrambled to her feet and took off running down the hallway. She got all of ten feet before she was hit from behind.

Both men landed on her, taking her down, and she cried out.

ON the third floor, Creed jerked his head up, hearing the sound—half scream, half cry of pain—coming from somewhere above.

CHAPTER 15

SHE WAS AS GOOD as dead, and Cody knew it. Hashemi was bleeding where she'd caught him with the heel of her shoe, and if looks alone could have cut out her heart, she'd already be gasping her last breath on the floor.

They'd dragged her out of the hallway and slammed her into a chair inside one of South Morrison's apartments. She didn't know what floor she was on.

She did know she was losing the feeling in her arms. They'd jerked them behind the back of the chair and tied her with some cord that had been lying on the apartment's kitchen counter. They'd also tied her around the waist and secured both her legs to the legs of the chair. Like the rest of the building, the apartment had been ransacked, with its few shabby contents in pieces and the walls broken through.

Short and brutish, Akbar, the man who had been carrying her, had busted another leg off a different chair and was holding it like a baseball bat, as if he was going to bash her brains out. As a threat, it was very effective. She was hyperventilating herself right into a heart attack. Her mouth was so dry, it hurt.

She'd been vulnerable in Prague. Getting through the hours of her days had been like negotiating a mine field, always having a guard on her, always being at Sergei's beck and call; the nights had been even worse, with the incessant parties and tension-filled meetings Sergei demanded she attend with him.

But she'd never been helpless, not like this. She couldn't move, and her wits weren't going to be enough to save her—not with Hashemi pulling a knife out of his pocket.

He opened it with a touch. Switchblade.

Oh, God. Oh, God.

Keith O'Connell's was the only murder she'd ever witnessed, but she'd spent three months with the Russian mob, traveling all over Eastern and Western Europe under Sergei's "protection," and violence was their way of life.

Freedom. God, the price of her freedom was going to be her life. She'd known it for weeks, but thought if she could run fast enough, far enough, she could escape the Russian's net.

The more fool she.

Hashemi stopped in front of her, his lips thinned with fury, the knife balanced in his hand. He was taller and narrower through the face than Akbar, his dark eyes more deeply set between a prominent brow and his hawklike nose. Both men were wearing dark leather coats, but given the temperature in the building and the blizzard still raging outside, neither of them showed any signs that they were feeling the cold. Their focus was all on her—frightfully on her.

"Patrushev gave orders not to kill you, Dominika . . . not yet. He wants you back, you and the book, and has offered a generous reward, but I think taking a few small pieces will not distress him too much," Hashemi said, touching his fingers to the side of his face where she'd kicked him. They came away smeared with blood. He took a look and grimaced, his mouth twisting in anger before his gaze came back to her. "If you don't answer my questions, I will cut off your left ear. If you continue to refuse, I will cut off your right ear and then start on your fingers, one by one until you tell me where the book is, the one your father gave you."

His voice was cold and flat and as he spoke, Akbar roughly pushed her head to each side with the chair leg, pointing out the parts she would be missing.

Cody tried to duck away, turning her head to keep from getting hit too hard, and was only about half successful. Behind her back, she instinctively clenched her hands, drawing her fingers tightly together into fists, protecting them. Hashemi wasn't bluffing. He meant every word, and she knew it down to the depths of her soul. The world safe and secure for the price of her left ear? It shouldn't have even been a question in her mind.

But it was.

And her fingers? They ached just with the thought of being severed. It was an atrocity too horrible even to acknowledge.

"Reinhard Klein is h-here. In Denver. I . . . I saw him, and he wants me unharmed." She could barely speak, barely breathe around the knot of terror squeezing her heart—but she couldn't just sit there and wait for Hashemi to start cutting her up, or for Akbar to hit her hard enough to kill her. She had to stall them, and they knew as well as she who was on top of Sergei's food chain. Reinhard would always take precedence over the Taliban, no matter who they had killed for him.

As for Sergei, she'd been right. He'd realized what *Tajikistan Discontent* really meant.

"Of course Klein is here, along with the Iranians and the Zurich Seven," Hashemi said. "Sergei sent us to track you down. Akbar and I almost had you this afternoon at the post office, but we lost you in the storm, and the others didn't do any better, I see."

"The post office? Track me down?" What was he talking about? "How?"

In answer, he touched his knife to her ear and tapped her earring. It was all she could do not to cringe.

"Your jewels, little fool. Sergei had them bugged. We followed them across Europe to New York, and across the United States to Denver, but you were never with them. It was post office to post office only, until today." He lifted the knife a fraction higher, and touched the tip to her skin. "Very clever, but not so clever today."

For a second, Cody could only stare at him, stunned. She'd been bugged. Sergei liked "insurance policies," and that's what the earrings had been for him. He hadn't expected her to escape, not with his guards on her twenty-four/seven, but he must have figured only a fool would leave behind something as valuable and saleable as an expensive pair of earrings, if she did escape—and he'd known she was no fool.

"Untie me . . . now," she said, taking the only chance she had, "and I'll get you the book. I swear."

The library was probably still crawling with cops. It was the best place to go to buy herself some time. Maybe, with luck, Creed Rivera had gone back there. She'd give anything to be in his custody right now, to have him back by her side.

Anything, she thought again, realizing with startling clarity just how true it was. She needed a friend, and somebody who had fed her candy bars and saved her from Edmund Braun was as close to a friend as she'd had since Keith O'Connell. Even if Rivera was taking her to jail—and that was so pitiful; if she hadn't been on the verge of death and disfigurement, she would have been on the verge of tears.

"No, you will tell me where it is," Hashemi said, declining her offer. "Quickly, before I lose my patience."

She hesitated, despite his threat, but only for a second. She needed to pull her head together. She needed to make a deal, fast.

"You're right," she said, talking even as she formulated a plan. "I know where the bomb is, and I'm willing to work with you. We don't need Sergei Patrushev. We can make our own deal, and it'll be better than anything he offered. I guarantee it."

His answer was a short, humorless laugh. "You may be that stupid, Dominika, but I am not. Anyone who tries to take Patrushev's bomb will die an ugly death, and then their children will die. We wouldn't get two kilometers before he'd have our carcasses hanging from hooks. Not even my government would protect me. They owe him too much money. Everyone does, which is why no one double-crosses Sergei Patrushev. But you know this, don't you, Dominika?"

Before she could admit that yes, so help her God, she knew why nobody dared to cross Sergei, Akbar spoke up, saying something to Hashemi in Dari.

A sly grin twisted the taller man's mouth, and he reached out with the tip of his knife and snagged a piece of her fishnet. Cody's heart slowed to a near stop. Without understanding a word, she knew exactly what Akbar had said. The two had been notorious in Prague, widely known for their sexual deviances. It was said Akbar often flagellated himself afterward, in penance to Allah for his sins—and then the next night he would sin again, drinking the infidel's vodka and screwing the infidel's women.

Death, disfigurement, but first rape. She'd fallen into an abyss and was headed straight to hell.

Hashemi's dark gaze held hers, his smile fading as he said something back to Akbar, something the shorter man didn't like hearing. Akbar cursed and swung the broken chair leg, bringing it crashing against the back legs of her chair, knocking it over with her still tied to it. Her head snapped forward with the force of the blow. The breath was knocked out of her. She landed on her side, hard on her arm, facing Akbar, and had to bite back a cry.

Hashemi came around behind her and grabbed a fistful of her hair, pulling it back, exposing her left ear . . . *God save me*, she thought through a haze of pain and fear.

"Now." He ground the word out between his teeth. *"Tell me."*

She gasped as his fingers tightened and he jerked her head around. The stiletto length of his blade glinted in the light from the hallway.

She tried to speak, but her courage and her voice failed her. She felt sick with fear, the taste of it like bile in her mouth.

The Afghan shifted the knife in his hand, readying it to cut her.

And then he wasn't there.

Two shots sounded in near instant succession, a deafening blast in close quarters, and Hashemi jerked away from her. The knife clattered to the floor in front of her.

Oh, God. Dear God. Cody's heart was racing, pounding in her chest.

Akbar was screaming. Someone else shouted something she couldn't make out through the ringing in her ears, but she knew why Akbar was screaming. His kneecap had exploded.

Hashemi was dead, she had no doubt, and she was trapped. She tried to pull free, then froze as a dark shadow passed overhead.

Oh, God. Akbar's screams turned to gasping sobs and moans. She heard a struggle, heard muttered curses, and saw movement in the shadows.

Any second the shadow would come for her—and she was trapped.

She jerked her hands again and struggled against the bindings around her ankles. *Get out. Oh, God, get out,* she thought, the words ricocheting around her brain as every breath became harder to draw. The smell of blood filled the air, and a sob of pure panic broke free from her throat. She couldn't breathe, and her arm felt like it was breaking with her full weight on it. She couldn't move— and then it was too late.

The shadow passed over her again, stealing the faint

light, plunging her into utter darkness. A man bent over her. She could feel the weight of his presence, hear his breathing. *Oh, God.* If it was Reinhard or Bruno, she was doomed. With a soft grunt, the man shoved Hashemi further away. The faint stream of light from the hall returned, and she saw a bent knee and the drape of a dark coat. She hurt so badly, every muscle in her body, every bone.

Help me, she wanted to say. *Help me.* But her mouth was too dry, and she knew there wasn't any help to be had, especially when she saw the man's hand reach across her, holding a knife.

Everything was moving too fast. Blood was running across the floor, glistening in the low light.

Oh, God. She was going to be sick. She was going to faint.

Hashemi's killer leaned in closer behind her, the knife still in his hand, and Cody cringed.

"Hang on," he said. "I'll have you free in a second." The voice was rough-edged, rock-steady—and recognizable. Creed Rivera.

The sudden surge of relief she felt made her weak. He sliced through her bonds, first her hands, then her waist, and each of her ankles, each cut a single, swift stroke. She tried not to think about the blood on the floor, about what he'd done to save her. He *had* saved her, and nothing else mattered.

He pulled the chair away from her, but she couldn't move. Her arms and legs were numb. Akbar's moaning gasps and short, harsh screams were edged in pain, but all she could think was that she'd been saved.

"Come on," Creed said, hauling her up to a sitting position and propping her against the apartment wall. "Stay put."

The order was like a bad joke. Her limbs felt like dead weight. She wasn't going anywhere, not yet, not under her own power. She watched him roll Hashemi over, heedless of the bloody mess he'd made, and pat the man down, taking things out of his pockets and from inside his coat. It all went in his own coat, every paper, Hashemi's wallet, a set of keys, and something that looked like a wristwatch, only thicker, more like a hard plastic cuff with gadgetry on its face. When he was finished with Hashemi, he moved to Akbar, who wasn't dying, but was handcuffed with the same plastic cuffs Creed had used on her. Blood flowed down the side of his face. His leg was shattered, but his eyes were wide open and full of pain and fury.

Creed said something to him, his voice low and hard-edged, and Cody would have sworn the language he used was Dari. Akbar certainly understood him. The smaller man went livid, his words coming fast and furious between his gasps of agony. Creed ignored him and just kept patting him down, relieving him of all his possessions. Every movement was controlled, his actions swiftly executed and efficient. He had both men stripped of their goods and was back by her side in less than a minute.

"You okay?" he asked, pulling Hashemi's strange watch out of his pocket and pressing a button on the front.

When she didn't immediately answer, he lifted his gaze to hers, and she nodded, a single, automatic movement.

"Good," he said, returning his attention to the watch. A red light blinked on in the center of it. There was no time display, just a bunch of dials and small buttons, which he spent a few seconds adjusting. When he lifted it to her shoes and began slowly running it up her body, she suddenly understood what he was doing.

"It's the earrings," she said, her throat so dry it hurt. "Hashemi told me it was the earrings they'd all been following." The earrings she'd gotten out of the package she'd picked up this afternoon at the post office. She'd no sooner told him than the red light stopped blinking and went full-out solid, right when he passed the tracking device past her ear.

"Sure enough," he said, dropping the tracker in his pocket and reaching for the earrings. In seconds, he'd removed them, an exquisite set of ruby-and-diamond-encrusted crosses by Olena, a Ukranian designer. They were worth two thousand Euros in Prague, but to Creed Rivera, they weren't worth the risk. She watched with a mixture of dismay and relief as he leaned over and tossed them down a broken, exposed pipe jutting out of the wall. The tiny clatter of their fall didn't last more than a second or two, before they were lost to the world.

The sound of voices in the hall brought her moment of dismay to a sudden halt. Her adrenaline spiked, and she tried to get to her feet. Creed was way ahead of her, scooping her up into his arms and whisking her through a wide gash in the wall behind them where a door had once been. The hinges were still hanging on what was left of the jamb. In two steps he had them hidden in the shadows and rubble of the dark room. There was no outside door in this room—a bedroom, she figured—and the window had been busted out, leaving it open to the weather and the wind howling outside. Snow swirled across the carpeting and drifted in the corners. There was no furniture, just piles of trash and junk. He let go of her legs, letting her feet slide to the floor, but kept his other arm tightly around her, holding her up.

She clung to him, terrified of who might come in the apartment with another tracker in his hand—but nobody did. The voices went on by, laughing and swearing in good old American English, two guys talking about a girl. She didn't relax, though, not for a second—because he didn't. Every muscle in his body was on alert, tensed, ready for whatever the hell happened next.

Well, so was she, so tense and ready she felt like she was going to snap.

In another couple of seconds, all that nauseating tension proved justified. A new set of voices came down the hall speaking German.

Reinhard.

Her blood ran cold. She would know his voice

anywhere, in any language. She heard it in her nightmares, sneaking up on her in the dark, whispering in her ear, threatening her.

More voices joined in, more than she could distinguish from each other, all of them getting closer to the apartment. She and Creed Rivera were horribly outnumbered—and oh, God, he'd killed Hashemi.

The Afghan had said the Zurich 7 were in Denver. It could be them coming down the hall with Reinhard. She'd never seen the Zurich 7, didn't even know if there were actually seven of them or not and seriously doubted that any of them were from Zurich. All of their dealings with Sergei had been encrypted and sent over the Internet, the amount of money they had been able to secure effectively pushing out all of the smaller buyers, except the Iranians, who were hanging on by a thread but didn't really have a chance against the major players.

An arc of light sliced through the gash in the wall, and a man said, *"Scheisse!" Shit!*

Cody knew how awful the whole thing looked, with Hashemi dead and his blood everywhere and Akbar screaming and writhing on the floor. She heard a shout, sounding like Akbar, and then the apartment was overrun.

She gasped as Creed tightened his hold on her waist and ran for the window. He was damn near crushing her, but the worst was the window.

He shoved her out ahead of him onto a rickety old fire escape, and *oh, God*—she felt like she was going to die. The bitter wind slashed at her skin, each snowflake feeling like the cut of a knife, the fishnet giving her no protection at all. The air was too frigid to bear, too raw. She was too exposed, her heart racing, her head pounding, her muscles throbbing, tingling, trying to come back to life and failing against the sheer fierceness of the blizzard. Her last ounce of strength was torn away from her by the icy maelstrom, and then she was falling.

CHAPTER 16

CREED SWORE, catching her as her knees buckled and swinging her back up into his arms. He'd had a fistful of fishnet, holding onto her while he'd ducked through the window after her, but he'd still almost lost her. *Geezus*—the friggin' window. It hadn't been his first choice. Going back into the apartment, pumping shells through the shotgun, that would have been his first choice if he'd been alone. Of course, if he'd been alone, there would have been no reason to go back in with guns blazing, because all the tangos in South Morrison would have been someplace else chasing after Cody Stark.

And they were tangos. Every damn last one of them. He'd read their files, and he knew Reinhard Klein billed himself as an international businessman, but anybody who dealt with the Taliban and the likes of Ahmad Hashemi and Qasim Akbar was a terrorist in his book.

Geezus. Selling guys like Hashemi a friggin' nuclear warhead was like signing a death warrant for New York, or London, or any of half a dozen major cities in the world. Let the Chechens buy it, and you could say good-bye to Moscow. Give it to Jemaah Islamiah and say so long to a big chunk of Indonesia. Al-Qaeda didn't bear thinking about. Hamas or Hizbullah would blow Israel right off the map. It would be Holocaust on a global scale. There would be no end of destruction if a rogue nuclear bomb was set off.

So what did that make the woman freezing to death in his arms?

Tango with a capital T.

Fuck.

And what all the assholes in the apartment had not been able to do, he was going to manage without even trying—namely, be the death of her. Her outfit put a whole new spin on the term "scantily clad." He'd lost her clothes somewhere in the basement, dropped them when he'd dragged out the Mossberg. It had seemed like the smart move at the time. Funny how things changed. Clothes looked like a good idea about now, with her shivering to pieces—and she *still* had half a dozen bad guys on her ass.

He only made it down two floors before deciding that the fire escape idea had been one of his worst of the night, and that was saying a lot, considering how things were turning out. The whole damn thing didn't have more than two bolts in it, and besides being icy as shit, it was swaying in the wind. A silenced shot coming from above and pinging off the outside rail gave him the last little bit of incentive he needed to get the fuck off it.

He kicked in a window and knocked the remaining shards off with his shoulder as he pushed inside. She groaned, which he took as a good sign, which just once again proved how quickly the night had gone to hell. Dylan was going to have his ass if anything happened to her, and he'd be welcome to it.

Moving fast and avoiding the hall, he carried her through to the next room, and the next, and the next. Most of the walls separating the abandoned apartments had been at least partially destroyed. Others had doors in them. He managed to get quite a ways before he dead-ended and was forced to move back toward the hall.

She'd roused herself enough to put her arms around his neck and hold on to him, but he wasn't inclined to set her down anywhere while he did recon. She'd proven damn slippery so far, and he was done with chasing her. All he wanted now was to get her to Steele Street and hand her over to Dylan.

Well, it wasn't all he wanted, but it was all he was going to get. The rest of it was too damn crazy, especially the god-awful urge he had to press his face into her hair, to somehow reassure her, to—*fuck*—reassure himself that she really was okay. That Hashemi hadn't cut her.

He could feel her breath on his skin, soft and shallow and warm. *Damn*.

He needed a new line of work, really. Just because the Afghan had been ready to start carving her up was no reason for him to get his boxers in a wad. It was no reason for him to have had a fucking heart-stopping flashback starring him and J.T.

But he had. Fiercely intense, like running smack-face into Hell and having your guts ripped out in half a second flat.

He was still sweating, his hands shaking. *Geezus*. It had been so real, the heat, the smell—J.T. screaming.

He'd heard Akbar say he wanted to fuck her, but he'd been hearing it from a thousand miles away, still reeling from the sudden burst of heat and pain and raw emotion that had seared itself across his brain. All because Hashemi had put a knife to her throat.

Yep. He definitely needed a new line of work. Flashbacking commandos were dead commandos, and they sure as hell weren't any good to anybody else. He'd hesitated. With Hashemi threatening her, and Akbar going freakin' nuts knocking her around, it had taken everything he had to drag himself back to the present, to focus on what was happening *now*.

Fuck! He stopped just inside the door and slammed his back up against the wall, his arm tightening around her waist as he let her feet slide to the floor.

He was losing it, and now was *not* the time, and this was *not* the place to be losing anything.

A snick of sound at the back of the room had him whirling around, the Glock leveled and loaded, his finger on the trigger.

A derelict shuffled out of the shadows, completely oblivious to the fact that his life was a mere two-and-a-half pounds of pressure away from getting blown to smithereens.

Creed didn't even want to think about how he'd missed something as big as a wino in the room. The old guy was mumbling to himself, struggling to get the screw top off his bottle of hooch, and Creed felt like his heart was in a vise.

"Get out," he growled when the man looked up.

The guy didn't need to be told twice. Staring down the handgun's bore, his rheumy eyes went as big as saucers. He wrapped his arm protectively around his bottle and shuffled off, going back the way Creed and Cody had just come.

Bad choice, Creed thought, but he wasn't getting paid to save winos tonight. He was getting paid to save her.

And it was time to earn his keep.

The sound of men talking, searching, coming through the apartments behind them and down the hall was narrowing his options pretty damn fast.

Shoving the Glock back into its holster, he pulled out the shotgun and put it firmly in her hands.

"You've got six shots," he said. She'd never be able to

reload. She looked shell-shocked, her lips white, her gaze dull. "That's more than you think, so don't be shy about using them. All you have to do is point this thing even remotely in the general direction and pull the trigger. Trust me. You're gonna hit something, and if you keep pulling the trigger, you're gonna hit everything."

He shrugged out of his coat and lifted it onto her shoulders, then helped her get her arms through the sleeves, always bringing her hands back onto the shotgun. She needed to know what she had, to get a grip, literally and figuratively.

"Get back in the corner, into that pile of junk, and shoot anything that comes through the door in the next two minutes," he continued, hating himself for even having to give her such crap advice. He should never have brought her here.

"Wh-where are you going?" Her teeth were chattering, her body trembling.

He jerked his head toward the darkened hall. "I'm going to draw them off to the apartments on the other side. Work my way back to the front of the building."

"N-no . . ." She shook her head. "Don't leave me."

"Don't worry. The good guys are on their way, and they're gonna be looking for this." He pulled his cell phone out of his pants pocket. A blue light cycled across its screen. He dropped it into one of the pockets on his coat. He'd put a 911 call in to Skeeter on his way up the stairs that would have lit up every computer screen at SDF's headquarters.

"B-but . . . but what if it's you who comes through the door?"

"Odds are I won't be making it back this way," he said, buttoning the top button on the coat to keep it from falling off her.

Her hand came up and wrapped around his wrist. "N-no . . . you can't . . . can't leave me here. I haven't . . . haven't ever shot anyone."

Okay, time to backpedal, big-time. "It's not as bad as I said before, when we were on the roof. Honest." He pulled the coat more tightly around her and buttoned the next button. "You've got to be sharp. Okay? Because if any bad boys show up at the door, it means I'm gone. Really gone. No coming to the rescue. Okay?" He ducked his head to look her straight in the eyes. "Six badass shots, babe," he repeated. "Six. Use them. And if my buddies don't get to you and you still get out of here, turn yourself over to the FBI, or the cops, CIA, somebody, please. It's the only chance you've got. Swear to God, you're never going to make it on your own, not with these guys after you."

"You don't even know me." She sounded so distraught, so heartbroken, he didn't have the heart to tell her that knowing her wasn't the point. He didn't need to know someone to lay his life on the line for them. It was his job to lay his life on the line, whatever line Uncle Sam drew, whenever and wherever he drew it.

No, he wasn't going to tell her that. So all he said was,

"Not yet." And then he kissed her, bent his head down and opened his mouth over hers.

Talk about a heart attack. Her lips were cold, but the inside of her mouth was sweetly warm and unbelievably welcoming. She melted for him. She melted on him. She melted in him—so instantly, so perfectly. A soft groan, the catch of her breath in her throat, her body leaning into his. It was more than he'd expected and all he needed to know.

He'd be coming back for more of this, come hell, high water, or Reinhard Klein.

"Gotta go," he said, pulling back just enough to whisper against her lips and steal another kiss.

The voices were drawing nearer, the sound of the search intensifying. He hoped to hell the wino had gone to ground.

Setting her aside, he drew the Glock and checked the hall, one quick line-of-sight glance. They were down there all right, moving shadows in the darkened building.

Without another word, he slipped across the hall, moving swiftly, silently, keeping low. Forty seconds later, he let loose with his first shot and heard Reinhard and his posse take the bait, coming after him.

WHAT the hell is that?" Tony Royce asked, his head swiveling from side to side as every computer in the Steele Street office suddenly went off like an alarm clock on steroids. He could even hear the computers in Hart's office going off.

Mathers leaned over the nearest keyboard. The other agent, Bracken, moved to the computer nearest him. Royce looked from one screen to the other, watching as flashing horizontal lines disintegrated into a city map. It took him all of five seconds to figure out what he was seeing.

"Somebody's in a shitload of trouble and sending out an SOS," Mathers said.

"Yeah." Royce grinned. "I'd say we've got our guy. Let's just hope to hell he's got Dominika Starkova. Get a lock on his position and let's go."

"What about Hart?" Bracken asked.

"Screw Dylan Hart. He can play catch-up for a change." Royce knew the stories, and in his book, Dylan Hart should have been locked up years ago, right about the time he'd gotten nailed in Moscow carrying way too many U.S. government classified documents. Hart had been twenty-two at the time, plenty old enough to take a fall. As for SDF, it shouldn't even exist. A bunch of car thieves and ex-cons. That's all they were, all they'd ever be. Royce knew General "Buck" Grant. He knew the kind of pull the old man had, but not even a legend like Buck Grant could have been solely responsible for saving Dylan Hart's ass and setting up Special Defense Force. That had taken some real power, and someday Royce was going to find out who had been wielding that power.

"What about Ms. Bang?" Mathers asked.

"Screw Ms. Bang." Skeeter Bang was nothing but a Grade A juvenile delinquent, straight off the streets with more attitude than she had a right to claim.

"Yes, *sir*," Mathers said with just a shade too much enthusiasm for anybody to miss his point.

"Hot, very hot," Bracken agreed.

"*Torturously* hot." Mathers's grin was a mile wide.

Dickheads, Royce thought, giving them both a cold, blank stare guaranteed to get them back on track. He asked for agents, and they sent him dickheads.

YOU quit smoking," Dylan said as he turned the Humvee onto Platte Street.

Behind her sunglasses, Skeeter's eyebrows went up half an inch. She slanted him a quick glance—about her eight hundred and twenty-eighth quick glance since they'd gotten in the monster vehicle. How in the hell had he known she'd quit smoking? She never had smoked in the office, only in the garages, which had been no skin off her nose considering that the SDF headquarters was nothing but one garage on top of another with a couple of floors of lofts and offices on top. Okay, half a dozen floors of lofts and offices, but still, the building was mostly filled with tires and iron.

"Uh, yeah. Superman and I, we decided it was bad for our health." Actually, Superman had decided it was bad for her health, a conclusion he'd come to a few months after he'd decided it was bad for his health and quit—which coincidentally had been the exact same time that he'd found true love.

Skeeter didn't much buy into coincidence of any sort, so even though it had been sort of a stretch of the laws of probability that not smoking and true love were somehow connected, she'd gone ahead and quit anyway, to get Superman off her butt and on the off chance there was something to the love thing—and lo and behold, here she was in a car at night with Dylan Hart.

"Well, congratulations. I know it's not an easy thing."

"Thanks." She'd done tougher. They both knew it, but her smoking career was a far more comfortable subject than her family life or her graffiti convictions or those months she'd spent on the street. And as far as she knew, Dylan didn't have any of those things to talk about—no family life, no convictions, and no actual time on the street. According to all she'd ever been able to get out of the guys, it was as if Dylan Hart had dropped into lower downtown from out of nowhere at the ripe old age of fifteen with plenty of cash and a plan in hand. He'd culled Sparky Klimaszewski's garage and the craps games for his crew, and set himself up in business selling chopped car parts across the western United States from Chicago to L.A.

"You know, you're welcome to have your friends over," he spoke up again. "You don't have to just hang out with the operators and SDF stringers. I've been thinking about putting a pool table and maybe an ice-cream fountain down on the second floor, move some of Quinn's Chevys up to the third."

Eyebrows angling toward the stratosphere, she slanted him glance number eight hundred and twenty-nine. Move Quinn's first-generation Camaros? Was he nuts? She had most of those cars broken down to their frames. The last thing she wanted was to start frickin' *moving* them anywhere. And ice cream? What was that all about?

"Uh, thanks." Honestly, they had more important things to be thinking about right now.

Or so she thought.

To her everlasting amazement, her answer brought a relieved-looking smile to his mouth, as if he'd been worried that she'd been pining for the gang-bangers, street-walkers, and cokeheads she'd done her best to avoid when she'd bottomed out on Wazee.

"Great," he said. "We'll get started on it right away."

Over her dead body.

"How's your coffee?"

And now her coffee?

"Uh, fine. How's yours?"

"Great. Really great."

Oh-kay. This conversation was going nowhere fast, which flat-out fascinated her. Dylan Hart was not one for small talk, but here he was, chitchatting his way right into a dead end, a fact she would have loved to explore, but right then the computer alarm in the Humvee went off.

Her heart instantly dropped to her stomach. *Oh,*

damn. Oh, crap. Oh, double damn crap. It could only be Creed, and he had to be in it up to his neck to have dialed in a 911.

"Son of a bitch," Dylan swore.

She leaned forward and quickly worked the keyboard to pull up the incoming map. She should have gone with him. She'd known it. So help her God, she'd known it. She should *never* have let him go alone.

She'd read the files. She knew how many bona fide international crime lords and terrorists were trying to buy the nuclear missile. Way too many, if Creed Rivera was calling for help. *Shit.*

She and Dylan had been tracking Angelina through the Humvee's onboard computer, but a 911 call shot the night's mission directly into the personnel-in-peril category, and what she needed now was a lock on Creed's GPS cell phone. She didn't need his car anymore. She needed *him.*

"There's Angelina," Dylan said.

Sure enough, the Chevelle was parked in front of North Morrison with snow drifting up to her rims.

"Keep going," she said, connecting her customized PDA handset to the computer and running a quick program to download the coordinates of the call's origin. "He's farther west."

The Humvee's tires crunched on through the snow.

"Take a right," she said, keeping her eye on the computer screen and silently urging the program to download faster.

It finished in seconds. She quickly unhooked her handset and looked up through the windshield—and there it was in all its dilapidated glory. South Morrison.

Damnit.

"He's at the party," she said. At the party with untold hundreds of party rats and at least one terrorist with enough firepower to back him into a corner.

"Stick close to me," Dylan said, pulling to a stop and throwing the Humvee into park.

Like white on rice, she thought, jumping out of the Humvee and taking off at a run, pacing him as he headed toward South Morrison's front door.

CHAPTER

17

Cody FLINCHED AT the shot. She hadn't moved, and she needed to move. She needed to hide, but the gun Creed had given her felt like a long lead weight in her hands, heavy, unmanageable—like the death of her.

Reinhard shouted out in the hall, swearing at his men to go, go, go, and the sound of his voice was enough to finally startle her out of her inertia.

She'd lost seconds, precious seconds.

Head pounding, her arm aching, she forced herself into action, heading for the pile of junk and trash in the room's far corner. The biggest piece of junk turned out to be an overturned cast-iron bathtub. Sinking down behind it, she pulled a couple of pieces of cardboard close around her, making sure she could still see the door. Finger on the trigger, she rested the barrel of the gun on the edge of the tub.

Six shots—all of them with Reinhard Klein's name on them, if he came through the door. She swore it.

Please, she thought, but couldn't have said if it was please keep him away or please bring him into her sights.

She wouldn't miss. She knew that. Creed had told her she'd hit something, everything.

A wave of dizziness and nausea washed through her, making her hands shake. She tightened her grip and gave her head a shake, trying to clear it.

Reinhard Klein—she needed to concentrate. She needed some grace, an angel to exorcise him out of her memories, to get the taint of him off her skin, but the only angel she'd ever met was sacrificing himself to save her pitiful life.

Another shot sounded from her end of the building, followed by a barrage of shots coming from down the hall. A man cried out, and a sob caught in her throat. *Oh, God. Oh, God. Oh, God.*

She tightened her hold on the pistol grip of the shotgun with both hands, her fingers stiff and cold, trying to hold it steady and keep the muzzle up.

Another shot was fired off. *God help her.* She couldn't do this, couldn't live like this anymore, hiding, running . . . losing. Karlovy Vary had stripped her to the bone, taken her last ounce of innocence and shredded her self-respect into nothing. She didn't have a fragment of it left. Now she knew what she'd do to survive, how low she'd sink, and it was as sordid as anything she'd ever imagined.

A gust of wind blew through a broken window behind her, bringing a sweep of snow inside to swirl around her feet. She glanced down, barely a second's worth of inattention, and it was all over.

A hand grabbed hers on the gun, disarming her, another went over her mouth, and she was hauled to her feet. The person who had her pulled her out from behind the tub and into the light coming in from the hallway.

Good Lord. She hadn't seen anybody enter the room. Hadn't heard anyone. They'd moved like shadows.

"Creed's coat," a woman said.

"Creed's gun," a man answered.

They were frisking her, patting her down. A hand went into the coat pocket and came up with his cell phone.

"Creed's frickin' phone." The woman didn't sound any too happy about that piece of information.

"But no frickin' Creed," the man added, handing the woman the gun while he continued frisking Cody down. She thought about struggling, but didn't have the strength or the energy to give it more than a thought. There were two of them, and they were both bigger than she, stronger, and sounded very sure of what they were doing. "A few hundred in cash and miscellaneous documents. Keys. A tracking device."

She heard the man flip through the money. Creed had found her stash. She'd known he would.

"Where is he?" the woman demanded, addressing her directly for the first time.

"And who the hell are you?" the man asked.

"It's Starkova," the woman answered before Cody could, sounding damn sure of herself.

"Not according to the photographs I was given."

"It's her," the woman insisted. "I've got a vibe a mile wide on this one."

Cody was trying to see their faces in the faint light, but it wasn't easy. The man was behind her, holding her, and the woman was dressed in black from the top down, the only noticeable break in the darkness being the long, platinum blond ponytail trailing over her shoulder and hanging to her waist.

Oddly, she was wearing sunglasses and had a ball cap pulled low on her face.

"An ice-cream fountain?" the woman asked from out of nowhere as she opened the chamber on the shotgun, checked it, and closed it again. The whole process was one smooth action.

"For milk shakes and things." The man sounded slightly defensive.

The woman snorted.

What in the hell were they talking about? Cody wondered.

"He . . . he needs help," Cody finally got out. These had to be the "good guys" he'd told her were coming.

"Can you handle her?" the man asked.

"Can Superman kick your butt with one arm tied

behind his back?" the woman replied. "She's half dead, Dylan, and the other half of her is in shock. I can handle her."

"Go back the way we came. It's clear. Take the Humvee," the man said, and then he was gone, as invisibly as he'd shown up, like a shadow.

"Okay, babycakes," the woman said. "Let's get you home before you croak on me."

CHAPTER

18

S KEETER BANG.

The woman's name was Skeeter Bang, except she was a girl, not a woman, little more than a teenager, but built like an Amazon—sleekly muscled, slim-hipped, and amazingly curved from the waist up. Cody was completely done in, weak from the inside out, and Skeeter looked like she pumped iron in her sleep.

More importantly, Skeeter was who Creed had sent after her, the only connection she had to him—and she had no place left to run, no reason to escape. She felt that truth down to her bones. She'd come to the end of the road.

The place they were going—Steele Street, Skeeter

had called it—was her last stop before the CIA hauled her off to Langley and whatever fate awaited her there. It wasn't going to be pretty, or pleasant, or necessarily legal. Not with a nuclear warhead on the auction block. She knew that much. And when the CIA was done with her, Sergei and Reinhard would find a way to get to her.

And then her nightmares would all come back to life.

An involuntary tremor went through her.

She clenched her hands together and glanced out the window. The streets around South Morrison had been dark, but Skeeter had driven back into downtown and all the city lights, the Humvee churning through the snow as if it wasn't even there. Inside the huge vehicle, she was finally thawing out. The huge four-wheeler had heated seats, and her butt was warm, an odd blessing to be granted when she felt like her whole world had been torn apart.

Skeeter had handcuffed her, real handcuffs, not the plastic things Creed had been using all night.

Creed Rivera.

She dragged in a shuddering breath, holding back a well of emotion she couldn't begin to explain. He'd kissed her again, really kissed her this time, and she felt confused as hell about it.

What had he been thinking?

For that matter, what had she been thinking? And why had his kiss felt like a moment of hope in all the bleak awfulness of the night?

She was almost too miserable to care. She'd lost

everything. Been lucky to get out with her life—if she had. She really wasn't sure, didn't know who Creed and Skeeter and the man in the shadows—Skeeter had called him Dylan—represented. Creed never had confirmed a connection to the CIA, and he'd told her to turn herself in to the FBI first, then the police. Skeeter sure didn't look like a government agent. For that matter, neither did Creed Rivera.

But there had been that kiss.

Creed.

Her next breath caught in her throat, and she tightened his coat around her. It smelled like him, which surprisingly brought her some comfort—and she couldn't explain that, either. Her life had been a roller-coaster since he'd shown up in the library.

But if he hadn't shown up, she'd probably be dead. He'd saved her life how many times tonight? She'd actually lost count.

From where she was huddled in the passenger seat, she looked up through the window. The weather had changed since they'd been on the fire escape. The snow had stopped. A warm wind had blown up from the south, and the temperature had risen. She'd felt it when she and Skeeter had crossed the courtyard. The storm was over, and the streets would be running wet come morning.

"There was a lot of shooting before you showed up," she said.

"We heard some of it," the girl said.

"I . . . I heard a man cry out, as if he'd been hit."

"With Creed shooting, I'd be surprised if a whole lot of guys didn't get hit."

"So you don't think it was him who was hurt?" That had been the burden in the back of her mind. That he'd been shot, maybe even lay dying in South Morrison. The thought was too horrible to bear, so she'd just been shoving it to the back of her mind, right along with the question of why she cared so much.

"No," the girl said without hesitation. "It wasn't him. If Creed had been hurt, I'd know it, and you and I wouldn't be moseying our way back to Steele Street."

The utter certainty in her voice made Cody almost believe her, although she would have begged to differ on the word "moseying." Skeeter Bang drove like a bat out of hell, with the Humvee well suited to her tank-girl style.

"Why not?" she asked.

Skeeter cut a sharp right into a darkened alley. Cody barely caught the street sign out of the corner of her eye. It said "Steele Street."

"Because we'd be too busy kicking ass and taking names in South Morrison," Skeeter said. "Don't worry. Dylan will get him out of there in one piece."

Cody prayed so, even as she wondered where they were going. There wasn't anything of any note in the alley, and it was getting darker, feeling narrower by the second. She didn't think it had been built with Humvees in mind. Skeeter reached up and pressed a control on the visor, and a large square of light opened up ahead of them on one of the buildings. A garage door, Cody realized. Beyond it, she could see an amazing, open metalwork contraption attached to the side of the building and disappearing along with the top floors into the darkened sky. It was girders and cables and thick mesh cages, a platform that looked to be made out of steel plate, the whole of it reminding her of an upended suspension bridge, if a suspension bridge could have been dropped into lower downtown and bolted onto the side of one of LoDo's historically old brick buildings.

"What is that?" she asked.

"A lift," Skeeter said. "A freight elevator. We use it to get cars off the streets and to move them between garages."

Garages? Cody looked more closely, and sure enough, could see what looked to be black metal garage doors opening onto the lift on every floor. Ice clung to their edges and frosted their fronts, giving them a dull shine in the low light.

They passed an alley-level door with the numbers 738 above it, an iron door with bolts in a grid pattern across its face. Next to the door was an old metal sign with the word WEATHERPROOF painted across it.

"Seven thirty-eight Steele Street," she murmured.

"Home sweet home," Skeeter replied, then cranked the wheel hard, barely bothering to slow down as she turned the Humvee into the lit opening. They were no sooner inside than the garage door slid shut behind them, blocking out the night.

The only concession Skeeter made to being inside was to turn off her lights. She didn't slow down, just drove like a maniac through the rows of cars, until she apparently found a spot she liked and turned the Humvee in for a sudden, jarring halt.

Cody's heart was halfway to her throat, but they hadn't hit anything, and they were now stopped.

Home sweet home, indeed, she thought, looking around her at all the cars, and in at least one case, the skeleton of a car.

"What happened to that one?" she asked, nodding toward the blackened wreck. It looked melted from the inside out and charred from the outside in.

"Jeanette?" Skeeter asked, turning in her seat to see the burned-out hulk. "Jeanette the Jet gave up her life last summer in a warehouse at the old Stapleton Airport. She blew up when she hit a rack of fuel barrels. Come on, let's get you upstairs."

From where they came out of the elevator, Skeeter directed her toward a bank of well-lit offices cantilevered half a floor up over the garage floor—a garage floor full of cars, expensive cars with gull wings, European cars, a whole row of Porsches, cars that looked like Angelina, classic muscle with big tires and probably even bigger engines.

"The CIA was visiting earlier," Skeeter said, keeping them in the shadows on the far side of the Porsches, "not very nice guys, so it's probably best if we go in the back way and you stay out of sight, at least until I can figure out if they're still here or not."

Cody couldn't have agreed more, but Skeeter's advice only increased her questions about who these people were, and who they really worked for—which apparently was not the CIA, thank God.

"What do you do with all of them?" she asked, gesturing with her cuffed hands at the seemingly endless expanse of automobiles.

"Drive them, fix them." Skeeter shrugged. "Maybe race them on Saturday nights, but you didn't hear that from me. And we sell them."

Car salesmen—*right*. Now Cody had heard it all.

Warmed up, she was reconsidering her options, starting to believe she actually had options. Skeeter was strong, but Cody might be faster. There was the problem of the handcuffs, but that wasn't enough to stop her. They'd come through downtown, so the library wasn't too far away, and her car was there, and she had the money Dylan had left in Creed's coat.

"Don't," Skeeter said, guiding her up a set of back stairs.

"Don't what?"

"Don't try it."

Was the girl reading her mind?

"Creed is big enough to stop you without hurting you, but I'd have to hurt you, and it looks to me like you've already been hurt a few times tonight."

Definitely reading her mind.

At the top of the stairs, Skeeter opened a door onto one of the offices. It was separate from the offices Cody had seen overlooking the garage. Its only windows opened out onto the alley, not the cars. The room was exquisitely spartan, luxurious in the quality of the furniture and materials used. Two black laptop computers commandeered a center desk made out of pale beech, which matched the filing cabinets and the bookcase. There was only one chair, and it took Skeeter less than a minute to release one of Cody's hands and handcuff her to it.

"Stay put," she said.

Can do, Cody thought, but as soon as Skeeter left the room, even though the girl didn't close the door, she opened the desk drawer and started looking for something to use as a lock pick, or a screwdriver. The drawer was incredibly tidy, like the office, but there was a letter opener. Sterling silver and gold inlay, she'd say, with a heart monogrammed on it, along with the letter H.

The trouble was the chair. The frame was one long extruded piece of bent aluminum without a screw on it, so even if she got the cushions off, she'd still be dragging around a chair frame. She had a feeling Skeeter had known that when she'd handcuffed her to it. Jiggling a paper clip in the cuffs' lock didn't get her anywhere either.

And maybe, just maybe, that isn't such a bad thing, she thought, tossing the paper clip on the desk with a sigh. No one at Steele Street was out to kill her, or torture her, and the streets of Denver were crawling with people tonight who wanted to do both.

God. Letting out another weary sigh, Cody laid her head on the desk—and that's when she saw it, the stack of photographs lying on the other side of the two laptops. There were a lot of them, all eight and a half by eleven inches, black-and-white, a little grainy from the looks of them.

Curious, she reached out and pulled the stack closer, turning it so the top photograph was right side up—and instantly wishing she hadn't.

The image hit her like a wall of painful, searing heat. Her face flushed with the force of it. Her mind balked. For a few seconds, she couldn't breathe, and then her breath left her all at once on a strained gasp.

Karlovy Vary had been a nightmare, but this . . . this was inconceivable.

There were three men, one nailed to a cross and cut open, his whole chest; another with the knife still in his hand, blood running off the blade; and the third chained on his knees in the mud, naked and bleeding from three long gashes across his upper arm and a deep cut down the side of his leg.

Her gaze skittered from one man to the next and back again, her heart racing. The killer was grinning, his nose flat and broken, his skin pockmarked, a deep, disfiguring scar running from the corner of his mouth and along his jaw. At the bottom of the page was a name, written in black ink—*Pablo Castano/NRF/Colombia S.A.*—and a date from last summer, in early July, digitally imprinted on the frame by the camera. The dead man was identified as J.T. Chronopoulous.

And the third man, she knew. Without even looking at the name, she knew—Creed Rivera. He was smeared with mud, his face and hair caked with it, but there was no denying who it was, and there was no denying his anguish. His pain was palpable, his mouth slack, his gaze straight ahead . . . watching, watching the other man die . . . blood and sweat running down his face and body. His shackles were thick and heavy, on both ankles and wrists, chaining him to a vehicle sunk into the mud behind him—and still he strained toward the crucified man, his muscles tight with tension, his fists clenched.

Dear Christ.

In the next picture, she could tell he was screaming. His mouth was open, his teeth bared, his expression terrifyingly fierce—his body language the epitome of frustration and rage.

She kept going, moving each picture to the bottom of the stack, held by the horror of them, like Creed, bearing witness to the inhuman deed, except it *was* a human deed. It was Hashemi and Akbar in Karlovy Vary, only worse, bloodier, more barbaric.

She stopped at a close-up shot of Creed and felt her heart break in a thousand different ways. Desperation marked every curve of his face, desperation and panic and agony.

This, then, was the man who had saved her. This was Creed Rivera stripped to the bone. *Sweet Jesus.*

It was more than she ever would have wanted to see. Creed so defenseless, so utterly destroyed. How did he bear it?

She kept sorting her way down through the stack. A new series started in color, and again there was a name, place, and date at the bottom of each of the pictures: *Manuel Garcia/Peru S.A./December.* He'd been shot between the eyes and was lying in a road. Part of a tire and the front of an automotive grill were visible in the photograph. The second photograph was more gruesome: *Pablo Castano/Peru S.A./December.* He was lying in the dirt, with small patches of snow caught in the sparse vegetation surrounding him—and his throat had been cut. Blood darkened the ground around his head and shoulders.

His throat cut with a knife—a sharp blade wielded with lethal skill.

She pushed the photographs away, heartsick. No one lived through that kind of an ordeal without being changed forever, down to their soul, the way Karlovy Vary had changed her.

Trying to force the horror from her mind, she looked around at the office again. The room was sparsely decorated, but every piece was exquisite, expensive. From what she could see through the open doorway, the rest of the offices were even more luxurious. And the cars—

there must have been hundreds of thousands of dollars' worth of cars on the lower floors, maybe millions.

Skeeter Bang was in the outer office, standing in front of a bank of computers, actually working two keyboards at once, with no sign of the CIA, or anybody else for that matter, in sight, and for that Cody was grateful.

Despite her youth and her appearance, Skeeter and the man in South Morrison had sounded like a team. He'd treated her like an equal.

She was definitely one for the books with her leather pants, fur-lined black jacket, ball cap, sunglasses, and lightning-bolt T-shirt. The fur looked like sable, very expensive. She had a sheathed knife on her hip and was wearing clunky, thick-soled work boots, but even those looked designer made. She'd certainly known her way around Creed's gun.

And the attitude. Man, she had it in spades, calling the CIA "not very nice guys." The fact that she even knew a CIA agent put her in a category most kids her age couldn't claim.

A small pain tightened in Cody's chest. Keith O'Connell had been a nice guy, smart, professional, and he'd done his best to bring her in from the cold. She'd told him everything, all about *Tajikistan Discontent* and her father's death while he'd been leading Sergei's men into the Tajikistan mountains, and she'd given O'Connell the names of all the buyers who had come to the house to deal with Sergei.

How much of her information had gotten through

before O'Connell had been killed, she didn't have a clue. Enough, she guessed, that the CIA had shown up here, looking for her. Enough to put Creed Rivera on her trail.

She'd learned her lesson from O'Connell's death, though. Learned it well: Don't talk. Run.

Out in the main office, Skeeter grew suddenly still, her head coming up, her gaze seeming to fix on some point out in the garage. It was another full minute before Cody heard it—the sound of cold metal grinding, screeching, of cables straining and shuddering against a great weight being lifted.

The freight elevator.

CHAPTER

19

OKAY, HE WAS FREEZING his ass off, and Dylan wanted to talk about ice-cream fountains? What the hell was up with that?

Creed wrapped his arms more tightly around himself and vowed to put a little more effort into Angelina's heater, instead of spending all his time porting her heads and tuning her to within an inch of her life.

"Yeah," Dylan said, relaxing back into the Chevelle's passenger seat as they slowly crawled up the side of 738 Steele Street in the old freight elevator. The new get-you-to-the-top-in-sixty-seconds-flat freight elevator, the one with heat, was deep into repairs. "A regular, old-fashioned soda fountain, banana splits, sundaes, milk shakes, the works."

"I'd rather have a Scotch."

Creed didn't want to hear about milk shakes. He'd just tagged and bagged a Taliban terrorist and gotten away from God only knew how many of the rest of them by the skin of his teeth, all on a mission where there hadn't been any clearly defined Rules of Engagement, because he wasn't supposed to have actually *engaged* anybody.

Hell, he'd done nothing but *engage* all frickin' night long.

Dylan slanted him an annoyed look. "Not everybody at Steele Street is old enough to drink."

Yes, they were. Everyone except Skeeter.

His gaze narrowed, and he looked over at Dylan, looked very carefully. Skeeter?

He wasn't going there. No way. And Dylan shouldn't go there, either. Not Skeeter. *Geezus.*

"So what's the score tonight?" They'd gone over it twice already on the drive home, but Creed needed to hear it all again.

"The CIA has come up empty-handed. The Denver Police Department's finest, the lovely Lieutenant Loretta Bradley, is claiming Edmund Braun, and she picked up two Iranians in the stacks—so she's pretty damn pleased with the night so far. I think she's going to go for a Homeland Security Award or something. It's a toss-up over who's going to get the Afghans, but nobody who was after you in South Morrison is going to have time to go back and get the wounded one without getting busted." Dylan had put a call in to Loretta, who, it seemed, was having trouble shaking the CIA agent she'd had to arm-wrestle for Edmund Braun. A dead Taliban terrorist was really going to have them at each other's throats, but Creed's money was on Lieutenant Loretta. He'd given Dylan the address to Cody Stark's apartment, and Dylan had passed it on to the good lieutenant and suggested she pass it along to the CIA to soften them up a bit. They were definitely going to want a piece of that action.

"Tony Royce is the agent who showed up at Steele Street tonight?"

Dylan nodded. "With his name written all over Dominika Starkova. He wants you to back off and turn her over."

"What do you want?"

"I want to follow orders, which means she goes to General Grant, not the CIA."

That sounded damn good to Creed, but there was a problem. There was *always* a problem. "She was in Karlovy Vary. I think she saw the whole thing; she said Reinhard Klein was there. She even offered to tell me all the details if I'd let her go and give her some spending money."

Dylan winced at the news and brought his hand up to rub the bridge of his nose.

"Damn it," he swore under his breath. "Keith

O'Connell. So this isn't just business for the Agency, this is personal."

"Real damn personal," Creed confirmed. Everyone knew what had been done to O'Connell.

"She must have talked," Dylan said, lifting his gaze to meet Creed's across the inside of the Chevelle. "O'Connell must have been trying to bring her in, and she must have talked. That's got to be where the Pentagon got the information we have about the arms buyers. Maybe the CIA is way ahead of us on this."

"Not tonight, they aren't," Creed said. "Because we've still got her. Right?" That's the part he'd actually needed to hear again, the only part. He needed to hear it until he saw it with his own two eyes: Cody Stark safe in SDF's headquarters at Steele Street.

"Yeah, we've got her," Dylan said. "As of Skeeter's last call, she's still handcuffed to the chair in my office."

"Good." Damn good. She was out of his hands now. He could live with that, but he damn well wanted to know she was out of Klein's hands as well, and Walmann's, and everybody else's. "If she talked to O'Connell, then she was cooperating. Make sure Grant knows that when you hand her over." Considering what was on the line, it wasn't going to buy her out of the mess she was in, but cooperation was always worth something.

Geezus. He'd kissed her. Again. What was up with him?

"And she's American?" Dylan asked. "You're sure?"

Creed nodded. "Cordelia Stark of Wichita, Kansas,

but we need to double-check the details. She went to visit her father in Prague, a Dr. Dimitri Starkova, who also definitely needs to be investigated." He lifted his hips off the seat and pulled a photo out of his back pocket. "This is her school picture."

"Damn." Dylan swore again and looked down at the photo. He was quiet for a second, then asked, "Are you sure this is her?"

Creed knew what he meant. There was no resemblance between the school photo and the picture they'd been sent of Dominika in her ass-hugging little silver dress. Neither was there much resemblance between the photo and the punked-out raver Dylan had picked up in South Morrison. Creed hadn't really had a chance to fully describe the beauty of her mousy-librarian and homeless-boy incarnations.

"It's her," he said. "Look at the eyes and the cheekbones, forget the hair."

Dylan studied the photograph for a moment, then glanced up. "I'll get Skeeter to morph them."

"Sure," Creed agreed with a shrug. "Then maybe you can take her out for a milk shake or something."

His comment hit a wall of silence.

"Kids like milk shakes," Dylan finally said, sounding far too defensive to be anything except defensive.

Creed hated to be the one to burst his bubble, but Dylan had obviously fallen out of the loop on this one.

"Skeeter is no kid."

"Sure she is."

"No," Creed corrected him. "No, she's not. No more a kid than you were at her age. But she is Superman's baby chicken."

"Which means?"

"Absolutely nothing, except if I was fishing for shark, I'd keep one hand on my *cojónes*."

Nothing but the sound of the old elevator straining up to the seventh floor filled the ensuing silence.

"So when did you get so friggin' inscrutable?" Dylan asked after a moment.

"Three hours ago." On the roof of the Denver Public Library. He knew it to the minute.

"Christ," Dylan said, dropping his head back on the seat and letting out a short burst of laughter. "It's been a crazy night."

"Fucking *insane*," Creed agreed, shaking his head and fighting back a grin.

FIVE minutes later, he was in no condition to alter that statement.

He'd steeled himself all the way across the garage, parking Angelina at the far end of the seventh floor and walking the length of the bays toward the main offices— and he still felt gut-punched when he walked in and saw Cody Stark sitting in Dylan's chair, handcuffed to the frame.

She was such a lovely mess, her spiked hair falling over her face and going every which direction in the back and on the sides, glitter drifting onto her skin, her cheeks pale, mascara smudged beneath her eyes—but still so beautiful it was all he could do to drag his gaze away from her.

Not good, he thought, taking in a deep breath and forcing his attention to Skeeter, who was striding toward Dylan's office, a concerned look on her face, her brows knitted together beneath the brim of her hat. She breezed through the doorway, shrugging out of her jacket and tossing it on Dylan's desk, disturbing a pile of papers or photos or something, then all but throwing herself into his arms.

"Creed," she said, wrapping her arms around his neck.

"Baby Bang." He held her close, thinking back to those fifteen phone calls he hadn't bothered to answer and feeling a little guilty. She must have been more worried than he'd thought. He didn't like to freak her out. She was too good a kid to deserve that.

Okay, so he thought of her as a kid, too, but he really did think of her as a kid, and only a kid—regardless of her absolutely amazing body, which was pressed up against him all over the place.

He looked up and found Dylan's gaze boring into him like a laser beam on Death Blast, and he couldn't help himself. He grinned.

Skeeter pulled away after giving him a tight squeeze, and they slid their palms off each other. A quick slap and a tap of their fists later, the formalities were over.

They were both so full of the street.

Creed knew his name was still whispered in lower downtown's darkest alleys, and that suited him just fine, but he'd never killed anybody until Uncle Sam had put a gun and a seven-inch Randall knife in his hand and taught him how. He'd be the first to admit that it hadn't taken much. He'd been a natural.

"Where's Royce?" Dylan asked.

"On your butt." Skeeter turned to him. "I pulled him up on the computer, and you barely beat him back. Creed's 911 must have sent them racing out of here like rabbits at the track. I show them hitting South Morrison about twenty-five minutes after we did and turning tail about three minutes later. I'm thinking they didn't even get out of the car, unless they left somebody behind."

"You put a tracker on a CIA agent's car?" Creed asked.

"You bet," Skeeter said. "SOP." Standard Operating Procedure.

"And they're headed back here?" Dylan asked.

Skeeter looked out toward the garage. "Any second now we're going to get a call to open the alley garage door and let those bad boys back in."

"Three minutes at South Morrison and they leave?" Dylan looked over at him. "When there's live fire and they think Dominika Starkova is inside with you?"

Creed knew what he meant. It didn't make sense. The party boys and girls in the basement wouldn't have heard the gunshots, but anybody outside the building would definitely have heard the pistol fire.

"Somebody jerked their chain, hard," he said.

"Only one person can jerk Tony Royce's chain that hard," Dylan said. "Daniel Alden, the director himself. But why would he pull his men off the case? They wouldn't use a retirement option, unless . . ." His gaze slid to Cody Stark for the barest split of a second, while everything inside Creed ground to a sudden, wrenching halt.

Unless they were just going to let the terrorists have her. Unless they wanted her dead—and that really didn't make sense, because unless something had drastically changed in the last three hours, she was still their best bet for finding the bomb.

Geezus. The CIA wouldn't walk away from her. They couldn't let Reinhard have her—but even as he thought it, he knew they could.

"Well, they sure didn't waste any time getting back here," Skeeter said, forcing a bright note into her voice and looking everywhere except at Cody Stark.

Geezus.

The phone rang, and Skeeter glanced at Dylan, who nodded. She picked up the receiver.

"Uptown Autos, we only sell the best," she said, keying a code into Dylan's laptop and firing it up.

Dylan turned his attention to Creed, whose heart had started back up on a painful, unsteady beat. He didn't know how long he could protect her if the CIA wanted her dead, but he knew she deserved better than to be shoved out in the cold so Reinhard Klein or some Middle Eastern bastard could gun her down and do the Agency's dirty work for them.

"So what's changed since I was sent out four hours ago?" he asked. Four hours ago, she'd been a top priority capture-and-recovery—and now they wanted her eliminated?

"Maybe nothing," Dylan said. "Maybe it is what it was."

That was no answer. If they'd wanted an assassin, they wouldn't have sent him. They would have sent one of those never-seen-them-because-they-don't-exist CIA spooks whose pasts were so shady they couldn't have gotten a job before 9/11, the kind of guy whose résumé was half rap sheet. General Grant knew the score. And if they'd wanted somebody to screw up enough that the tangos would get her—well, they wouldn't have sent SDF.

His mission had been to recover and protect, and he'd done it—and he wasn't at all inclined to stop doing it now.

"We've got a potential ID on Klein, Walmann, the Braun twins, and the fact that there were two Iranians in the library tonight," Dylan said, ignoring the questions burning between them and getting back to the answers they already had. Creed agreed with the tactic. Cody didn't need to hear that her government might want her dead. "We're assuming the Iranians the Denver police picked up are Khalesi and Hafiz. The two guys speaking

Dari and interrogating Dominika Starkova with a knife have got to be Hashemi and Akbar. They were all known buyers." He turned his attention on Cody. "Can you verify any of those names?"

Her gaze slid to his, looking for something Creed wasn't sure he could give her. She looked scared, and she had every right to be as scared as she could get if what Dylan had suggested was true.

"You've lost," he said, foregoing reassurance in favor of unadulterated bluntness. They were hell-and-gone out of time for reassurance if the CIA wanted her dead. "All we can do now is control the damage." And maybe make a run for Mexico.

When she still didn't say anything, he gave her the best advice he could.

"Tell us everything, Cody, and maybe I can help you. Without your cooperation, there's nothing I can do."

After another long silence, she finally spoke. "Everyone you mentioned is in Denver. Every man you listed, except maybe Hafiz. I don't know for sure about him," she said, glancing back at Dylan after another slight hesitation. "He never spoke during any of the meetings with Sergei Patrushev. So I wouldn't recognize his voice, and I didn't actually see the two Iranians in the old library. I can only confirm that someone who sounded like Khalesi was there with another man and they were speaking Persian."

Creed was impressed. That kind of discriminating analysis was just what they needed. They just needed more of it, hopefully the kind of analysis that would include the location of a nuclear warhead.

"What about in South Morrison? Who was threatening you with the knife?" Dylan asked. "Hashemi or Akbar?"

"Ahmad Hashemi. He's the one who was killed." Her gaze slid back to him, and he wasn't sure what he read there—relief, revulsion, or maybe gratitude. It hadn't been a pretty death, and she'd been trapped right in the middle of it, a bad bit of timing on his part, but he'd had that little problem with the freakin' flashback.

"So, basically, Denver is Tango Central tonight." There was no ambivalence in Dylan's expression. He was disgusted. "That must have been one helluva tracking device on your earrings, to have pulled people all the way from Prague." Creed had given his boss a complete rundown of the night. "Is there anybody who *isn't* here tonight? And that is not a rhetorical question."

"I haven't seen Hamas, Jemaah Islamiah, Prince Abdullah, the North Koreans, or the two men from Chechnya, but Hashemi said the Zurich Seven were in Denver, and there were people speaking German with Klein in South Morrison."

Dylan grew noticeably quiet in his body language as Cody spoke, which Creed did not take as a good sign. True, she was talking her head off, confirming everything Dylan asked, but he hadn't asked her for anything other than what they'd already guessed or knew from the files. But that was all just the warm-up, and Creed could tell everything was about to change. "Bad cop" Dylan was about to make his appearance.

"A global signal tracking device on a pair of earrings?" Skeeter asked, turning away from the phone for a second and putting her hand over the receiver. "I'd like to see them."

"I dumped them down a steam pipe on South Morrison's fifth floor," he said.

"Holy crap, Creed," she said, a look of disappointment crossing her face.

"Sorry, Skeeter. I didn't have time to debug them." A weak excuse in her book, he knew. Skeeter loved tracking devices. She collected them like stamps, and liked nothing better than to stick them on something and find out where they went.

She gave her head a sad little shake and turned to Dylan. "What do you want me to tell these guys?" she asked, holding up the phone receiver. "They've made it clear that they don't want to buy a car, but they still want to see the merchandise."

Yeah. Creed bet they did, but he hoped like hell Dylan wasn't going to show it to them. The situation was going to get real complicated real fast if Dylan decided to wash his hands of this mess and hand her over to the CIA. He wouldn't blame the boss, not really. O'Connell's murder had been bad, bizarre, and Cody Stark was the one who could tell Royce and his team exactly what had happened and who had pulled the trigger. That made her theirs.

He did know one thing. He wasn't going to let Tony Royce have Cody Stark. No way in hell. Witness or no witness, he couldn't let her go, not tonight, with the city in chaos and the mission looking damned ambiguous. Ambiguous missions were fucked missions. People got hurt—and he wasn't going to let one of those people be Cody.

"Whoa," Skeeter said, her hand coming up to her chest, the brim of her hat turning toward him. "Creed?"

Hell, this was a fine time for Skeeter to go all spooky and clairvoyant on him. He was having trouble breathing. Too many things were crashing in on him, and he was just about ready to grab Cody and run.

Of course, there was the one little problem of the handcuffs. *Shit!* Now he really couldn't breathe.

"Give him the key, Skeeter." Dylan's voice cut through the clamoring in his brain—steady, measured, utterly calm. "Creed, get Ms. Starkova out of here. We'll sort this out later, after Royce and his agents are gone. Leave your coat."

Skeeter pressed the key into his hand and kept her fingers against his palm a little longer than necessary, long enough to remind him that he wasn't alone here tonight.

"Sure, come on up," Skeeter said into the phone, letting him go.

He had Cody released in seconds.

"You should see door number two opening now," Skeeter continued, working the laptop's keyboard.

He helped Cody as she shrugged out of his coat, knowing full well why Dylan wanted it. The pockets were stuffed with the night's work.

And he tried not to stare as the coat came off—but it was impossible. In full light, her fishnet cat suit left very little to the imagination, and she had more curves than a pony car on slicks.

His gaze dropped down her body, from the slope of her shoulders, over breasts and hips and the sleek length of her legs, and he felt poleaxed. Here was Dominika, club scene princess and punk rock baby, all sex and come-on with her spiky hair and kohl-rimmed eyes. The mousy librarian had been a first-class illusion. The lost boy had never existed.

But Cody Stark did, and she still looked scared.

"Skeeter," Dylan said, his voice sounding strangely far away. "Remember, as far as Royce is concerned, we never left the building tonight. We came back downstairs, and they were gone. We're still waiting for Creed to bring in Dominika Starkova."

"Sure." Skeeter sounded kind of far away, too.

But Cody was close, where he needed her. Her hand in his. Her gaze locked onto his.

He wasn't going to kiss her again, no matter what she looked like, no matter how poleaxed he felt. Hell, he could hardly breathe, and kissing her wasn't what this was all about. She was a target. She needed protection, and that's what he did better than anybody, protect, whether it was Uncle Sam's best interests or a life put in his care.

Keeping hold of her hand, he quickly led her out into the main office and toward the elevator.

Yeah. Close was where he needed her. Close and going home with him.

CHAPTER

20

"Wow," Skeeter said as soon as they were gone. "Did you feel that? What was that?"

"A guy who has had enough for one night," Dylan said, knowing exactly what Skeeter was talking about. Creed had been about ready to jump out of his skin. "We send him down to the library to pick up a woman, and nobody seems to know that half the tangos from Berlin to Tehran have invaded the country? Or if they did, they forget to tell us. *Geezus*."

"Who killed this Hashemi guy?" Skeeter asked.

"Who do you think?" *Shit*. If he'd known how screwed up the night was going to get, he would have picked up Dominika Starkova himself. He hadn't been that late getting in from D.C.

"You think that's what's bothering him?"

Hell, no.

"It never has before." Killing bad guys was what they did, and there wasn't a commando in the employ of Uncle Sam who couldn't do it coolly, calmly, with utter precision and no fucking regrets all day long, including every one of the SDF operators. Winning the gunfight or the knife fight was always a good thing—and Creed had won every fight he'd been in tonight, for which every cop in the city of Denver owed him one huge thank-you.

"So what's up?" She was concerned. Rightly so. Creed had been a little wild-eyed there for a minute.

But the jungle boy wasn't that complicated. Right, wrong. Good guys, bad guys. More than any of the rest of them, Creed had a certain innocence about him, a purity of purpose—not that Cesar Raoul Eduardo would ever have seen it that way. But Dylan knew it, just like he figured he knew what had set Creed off.

"Hashemi had Ms. Starkova down with a knife to her ear, right on the vein, threatening to cut her up from here to Sunday and send her home in pieces, the same way J.T. was sent home."

Skeeter's face fell, her skin turning even paler than normal, her soft mouth softening even more.

"*Geez,*" she said, swallowing.

"Yeah. Geez. And I don't think he can take anybody else dying on his shift—especially if they're butchered by some psychopath with a knife. That would be enough to push anybody a couple of degrees south of normal."

"Not you," Skeeter said, sounding so very sure. "Nothing pushes you over the edge."

Except you, he thought, dragging his gaze away from her. She'd been superb in South Morrison, the perfect partner: followed orders, held up her end, done the deed, and fulfilled her mission. Christian Hawkins was doing one helluva job training her, but Dylan still wasn't happy about it.

True, she didn't spook as easily as she used to, wasn't nearly as jumpy, and he was glad about that. Really, he was. He'd hated seeing her live inside a nervous shell— but maybe Hawkins had gone too far, the way she'd strapped on that 9mm like it was a second skin. He'd heard she'd pulled a knife on Gino Cuchara last summer and lived to tell the tale. When she'd been tagging, she and her crew had been more like shadow wraiths than graffiti vandals. No one had seen them, not the cops or the gangsters. The police had gotten lucky a couple of times, but mostly it had been as if SB303 had shown up out of nowhere, painted all over the city, night after night, all on its own.

But now. Hell, she had more balls than Toys "R" Us.

Baby Bang, Creed had called her, a name she'd brought with her off the street. He knew both Hawkins and Creed had laid down the law from West Denver to East Colfax: Mess with Baby Bang at your peril—your guaranteed peril.

Well, it was a warning he needed to heed, pronto. This ache he had for her, it needed to go away.

He wanted her. There was no denying it. He wanted her lightning-bolt tattoo and long legs wrapped around him. He wanted her under him and his mouth on hers. He wanted all that spooky psychic energy focused on him, getting under his skin, figuring him out, letting him in. He wanted to be so incredibly close to her it scared the hell out of him—but it would reach an end, and when it did, there would be way too much hell to pay.

So he stayed away—a tactical strategy that had been working really damn well for him, up until tonight. He felt burned just looking at her.

"Thanks for that . . ." He gestured at the desk, where she'd thrown her jacket over the photographs from South America. The coat had been a present under the tree to her from Santa Claus this year. He'd seen it in a shop on Larimer Square, sable and leather, and known she would love it. He'd been right. From himself, he'd gotten her a set of wheels for her 350 Boss Mustang, Babycakes.

"Yeah, well, he doesn't need to see that," she said. "Not ever again."

Santa Claus. That was him all right. And as long as Santa stayed out of Victoria's Secret, he might be able to maintain his cover.

"Did you . . . uh . . . happen to see her butt?" Skeeter asked.

A grin flashed across his face. Yes, he'd seen her butt.

"Saturday," he said, his grin widening.

Skeeter grinned back. "Yeah. Saturday."

CREED wasn't going to kiss her.

Right.

He was so glad he had that straight in his head. So little was straight in his head these days.

He'd held her hand all the way up the elevator. It hadn't been necessary. She hadn't offered any resistance. She had no place to go, and actually, holding someone's hand, while incredibly effective as a defense move, wasn't exactly the best way to hustle someone down a hallway. A firm grip on their upper arm gave a person a lot more leverage, a little more control over a perp's speed and direction.

But he'd held her hand—was still holding her hand.

He'd also used the brilliant strategy of maintaining absolute silence. He was sure she was impressed.

Not.

But she had to be impressed with the hallway. He called it Superman's Annex. Hawkins had more paintings than he had walls up on the eleventh floor, and a lot of very fine art had ended up in Creed's hallway. Polished oak floors, cream-colored paneling, discreetly appropriate lighting, and Christian Hawkins's discriminating taste in Cubist Modern. It was all very cool.

So was the door into his loft.

He pressed his hand on a freestanding biometric

scanner, and the embossed steel door slid open, retracting back into the wall.

"This is my place," he said. "You'll be safe here." At least for a while. He honestly didn't know what was going to happen to her, or how much, if any, control he was going to have over it.

Once inside, he pressed his hand to another biometric screen, and the door slid closed, nearly silent, leaving them in the dark. He pressed the blue screen again, pushing down with his fingertips, and a pair of bolts slid home with a solid *thunk thunk*, locking out the rest of the world.

A boatload of tension drained out of him at the sound. Home. Safe. There was nothing and no one who could invade this place.

He lowered his forehead to the door and just rested for a moment, letting the quiet and the warmth seep into him, still holding her hand, still keeping her close. After a couple of seconds, she leaned back against the door, too, and let out a soft breath. He looked over. Her eyes were closed, her expression still tight, but not quite so strained as it had been in the office, as if she knew that for a while everything was going to be all right.

Watching her, his eyes slowly adjusted to the faint glow of the city lights filtering into the cavernous room through the windows. There were two floors of them, thirty feet of iron-bound glass extending the full length of the south wall. A full moon was visible in the clearing sky. The sound of free-running water, a lot of it, coming from the far end of the loft, was unmistakable.

"Did you leave a faucet on?" she asked softly, a slight tremor in her voice.

"Sort of." The steel was cool against his skin. Her hand was warm in his, and with every breath she took, an irrepressible longing was building inside him, making his chest tight.

"Should you turn it off?" she said after a moment's hesitation, as if afraid to mention something so obvious.

"It'll be okay." But he wasn't sure he was going to be, not with her wearing a push-up bra.

Black satin.

With silver stripes.

Yeah, he'd noticed. The same way he'd noticed Saturday written across her ass and that she was holding his hand, too.

Now that he could breathe again, everything was starting to fall into place in a little bit different order, stacking up to one undeniable truth: He wanted her.

God, it had been so long since he'd wanted a woman. Well, he always wanted one. He just hadn't bothered lately to find one, something he used to do without putting out too much effort. Usually, the women were just there—beautiful, warm, soft, sweet, funny, sometimes a little bitchy, and sometimes he didn't mind. And usually they found him.

But if they'd been anywhere lately, he hadn't noticed, not since Colombia.

He'd noticed her, though. Noticed her in a way that was impossible to ignore, deep down in his gut, viscerally. With the snow falling on her hair and melting against her cheeks, she'd looked up at him, and he'd suddenly noticed everything about her—the thickness of her lashes and the softness of her breath, the paleness of her skin and the racing of her heart, and he'd wanted her, the baddest badass girl to ever hit his part of town. She was so off-limits, she should have come wrapped in concertina wire—and he wasn't sure even that would have been enough to hold him at bay, not tonight.

He rubbed his thumb across the back of her hand and let out a heavy breath. Okay. What was he going to do here? He'd never out-and-out fraternized with the enemy before, but right now, every cell in his body was consumed with the thought of doing a whole lot more than that.

His gaze drifted over the little triangle of black satin clinging to her hips and the absolutely amazing sight of her breasts practically spilling out of her bra, and it tied him in knots. Just watching her breathe made his skin hot.

Covert war was like rugby, he thought. Women shouldn't even be allowed on the field, because it made the game impossible to play. He was supposed to bring her down, just like any other tango, and turn her in, and all he could think about was touching her, getting his mouth and hands on her, getting inside her.

Oh, yeah. Inside her, that was the picture hardwired

in his brain and short-circuiting his common sense all the way down to his groin.

A black-market arms dealer, *geezus*. He was a highly trained special ops warrior. He was supposed to know better than this. He killed guys like her.

But he wasn't going to kill her, no matter who ordered it, and he'd be hell-and-gone damned if he was going to let anybody else, either, because somewhere, deep inside, he was having serious doubts about her involvement in this mess. She'd been bugged, and nobody bugged their partner.

You are so fucking crazy, he told himself. He couldn't think of a damn thing she'd done to slay him like this. In truth, she hadn't done anything except run for her life all night long—but he was slain, at her feet. All she was doing was holding his hand, and he was getting hard.

Perfect. He wanted to groan with the absurdity of it.

CODY felt his fingers twine through hers, felt the silky length of his hair slide across the top of her cheek where they stood so close together—and it was all she could do to keep breathing. Her heart was racing so fast.

O'Connell had told her if she didn't cooperate it might become expedient for the CIA to "retire" her. She knew exactly what "retire" meant, and the minute Dylan had spoken the word, her blood had run cold.

It was still running cold—dead cold, if she couldn't

find a way out. Time had escaped her, all of her time, all at once, and she was alone, except for Creed Rivera.

She'd missed him, her guardian angel. She hadn't known how desperately, until he'd walked into the office, bruised and cut across one cheek, his pants torn. She hadn't expected to see him again, ever—but he was here now, holding her hand, and she was loathe to let him go.

She tightened her hand around Creed's. She could feel his pulse, feel his strength—and she could feel the sharp edge of panic snaking through her gut.

Everybody wanted her dead—except for Creed Rivera.

"Would . . . would you kiss me?" The words came out softly, barely audible, almost taking her by surprise, but not quite. She knew why she wanted to kiss him again—and it was all selfish, but she wasn't going to take the words back. The place they were was warm and dark, and he was close, and this was it, as safe as she was ever going to be for the rest of her life, in this room, with him.

He'd kissed her in South Morrison the same way he'd kissed her on the roof of the library, with more tenderness than she'd had in too long to remember. It had been instantly consuming, the taste of his mouth, the softness of his breath upon her skin, the sheer heat of it washing through her and making her melt.

She'd like to melt now, or at least feel warm, and he was a wall of warmth standing beside her, almost face-to-face, his chest almost touching her shoulder. He was alive, and her life was slipping through her fingers. She looked up and saw him silhouetted in the shadows with moonlight limning his face and running like silver down the bare skin of his throat, and everything inside her ached. He looked like an angel, a ruthless, heartbreakingly beautiful angel, and he'd killed a man to save her life.

A weary sigh left him before he turned and met her gaze.

"You don't owe me anything."

She nodded slowly in agreement. She didn't owe him anything, but she couldn't forget what he'd been through, the look on his face in those photographs as he'd watched J.T. Chronopolous die.

"And I can't be bought," he said, his voice a little firmer, his gaze more direct. "Not like this."

"I'm not buying." She didn't know how to explain everything to him, how to tell him what she needed, what she was feeling—which was awful, and scared, and so horribly alone. "I'm . . . I'm trapped."

She wasn't going to cry. The last thing she wanted was his pity. She'd weighed her options and her chances in Prague—and she'd miscalculated everything.

She hadn't really expected to die.

She hadn't expected to meet anyone like him at the end.

"Cesar Raoul Eduardo Rivera."

A slight grin twitched the corner of his mouth, and his thumb slid across the back of her hand again. "Nobody calls me that, not even my mother."

"*Creed*," she whispered, letting the name fill her heart, feeling the strength and warmth of his body so close to her, but not close enough, not yet. It had been so long since she'd had anyone of her own, and she didn't want to die with the sins of Karlovy Vary still on her. "Please."

PLEASE. *Geezus.* Everything Creed knew, everything he stood for was telling him this was just one big mistake, but *God*, being with her felt so right.

And she'd said *please*, which tore him up. What was she thinking, to ask a stranger for sex? Because she had to know that's where it was going to end up—the two of them hot and naked and all over each other. He didn't see any way around it.

His gaze went over her again, up the length of all her fishnet-covered curves to her face.

Yeah, she knew. He could see it in her eyes.

He was doomed.

He brought his hand up to her face and gently cupped her cheek, then leaned sideways and pressed his mouth to her temple, just to feel the softness of her skin—and she was soft, incredibly, seductively soft, so female. He slid his mouth lower, closer to her ear. Her hair was damp and cool where a stray tendril curled onto her cheek. The flowery scent of her hair spray had faded. In its place was a more complex mix, a light, windblown muskiness that said "woman" to him, one-hundred-percent pure girl; a deeper, unnameable essence that was simply, irrevocably *her*—and the trace of fear he'd known was there. He could always smell fear; from fifty yards he could smell someone's fear.

He'd smelled J.T.'s, and it had smelled like his own, the scent binding them across the short, muddy stretch of the guerrilla camp that had separated them—separated life from death.

But this—he squeezed his eyes shut—this didn't have anything to do with J.T. This was about her and what she made him feel.

He breathed her in, letting his mouth roam even lower, down to the delicate angle of her jaw and the tender skin of her throat, lower still across her shoulder—and satisfaction flowed into him. Her clothes, what little there were of them, and her skin, smelled like him, from his coat. He inhaled more deeply. He liked smelling himself on her. He liked it a lot.

Moving back up, he nuzzled his face into the curve of her neck, and his satisfaction deepened, a new scent coming into play. She was trembling, her pulse fluttering, and she was softening ever so slightly, becoming . . . amenable.

Please, she'd said, and he'd wanted to devour her.

He'd won her tonight, through strength and cunning and skill. Fought for her and won.

He wasn't completely uncivilized, not here in this place, not like he'd been in other places, at other times—

but he'd still won her, and he wanted to claim what he'd won.

Smoothing his hand up into her hair, he lifted his head and met her gaze for one more moment. It was her last chance to stop this, and when she didn't, he lowered his mouth to hers and gave himself up to the biggest mistake of his life. It was the sweetest thing he'd ever done—to sink into her kiss, to lick her mouth and feel her teeth with his tongue, to lave her lips and hold her close. The smell of her was like a balm to his soul, soft skin, warm scent, sweet woman sighing in his mouth and firing up *all* of his cylinders. He pulled her close, loving the feel of her, the life of her.

It had been too long since he'd done this, lost himself in a woman.

He was in so much trouble. Where the hell was Dylan? Or Skeeter? He needed the cavalry, right now, somebody to come and save him—because he wasn't going to save himself. Not when Cody Stark tasted so beautiful, like sex and heaven.

No way. Not tonight.

I'M worried about Creed being upstairs with that woman," Skeeter said, flipping open the wallet she'd just pulled out of Creed's coat. "I think it's just asking for trouble."

They were working fast, getting everything out of the pockets, seeing what the jungle boy had come up with for the night. Dylan figured they had about five more minutes before Royce and his gang made it to the main office.

"Trouble?" He looked up from a folded piece of stationery. There was a phone number written on the front, along with a few words in Dari on the back. "What have you got?"

"Bruno Walmann's wallet."

He grinned. Creed was damn good. "You said yourself that she was done in. There's no way in hell she can get away from him, not here."

"Well, that's the problem," she said, setting the wallet aside and digging her hand a little deeper into the same pocket. "I don't think she wants to get away from him."

"What do you mean?" he asked, watching her pull out a blocky-looking wristwatch.

Her eyes lit up. "Yikes."

"Put it on the desk and forget it," he ordered. The last thing he needed right now was for her to get sidetracked on the tracking device somebody had used to chase down Dominika Starkova. A.k.a. Cody Stark.

With obvious reluctance, she set the tracker aside and dug back into the pocket. "She didn't take her eyes off him, not from the instant you guys walked in," she said, pulling out a soft, crumpled-up bit of something that was very white.

What in the world? he wondered, watching her untwist the small item.

"What is that?" he asked when she held it up and he still didn't have a clue what it was.

Amazingly, Skeeter took off her glasses to give the thing a closer inspection before she answered him. She stretched it out a little, and a funny look came over her face before she lifted her pale blue eyes and met his gaze across the length of the desk. He could just see the end of her scar under the brim of her hat, where it cut across her eyebrow, but her nose was so cute—kind of short and kind of a button—and her cheeks were so baby soft, there was no help for it, he felt like a pervert. When all a guy could see was her body, black leather, and tattoos, it was easy to forget how young she was.

But that face. God, twenty years old or not, scar or no scar, that face made her look like jailbait, and "jailbait" was looking utterly dismayed by the thing in her hand.

"This . . . this is what I'm talking about," she said, giving the thing a little shake where it dangled off her fingertips, her voice rising a bit at the end. "This is *Tuesday*. Saturday's cousin."

Oh.

Oh, shit.

He didn't have to ask what Creed was doing with Dominika Starkova's underwear in his pocket. He was a guy. He knew—and he couldn't believe Creed was going there.

Well, Creed wasn't, not on this op. No way in hell. Women like Dominika Starkova ate jungle boys for lunch. Hell, she'd been running with the Russian Mafia for months.

Son of a bitch.

"Don't worry," he said, his words strong with conviction. "They're not going to be up there long enough to get into trouble."

Skeeter arched a brow in his direction, her expression one of pure incredulity.

"Okeydokey, Mr. Know-it-all, but the way they were looking at each other it sure looked to me like they needed Commando Condoms 101 and a safe sex lecture. Didn't you feel the vibe coming off the two of them? Fifty bucks says he's already kissing her."

Dylan didn't know what bothered him more: Skeeter referring to him as Mr. Know-it-all, or the word sex coming out of her mouth.

"Creed is a professional."

"Creed is a man."

He wanted to ask her what she knew about men, but he didn't dare for fear of what she might say. He didn't want her knowing anything about men—especially men with women's underwear in their coat pockets.

What in the hell was Creed thinking?

CHAPTER

21

BLACK SATIN, *soft skin, silky mouth*—Creed was going down in flames. Everything was moving so fast. They were up against the door, and she had her tongue in his mouth and her hand halfway down his pants, and he was nearly electrified with pleasure.

Geezus. How could he have forgotten what this felt like? How incredibly, mind-blowingly good it felt to have a woman touching him?

He needed to slow things down a little, though, help her out. She was a panic attack in the making, all over him—which he loved, but at this rate, and if she actually got her hand all the way down his pants, it was going to be over in about two minutes whether he figured out how to get her out of her fishnet or not.

And he had just enough clearheaded thinking left in his brain to know he didn't want that. It would be so freakin' stupid to come in her hand, when he had the chance to come inside her.

Just the thought sent another wave of heat surging through his body. He rocked against her, all but begging her to find those last few inches down to home base.

But the fishnet—*cripes*. No zipper, no buttons, no snaps, no nothing, and not enough stretch. How did she get into the thing? Paint it on?

"Cody, I—" He was starting to ask that exact question when something gave way, some little cut thread at the top, and suddenly the whole bodysuit was unraveling faster than he could keep up.

"Oh," she said, grabbing for her waist, but she was way too late.

Oh, yeah. This was amazing. He had a handful of black thread with more falling off of her every second, and the more he tried to stop it, the faster it came undone. It was like watching a runaway train, and in less than a minute he was left holding a whole lot of ruined fishnet, and she was left with her outfit in shreds.

He loved it.

"Wow." She looked even more naked with only half the fishnet—and what was left wasn't going to last long.

He let the ruined part fall and slid his hand around her waist. She was so soft and sleek, nothing but smooth curves. He followed them around over her hip to the small of her back and lower, onto the little triangle of black satin with the word *Saturday* racing across her ass.

She stretched up on tiptoe to kiss him again, and it was all so perfect.

So almost perfect.

Something was wrong. He could feel it. He'd had desperately hot and fast sex before, and yes, he'd had it with a stranger once—a memory which regularly played on his surefire fantasy hit list. That night in the women's bathroom at McDaddy's Bar and Grill, him in the last stall on the right with Miss February and a condom, had been every twenty-year-old homeboy's dream come true.

But this was different. The stakes were higher, incalculably higher, and he knew a whole lot more about Cody Stark than he'd bothered to find out about Miss February.

Women came onto him all the time, and those women had moves, moves Cody Stark didn't have. Her kisses were too short, and her hand never had made it to where it needed to go. If this was a "kiss me, Creed, please" seduction, she could have given him a long, slow, wet, deep, drugging kiss, unzipped his pants, and had him on his knees.

But she hadn't.

So he slowed things down. He didn't want everything to go so fast that she didn't have any fun. Once with Miss February had been enough. He was older now, wiser, and he wanted to play with Cody Stark all night long.

And then he was going to want to take her to Mexico.

Shit. He could see it all now: weeks on the run, making love on the beach, and a Butch and Sundance end.

What in the hell did he think he was going to get away with? And when had desperately hot sex turned into making love?

He was so screwed up, he needed a warning label.

And she needed a little help. So the next time she went for his mouth, he slid his hand up under *Saturday*, pulled her close, gave her one of those long, slow, wet, deep, drugging kisses, and felt her die a little in his arms. She groaned, such a sweet sound, and it did nothing but make him harder.

He wasn't just going to take her. He was going to make her his.

Sliding the black satin straps off her shoulders, he pushed her push-up bra down, and when she tried to go all shy on him, he bent his head and sucked on her until she went molten in his arms.

This was all working out so well. He had her breast in his mouth, and his hand all over her ass, and when he slid his fingers between her legs, so slowly, so gently, and pressed up against all the soft wonderfulness of her most private parts, she trembled all over.

"Creed," she whispered his name, and her hands went to his shoulders, then slid up into his hair, holding him.

Yes, everything was working perfectly, until he slid

down her body and pressed his mouth to the juncture of her legs, and she balked.

"No, I . . . What are you doing?" she gasped.

What was he doing?

Well, now there was one for the books. In the not-so-distant past of his teenage years, he'd known seventeen-year-old good girls who'd known exactly what he was doing and loved it—and bad girl Dominika Starkova didn't know what he was doing?

Maybe he'd misunderstood.

He started to pull down her panties, those black satin ones, and she clamped her legs shut tighter than a vise. Fortunately, his other hand was still in there from the Saturday side, so there were some compensations.

"I . . . I don't like that," she said, but she didn't sound too sure to him.

Taking a deep breath—but not getting off his knees, because he still had high hopes for this pivotal part of his plan to "make her his"—he rested his forehead on her stomach, her lovely, silken stomach.

"Have you ever tried it?" he asked.

"N-no. Well, once, maybe . . . almost."

Sweet Jesus. His eyes closed on a silent invocation. When he opened them, he let his gaze linger on the few dark curls he'd revealed, and his heart slowed for the space of a breath.

Virgin territory.

He and Cody had fallen way out of the boundaries of desperate hot sex. It was impossible to have truly desperate hot sex with someone who was so inexperienced they'd only "once, maybe, almost" been gone down on, and there was really only one way for a guy to screw up what was basically a fairly straightforward deal and turn it into a "once, maybe, almost." Some idiot lover of hers, of which she couldn't have had very damn many, hadn't liked it—which boggled Creed's brain. He was pretty much riveted by all the possibilities between a woman's legs. Everything was so soft, always warm, smelled like sex, and tasted better.

What wasn't there to love?

"Come on," he said, rising to his feet and snapping her panties back up around her butt.

"Ouch."

He grinned and took her hand in his to lead her farther into the loft. His bad girl wasn't so bad after all, and why that should have him grinning like a fool, he didn't have a clue.

"Where are we going?" she asked, staying close to his side. He noticed she'd rearranged her bra back into place. Damn.

"For a long hot soak in a waterfall." He needed it. The night hadn't been without its fair share of dings. Edmund Braun had gotten one good hit in. He'd cut himself on a frozen edge of that friggin' fire escape, and played a game of real rough-and-tumble leading Reinhard Klein and his gang through South Morrison.

She'd had her hurts, too, and he felt bad for having

forgotten them. He should have taken care of her before he'd started taking her clothes off.

"That's what I've been hearing?" she asked. "A waterfall?"

"Uh-huh. With a jetted pool. It'll feel great."

CODY believed him. After the way he'd held her and kissed her, she was inclined to believe every word he said. It was absurd, she knew, and something she'd definitely thought she'd outgrown, but she felt like she had a crush on him, a mad kind of crush on the maniac wild boy who'd been dragging her around and saving her life all night—the kind of crush that left her a little dizzy and overly thrilled and thinking he was way too cute to be real—which was so much easier than thinking about everything else, about the men after her . . . about actually making love with him. She didn't think her reaction to him was that captor/captive attraction that sometimes happened.

They hadn't been together that long, only a few hours.

But cute? This was the man who had killed Hashemi and broken Edmund Braun. There was nothing cute about him, except for his long, surfer-boy hair, the dreamy, washed-out color of his eyes, and the erotic fullness of his lower lip, nothing except the arch of his cheekbones, the lines of weariness marking his face, and the short scar across the bridge of his nose. If cute had a hard, rough edge, it was Creed Rivera.

She was worried about the sex, though, real worried. Everything had been going great, until she'd been such an idiot. She couldn't afford knee-jerk reactions. She was running out of time. And as far as oral sex went, she knew lots of men liked it, liked giving it—her ex-fiancé, Alex, being the exception, for reasons he'd taken great pains to explain. Hell, by the time he'd gotten done, she hadn't blamed him for not liking it. So she'd spent four years in the approved missionary position, and the sex had been okay, because she'd been in love and had loved being so physically close to him, to share all that time under the covers. She hadn't realized what a truly sanctimonious bore he'd been until long after he'd left her and she'd been swept up into Sergei's world.

Of course, if Alex hadn't left her, she never would have left Wichita and gone halfway around the world to find a father she'd never known, looking for adventure and some relief from her broken heart.

Women settled for too little too much of the time, but here she was again, willing to settle for anything Creed Rivera would give her, because even though she rather desperately wanted to have sex with him, what she wanted wasn't about sex.

She needed redemption, and he was her last chance, and those facts far outweighed any moral disquietude she felt about making love with a virtual stranger. It wouldn't be the first time—and that was the problem, the sin that ate at her. She wanted Reinhard Klein and what he'd done to her, what she'd let him do to her, wiped off her slate, or at least pushed back into history. For whatever future she had left, she wanted Creed Rivera to be her memory of what could be shared between a man and a woman. She wanted a hero. She wasn't going to call it love, any more than she could call what Reinhard had done to her rape—and even though she tried not to, she hated herself for that.

She could have told Reinhard no and taken the consequences. But with Keith O'Connell's body hanging from the rafters behind her, and the air filled with the scent of gunpowder, and his blood everywhere, a pool of it on the floor, the taste of it in the air, terrifying her, horrifying her, she'd taken the easy way out.

Except it hadn't been easy. Reinhard made her skin crawl and her stomach churn, and every time she'd had to be in the same room with him after Karlovy Vary, she'd wanted to scream.

The only easy thing she'd done since her father had delivered her to Sergei Patrushev was kiss Creed Rivera and be in his arms.

She followed him down a short flight of stairs, into the main living area. There were a lot of large, looming shadows in his apartment, and as they passed beyond the first set of them into the wan light coming in through the windows, she was able to see what they were.

"Trees," she said, looking over her shoulder, then back

all around, flabbergasted. "You have an apartment full of trees. Huge trees."

Palm trees, some of them scraping the ceiling which was maybe thirty feet above them. A couple of the palms seemed to actually disappear up into the ceiling. There were ferns everywhere, and giant philodendrons, the kind that came from the tropics. Her only excuse for missing all of this at first was that it was dark and she'd been so focused on him. He hadn't turned on any lights, which was fine with her. She didn't want to have to face anything too clearly. But she had noticed how warm and humid it was when they'd first entered his apartment— or maybe loft was a more accurate description. There didn't seem to be any walls, anywhere . . . only trees.

"Skeeter's been running an experiment in here for the last couple of years," he said, "and I think the plants have won."

"Where do all the stairs go?" Looking around, she could see three swooping iron staircases, freestanding, winding up through all the vegetation. The whole place was simply amazing.

He nodded toward the staircase closest to the windows that took up one whole, huge wall on the far side of the room. There must have been a hundred feet of thirty-foot-tall windows, if not more.

"That one goes to my bedroom. The other two lead to a bedroom and an office, all at different levels. The kitchen is behind us on the main floor, and the bathroom is up ahead."

"With the waterfall." Unbelievable.

He grinned down at her. "With the waterfall."

"Did Skeeter design the whole loft, or just the jungle?" The girl seemed immensely talented.

"She's just the jungle girl. Superman and I built the original platforms and the staircases years ago. The walls on the platforms move, very Japanese. You can have privacy if you want, but usually the whole place is just open."

"Superman?" She wanted to know everything about him, or as much as she could, and as long as he was answering questions, she was going to ask—and she wasn't going to quit holding his hand. If they were touching, she felt like she still had a chance at redemption.

"A friend," he said. "More than a friend. A brother."

"Like Dylan," she said, remembering how the two of them had come in together, the easy way they'd been with each other—up until the CIA had come into the conversation.

"Like Dylan," he agreed.

"What about Skeeter?" The girl fascinated Cody, the way she looked and the way she fit into this place with all its high-powered cars, high-tech equipment, and highly skilled warriors. This building was luxuriously expensive. The art in the hallway outside Creed's loft was of museum quality. Everything in the building was unique, from the cagelike freight elevator crawling up the side of the building, to this indoor jungle, to the men who lived here, to the girl.

"Skeeter's our wild card. She's only been with us a couple of years, but she's taken over the whole place."

"She scared me a little."

"Yeah, well, you're small. She could have taken you."

"That's what she said."

"You tried something?" He didn't sound at all happy about the possibility.

"No."

"Why not?" And he sounded intrigued by that. "You didn't waste any time ditching me."

She shrugged, a small gesture. "I was afraid." Afraid of escaping only to find out she had no place left to go. Afraid of Reinhard finding her. Afraid of never seeing Creed again, but she doubted if he'd make that inference.

"You're safer here than anyplace else in the world tonight. I can guarantee it."

Since he'd been the only guarantee of safety she'd had for months, she didn't find his statement too hard to believe, but there was a problem, and it was only two floors away.

"What about the CIA? Is Dylan going to tell them I'm here?" It would be the end of her if he did.

NOT tonight," Creed said and hoped to hell it was true. She was hanging by a thread no matter how anybody looked at the situation. The best he could do was catch her if the thread broke or if somebody out-and-out took a machete to it.

A sudden breeze drifted through the trees, setting leaves in motion and fronds swaying.

"Wind?" she asked, a small laugh escaping her. "Can you make it rain, too?"

"As a matter of fact, yes. The fans cycle every fifteen minutes, and there's a sprinkler system to make it rain for three minutes every eight hours." They were almost to the pool, or the lagoon as Skeeter called it. It was the deepest, darkest jungle in the loft, with the trees and ferns planted close together to create at least the illusion of privacy, if not the reality.

"It smells good in here," she said. "Different."

He knew what she meant. The loft smelled green. He'd always had the largest apartment in the building and had long ago dismantled part of the ceiling to open it up to the tenth floor. It was a cavernous living space, but it was Skeeter who had added the fans. Skeeter who had started at the copper and iron waterfall he and Hawkins had welded together as kids and begun transforming the industrial ambiance of his multiplatformed loft into a literal urban jungle.

The place seethed with life.

He could feel it around him. Smell it. The greenness rich and decadent. It had driven him a little crazy at first, when he'd realized what Skeeter was doing to his place. Every time he had come home, there had been a new layer of forest added to the last, another wall of vegetation encroaching on his few pieces of furniture, another tree towering over his bed.

Now he depended on it. He was living in a garden of Eden, and he'd just brought home Eve in torn fishnet with sparkle gel in her hair.

CHAPTER

22

So what have we got?" Skeeter asked.

"A thousand dollars," Dylan said. "Half of it in Euros."

"Check." She marked it off on her list.

"Four wallets."

Skeeter grinned. Creed was so smooth. He'd made a damn good living as a twelve-year-old pickpocket before he'd started boosting cars and working with Dylan at the chop shop. She'd heard the stories. It was that sweet face of his, or at least she guessed his face must have looked sweet at twelve. Now he looked like what he was—battle-hardened, street tough, and not to be fucked with—but in the right light, with a couple of beers in him, there was a little trace of sweetness still there.

Damn little, but it might come out with the right woman, who would *not* be Dominika Starkova. *Cripes*. Her underwear. Geez, for herself, Skeeter managed to remember the freakin' days of the week without having them embroidered across her butt.

"You wanna give me those names again?"

"Bruno Walmann," Dylan called out, opening each wallet in turn. "Edmund Braun. Ahmad Hashemi. Qasim Akbar."

Okay, so Creed had tagged two of those guys and bagged one. That still left Walmann as a very nice lift.

"Check. Check. Check. Check." She liked working with Dylan. They made a good team, and she'd been wondering like crazy if he'd noticed.

"Two sets of car keys."

"You want them to go to Lieutenant Loretta?"

"No," Dylan said, shaking his head. "I'd love to, but all this stuff will go to Royce."

"Why?" She looked up, surprised.

"It's a nuclear bomb we're looking for, Skeeter, not a couple of homeys with a gang vendetta. Loretta got to first base with Braun and the Iranians, but Royce will have them out from under her in less than an hour. He needs this information."

Well, that all sounded damn generous of him.

"And it'll get him off our ass."

Now that made sense.

"So we give him the trinkets, but we keep Dominika Starkova?" she asked.

"Until we hear from General Grant." He picked up the next item on the desk. "One tracking device."

"Chee-eck." One razzle-dazzle, supercalifragilistic, totally sick tracking device with the receiver embedded in a teeny-tiny pair of earrings which Creed had regretfully dropped down a heat vent in South Morrison. Dropped them and lost them.

Except, of course, it was impossible to lose an operating tracking receiver, and if somebody wanted to find those teeny-tiny earrings—well, there was the thingamajob that could do it. Sitting right in the palm of Dylan's hand.

"Don't even think it."

She jerked her head up, breaking her laserlike concentration on the big wristwatch.

"What?" she asked, giving him the most innocent look she could conjure up.

"Don't think what you're thinking," he said. "This all goes to Royce, every last piece of it."

"Of course." Well, duh. Like she didn't know that. The only things up for question were *when* it would all go to Royce and whether or not all the evidence would go at the same time, or if, possibly, one of the pieces might be sent along later.

A blinking light on the computer screen warned them their time was up.

"Royce is here," Dylan said, setting the tracking device back down on the desk. "Photograph and catalog everything. Run as much of it through the system as you can and let me know if you come up with anything, but first send it all over the secure connection to General Grant, all the pictures and information. When you're finished, box it all up and seal it. Work fast. Don't dawdle."

No shit, Sherlock.

"Yes, sir," she said, doing her damnedest to give the impression of someone who could be trusted to follow his orders to a T.

CODY had never known anyone who had a refrigerator in their bathroom, or anyone whose bathroom was a tropical rain forest, at least not until now.

Creed had touched a light pad on one of the few solid walls in the whole loft, and half a dozen lamps had gone on: two in the water, to softly light the pool; two in the trees, directed at the waterfall; and two on the solid wall, to light up a sink and cabinet area and a very sleek stainless steel refrigerator. The whole area was covered in light blue, iridescent tile, which made it seem like the place was under water. It was a magical effect.

"We have every fruit and vegetable known to man in those bottles," he said, gesturing at a stunning array of shampoos, conditioners, face masks, spa scrubs, and lotions lined up on the counter. She recognized a lot of the labels; all the products were first-class herbal organics.

"And flowers," she added, noticing small vials of lavender oil and rose oil, and a special brand of chamomile shampoo.

"Yeah, the way it smells in here sometimes, I'd say flowers, too. I think Skeeter has cat parties in the bathroom when I'm gone."

"Cat parties?"

"You know, when you get all your friends together and do stuff with shampoo and fingernail polish."

"You mean hen parties."

"No." He let out a short laugh. "There aren't any chickens in Skeeter's crowd. They're all cats. Probably bobcats, and wildcats, and I'm pretty sure there's a couple of real feral cats from her old crew. The kind of girls you do *not* want to meet in a dark alley."

"So Skeeter lives with you?" She'd gotten the impression that he lived alone, the way he'd said "my place," but she could easily be wrong. She had not gotten the impression that he had a girlfriend, not the way he'd been kissing her all night, but again, she could easily be wrong. Skeeter did seem to have the run of the place.

She wasn't going to be picky about it. She couldn't afford to be, and truth be told, she wanted him no matter how many other women had a claim on him. He could be sleeping with a hundred of them, and she'd still want him tonight, because he was her last chance, her only chance—which didn't really make it any less shameful.

God, her life had gotten so strange, was so different from what she had ever imagined it would be. The Central Intelligence Agency of the United States government wanted her dead. The only thing stranger was that from Russia to Denver, there were a whole lot of other people who felt the same way.

She was so scared, too scared not to hold on to the one sure thing she had: him. *Kiss me*, she'd asked him, and she might as well have said, *Save me. Save me if you can.*

"She has the loft above this one," he said, "but she does run things around here. She's a first-class mechanic and computer tech, and she's taking over Superman's job as majordomo of Steele Street—ordering in the food and organizing the houseboys."

"Houseboys?" she said, relieved. She didn't really want to share him, even if he was only hers for one night. But lord, he really did live rich. The elevator had shown thirteen floors, and she knew from the ground-floor garage how big each floor was. It must take a small army to keep up the building, especially if there were many lofts like Creed's, and yet the place was very quiet, as if it was resting, peaceful, until called upon to be otherwise—which sounded ridiculous, even to her.

CREED nodded and wondered why. It was true that Mama Guadalupe brought over a select crew once a week to do general housekeeping of the apartments on floors nine through thirteen. Floors three through eight were classified. No one got in there without specific orders and secure access codes. But none of that was any of Cody's business.

Shit. He was talking to her, and he shouldn't. He should be asking questions, hard questions, the kind of questions where he needed to sit her in a chair in an empty room and be a real son of a bitch until she broke—which was exactly what Hashemi had been doing. And yes, he'd always known that he had far more in common with the men he killed than the people he protected. That was the job. That was the life.

And that was why the few women he'd thought he loved had not stuck around. Too many secrets, too much leaving without a word in the middle of the night, too much maybe-I-won't-make-it-back-this-time. He hadn't blamed any of them for walking away, and neither had he missed them for too long—which had always made him wonder if he knew what love was, true love.

He was pretty sure it wasn't something that was going to hit a guy on a frozen rooftop with a woman who had a gun to his head, but he wasn't completely positive, which left him on shaky ground in the son-of-a-bitch department with her.

"Would you like something to drink?" he asked, foregoing one of those thousand and one hard questions in favor of an easy one, and sounding like a perfectly nice, normal guy who'd gotten lucky and brought a girl home.

Right, he thought, a perfectly nice, normal guy who'd killed someone tonight, and if he wasn't mistaken, gotten a piece of another one with his Glock.

"I've got all kinds of juice, beer, wine, probably some

organic smoothie things . . . shots of tequila." He could use a couple of those, but technically he was still very much on the job, in charge of a hardened international criminal, and though he had every intention of getting her into his bed, he'd probably be better off if he was stone cold sober when he did it. That way, at the court-martial, he'd have all his facts straight.

Kee-rist. He needed his head examined. Fortunately, he had an appointment later in the week with a Captain Teal, USN, to do just that . . . again. Honestly, he couldn't have too much left in there that somebody hadn't seen and probably already poked a couple of times, except for the stuff he wasn't letting anybody see—how it had been with him and J.T. at the end.

Shit. He brought his hand up to his chest.

"Juice, please. Orange juice, if you've got it."

Taking a deep breath, he left her by the side of the pool and walked over to the refrigerator. Skeeter did a helluva lot better job of keeping things stocked than Hawkins had ever done, and she bought all the really nice stuff. Superman had never ordered organic smoothies, which Creed had discovered he liked. It was Skeeter's bottles of watery stuff with leaves and whatnot floating in them that he couldn't take. Guaranteed to add years to his life and life to his years, Skeeter liked to say.

She could be such a dork. Years to his life, his ass. A Kevlar vest and a two-and-a-half-pound trigger pull added years to his life, not herbs.

But he was in the refrigerator looking for orange juice, just the thing to get a woman in the mood.

No wonder he hadn't been laid in months.

And today must have been houseboy day, because there was lots of new stuff in the fridge, and in an interesting twist, all the orange juice was in little boxes. Great, he was going to be offering her a juice box. How incredibly seductive.

Hanging on the refrigerator door, he gave in to a brief, but totally heartfelt sigh. His life had been falling apart in a lot of ways lately. Not the job—he'd kicked ass tonight, he was glad to say. But the rest of his life. He spent all his time in rehab, or at the shrink's, or under Mercy's hood, and he let a twenty-year-old girl do most of his shopping for him, so he ended up with juice boxes and forty-eight bottles of mango-papaya shampoo in his bathroom.

He grabbed an orange juice out of the fridge and was delighted to realize that each came with its own unbelievably tiny straw stuck right to the box—utterly fucking delighted.

Geezus. He did the deed, got the whole thing organized, then grabbed a few first-aid supplies and a bunch of towels and turned back to the pool.

"Thanks. That's . . . uh . . . sweet," she said, when he gave her the juice box.

That was him. Sweet.

He dropped the towels on the tile behind her.

"Let's see your arm." He'd noticed her favoring it in

the elevator, and then had conveniently forgotten all about it once he'd gotten his mouth on her.

He sat down cross-legged at the side of the pool. She'd taken off her shoes and had her feet in the water, but he was still in full battle gear, including the pistol-gripped shotgun strapped to his hip and Velcroed around his thigh—another real romance-inducing item.

Yessiree, he'd just about brought this party to a full freakin' all-out stop, and for someone who was still pretty much consumed by the thought of full body contact, hot, sweaty, lose-your-fucking-mind sex tonight, that couldn't be a good thing. God, he wanted to eat her, all of her. He wanted to lick her up one side and down the other, bury himself inside her and drive her crazy, right over the edge, and when she came undone all over him, he wanted to start over again.

He needed that, needed it like air—was beginning to think it was the only thing that could save him.

"I think it's okay, just sore," she said, lifting her arm, testing it, and not sounding like she had a clue what he was thinking. "For a minute there, in that room, I thought it was broken, but it's not."

"You're bruising." He could see it through the fishnet. Reaching up, he started easing what was left of the cat suit down off her arm. "I've got a cold pack to put on it for now."

"No." She shook her head, adamant. "No ice. I'm done with being cold tonight. I'm still cold, even in here."

Okay. He could let her get away with that.

"I'll be finished in a minute, then you can get in the water," he said. "That'll take the chill off." Especially once he got in there with her—at least he hoped they were still headed in that direction.

He got her sleeve all the way off, and then just didn't stop. There was no sense, to his way of thinking, in leaving those last few shreds of fishnet on her.

"Lift up," he said, and scooted what was left of the cat suit out from under her butt. From there it was one cheap thrill after another, rolling the rest of it off her leg. The other side had fallen apart at the door, so once he got to her ankle, it was a done deal.

He tossed the silky mess over by the cabinet and opened up a bottle of hydrogen peroxide.

"Let's see where you got hit in South Morrison. I saw you go down." And had gone ballistic. Nobody deserved to die because they'd hit somebody on the head, but Hashemi had proven himself willing to do a whole lot more, and Creed couldn't say he was sorry. He never was. If there was one thing he knew, it was the good guys from the bad guys, and it was his job to go up against the bad guys and win. Win at any cost, any way he could. There were no rules in his game, no code of conduct. It was win or die every single time.

Yeah, he knew who the bad guys were, and she didn't feel like one of them. He didn't think it was possible for him to be so horny he couldn't see straight, or for him to want a woman so much it would throw off his moral compass. That part of him had always run true, so even though all the facts lined up against her, his gut was telling him not to let the feds have her. That something didn't add up.

"This is going to hurt, isn't it," she said, turning her head and lifting up the back of her hair. She had a goose egg, all right, and a little bit of blood smeared behind her ear, and it pissed him off.

"No." Taking a slug hurt. Screwing up and getting cut by some asshole's knife hurt. Watching your best friend die hurt—but not hydrogen peroxide on a wad of cotton.

"Ohh, ouch, ow." She squirmed as he dabbed away, and he had to grin.

"Baby," he said, teasing her, then had to refrain from saying it again, but with his mouth on her somewhere, anywhere while he did it.

"Oh, do something," she said. "Blow."

And there was another one of those surefire winners on his all-time fantasy hit list, a beautiful girl in black satin underwear begging him to blow. He knew how to "blow" a girl, would love to "blow" her—blow her mind.

"Hold on just a second." Just a second while he let that image play in his mind a couple of times.

His gaze drifted to her lap while he dabbed, and suddenly he was right back at the door, on his knees, his gut in a knot, his chest tight. She was sweet. He knew it for a fact, and all he'd gotten was a promise more than an actual taste.

Taking a breath, he finished cleaning up the scrape on her head and made a three-pointer into the trash can with the wad of cotton. Then he gave her what she was really asking for, a little relief from the pain. He started blowing on the back of her neck and up behind her ear.

In seconds, she'd stopped squirming, everything about her telegraphing an unmistakable awareness.

Perfect, he thought. This was all going to work out perfectly.

He let his breath drift south, over her shoulder, and his mouth followed, pressing a soft kiss on her skin. This was where he'd needed to go. She was so smooth, and he was more than ready to cross the line again.

He moved aside her bra strap, letting it fall down her arm, and pressed another kiss to her shoulder.

When she turned to look at him, he lifted his head. Her eyes were a dark, verdurous green, and a little wary, which he didn't mind. Under the circumstances, wariness was a smart move. He wanted a lot from her, everything he could get and then some.

Would you kiss me? she'd asked, and there was only one answer: "All night long."

Careful not to hurt her, he slid his hand around the back of her head and brought her mouth to his. Her lips were soft, open, her tongue warm and wet sliding along the length of his, instantly turning him inside out, turning him on. Yeah, this was the kind of kiss he'd needed, hot and deep, not desperate. Hell, they both had enough desperation in their lives. What he needed was time out from everything else on the planet. He needed a break.

So did she.

Moving his hand to his hip, he double-checked the safety on the Mossberg, then unclipped his gun belt, pulled the Velcro apart, and laid the whole holster off to the side.

He didn't particularly want her to see the Randall fighting knife, so he opened his mouth wider on hers, took her a little farther, held her to him tighter, while he undid the strap on his ankle and gave the knife and sheath a good shove off into the shadows. Next came his boots and socks, all of them tossed off to the side.

The kissing was great, sweet and slow, his teeth grazing her lips, her breath soft on his skin, and him being careful not to give in to the urge to shove his tongue halfway down her throat and just do the caveman thing on top of her.

No, he was cool, letting her take the lead while he got rid of his weapons and clothes. She'd turned more toward him, leaned in, and he had his hand up under her arm, his palm cupping the side of her breast. She wasn't very big on top, even in her push-up bra, just perfect, and he couldn't wait to kiss her there again. She'd been so responsive.

Reaching up and back between his shoulders, he grabbed a handful of sweater and T-shirt and pulled both of them off over the back of his head. With an overhanded toss, he lofted it all toward the sinks and countertop.

He was committed now, with her small hands touching his skin, sliding over his shoulders and up into his hair, her mouth coming back to his for more of his kiss. He ran his hands over her, from under her arms all the way down to her incredible ass. She was so curvy—sleek rib cage, small waist . . . hips. God, he loved a woman's hips. She pressed against him, bringing her satin bra in contact with his chest, rubbing against him ever so slightly, and heat flowed down into his groin.

"Come on," he whispered, pulling her to her feet.

He stood with her in front of him, one hand around her waist, keeping her close, the other undoing his pants. He shucked out of them and his boxers, then took her hand and slipped into the pool. The water felt great, swirling around him as he led her back toward the waterfall.

It wasn't far. The whole lagoon wasn't much bigger than two or three good-sized hot tubs, big enough to hold quite a few, but he'd never had more than one in it with him, sometimes a woman, and lately Skeeter. He'd never been one for crowds of any kind.

He noticed Cody didn't drop her gaze below the water line, which made him grin. He'd like her to look. It was always such a turn-on to have a woman check you out, but since he was pretty turned on already, maybe her shyness was for the best.

What he really wanted was for her to relax. He wasn't sure he could get everything he wanted if she was too nervous, and for all her wonderful kisses and pressing up against him, she was nervous.

Well, he could probably help her out there. Leaning a

little ways away from her, he cut his hand across the top of the water and splashed her. The small wall of water caught her all the way down the front, drenching her from the top of her head to her waist.

She sputtered, instantly indignant, and when she gave him the "you're in trouble, buster" look, he grinned and did it again.

Before she could retaliate, he dropped her hand and dove under the water—and circled her like a shark.

Even under water, he heard her squeal, could see her feet tap-dancing on the pool bottom, while she tried to decide which way to make a dash for it—it was such a primal response, absolutely predictable, but there wasn't going to be any escaping. He was a good shark, and when he zeroed in on her, she didn't have a chance. Like a shot, he went for her legs, grabbed her, caught her as she fell, and dragged her under.

When he brought her up for air, they were on the far side of the waterfall, with steam and mist rising up around them and the water sheeting into the pool behind them, creating a liquid barrier between them and the rest of the room, between them and the rest of the world.

"You're—" she gasped, laughing, water running down all over her. "You're . . ."

"Stupid," he said, shoving his wet hair back off his face with both hands and grinning. "I know."

"And . . . and—"

He lifted her out of the water and set her on a stone

ledge in front of him, bringing them face-to-face. Foliage and palm fronds curved around them. Ferns arced down from the rocks above, dripping with water. With one, smooth twist of his fingers behind her back, he had her bra undone.

"And . . . and you're taking off my underwear." She laughed again, incredulous, her arms coming up and crossing over her chest.

"I want to see you."

"Well . . . yes . . . I—"

He moved in closer and dipped his head slightly to look her in the eyes. "I want to make love with you."

And he did. As much fun as it could be, he hadn't really wanted to just do the wham-bam thing up against the door. He wanted more than to just get off on her. He needed more.

She stared at him, speechless. "I . . . I—"

"Are you warm?" he asked, so smooth, going for her panties, those Saturday panties. "Lift up."

To his everlasting satisfaction, she did, first one side and then the other.

"Y-yes," she said.

She wanted this, all of her actions said so, but he hadn't exactly figured out why. The attraction was there; he could feel it pulsing between them. But there was something else.

"How old were you in that school picture?" He slid the panties off her legs and tossed them behind him into the pool.

"Seventeen," she said. "How did you *get* that school picture?"

He saw her gaze follow the short arc of her underwear into the water, before returning nervously to him.

"I lifted it off Bruno Walmann. It's the one he was showing around the library."

"You stole a photo from Bruno? Right off him, and he didn't, like, grab it back?"

"Pickpocket," he confessed. "Bruno never even knew. Old school skills, right out of west Denver, when I was a kid. If we got lucky, we ate. If we didn't, we'd go hang around the back door at Mama Guadalupe's restaurant. She never let us go away hungry."

"You . . . you were homeless?" She sounded truly shocked and a little dismayed. "But . . . but all this." She gestured at the loft.

"I had a home." He shrugged, not too worried about the past. "There just wasn't any food there, so lots of the time it was better to just cruise the streets a little, see what I could come up with."

"What about your parents? Didn't you have brothers and sisters?"

There had been plenty of siblings, which had only made things worse. During those years, everybody had been struggling.

"I was the last of the litter," he said, "and my dad took one look and decided I wasn't his." He scooped up a handful of water and ladled it over her shoulder. A slight grin curved his mouth. "I think it was the blond hair and blue eyes that gave me away. It didn't matter that Mom weighed me down with Cesar Raoul Eduardo—the old man wasn't buying it. I was the whitest boy in the 'hood."

"So your mother is Anglo?"

He nodded.

"Do you know who your real father is?"

He shook his head. "Mom has never said."

"But you see her."

"Sometimes. I'm out of town a lot." And this conversation was quickly coming to an end. He wrapped his fingers around one end of her bra and started to pull.

She tightened her hold on it, still covering her breasts with her arms.

He had to keep himself from grinning. Women were such a mystery, such lovely mysteries. He already had her out of her underwear. She was completely naked except for this one little scrap of satin that technically wasn't even on her body any more.

"It's okay, Cody," he said, looking up at her and giving her the grin he couldn't resist. "It's just us." He didn't want her scared, he just wanted her, and after another moment of hesitation, the bra started coming away. He watched it unthread from between her hands.

CODY watched him watching her, watched his eyes darken in appreciation, watched the subtle deepening of his breath, and felt the heat of his gaze warm her skin.

Just us, he'd said, and suddenly, she believed him. The

whole rest of the world had fallen away, simply disappeared. It was magic. There was no one, ever, anywhere, just the two of them in this hot, tropical pool, drenched in steam and surrounded by the rich greenness of the jungle.

It was Eden, and he was so beautiful, such a fascinating mix of tenderness and ferocity, of sweetness and seduction. She knew he was dangerous. He killed without hesitation—but he'd put his life on the line for her the same way.

Pulling the last of her bra free, he dropped it into the water and moved closer, stepping between her legs, smoothing his hand down to her ankle and lifting her calf up around his waist.

She felt him come up against her, felt the head of his shaft press into her curls, and her breath caught in her throat, stolen by the fierce edge of desire that cut down her center to her core.

"*Creed.*" She could barely speak his name.

"You're so beautiful," he said, rocking against her, his voice husky, his other hand going around her back, supporting her.

He lowered his mouth to hers and simply consumed her, sucking on her tongue, gently biting her lips, turning her deep into his kiss—and all the while rubbing himself against her, enthralling her with his power, his need, with the size and heat of him. God, he was . . . everything. When his hand came into play, his fingers teasing her, his need suddenly became hers.

"You're so soft," he whispered, running his nose down the length of hers, his mouth barely grazing her cheek, her lips. "I love touching you like this."

And she loved being touched by him; the sheer intimacy of it felt like a gift, to be so close to someone after being alone for so long. She opened herself to him, opened her legs, opened her mouth and captured his lips with her own, his name running through her mind— *Creed.*

The kiss was endless, sensually charged, mind-drugging, and she was dying with wanting him. Her head fell to his shoulder, her hands tightening on his arms. She hadn't expected such aching pleasure, only the deed, to have him inside her, making her whole, but here she was, melting into him, her body limp with the pleasure he was creating. She wanted to swoon with it, and when he started to push up inside her, she almost did. All he had to do was be there, pressing against her, and she was mesmerized.

"Creed . . . I—" She didn't know what to say, but needed to say something. She should tell him the truth, before he went any further, but she couldn't, not when he felt like this and it all seemed so much more than she'd planned.

"Shhh, everything's okay." He brought one of his hands up to the side of her face, cupping her cheek with his palm, kissing her once, so gently.

On his next push, he slid deeper, and she watched, entranced, as his pale gray eyes slowly drifted closed, his dark lashes coming to rest on his cheeks. His head came forward, bringing with it a long fall of sun-streaked hair, a harsh breath escaping him as he moved inside her, hitting every nerve ending she had and all the tender places in her heart, and oh, God, it was all so much terrible trouble—to really need him, to need him like her next breath.

He felt so incredibly good, one soul-shattering sensation after another, thrust after endless thrust taking her someplace she'd never been, his hands all over her, his mouth burning a trail on her skin, leaving her dazed. His body was so tight and hard beneath her hands, one set of lean muscle layered over another. She loved the way he tasted, the way he smelled . . . the way he moved, pushing into her, holding her close. She tangled her hands through the long, silky strands of his hair, buried her face in the curve of his neck, felt the strength of his arms around her—and died a little just for the wanting of him.

Then, between one breath and the next, desire caught, every place he touched her suddenly taking her higher, until she couldn't take any more. It was the last thing she'd expected.

"*Creed* . . ." She gasped his name, every cell in her body pulsing with the sudden sweetness of release. *Oh, my God.*

A soft groan escaped him, and he buried himself deep inside her, his hips coming up flush against hers, his body going rigid in her arms. *Oh, God.* His breath was so hot on her neck, his arms so tight around her. She could feel the pounding of his heart, feel the pleasure coursing through him—and she was lost.

At the end, all she could do was cling to him and try to breathe. He had her in such a death grip, his arms like a vise around her, his body a rock solid wall of heat and power up against hers—and she never wanted him to let her go. Never.

After a long, intense moment, in which he didn't move, he sank to his knees in the pool, taking her with him. Water lapped at her chin as he rolled onto his back and drifted up against the base of the waterfall. He leaned back into a bed of ferns, still inside her, still holding her.

"Shhh," he said, when she would have changed position. "Don't move. Not yet."

Then he kissed her, over and over, his mouth opening on her forehead, her eyebrow, the side of her face, soft kisses, gentle kisses, each one of them making her feel more loved than she knew she had a right to feel.

CHAPTER

23

SKEETER LOOKED MUTINOUS. Her arms were crossed. Her legs were crossed. Hell, for all Dylan knew, her eyes were crossed. But he couldn't see her eyes. Her ball cap was pulled down so low and tight on her head, he could barely see her sunglasses.

"You don't want me to have to take this place apart," Tony Royce said, putting a new twist on the same threat he'd been making for the last half an hour, ever since he and his guys had made it back to Steele Street.

"No," Dylan admitted, not too concerned about the possibility. Skeeter had sat her mutinous butt right in front of the main motherboard, and with a couple of keystrokes, she could shut the operation up tighter than lockdown at the state penitentiary. Tony Royce would be lucky to get out, let alone get farther in.

But he didn't think that was what was bothering Skeeter. She'd come out of the office and signaled him that they needed to talk, but before he'd been able to extricate himself from Royce's tirade, she'd gone all spooky on him, glancing toward the ceiling and sitting herself down in the chair and getting silently, seriously wound up. Something was going on, and something was going to snap if she didn't lighten up.

He glanced back over at her, and watched, fascinated, as she mouthed the word "sex" at him and jerked her head toward the ceiling. It was unmistakable, she'd said sex, and it had an equally fascinating, if inappropriate effect on him. He knew what she was talking about, and despite his reaction, it didn't have a damn thing to do with the two of them getting hot and naked.

"No way," he said. Impossible. Creed and Dominika Starkova hadn't been upstairs that long. He knew women found Creed damn near irresistible, but Ms. Starkova had looked like a drowned rat, and Creed had been way too strung out to put together any sort of "this is my place, can I get in your pants" scene.

"No condom," she said with a tight little shrug, so angry it looked like she could spit.

Again, absolutely impossible. There was no way in hell for her to know something like that. He didn't care how "spooky" she was.

"No way."

A strangled cough, coming from his right, drew his attention to Agent Mathers, whose gaze was riveted on Skeeter, everything in his expression saying "Yes, way. Anyway you want it way. With or without a condom, I'll go upstairs and have sex with you."

Dylan had already been thinking he might have to kick Mathers's ass, because of the kid's fascination with Skeeter's breasts, and now he was convinced. It was just a matter of time.

"Do . . . uh . . . you two need to clear something up, so we can focus on what's happening here tonight?" Royce asked, sounding about as disgusted as Dylan suddenly felt.

He never got off track, and Skeeter had just sidelined him into the bleachers.

"Yes. As a matter of fact, we do," he said, heading for his office and gesturing for her to follow.

She was off her leather-clad butt in a heartbeat and right on his ass all the way into his office.

SOMETHING damn fishy was going on, Royce thought. Something about as fishy as what he'd found at South Morrison. He and his guys had hardly gotten out of the car before they'd been called off by the director himself.

Called off when there'd been goddamned gunfire coming right out of the goddamn building. All under control, Alden had said. Another set of agents was on the job.

Bullshit. There was only one reason for another set of agents to have been "on the job" at South Morrison: The "prongs" in Alden's multipronged approach to the Dominika Starkova operation were starting to trip over each other. Royce could see the writing on the wall. He'd been sent as a frickin' decoy to rattle SDF's cage and draw them off, while some other guys grabbed all the glory and Dominika Starkova.

Well, fuck that. This sort of snafu should have been all sorted out between the Pentagon and Langley before it ever got down to agents being deployed in the field. It was always a potential difficulty with clandestine operations, that one hand wouldn't know what the other was doing, and the kind of rogues the CIA had been recruiting as agents since 9/11 only compounded the problem. Nobody knew what in the hell some of them were doing. For a few years, Agency work had been a fairly clean operation of signal interception, electronic surveillance, and technical information gathering. They'd cut back on the less savory aspects of human intelligence gathering and lost most of their special forces capabilities, but gained respectability.

Of course, it had all been so damned ineffective, even Royce had balked at some of the changes. It was a well-known fact that if your enemy was in the sewer, you had to have a few rats on your side, the kind of rats who knew how to infiltrate enemy organizations.

Well, Royce smelled a rat, probably more than one, and while they were snatching Dominika Starkova and taking down terrorists, he was stuck in this friggin' impregnable building, watching his guys drool over a street punk and praying to hell he wasn't getting outplayed by a man who should have been sitting in Leavenworth for the last nine years.

He needed something to break—and if it couldn't be Dylan Hart's special status at the Department of Defense, he sure as hell would like it to be Creed Rivera's ass.

SEX?" Dylan said, shutting his office door firmly behind him. "And what's this about a condom? You can't possibly know that."

"Oh, yes, I can," she said, facing him with her hands on her hips. "There hasn't been a condom in Creed's loft since I took over requisitions. Every week, I send out the list, the same list you get, and right there under Grooming and Hygiene is a little box for condoms—and it is *never* checked. Never. There isn't a condom on the ninth floor."

Dylan stared at her, stupefied. Yes, he'd seen her unbelievably detailed requisition list. He got it via e-mail every Sunday, and every now and then he ticked off a couple of items: espresso, steaks, cordon bleu, croissants, maybe some of that special shaving cream he liked.

But he never checked the box for condoms.

"A guy can buy his own condoms," he said. As a matter of fact, a guy *preferred* to buy his own condoms. He could A-1 guarantee it.

"Could," she agreed. "But why? I've got all the options. There isn't anything you could want that I don't have on the list: cherry-flavored, ribbed, magnum, whatever. It's all there."

Yes, he'd noticed all those options the first time she'd sent out the list, and he'd tried damn hard not to notice them ever again—and the very last conversation he wanted to have with her was the one that included cherry-flavored ribbed condoms.

Jesus. It was giving him hot flashes.

He turned away from her and walked over to his desk.

"It looks like Royce and his guys are here for the long haul," he said, sitting down and opening a new document on his computer, and doing his best to just forget about condoms. "Unless we can draw them off."

He wanted the bastards gone. It wasn't just professional. He couldn't really fault Royce for trying to do his job—but Mathers was skating on thin ice, and he didn't want the guy hanging around Steele Street all night staring at Skeeter's ass.

"I'm going to go—no, I'm going to send *you* to police headquarters, over on Thirteenth and Cherokee. Take the Humvee." There wasn't anything that could get to her or stop her in the Humvee. "Drop off all the intel Creed collected tonight. Give it directly to Lieutenant Bradley. I'll send instructions for her to make sure it gets to the CIA guy she's been arm-wrestling with all night. It won't take him long to call Agent Royce, and then they can all go hole up somewhere else and go through their goodie bag. And make sure Loretta gave them the address to Dominika Starkova's apartment. They can have that, too. All we need is the girl."

"Won't Lieutenant Bradley think that's all kind of roundabout?"

"Loretta owes me, big time. It won't matter what she thinks; she'll do it."

Royce had been chasing his tail all night long. Dylan could guarantee that he'd jump at the chance to get ahold of something besides his dick tonight.

"Once Royce is gone, I promise you, I'll save Creed from Dominika Starkova's evil clutches."

He didn't know how. Hell, if Creed was that far over the edge, it was going to take more than a well-intentioned friend, a direct order, or a bucket of cold water to stop him.

"Now what else do you have for me?" he asked. "You came out of the office with something on your mind."

Her face cleared in an instant. "Yeah, right. Wow. You won't believe what I found when I started running some of this stuff through the computer." She came over to the desk and leaned down next to him, sorting through the top layer of papers strewn everywhere.

She smelled good. Real good. She always did. It was one of the fascinating things about her, how from a distance she could look like such a piece of street trash, but up close, everything about her was squeaky clean, buffed, polished, shined, every bit of chain mail, every bit of leather, that silky fall of platinum hair—her sweet face.

Her mouth.

And she always smelled good.

Honor. Duty. Loyalty. He read the Chinese tattoo inked into the skin of her upper arm. She'd gotten it long before she'd come to SDF, back when she'd still been a wallbanger.

He understood honor among thieves. He and the rest of the SDF guys had epitomized the credo back in their chop-shop days. The same with loyalty. They'd each put their lives on the line for each other at some time in the last sixteen years.

But duty. That one threw him. What "duty" did a wall-banger have? Or duty to whom? He'd never boosted a car out of duty. He'd chopped a few when he would have rather sold them whole, in order to meet a quota or smooth over a rough deal, but he'd always called that "covering his ass," not duty.

He would have to ask her about it sometime, if he ever allowed himself to be alone with her in a quiet place without a crisis raining down on their heads.

Nah, he decided. *Bad idea.*

"Here it is," she said, a thread of excitement running through her voice. "This is so cool . . . well, not cool. It's kind of bad news, but it's bad news we've got, so in a way that makes it good news. Right?"

"Right." He guessed.

She picked up a copy of Bruno Walmann's business card and the sheaf of papers underneath.

"I ran this company name and hooked into their office in New York. They sell computer parts, hardware, all legit as far as I can tell. But they've got a couple of subsidiaries and one of those is a dummy corporation out of the Dutch West Indies. Interestingly enough, it's got a few subsidiaries of its own, including a corporation headquartered in London with branch offices all across the United States, including Atlanta, Cleveland, Chicago, Seattle, Phoenix, Los Angeles—"

"And Denver." Amazing. Not the information, but that she'd gotten it all in less than half an hour.

"Yeah. They've got a small warehouse on the north side."

"How . . . how did you get this so quickly?" Frankly, he was stunned. Nobody worked that fast.

"Followed my nose," she said, as if it was nothing. "Broke a couple of codes. Didn't *dawdle*." A smile curved her lips, and it took everything he had not to just reach up and kiss her.

He should marry her. That's what he should do.

"This is incredible work, Skeeter." He looked through the papers, following the trail she'd discovered. "Really incredible. I need to give you a raise."

"No, you don't."

"I don't?" He glanced up.

"No," she said, her smile returning. "You already over-pay me. Superman and I made sure of it."

CHAPTER 24

WARM BRIE, French bread, lobster bisque, fresh pears—Cody felt like she'd died and gone to heaven. The whole meal had been prepared and waiting in Creed's refrigerator, inside a white box tied with a gold ribbon with *Chez Paul* swirled across the top in gold ink. On the side of the box, *738 Steele Street* had been scrawled in black Magic Marker, along with the day's date and the instruction for "Lunch Delivery." Another box, this one paperbag brown with *Wolf Creek Café* printed on top and 738 Steele Street and the day's date written on the side, along with the word "Dinner," had contained beef tenderloin cooked medium rare, with mashed potatoes, baby carrots, summer squash, and chocolate cake.

"Open your mouth," he said, not for the first time, and when she did, he fed her a particularly tender piece of the steak, then leaned over and kissed her cheek.

God, he was so sweet, and she was drifting in the most ridiculous postcoital haze. She felt drugged with it, couldn't get a grip on herself, and every time he kissed her, the haze thickened, like fog on her brain, some kind of sex fog the likes of which she hadn't known existed.

People could fall in love like this, she thought, because of sex like they'd had in his jungle pool. He was close enough for her to smell him, and he smelled warm and safe, unbelievably erotic, and like he belonged to her. She could still feel where he'd been inside of her, still almost taste him.

She was trying not to fool herself. She knew he was a stranger and what they'd had was crazy wild sex on a desperately crazy night, but she'd melted into him, disappeared inside of him, and for a few moments had been more with him than she'd ever been with anyone else in her life. Right or wrong, the feelings were there, and they were real, and God, she just wanted to bury her face in the curve of his neck and start the whole thing all over again. She hadn't known she could be so shameless—and she was, utterly unashamed. All she wanted was more. Every time she looked at him, heat washed into her cheeks.

He'd given her a T-shirt and a pair of his sweatpants, and they were sitting in his kitchen at the counter on a pair of tall stools, the overgrown jungle of his living area encroaching on all sides, except where the tall bank of windows opened out onto the city night. He was facing her, very close, his legs on the outsides of hers, with the boxes of food spread out on the counter next to them.

He'd put on a pair of low-slung jeans and a softly worn cowboy shirt, but hadn't bothered to snap the shirt closed. In between the open sides of the faded blue plaid material was an erotic landscape of golden skin with a light dusting of dark brown hair that thickened and swirled around his navel. A silver crucifix and a saint's medal hung from a leather thong tied around his neck.

"Catholic?" she asked, lifting the cross and smoothing her thumb over its ornate surface.

"Very," he said. "Not a very good Catholic, just very Catholic."

"And is confession good for the soul?" she asked, looking up to meet his gaze.

"Sometimes. Most times," he said, a small grin coming into play as he leaned closer. "Tonight, you're good for the soul."

Good for the soul, good for love, good for kissing— she couldn't resist. She met him halfway, her hand sliding down his chest, her mouth opening under his.

This is what she'd wanted again.

Sliding off the stool, he lifted her into his arms, their dinner forgotten. The iron staircase leading up to his bedroom was only a few feet away, and as he carried her higher into the trees, she gave herself over to kissing him. She loved the texture of his skin, the softness of his lips, the warmth of his body. He'd pulled his hair back and bound it into a low ponytail, and now she slid the band off, letting his hair fall loose and silky over her hands.

The stairs ended at a wooden platform overhung with palms. Lush, green fronds brushed the wooden headboard of his bed and arced over the sides of the platform's surrounding iron rail. Vines twined themselves through the spindles. Light from the bathroom drifted through the trees, revealing low stacks of wooden Japanese boxes all along one edge. The only other piece of furniture was the bed. She would have expected something simple—and she would have been wrong.

His bed was decadent, antique, with massive wooden pillars and piles of pillows. He laid her in the middle of them and followed her down, winding his legs through hers, drawing her back into his kiss. Everything on the bed was soft and cotton—the sheets, the pillows, a comforter—the colors all in pale greenish blues and grays, like his eyes.

He smiled at her when she pushed his shirt off his shoulders, then helped her by kicking out of his jeans. He'd gone commando after the pool, so there was nothing more before he was naked and stretched out by her side, six feet of beautiful male animal, all lean strength and hard angles.

She ran her hands over his hip bone and up to his

shoulder, then paused, her wandering brought to a sudden halt when her fingers slid over three thick ridges, one brutal stripe next to the other, just like in the photographs from South America.

Every one of them cut her to the quick—but she said nothing, just remembered the fierce rage on his face and kissed his mouth, remembered the ungodly pain of his suffering and slid her hand lower, all the way down his chest and into the dark hair spreading out from his groin.

She took him in her palm, stroking him, loving him, and a soft groan sighed from his lips.

"Cody," he whispered, resting his forehead on hers, moving into her hand, his own hand slipping under the waistband of the sweatpants and down between her legs.

This was love, she knew it, as close as she'd ever been, this melting sweetness, the bone-deep longing for more, the simplicity of the seduction—he touched, she yearned. It was so easy.

CREED kissed her, letting himself sink into her, consume her. She was so sweet—so instantly wet when he touched her. So slick and hot, it made his brain buzz. He could hardly think for wanting to be inside her, but man, he wanted something else even more.

Slipping his fingers farther down and gently up into her, he moved down the front of her body and opened his mouth between her legs, putting his tongue on her before she had a chance to say no. She gasped, and he licked her—just once, so slowly, so gently. A small tremor went through her body, and desire slid down the length of his spine and settled deep in his balls. *Oh, yeah*, this was the place. There would be no resistance. He pushed the sweatpants completely off, while his tongue played her, teased her. With the pants gone, he moved between her legs, letting her thighs rest on his shoulders, on either side of his face, and he was surrounded by sex—her sex. Nothing tasted and smelled like a woman, nothing was as soft, and she was his.

Time drifted into another dimension, his whole world narrowing down to loving her and the hard ache between his legs. At some point between bliss and heaven, she came undone, a soft moan, the tightening of her thighs, a slow grind upward into his mouth, and then complete and utter surrender. God, he loved it.

He played her out before moving back up her body and thrusting inside. The latent ripples of her orgasm pulsed around him, winding him up, making him harder. Sealing his mouth over hers, he let her taste herself on his tongue, and he thrust again, loving all the hot softness of being inside her, and again, over and over, until he came, his hands in her hair, his mouth on hers, breathing her in as he poured himself inside her.

SKEETER crossed the street in front of Denver Police Headquarters and made a beeline for the Humvee.

Once locked safely inside, she breathed her first easy breath of the last half hour.

Cripes. There was nothing like a little visit to the local precinct to get a girl's blood pumping. Lieutenant Loretta was okay, but all the other boys and girls in blue made the hackles rise on the back of her neck. She'd spent too many years outrunning and outsmarting Denver's finest to feel good offering herself up like a bit of nosh on a toothpick.

She had a reputation, and cops were like elephants. They never forgot. She'd seen a couple of them eye-balling her. They knew who she was. Hell, city crews were still scrubbing SB303 off the sides of buildings, and she hadn't tagged in over two years.

Nope, she'd been too busy tearing down engines and building computers. Way too busy organizing the SDF offices and having just a little bit too much fun learning about and building tracking devices.

She was the master.

And she had a little time on her hands.

And a foreign tracking device was languishing in a condemned building not more than a stone's throw away.

She pulled the wristwatch receiver out of the pocket on her coat. It took her all of five seconds to figure out how to turn it on, and less than a minute to decipher all its dials, turn it back off, and be on her way to South Morrison.

She was in business. All systems go.

———

CODY lay propped up in his bed and was letting him feed her another baby carrot. Surrounded by pillows and the latent heat of his lovemaking, she never wanted to leave. Not ever.

"How much to sublet the platform in the tree next door?" she asked, reaching for a piece of French bread. She dipped the end of it in the lobster bisque and popped it in her mouth.

He looked up from where he was taking the lid off the chocolate cake. "You need to stay here, in my treehouse," he said, his expression completely serious.

"Don't you want to be neighbors?" she teased.

"No," he said, still so very serious, setting aside the cake. "I want to be lovers." From where he was sitting on the bed, he moved to all fours and knelt across her body, then cupped her face in his hands and kissed her on the forehead, both cheeks, and the tip of her nose. "Sleeptogether lovers. Wake-up-together lovers. One bed."

Oh, God, she was going to fall in love. She could feel it happening, feel it in her heartbeat, feel it echoing through her pulse.

"In real life," she whispered, her eyes closing as he continued to kiss her face, "in real life, I really am a librarian."

"I like librarians," he said, brushing his lips over her cheek and sliding down toward her mouth. "I like the way they *taste*."

Oh, God, oh, God, oh, God, she was drowning in him. Lost again.

IT was official. She'd now had more orgasms since she'd entered Creed Rivera's jungle apartment than she'd had the whole last year with her fiancé, and she needed to get a grip.

Mind-blowing sex did not a permanent relationship make—at least, she didn't think so. Her experience in the mind-blowing sex department was fairly recent, and she had absolutely no business hanging out in the permanent relationship department. She'd be lucky if "permanent" lasted until dawn—a fact she was finding harder to ignore with every passing minute

They couldn't have sex all night long. It had to be humanly impossible. Wasn't there something called "recovery time"? But if there was, why didn't he seem to need it?

She did. She needed to get ahold of herself.

"Pass the cake, please."

He did, while finishing off the soup, drinking the last of the bisque out of its paper to-go bowl. They'd just made incredible love again, with all the food on the bed with them, without spilling so much as a drop of anything, because what he'd done to her . . . what he'd done to her had been so *primal*.

A wave of heat went through her just thinking about it.

He'd rolled her over and pinned her against the bed, hardly letting her move. It had been bondage without the bonds, with his right hand encircling both her wrists and his left hand underneath her, between her legs. His mouth had been open on the nape of her neck, his teeth grazing her skin, and holding her like that, he'd had his way with her until she'd wanted to howl.

From the very, very satisfied look on his face, she probably had howled. She'd been in such an overheated state by then, she could have done anything.

His eyes met hers over the top of the bowl, and a wicked grin curved the corners of his mouth. Warmth flooded her cheeks. He knew things about her she didn't know herself, and that had to be dangerous.

He had no rules. That was the problem. No rules and no hang-ups, and there wasn't an inch left on her that he hadn't explored.

He'd marked her. She knew it. Marked her as his own, and God forbid if they ever left the loft, the rest of the world was going to know it, too.

And where that left them, she hadn't a clue.

CHAPTER 25

SOUTH MORRISON WAS still rocking when Skeeter pulled up outside. Cars were parked everywhere, packing the streets and jumbled up in the courtyard. By sunrise, there'd be nothing left but tread marks, candy wrappers, and beer bottles—and one less pair of earrings.

She knew South Morrison inside and out. The party had been going on even when she was on the street. It had gotten bigger this last year, the bands better, with a few "entrepreneurs" trying to improve the venue, bring in premium kegs and hustle a few thousand dollars every Saturday night dealing dope at the back door. That the entrepreneurs were Duce Nine Lords was a real testament to their strength and their enduring victory in last summer's turf wars. They'd taken Platte Street south of Fifteenth and were holding it. Still, by long-standing tradition and necessity, South Morrison itself, and especially the party, was open real estate. Excluding anyone, or making it too tough for the specialty boys to do business, only cut into the crowds and everybody's profits. Saturday nights at South Morrison were all about free trade and capitalism in action.

For herself, Skeeter had no vendetta with the Lords, and more importantly, they didn't have one with her. She'd never crossed out their work or trespassed on West Twenty-ninth. So when she walked through the front door and the first thing she felt was a warning skitter up the back of her skull instead of the music pounding up through the floor, it gave her pause.

She had a blade on her hip, her piece resting in the small of her back, and a tool belt she'd picked up in the garage before she'd left Steele Street. The HK 9mm alone was enough to keep her out of somebody else's trouble and to keep them out of hers. She hadn't felt any warning when she and Dylan had showed up to help Creed.

So what was going on? she wondered, looking around. Nothing in the lobby had changed in the last two hours, including the two kids passed out just inside the door. This week's gate, the chain-link barrier guarding the entrance into the party, was still hanging half off the wall. Strobe lights still flashed up through the stair-well. Music was still making the floor hum.

Disobeying Dylan was probably worth a warning skitter or two, she decided, which was why she'd taken the precaution of turning off her cell phone and the on-board computer in the Humvee. Disobeying him was one thing, getting caught was another—and she had no intention of getting caught. He hadn't precisely told her not to go to South Morrison, but that would be a damn poor defense if he ever found out.

As far as the tangos they'd been up against earlier were concerned, well, she was the one who belonged on Platte Street on a Saturday night, not them. She looked like every other girl at the party, a little Goth, a little punk, and like more than a little bit of trouble. The tangos were the ones who would stick out like sore thumbs. If they were even still in the building, she'd see them long before they saw her. Besides, there was no reason for them to be looking for an ex–street rat prowling the halls. The bunch of wild Germans and miscellaneous terrorists Creed had been after all night didn't know Skeeter Bang even existed. She didn't show up on any-body's radar. Dylan and Hawkins had made sure of that. Up until Dylan had used the title of personal secretary to describe her, even Royce had figured she was just the kid who swept out the garage.

Now she was here to sweep out South Morrison and sweep up a pair of earrings.

Creed had said he'd dropped them down a steam

pipe on the fifth floor, and all the steam pipes in South Morrison eventually ended up in the boiler room in the basement. She'd start there and work her way up.

Snapping the tracker around her wrist, she hit the "on" switch and headed for the stairs.

UP on the fourth floor of North Morrison, in Cordelia Stark's apartment, one half of the group known as the Zurich 7, code name Hansel, glanced at the GPS tracking device on his wrist.

"Son of a bitch," he said under his breath, looking over at his partner, Gretel.

"What?" The woman rose from where she'd taken a small jewelry box out of a cardboard box on the bedroom floor. It had the name Olena in gold script written across the top.

"Hashemi's tracker just came back on board."

"Where?"

"Close," he said. "Damn close. Like maybe back in the building we just got out of by the skin of our teeth."

"Well, it sure as hell isn't Hashemi carrying it around. He's dead." She opened the jewelry box, then closed it and dropped it back in the cardboard box with a short sigh. The jewelry box was empty, and they hadn't found a trace of *Tajikistan Discontent*, not even after tearing the dingy little apartment apart. Nothing had been overlooked or left untouched.

"Akbar said the guy who waxed Hashemi took his tracker."

"The same guy who took down Edmund Braun and just led all of us on one big wild-goose chase?" Gretel asked, a small grin playing on her lips. "Now there's a bad boy I'd like to meet."

"Rein in the hormones, babe. We're only assuming it's all the same guy, and the only thing we need to meet is a nuclear bomb."

"You always did know how to show a girl a good time." She smiled, then walked over toward the man standing by the front door. Two Denver policemen were lying on the floor near his feet. "Well, Reinhard. You've lost her."

"We've all lost her," Reinhard said, and Hansel watched the older man's gaze go over her from top to bottom. "She's either ditched the earrings, or they've stopped transmitting."

"They wouldn't stop transmitting," Gretel said. "The signal might have gotten too weak to read for some reason, but it's still there. I can guarantee it. Our best man made those earrings for Sergei to give her."

"Your best man," the German grouched. Reinhard Klein was made of money, and it showed. And as Sergei Patrushev's right-hand man, he held Hansel and Gretel's deal of a lifetime in his hands, but if the bastard hit on Gretel one more time, Hansel was going to clean his clock. He'd liked dealing with the guy over a secure Internet line a lot better than face-to-face—but once

Dominika Starkova had flown the coop, the whole game had changed. Suddenly, he and Gretel had been forced out of their cozy Eastern European apartment, and sent front-and-center into the action.

Gretel, the wily, wonderful witch, just smiled. "We've just gotten a new lead. You're welcome to play it out with us . . . for the price of consideration."

That was a good way to put it, Hansel thought. For the consideration of making damn sure that Sergei Patrushev blew off all the other buyers and sold his friggin' nuclear bomb to the Zurich 7—Hansel and Gretel, who were most definitely *not* lost babes in the woods, not when the woods involved black-market arms deals. They were the masters of the trade, and this was the deal of the century.

"Consideration?" Reinhard repeated, one aristocratic eyebrow lifting. "That you've gotten this far proves both Sergei's and my consideration."

"We want the warhead, Reinhard, a fact we believe we've proven with our offer," Gretel said. "No one else can meet it. Certainly not Hamas or Jemaah Islamiah. Patrushev isn't going to sell it to the Chechens and have it blow up in his backyard—and the same goes for the Taliban. The only way they'll meet his price is by partnering with al-Qaeda—and he's not that big of a fool. The Iranians didn't get out of the library, which has to make you wonder if either one of them could even pull off this deal. The Zurich 7 are the only ones you can count on to make it to the closing table and to continue to protect both your and their best interest long after the deal is done."

"You didn't kill the policemen," the man standing behind Reinhard Klein said.

Hansel noticed that Gretel didn't blink an eye or shift her attention away from Reinhard. Bruno Walmann could suck eggs. It would take more than he had to throw Gretel off her stride.

"Anywhere in the world," she said, "people who kill policemen suddenly exist. They're hunted. Zurich 7 survives by not existing. We are the hunters, Mr. Klein, always—never the hunted."

"What's your new lead?" Reinhard asked, bypassing Walmann's dissent and Gretel's barb.

"The man who killed Hashemi," Gretel said. "We believe he's still in the building next door."

"And Dominika?" Reinhard asked.

"We don't know for sure, but he's still our best bet for finding her."

That was for damn sure, and Hansel had only himself to thank for being the only one with the capability of tracking not only the earrings, but the other tracking devices. It didn't pay to play in the black market arms trade without a lot of connections. There wasn't an aspect of this deal that he and Gretel hadn't brainstormed and controlled to the limit of their ability. The only thing they didn't know, the only thing Hansel was afraid nobody knew, was the location of the missing warhead.

But if he could get his hands on Dominika Starkova,

it wouldn't take him long to get his hands on the book Sergei was certain contained the warhead's location.

"If you can bring me Dominika, I'll reconsider your offer," Reinhard said, which was as close to a commitment as they'd been able to get out of the bastard in three long months. But by anybody's estimation, the deal had reached a crisis point.

Hansel caught Gretel's eye; she was smart enough not to give anything away, but he saw the satisfaction in her gaze. They weren't going to lose this game, no way in hell.

"Let's go find our lost girl, then, gentlemen," she said, lifting her hands and gesturing for the door.

Hansel fell in behind her, stopping only to retrieve the tranquilizer darts she'd used on the cops to clear their way into the apartment.

DEEP in the bowels of South Morrison, the "lost girl" was following her nose and the tracking device through a maze of rusted out pipes and corroded machinery. The party was long behind her, but the pounding beat of the music resonated through all the metal, and she could still hear the crowd and a few people here and there above her on higher floors. South Morrison was fairly porous with all the holes in its infrastructure, walls that just weren't there anymore, big gashes in the floors and subfloors. The basement itself had turned out to be a whole helluva lot bigger than she'd thought—or at least it looked that way in the beam of her flashlight, like there were whole worlds lost in the shadows.

As a bonus, she was ankle-deep in rats. Beady eyes shined at her out of dark corners. The scrabbling patter of little feet rushed away in front of her, which she appreciated, but it also closed in behind her, which was definitely creeping her out. She was starting to feel a little herded.

Oh, great. Now there was a thought to give a person the heebie-jeebies—being herded by a bunch of rats to God knew what end.

She took a breath and tried to let the idea go.

There was ice on the floor in some places and standing water in others, which kind of mystified her. She was freezing her ass off. It occurred to her that the entrance to Hell might be in South Morrison's basement, with a few hot spots leaking through.

Another comforting thought.

Geez. She just needed to find the damn earrings and get out.

CHAPTER

26

SON OF A BITCH, Dylan thought, closing the door behind Tony Royce. She hadn't come back.

Royce had gotten the call from his agent in the field and lit up like a Christmas tree. Without giving anything away, he'd grabbed Bracken and Mathers and hightailed it out of Steele Street, promising to be back.

Dylan doubted it, not tonight. There was enough stuff in the box to keep Royce busy for weeks, with the added bonus of Dominika Starkova's address, which wasn't nearly the priority it had been, because Skeeter hadn't come back. She'd had plenty of time to get home, even if she'd kept the Humvee in first gear. So if she hadn't come home, where had she gone?

He had only one answer for that, and it made his jaw tight.

He crossed over to the computers in the main office. If it had been anyone except Skeeter, he would have said no way. No one else would have so blatantly disregarded a direct order, so willingly disobeyed him, so blithely put themselves in so much danger—all for a tiny piece of electronics.

But this was Skeeter, and she knew where the electronics were, in the bottom of a steam pipe off the fifth floor in South Morrison, and he'd stupidly left her alone with the tracking device that would lead her right to them.

Except it wouldn't be that easy.

And she wasn't the only person who might be after the earrings.

He typed the Humvee's access code into the computer at the same time as he called her cell phone to tell her to get her butt home. Both procedures got him exactly nothing.

Okay. Now she was really in trouble.

He picked up the house phone and dialed the ninth floor.

Really in trouble, like trouble so deep she'd be lucky to dig herself out by the Fourth of July.

"Yo," Creed answered—thank you very much. Dylan really hadn't wanted to have to go up there and do the bucket-of-water thing, because however skeptical he had been with Skeeter, he figured, unbelievably, that she'd called that one right. Sex with an international criminal. If he hadn't thought Creed was crazy before, he did now.

But that was a whole other set of problems.

"How's it going up there?"

"Good."

Okay. Fine. Creed never had been very chatty.

"Dominika still under wraps?"

"Got her right here. What's up?"

You tell me is what Dylan wanted to say, but they had a bigger problem than Creed sleeping with a black-market arms dealer who was trying to sell a multimegaton nuclear warhead to the friggin' Taliban.

Jesus.

"Skeeter went after the earrings."

Creed swore, one succinct word that pretty well summed up how Dylan felt, too.

"I'll go pick her up."

"No," Dylan said. "I'm going after her, but I need you down here, manning the office. If she shows up while I'm gone, I want to know it ASAP."

"She might not be the only one who went back to South Morrison," Creed warned him.

"I can handle it."

"No, I—"

"I can handle it," Dylan repeated. "And if I can't, I'll call you." They couldn't leave Dominika Starkova, or Cody Stark, or whatever she wanted to call herself, alone in Steele Street, and they sure as hell couldn't take her with them, and he wasn't willing to turn her over to anyone else, not yet—those facts narrowed down their options to just one.

"I'll be locked and loaded."

That's all he asked. Creed Rivera locked and loaded was more backup than most people ever needed.

"Has Ms. Starkova volunteered any useful information yet?" he asked, which was about as euphemistic as it got for "Where the fuck is the map we've been busting our asses to find all night?" SDF wasn't in the business of waiting for bad guys to "volunteer" information. They were in the business of *getting* information, and under normal circumstances, they got it any way they could.

"I'm on it," Creed said.

"Good." That's what he'd wanted to hear. He hung up the phone, and on his way out of the office, grabbed four extra magazines for his 9mm.

CREED was as into reality as the next guy, but tonight, reality was a bitch. He was sitting at the bank of computers in the main office, ready to track the Humvee or Skeeter's cell phone, whichever she turned on first, and maintaining a direct feed to General Grant's office at the Pentagon on another.

"The more information I have, the more I can help you, Cody," he said. It was true, but he still felt like a son of a bitch asking the questions. "You've already told me you were at Karlovy Vary. Why don't you tell me what happened."

Debriefing—now there was some harsh, cold, stark reality. He was debriefing the woman he'd just had the hottest sex of his whole life with—sex he'd had without a condom.

That was right. No condom. And how was that for some cold stark reality?

He'd flat-out forgotten to use one, but even if he'd remembered, he had a feeling he would have been out of luck.

If he'd thought about it, he could have borrowed a few condoms, he supposed. Kid probably had a couple hundred of the damn things up in his loft, but Creed had been in Kid's loft, and a person's chances of finding anything smaller than a kayak were between slim and none. Kid had only two categories of stuff: things that needed ammo, which he was obsessively careful with, and things that didn't need ammo, and if it didn't need ammo, it could be anywhere.

That would have left Dylan, and Creed could think of few things that would have lit a three-alarm blaze under the boss's butt faster than him calling down for condoms with Dominika Starkova holed up in his apartment.

Of course, it was all moot, because he hadn't remembered to take precautions until they'd hit the cold, stark reality of the SDF office—where, coincidentally, he'd hit a cold, stark wall.

She wasn't giving anything away.

Kissing someone wasn't listed anywhere in the commando interrogation manual as a verified method of softening up a detainee, but he still wanted to do it.

"Cody? Honey?"

Calling a prisoner "honey" also was not listed in the interrogation manual.

"Sweetheart?" *Nada*. Not listed.

He was teasing her a little with the endearments, trying to get a reaction, not that he didn't like them. She could be his sweetheart. He could see it, easy, but she hadn't looked at him since they'd walked out of the elevator, which was driving him nuts.

"*Querida?*" My love.

That one finally got him a flicker. Her gaze lifted to his for a fraction of a second before dropping again.

"I . . . I can't tell you anything," she said.

"Why not? You're going to end up telling somebody everything, and it really would be for the best if you started with me." He would protect her any way he could, and he doubted if anyone else would bother. "There might be a way out of this, Cody, but I won't know if you don't help me."

She let out a weary sigh and finally met his gaze. "I told Keith O'Connell everything, and he ended up dead. That's not a chance I'm willing to take with you."

And that was good news. Sort of. In a roundabout way that didn't do him a damn bit of good. He didn't mean to brag, but he'd been freakin' unstoppable tonight. She must have noticed.

"I'm a highly trained operative of the United States government, Cody. I can take care of myself, and you, if you'll let me. Keith O'Connell was a State Department attaché who shouldn't have tried to take things as far as he did."

"No, he wasn't," she said, taking the misinformation bait. He felt like a jerk for doing it to her, but it looked like it was going to get them off square one. "He was CIA. If you look deeper, you'll find it. I swear. And he was also highly trained, and they hung him up by a rope and shot him until there was nothing left. I *was* there, and I saw it, and he was helpless, and I . . . I was useless." She looked at him, her frustration palpable. "I tried. I begged, and they killed him anyway, and they kept killing him, over and over and over."

Well, for someone who wasn't going to tell him anything, she'd just said a mouthful—and he'd just fallen into déjà vu quicksand. He knew all about being helpless and useless.

"Who shot him, Cody?" He needed names.

She shook her head, her frustration turning to anger. "Don't make me do this. I don't want you hurt."

"You're on home ground, now, with the full power of the U.S. government on your side. If you give me something to work with, we can stop them cold." He believed it, because that's what he'd been doing for the last ten years, stopping the bad guys cold, without question, except for one godawful failure in Colombia. "If you tell me everything, and I mean *everything*, maybe we can walk away from this together."

"*You* can walk away now, and that's exactly what you should do."

God, she could be stubborn.

But he no longer believed she could be a terrorist. No way. And that wasn't just the sex talking. At least he hoped it wasn't. Nothing about the way the night had gone down pointed to anything except her being on the run, without the skills and resources to be successful.

For that she needed him. He had the skills and the resources, and if he decided to make a run for it, there wasn't anybody who was going to catch him. Unbelievably, against every ounce of his better judgment, that's exactly what he was beginning to decide.

"Give me the location of the bomb, and I can use it to cut a deal." There, it was out in the open. "I'll take you someplace where they'll never find us, not if they look for the next fifty years." He could guarantee it, but so help him, God, once he crossed that line, if he crossed that line, there'd be no turning back.

She looked up, and he was amazed that such a soft mouth could be set in such a hard line.

"We're having our first fight." It had just dawned on him. "If you come away with me, we can do this whenever we want."

From the look on her face, that wasn't the big selling point he'd hoped it would be. "And *why* would I want to go away someplace and fight with a crazy man?"

"Because I make you hot."

"Other people make me hot, and you don't see me running away with them."

"Liar." He moved in close. "Nobody makes you hot

the way I make you hot. Come on, Cody, take the chance. It's the only one you've got."

He needed a chance, too, and it wasn't just because of the sex. He wasn't that big of a fool, and sex had always been easy for him to find. This was something else. He didn't know what, couldn't put a name to it, but whatever he'd seen in her on that rooftop had been profound. It had compelled him. It still compelled him.

"Please." He didn't want this to end, not tonight, not with her going into lockdown for the rest of her life, and him going into therapy until his teeth fell out.

"Hashemi," she finally said after a long pause, looking like she already regretted telling him. "And . . . and Akbar. They were the ones who actually pulled the triggers."

It wasn't a map to the warhead, but it was a start, the start down a long road of no return. If he saved her, he'd be a fugitive, too. But if he didn't, he had no future at all, because he wouldn't be able to live with himself.

"Who else was there?" He reached over and turned off the computer connecting him to General Grant's office and picked up a pencil and notepad. He'd decide later how much information to disseminate and when, and if that didn't smack of high treason, he didn't know what did.

"Sergei Patrushev, Bruno Walmann, and . . . Reinhard K-Klein were all there, and the Braun twins." The litany of names came pouring out of her, one after another, each one of them marking a man as an accessory to murder.

"Patrushev," he said when she finished. "Tell me about

him. How you got involved with him. The work you did for him." He'd get back to the map.

"I never worked for him. I was his prisoner. When I was able to escape, I did."

"Prisoner?" She'd dumbfounded him again. No one had thought to follow that angle. "How? Why?"

"My father, he, uh, owed Sergei a lot of money."

Which meant what? he wondered. "He sold you to Sergei?"

Oh, man. This was going to get bad. He felt it in his gut.

"Not sold, exactly. It was more like he used me for collateral."

Same difference in his book, the bastard.

"If you were a prisoner, how did you end up in the middle of the negotiations for the nuclear deal? We've got photos of you with almost all the buyers, sometimes at a party, but sometimes just entering a building with one or more of them."

It was what had sealed her fate, her high profile with all the terrorists trying to work a deal with Sergei.

"That's what I was collateral for, not the money my dad owed, but the nuclear warhead he had been responsible for when he'd been a general in the Soviet army. He's the one who took it off the military base in Tbisili and hid it in Tajikistan."

Tajikistan.

Bingo. Big, huge freaking bingo. That was it, the information they all needed.

"Do you have the exact location?"

And oh, hallelujah, she nodded her head. "It's in a book of poetry my father gave me."

"And where's the book?"

His question hit a wall of silence, a solid brick wall of silence.

"Cody?" She couldn't clam up now. "Come on. You've got to tell me."

Or not.

"No," she said, her voice distressed. "O'Connell was killed for knowing about all this."

And everything O'Connell had known should have been in the intelligence reports, but a couple of big pieces were missing out of those reports.

"You told him about your father? About the book?"

"Yes."

Damn CIA. They'd probably considered those two huge facts proprietary information and given them to their own guys, but not to anybody else. It was one way to keep people from trampling all over an investigation, but it made it damn hard on other people who were out there in the field, people like SDF.

It looked like SDF was going to ace them out anyway—maybe. He decided to go back around to the beginning.

"What else can you tell me about Sergei Patrushev?"

"He's rich, obscenely wealthy, but you probably already know that, and he likes to party. There's always a crowd with Sergei."

"Which included you, most of the time." It wasn't a

question. She'd been seen everywhere these last few months.

"He liked to keep me with him. I was a valuable commodity."

He'd seen her in the little silver dress. He knew exactly why she'd been so valuable, and it hadn't all been about the warhead. If she hadn't been an asset on the party scene and with the buyers, Sergei would have kept her under wraps.

"As dumb as it sounds, in pretty short order, I was the most famous party girl in the Czech Republic, even made it into a few magazines, quite a few, actually."

"So does this mean we can look forward to an accidentally released Dominika Starkova video sex tape showing up on the Internet?"

To his amazement, her smile faded and a wash of color came into her cheeks.

Whoa. Some of the air went out of him. He'd only been teasing her.

"Cody?" This he had to know.

"No," she said. "There's no sex tape."

"But there's something."

"No. Nothing." She shifted her gaze to the computer screen and took hold of the mouse.

"You're the worst liar I have ever seen."

There was something, all right. Something he wasn't going to like. He could tell, because without even knowing, he wanted to hit something, like the desk, or the wall, or probably some guy, because her "nothing" did not sound like a simple ex-lover, sex tape or no sex tape.

"What kind of nothing?" he pressed a little harder.

"How about a none-of-your-business nothing." She wiggled the mouse around, avoiding his eyes.

"How about an I'm-making-it-my-business nothing. And if you were wondering, this counts as fight number two. Dish it up, babe."

She met his gaze with a much maligned sigh. "You're being . . . being—"

"Proprietary?" He helped her out. "We made love, Cody. That makes you mine for as long as I can hold you, even if it's only for tonight. Territorial? Damn straight. Ridiculous? No. Vengeful? In a heartbeat, if someone has hurt you."

"How about nosey?"

"Definitely. I need to know everything about you, for your sake. For mine."

"*Oh*. Oh, I see." Her expression instantly changed.

She'd just had an epiphany. He didn't know what the hell about, but he knew an epiphany when he saw one.

"Of course, well," she continued. "I haven't . . . well, so I didn't, but, well—"

He leaned forward, resting his elbows on his knees, watching her, fascinated. He'd said something to make her blush, and he couldn't wait to figure out what exactly that had been. His "getting to know everything about you" line had been pretty straightforward since they'd left the loft.

"Well." She let out a breath, as if steeling herself. "To begin with, there was this boy, very sweet, but it was his first time, too, and we weren't together that long."

Oh, wow. She was going to give him her sexual history, literally from the beginning. No one had ever done that before. He sat back in his chair, completely nonplussed. He usually didn't do this scene at all. He was usually careful enough that he didn't have to do this scene. Yeah, he definitely wanted to know what had put that look on her face when he'd joked about the sex tape. Something had happened to her, something sexual that had made her very uncomfortable, and he needed to know what that had been, for her sake, for his sake, just like he'd said—but this litany-of-old-lovers thing. He wasn't going to stop her, because the more she talked, the more he learned, and that was his job, but God, she was actually starting from the beginning.

"And then there was another boy, but again, nothing to worry about there, and then I was engaged to Alex for four years. He was a professor of cultural anthropology."

Okay. They'd just covered a whole lot of ground without much action, and nothing sounded too freakin' bizarre yet, unless the anthropology thing was going to include the sexual initiation rites of some obscure Bohemian hill tribe in which the professor had forced her to participate. That would be bizarre.

"We broke off just before I went to Prague to visit my father." She gave him a quick glance.

Okay. Things happened. Guys left, and he couldn't

say he was anything but damn glad that the fiancé had split.

"So what about you?" she asked, and he felt a little something shift and quake inside him.

"Seven," he said, and that was all he was going to say. He'd read somewhere that seven was a workable number of ex-lovers to admit to having—not too wild, not too tame.

Seven, and he was sticking to it.

"Seven?"

"Seven." He wasn't going to go into this, ever. He was not a kiss-and-tell kind of guy. Problems he'd had with relationships were fair game, but not the sex.

"So what happened after Alex?" Who he was guessing was the dumb guy who didn't like going down on girls.

"I was alone after Alex, and after a few months, I went to Prague."

And before Prague, had what? Jumped a girlfriend? He could live with that, even if it was going to give him crazy ideas which a smart guy would just keep to himself.

"Of course, in Prague everybody thought I was sleeping with everybody except them. It's just what people think at these parties, and . . . um . . . one guy in particular really had a problem with that, and with me always turning him down."

Okay. Now they were getting somewhere. This was not going to be one of those stories with a kinky, but basically harmless ending. He took a breath and shifted in his chair.

"Who was it?"

"I don't think the name is important, it's just—"

"It is," he said. Damned important.

"Creed." More color washed into her cheeks, which simply fascinated him. She had the softest skin, and if some bastard had hurt her, he was going to have to work damn hard not to hunt him down. He was an operator, not a vigilante—and he needed to keep reminding himself of that. Still, he wanted the name.

"Yes?" he said, when after a few more seconds she didn't go on. What? She thought she could stop now?

"I'm sorry." She made a small dismissive gesture with her hand. "I shouldn't have brought it up. It doesn't matter."

Wait a minute. It did matter.

"You didn't bring it up. I did, and you need to tell me what happened." She could not leave him hanging like this. "If you were hurt, I need to know." It was a rule somewhere, in the good-guy handbook.

"I wasn't hurt, not like you mean, so it . . . it isn't anything you need to worry about. It wasn't rape."

The pencil snapped clean in half in his hand.

Well, he was really fucking glad to hear that.

He tossed the broken pieces of the pencil onto the desk and forced himself to take a breath.

"I'm sorry about forgetting to use a condom with you, but I didn't have one," she said, coming way out of left field again and pretty much blindsiding him.

"That's my line. All the way." And he meant it. He should have been more responsible. But they needed to get back to this guy, and this "wasn't rape" thing. What the hell did that mean?

"You don't need to worry. That man used a condom. Actually, he used two, because he was so sure I was sleeping around."

Geezus.

The color in her cheeks wasn't because of embarrassment about her sexual history. It wasn't embarrassment at all. It was pure distress about this guy and whatever he'd done to her, which she *was* going to tell him.

"Why wasn't it rape, Cody?" He had a pretty strict interpretation of the crime, and it came down to one thing: If a woman didn't want you, you needed to back off and rethink your plan.

"Because I didn't say no." She did her best to meet his gaze, but only about half succeeded, which made him feel badly for her. "It was that night, at Karlovy Vary, and it was all so surreal—but I still could have said no, and I didn't."

The breath went out of him again. Karlovy Vary. He had an all-too-clear picture of what it had been like in the warehouse that night, and surreal probably didn't quite cover it.

"Did he threaten you?"

She shrugged. "With this man, every move he makes is a threat, every word he speaks. It's the way he is."

"Patrushev?"

She shook her head. "Sergei doesn't feel that way about me, not at all. He likes a different type of woman."

Okay. He was done. He knew who it was. He could see the whole thing, from start to finish, including the two condoms. It didn't take a genius to figure out how violence turned into sex, or to understand how easy it was to take advantage of a terrified, confused woman who couldn't figure out how to say no while someone was forcing themselves on her—not after what she'd just seen.

And the look on her face when he'd teased her about the sex tape? That had been pure shame.

"Without full consent, you don't have a mortal sin," he said.

Her gaze lifted to his from where she was perched on the edge of her chair.

"It's a very big deal, the full consent, and without it, you don't have a mortal sin. You can work this one off."

"But I'm not Catholic."

He lifted off the leather thong with his saint's medal and crucifix and slipped it over her head. "Now you are."

"I don't think it's this easy."

"Sure it is." He took her hands in his. "Repeat after me: Hail, Mary, full of grace; the Lord is with thee . . ."

CHAPTER
27

SKEETER WAS SO damn close to those earrings, she could almost taste them. Her tracking device had redlined, and she was standing right in front of a steam pipe that was coming straight out of the ceiling—probably all the way from the fifth floor, if her luck held.

Luck. Right. She wiped the back of her hand across her mouth. She was sweating. In a basement where there were icicles hanging from the ceiling, she was sweating.

She wasn't running on luck. She'd pushed her luck right over the edge and into a bottomless abyss. Every warning bell she had was clanging so loud in her head, the only way she could hear herself think was to focus on the earrings.

Get them and *go*—that was the message she was getting, but there was one slight problem. She was standing on tiptoe and holding the tracker as high above her head as she could get it, but there just happened to be an elbow in the pipe just past where she could see through the hole in the ceiling—which meant she had to get up there and take apart the pipe at the elbow. The earrings, if her tracker was as good as she thought it was, would be lying in the bottom of the turn.

She flashed her light around on the floor, until she found a few wooden crates piled up against the wall. The first one she moved set loose a flurry of rats. She danced around them a bit, and they scurried over her boots, and thankfully, disappeared back into the shadows. She didn't like rats, but she wasn't going to scream about them. She used to scream for rat encounters, but living on the street, it hadn't taken her long to figure out screaming scared her a whole lot more than it scared the rats.

Taking hold of the first crate, she dragged it over to the pipe, then hauled a second one over to set on top—which should just about do it.

Now all she had to do was get on the crates, shimmy up the pipe a little, find a place to set her flashlight so she could see what she was doing, and somehow take apart a corroded pipe that was probably four times older than she was.

Piece of cake.

That's why she traveled with a tool belt.

It took some doing, and about twenty minutes of

banging away and wiring up her flashlight, twenty minutes of bracing herself against the subfloor and hoping her right foot didn't slip off the crate or her left leg come off from around the pipe, but finally, finally, the damn thing was coming apart. She didn't carry a big old pipe wrench on her belt. Who would? So she'd had to make do, but making do was what all gear heads did.

Jerking and tugging, and being damn thankful for every pound of weight she'd ever pressed, she managed to get the pipe to turn enough that she could shine her flashlight down inside.

Ho-lee mo-lee. There they were: two shiny, sparkling, gem-encrusted crosses, each one no bigger than her pinkie fingernail. She reached down inside, caught them up in her hand, and was just giving herself a mental high five, when she felt the cold bore of a gun press against the small of her back.

The next sensation was equally ominous: Someone took her gun. She felt the lift of the weight, the slide of someone's hand, and the cold wave of dread that washed down her spine.

THERE was a bedroom in the office. As a matter of fact, there were three very elegant suites set up to accommodate overnight guests—but Creed wasn't going there. He was manning his post, and kissing Cody Stark, and trying to decide if he really had it in him to do it one more time.

Yeah. Sure he did, but this sort of half-arousal thing they had working, with her in his lap and his hands under her clothes and her mouth all over his face, nibbling on his ears, kissing him back—hell, it was great, kind of a long, slow hum where a guy could just float and really explore her body. Her breasts were so soft and full, not big, just full, her skin so silky. There was nothing on a guy's body that felt like breasts, and the way she was straddling him on the chair gave him full access to her amazingly curved tush—but he was showing a little caution there. If he got too far down her pants, his slow hum was going to turn into a John Frusciante riff and they'd be deep into achingly hot and sweet sex in a heartbeat.

Which maybe wasn't such a bad idea after all.

He'd no sooner had the thought, though, than the Humvee screen blipped on. Cody was kissing his neck, and he watched over her shoulder as a white-and-yellow-striped line undulated across a green skin.

"Hold on, babe," he said, kissing her cheek and wrapping his arm around her waist as he leaned forward to pick up the phone.

A couple of button pushes got him Dylan.

"Is that you at the Humvee?"

"Yes," Dylan said, not sounding any too happy about it.

"South Morrison?"

"Roger that."

Skeeter's ass was grass.

"Any sign of her?"

"No. I'm going in. What do you think? Start in the basement?"

" 'Fraid so, boss. Go straight through the party. There's a stairwell behind the stage, and the rest of the building lays out from there. You'll be looking for a boiler." The boss was the least mechanical of the lot of them. "Do you even know what a boiler looks like, Dylan?" Creed really had his doubts.

The boss's "Fuck you" cleared up some of his doubts, but not all of them. Dylan could scam his way through anything—but being a great con artist was not going to find him the boiler room.

"She hasn't turned on her cell phone, has she?"

"No, sir." Not bloody likely. The girl didn't want to be found out. She'd thought she could pull a fast one over at South Morrison and not get caught.

"If she should decide to call, tell her to—"

"Wait," Creed said, leaning forward and clicking the mouse to bring up another screen. "She's on. Do you want to make the call or—"

The decision was made for them when Creed's cell phone rang.

"Hold on, Dylan. I've got an incoming," he said, pulling his cell phone out of his pants pocket. "It's her."

Except it wasn't her. When he answered, he got a man's voice with a German accent.

"We've got your girl, your Skeeter Bang. If you want her back, you'll bring us Dominika Starkova."

Oh, Baby Bang, you've done it this time, Creed

thought, and felt his expression go from fucking grim to frightfully fucking grim in the course of a couple of seconds. He glanced up at Cody once, then focused his attention back on the call.

"You've got an hour," the voice said. "Call then and I'll give you directions to the drop."

The phone went dead, and Creed instantly went back to the land line.

"They've got her, Dylan," he said, his voice tight. "But they're willing to make a trade. It's a pretty straightforward deal—Dominika Starkova for the punk rock girl."

Geezus.

"Did you get a lock on the phone?" Dylan asked.

"Yes." He zoomed in on the computer screen, pulling up a map of the city. "It's on the north side. Up in Commerce City. West of Colorado Boulevard."

"Ten-oh-eight Robinson," Dylan said.

"Definitely Robinson, and I'll take your word on the ten-oh-eight." Creed was impressed. "How did you know?"

"Skeeter found a paper trail for one of Bruno Walmann's business cards. It ended up at a warehouse in north Denver."

Dylan's photographic memory would have done the rest.

"How do you want to do this?" They weren't going to give them Cody, Creed knew that, but there was no way in hell they were going to let them keep Skeeter.

"Full-court press. I'm calling Royce and Lieutenant Loretta. With dead foreigners showing up all over the city, everybody's on edge. When everyone is in position, I'll move inside, and we'll roll the circus straight down their throat."

Creed couldn't fault the plan, except for him not being part of it, but his priority tonight, his only priority, had been and still was to capture, detain, and protect Cordelia Stark. The whole "circus" idea would work. There was nothing like a hastily cobbled together interagency task force to create a diversion the size of Chicago. Inside the ensuing chaos, Dylan would be invisible. Skeeter hadn't nicknamed him "the Shadow" for nothing. Nobody moved with more stealth when the situation required it, and he'd have Skeeter on his side. The girl was far from helpless.

Superman had made damn sure of that.

SKEETER had been in worse places. The old flophouse up on Wazee had been a lot worse than this tidy little warehouse on the north side, but the company on Wazee had been better. A couple of these guys were major freakazoids, especially the one named Reinhard Klein. The gorilla-looking dude had to be what was left of the Braun twins, but he didn't worry her too much. Big dumb muscle wasn't dangerous unless it got ahold of you. Not that she wouldn't be pretty damn easy to get ahold of right now. She was tied to a chair . . . for the moment.

She was scared, but functioning. This wasn't the first

tight spot she'd ever been in. Nobody was insanely drunk or threatening to kill her. They would, if they thought it was to their advantage. She knew it. She wasn't stupid—or at least she hadn't been until she'd just had to go after those earrings.

She really needed to reorganize her priority list. Electronic gear, however attractive, was not worth her life. That was her new mantra: no dying for battery-operated devices. She needed to learn it and remember it.

That said, she had managed to slip the earrings into her pants pocket before they'd hauled her out of South Morrison, which was enough to make a girl wonder just how well she was learning tonight's little life lesson. But if push came to shove, she was ready to hand them over, so help her God.

As it was, she didn't think these tangos even knew she had the earrings.

Tangos, terrorists—yes, she was operating in real SDF territory now, even if this group didn't fit the hardened, moth-eaten picture she'd always had of terrorists. Almost everyone here tonight was in a suit. Freakin' three pieces on old Reinhard, with his slicked-back black hair and his cashmere overcoat. Definitely not the picture she'd had in mind.

Then there were the two MIBs, the Men in Black, except one of them was a woman. They all but screamed "cops," except they were better dressed. They had the look, though, and the attitude, the deliberate calm, the steady, modulated voices. Bruno Walmann was brooding;

the Braun boy was almost catatonic; Klein was moving and shaking, the power player; and the two MIBs were in control. If one of them actually did scream something, she was diving out of her chair, because something would *definitely* be coming down.

Reinhard stopped his pacing in front of her, for about the hundredth time, with his crotch right in her face. The rats in South Morrison had nothing on this guy in the creep department. He'd taken her hat and her sunglasses, which meant she was looking her worst, but that hadn't kept him from fixating on her.

He lifted her ponytail in his manicured hand. "For a moment, in the basement, I thought you were Dominika."

Her hair slid through his fingers, and all she could think was "double wash, double rinse."

"But you've been ruined. No, *liebling*?" He trailed a finger down her scar. "Too bad."

Ruined was what he said, but all the signals she was getting said she hadn't been ruined enough to turn him off. Hawkins had taught her how to work a situation like this to her advantage. It was kind of gross, but geez, he'd even made her come on to him, and if she could kissy-face flirt with Superman, who was practically her *dad*, then she could do it with gross old Reinhard.

Here goes, she thought, and lowered her gaze to his crotch. If this worked, she was going to lose all respect for men.

He chuckled, and ran his finger down her cheek. "How old are you? Fifteen?"

"And a half," she said, lifting her gaze back to his.

He liked that. He liked it a lot. She could tell.

Pervert.

But she could live with that, especially if it got her untied and alone in a room with him.

Her cell phone rang, and Bruno flipped it open. She had to grin. Somebody at SDF headquarters was marking her position every time Bruno got on the phone. Somebody else would already be on their way—and that thought was enough to wipe the grin off her face.

Man, she hoped it was Creed. She didn't want to have to face Dylan for a while. If she got out of this in one piece, he was going to skin her alive and nail her hide to the garage wall.

"Herr Klein, they are ready to deliver at a location of our choice."

"Perfect," Reinhard said. "Tell them we'll call them back in thirty minutes and tell them where to meet us."

Something told Skeeter it was going to be a long thirty minutes for her. Behind her back, she carefully slipped her needle-nosed pliers back into her tool belt. By her estimation, she'd gotten about halfway through the rope they'd used to tie her up. Maybe far enough to break it, but she hoped not far enough for anyone to notice.

They'd taken her gun in South Morrison, but not her tool belt—which had really made her wonder just how much these guys knew about tools—and because they hadn't taken her tool belt, they'd missed her switch-blade underneath.

"Ernst." Reinhard called the Braun guy over. "Take her into the next room. No," he said when Ernst reached for her ropes. "Keep her tied. Carry in the whole chair."

Tied? Just what in the hell did he think he was going to do to her tied to a chair? Her imagination, which was really good, came up with a few things without any trouble, but she refused to panic.

Then Ernst came up behind her and simply lifted the whole chair by its seat and carried her through the door.

She didn't even bother trying to catch the eye of one of the MIBs and give them a pleading look. Those two were running their own game here, and saving punk rock girls was not on their agenda.

Fortunately, this punk rock girl could save herself—she hoped.

After Ernst set her down, Reinhard followed him to the door and locked it behind him. Skeeter heard him slide the dead bolt home.

Perfect.

Once this thing started, she didn't want anybody else coming in.

CHAPTER

28

IN STEELE STREET, Creed was monitoring half a dozen devices on three separate computers. The Humvee was Dylan heading north into Commerce City to save Skeeter's butt. The cell phone was the location of the assholes who had taken her, and the third was an open-com setup where he was tracking everyone else who was headed up to the warehouse. He had the police radio on an open band. Royce from the CIA wasn't talking, but Creed knew by the tracker still on his car that he was definitely going in the right direction.

"You're amazing," Cody said, standing just behind him, watching him work.

Yeah, it was pretty impressive how he'd gotten this

all up and running in record time, and he thought it was cool that she'd noticed. He had the rep as SDF's jungle boy, but he had the rest of the gig down, too. He wasn't just good for swinging through the trees and booby-trapping the trails.

He'd been thinking, though, and he was thinking it was time to make a move. As soon as Skeeter was free, he and Cody needed to clear out, and get lost, and make damn sure they weren't found.

He knew the place.

He also knew a guy in Trinidad who could paint Angelina in an hour flat. She'd always wanted to look like Jeanette, and this was going to be her chance. Pure primer, baby. He was going to turn his show ride into a sleeper. Then it was straight to Mexico and the coast.

He always had two bags packed, ready to go at a moment's notice, one with clothes and stuff, and another with weapons. All he needed now was the moment, and something from her.

"We've run out of time, Cody," he said, watching the Humvee's white-and-yellow-striped signal come to a stop on the screen. Dylan had landed, but everybody else wasn't too far behind. "This thing with Skeeter has blown us up. We're not going to be able to hide out in Steele Street after Royce gets a load of what she's been up to. He's going to know I've got you, and it's going to be warrants for everyone's arrest. He's not going to be able to put me away, but it'll be the end for you—and I'm not willing to let that happen."

"I'm not sure you can keep it from happening." She leaned forward, resting her hands on his shoulders and pressing a kiss to the back of his head. "Or, if you can, that you should."

"Well, I can, and I'm damn sure I should." He hit a couple of keystrokes. Somehow, Royce's signal kept getting stalled. He was either hitting every red light in Denver, or ending up behind every garbage truck on the late shift, because the blinking light with his name on it was hardly moving. "If after a week, or two, or three, you decide you'd rather sit in Leavenworth than stand one more day of my company, I'll bring you back."

"Back from where?"

He looked up at her. "Paradise. You won't find it on a map, but I know how to get there. I wish I could give you a third choice, but I can't. I'd rather have you in Leavenworth than dead, and you won't last a week on your own. Not even if Dylan and the CIA get every tango in Denver tonight. Patrushev will just send more."

HE was right, and Cody knew it. She could run until she dropped, and there would still be somebody after her.

"There's a price, though, babe, and it's got to be paid," he said, swiveling around in his chair, the computers momentarily forgotten. "No compromise on this, Cody. I have got to have the book. You need to be as far away from it as you can get, and the U.S. government needs to find that nuclear bomb. The world can't have that threat hanging over its head."

He was right. Hiding the book was one thing, but it didn't make the bomb disappear. Somewhere in Tajikistan, it was waiting, and someday, map or no map, it was going to be found.

He was offering her a chance, the same way he'd offered her forgiveness for her sins. He'd lifted a weight off her shoulders, and he was willing to do it again.

"It's an awful burden, Creed." Truly terrible.

"I know, *querida*." He reached for her hand, then gently pulled her onto his lap and nuzzled her neck. It wasn't sexual. It was warm, and loving. It was being close, sharing the same space, and she'd never felt anything like it with anyone else, ever. "Come with me, Cody. Let's give them what they want and escape."

A few simple words would set her free, would be the end of it, and with his breath warming her skin and his body close, touching her, she found the strength to just let go.

"I hid the book in the library."

SKEETER looked down at poor old Reinhard Klein with his dick hanging out of his pants, and his glass jaw broken, and his four-thousand-dollar suit looking like yesterday's news, and she would have given away half her new Humvee for one can of spray paint. She'd bagged the bastard, and now she really wanted to tag him.

SB303. From the way he was moaning and groaning on the floor, she figured there was a good possibility that she'd actually broken his balls.

He had Superman to thank for that. She and Hawkins had spent enough time in Steele Street's fourth-floor gym to fill the basement with sweat—and tonight, it had all paid off.

You will *never* be hurt again, he'd told her. *Never.* And then he'd proceeded to make it so.

Poor old Reinhard. He'd never had a chance once he'd unzipped his pants. He'd thought he was going up against a girl. That's what he'd seen. What he hadn't seen was Superman's blood pumping through her veins, making her heart strong. No one could see it, but she knew it was there.

She looked around the office, but of course, there was no paint. Damn.

There had to be something she could—ah, she had it. Using her pliers, she snipped one piece of chain off her knife sheath, pried it open a little bit more, and then threaded it through his lapel button.

SB303, sucker.

From the pounding on the door, Reinhard's buddies had figured out all was not wine and roses in the love nest. It was time to get out of Dogville.

Stepping on the chair and the desk and up onto the bookcase, she climbed to the one window in the office, slid it open, shimmied her butt through it, and dropped the ten feet down on the other side. She landed soft on the balls of her feet, her knees bent, her mind clear.

DYLAN stood behind Loretta and the guys she'd brought from her SWAT team, which had not been his choice, but they were the ones with the breaching loads, so they got to blow the door. Supplies, that's all it was, simple supplies. The guys with the most toys got to play first.

He had breaching loads at home, and a Mossberg 500 Cruiser to deliver them, the operative words being "at home," as in "not here" outside this goddamn German warehouse, wading through snow up to his butt cheeks.

Four guys were lined up in front of him, each with their hand on the shoulder of the guy ahead of them. Everybody needed to know where everybody else was when the door went and they all peeled off into the dark building.

He was man number five, and he'd been told to stay put until he got the all clear, even though it was his employee, his *friend*, they were all there to save.

Actually, out of everybody sneaking through the dark and getting into position out here on Robinson Street, he and Loretta were probably the only ones who gave a damn about Skeeter. Everybody else wanted a piece of the action and their chance to do the deed, take down some assholes, get back at Osama, and hit one for the home team.

He didn't blame them; if it wasn't for Skeeter, he would have felt the same way.

But for him, this was about Skeeter, and his gut was in a knot of fear. He didn't want her hurt. If she was okay, then he got to strangle her himself, and that's what he wanted, what he needed. To have the luxury of shaking her until her teeth rattled and kissing her until she melted in his arms.

And then shaking her again.

CHAPTER 29

SKEETER KNEW AS MUCH about sneaking around in the dark as the next wallbanger, and man, was she sneaking tonight. The outside of the warehouse was crawling with cops. She'd slid by three before she reached the front of the building, saw all the cop cars lurking out on the street, and realized she'd been evading her rescue team, which wasn't such a bad idea from the looks of the combat-ready force assembled by the main door. When the SWAT team fired off their breaching load, she heard glass rattle in four directions. Live fire started up inside the building shortly thereafter. Cripes, was she glad she'd gotten out when she had.

What she needed to do was stay out of everyone's

way, and when she looked around, she saw the perfect place to stay safe and still be able to watch the action.

DYLAN could hear all hell breaking loose inside the warehouse. The breaching load had set everybody off. From the sounds of it, the tangos had decided to go out in a ball of flame and glory. It was the frickin' OK Corral all over again.

And Skeeter was in there. He waited another second—and then he was done waiting. Staying low, he crossed the threshold, and then the receiver buzzed in his ear: "All clear."

Hell. It was over. Fast and furious and short and sweet. He straightened up and headed for the light at the end of the rows of crates lining the walls. He could smell the gunfire, saw one dead body. It looked like one of the Brauns.

Boom! Another breaching load went off, and Dylan picked up his pace. The SWAT team had come up against a locked door somewhere, and he still hadn't found Skeeter.

At the end of the row of crates, the police were already cuffing a group of people. Dylan categorized everyone in one quick glance. There were two people he didn't know, a man and a woman who appeared to be negotiating their release before Loretta even had a chance to get in the building and book them. He heard the woman say, "Tony Royce," but didn't have time to look into that fascinating revelation just now, because there was still no Skeeter, and no Reinhard Klein.

He pushed past two of the SWAT guys to get into the room they'd just blown open, and there was Klein, flat out on the floor. He quickly scanned the rest of the room, saw the chair with a few lengths of cut rope dangling off it, noted that Klein had been worked over, and saw a black scuff mark high up on the wall next to the window.

Son of a bitch. She'd taken down Reinhard Klein.

He stepped over to the German. He'd been tied up, hands and legs, and was half stripped of his pants—and had a small metal ring looped through his lapel.

It wasn't a fashion statement.

She'd tagged him.

She'd taken him down and then she'd tagged him with a ring of her chain mail.

God, she'd probably wanted a can of paint.

The bastard was in a lot of pain, and nobody was bothering to untie him yet, but Klein was Royce's problem.

His problem was finding Skeeter. She'd gone through the window, and considering its location, she couldn't have been hurt, or hurt very badly, to have done it. She was probably hitching home, and at this time of night in Commerce City that could probably get her killed even faster than a bunch of tangos.

Turning and walking away, he started to feel pretty good about the night. Things had gotten a little hairy for a while, but were settling down now. His team had performed beyond expectations. Not Creed. He expected Creed to come out on top every single time. But Skeeter was a bonus. And to top it all off, they'd fulfilled their mission. They'd brought in Dominika Starkova and had her safely and quietly detained in Steele Street.

By anyone's estimation, the night was a Grade A success.

He'd parked the Humvee a ways up on the street and had to skirt a few cop cars to get to it. He needed to cruise the streets and find her, but for a moment, when he got inside, he just let go, slumped over the steering wheel, and allowed himself to feel the relief washing through him. She'd kicked Klein's ass and still had enough moxie to tag him, and enough physical strength to get herself out of a window ten feet up on the wall.

He really should marry her.

"Hi."

Shit! He jerked around, his heart in his throat, his hand going for his gun.

Shit! She'd drop-loaded two gallons of adrenaline into his system in less than half a second flat.

"Skeeter," he said, trying so hard not to sound even half as panicked as he felt that he damn near broke a vocal chord. She was tucked into the corner of the seat, and he'd been too wired even to see her.

Then it hit him.

She really was safe—he looked her over—and she wasn't hurt, and she was here, in the car, with him, and that bastard Klein had taken his pants down in front of her.

He couldn't do this. He couldn't feel this way about her and function.

"Big night?" he asked.

She nodded, and that's when he noticed she was trembling: her shoulders, her mouth—all of her was trembling.

He couldn't do this. Really. He was Dylan Hart, the cool one, the detached one, the brains of the operation. He was not the one who got swamped by feelings he couldn't control.

"Come here," he said, reaching for her across the front seat and pulling her into his arms. It was a helluva lot easier than he ever would have imagined, especially since she practically leaped over the console to get on his side of the car.

God, save him.

Her arms went around his neck, her face into the curve of his shoulder, her ass wiggling down behind the steering wheel so she could sit in his lap—and she was still trembling.

"Yeah. A really big night," she whispered, then let out a long sigh, and some of the tension left her body.

"Do you want to tell me about it?" He was so cool, Cool Hand Hart.

"It was scary and gross."

"How gross? Do I need to go back in there and castrate him?" He took a deep, easy breath to keep from giving himself away—that it wasn't a rhetorical question.

"No," she said. "They left me my tool belt. Left it right on me. Can you believe it? I'd already cut through half my rope before he ever started to *disrobe*. By the time he got his fly open, I was coming around with my first right hook."

"Good." Low-key, that was him. He started the Humvee, turned up the heat, and let out his own big sigh, in hopes some of the tension would leave his body. "In case you were wondering, you're grounded for eternity after tonight's escapade."

Escapade. Now there was a parent word if he'd ever heard one.

"You're not the boss of me," she said, her mouth brushing against his skin, and suddenly his brain was flooded with sex, every cell. It washed down through his body like a river of heat.

He couldn't do this, couldn't be her parent, or her friend, or her lover. There was no way for him to be with her that was bearable.

But he could hold her for a while longer, so he could remember, later, what it felt like to have her in his arms.

"You lost your hat." And her pony band. He'd never seen her hair down before, and it was like a curtain of silk falling across her shoulders. He picked up a swath of it and let it slide through his fingers.

"They took my sunglasses, too." She turned a little in his arms, so she could look up at him. "They're still in the warehouse, I'm sure, but I don't want to go back and get them."

"Neither do I," he said, realizing his reasons were probably different from hers. "You're beautiful, Skeeter."

He smoothed his hand up the side of her face, then lowered his mouth to her forehead and kissed her all along her scar, the whole length of it, down to where it parted her eyebrow. He took his time, but without lingering. He inhaled her, but in a way she would never know, and he gave her his heart with every kiss, because he didn't have a choice.

"And you're more trouble than you're worth," he said. "Now get your butt on your own side of the car."

He was done with this. Tonight had been hell. They were going back to Steele Street, and he was personally taking Dominika Starkova to General Grant in Washington, D.C., and then he was going to spend the next ten years telecommuting.

"Dylan?"

"Yes?" He put the Humvee in gear and looked over at her.

"You're beautiful, too."

Finished. Done. The end.

As soon as Dylan had called to tell him Skeeter was okay, Creed had grabbed Cody and they'd run. He was only going to get one shot at getting her out of town, and this was it.

The library. Son of a bitch. He'd practically been sitting on a map to the warhead the whole time he'd been watching her up in Reference. Except the map wasn't shelved in the new library. She'd hidden it in the old section, in storage—which was perfect, because at this time of night, it would have taken a court order or a very theatrical, highly gadgetized B&E, breaking and entering, to get into the new library.

Getting into the old library was going to be a breeze.

The lock he'd broken on the side door to get them out? He could guarantee nobody had fixed it in the last few hours. It would probably be days before they even knew they had a security breach.

They parked Angelina in the garage across the street, right next to Cody's Saturn.

All the cops were gone from Broadway and 13th, so they simply crossed the street and walked straight into the building. It amazed him a little, that she'd left the book sitting in plain sight in a public place, and that virtually anyone could have walked in and walked out with it.

Flashlight in hand, she led the way through the stacks on the main floor, and in minutes, he was holding the fate of the free world in his hands. *Tajikistan Discontent.* It wasn't very big.

Their plan was simple. The books in storage were often old and outdated, but sometimes people needed old, outdated information, and a number of the volumes did circulate, so a librarian was always assigned to the collection.

They left the volume of poetry on that person's desk, marked for Inter-Library Loan, with Dylan's name, address, and phone number listed on the ILL sleeve.

It was almost dawn by the time they finished, and Creed just had one more stop to make before they could leave.

THEY'RE not upstairs," Skeeter said, striding out of the elevator into Steele Street's main office.

"Are you sure?" Dylan asked, not quite believing it. Creed couldn't have left, not and taken Dominika Starkova, or Cody Stark, or whatever the hell he wanted to call her.

He couldn't have. It was tantamount to throwing his life away.

"Dylan, I even looked under the bed, no shit, and they are gone."

Skeeter was panicked. He could feel it rolling off of her in waves.

He was angry, and blown away.

Creed couldn't do this, not to himself, and not to the people who cared about him—and Dylan doubted very, very seriously if that included Cody Stark. She was using him, and Creed was in this bad place in his head and couldn't see it.

She must have fucked him blind.

Shit!

"Where would he go?" he asked, and by God, he expected an answer.

"He's got family in Mexico."

"Mexico is a big place, Skeeter," he said, tight-jawed. "Get on it."

She slid into a chair in front of the bank of computers and had started to work, pulling up Creed's files, when the screen next to her came on, and a purple line snaked out of the lower left-hand corner across a black screen.

"Dylan, look."

He went and stood by her side as she typed in 4167 and a map came up.

"*Christ.*" He put his hand on her shoulder and felt a tremor go through her.

"I guess he had to say good-bye," she said, her voice so soft he could hardly hear her, but he didn't need to hear her; the whole story was written on the map.

"Come on." He gave her shoulder a squeeze and wished to hell he didn't suddenly feel so goddamned awful. "We better go get him."

SHE had a good memory. Not photographic, but good. Good enough to save him.

From where she was sitting inside Angelina, Cody let her hand slide away from the dashboard keyboard. She hadn't forgotten 4167, any more than he'd forgotten his friend.

He was still by the grave site.

J.T. Chronopolous. She'd read the headstone: *Semper Fidelis.* Always faithful. He'd been thirty-four years old.

God, she hadn't even known him, and she missed him. She missed him for Creed.

This was the right thing to do. She hated it, but it was the right thing to do. He'd saved her life, absolved her from her sins, and she couldn't repay him by taking away everything he loved, everything he believed in.

Before they'd left Steele Street, they had gotten the

news that Reinhard and Bruno the Bull were in custody. Ernst Braun had actually been shot and killed. SDF, the team of operators he worked with out of the building on Steele Street, were amazing. They'd saved the world, and saved her.

Leavenworth was a risk, but one she was willing to take with Reinhard out of the picture. She didn't know why. Patrushev was no saint, but he also had less to prove. He'd have to go to a lot of trouble to kill her once she was in the hands of the U.S. government, utilizing time and resources that could be better spent making money, closing the next deal.

When she saw the Humvee pull to a stop up on the rise, she got out of the car and started walking back toward Creed. She wasn't going to think too much about what was happening, or about what was going to happen. She had a couple of minutes left with him, no more than that.

"Hey," she said, sliding under his arm and going up on tiptoe to kiss his cheek.

"Hey, yourself." He opened his coat and wrapped her inside. "Did you get warmed up?"

"Yeah."

The cemetery was pillowed in snow, the headstones sticking up through the mounds of white, the trees stark against a sky that was quickly turning blue.

He'd pulled his hair back in a low ponytail and hadn't shaved. She ran her fingers over his jaw, feeling the stubble, and when he grinned, she touched his lips.

"I think I'm in love with you," she said.

His grin broadened, and he tightened his hold on her, wrapping her more securely in his coat. "Good."

OH, cripes," Skeeter said, looking up into the rearview mirror.

Dylan dragged his gaze away from Creed and Cody Stark where they were standing by J.T.'s grave, and glanced over his shoulder—and swore.

"They got a tracker on you, Dylan."

"Me?" *Crap*. "How do you know they didn't get it on you?"

"Because nobody gets one on me."

This was it, then. He looked back at Creed, who still didn't know the game was up. The woman did, though. He'd seen her walk away from Angelina. She was the one who had turned on the Chevelle's computer.

She'd given herself up, and he could only think of one reason for her to do that.

Hell.

He and Skeeter waited for Royce to reach the Humvee, before they got out. The two "negotiators," the man and the woman who'd been inside the warehouse, were with him.

"I see you brought your rats," he said. It hadn't been too hard to figure out. The CIA had positioned their own people inside the whole Blond Bimbo with the Bomb operation. They'd had their own buyers in place, and probably given them an unlimited budget to make sure they were the ones who ended up with Patrushev's nuclear warhead. Assholes. That was the frickin' problem with the frickin' CIA. They never told anybody what they were doing.

"Yeah, yeah. Meet Hansel and Gretel. Hansel and Gretel, meet Dylan Hart." There were no handshakes. "Is that her?" Royce gestured down the hill at Creed and Cody.

"Dominika Starkova," he confirmed as another car pulled up behind Royce's, a late model sedan, pure FBI. Yet another car pulled up behind the sedan.

Yes, it was going to be a regular party here this morning, a lynching party.

A grim smile curved Royce's face. "It's been a long night, Hart, a damn long night." He started down the hill.

Dylan grabbed him by the arm. "You better let me go with you, or you'll be dead before he realizes you're one of the good guys."

Royce thought about it for all of five seconds. "Yeah," he said. "Good idea."

SHE was crying. Creed could taste it on her lips. One minute they'd been kissing, and the next she'd started crying.

"Cody—" He lifted his mouth from hers and started to ask her why—but then he knew. He felt it, and then he heard it, the sound of a car door in the distance, the low hum of voices.

He had another fight in him, easy, but he wasn't going to do it. Not now. God damn it. It was over.

"You chose *this*?" he asked, furious and frustrated and trying not to freak out. He was holding her too tight. He could feel it, but geezus, he wished she'd done anything else. "Why? I don't know if—" He stopped, took a breath, tried to get ahold of himself. How could he explain to her that he needed her? That she wasn't optional? "We could have made it. I swear. I wouldn't have ever let them catch us."

"I know." She wiped her cheek with the back of her hand, and then she laughed, one short sound. "God, it was a crazy night, wasn't it?"

"*Crazy*." Fuck. It had been more than crazy, and he did *not* want it to end, not like this. He wanted to kiss her. He wanted to hold her. He wanted to *escape*. "You've got to give me an hour, Cody, an hour to get the book out of the library. Don't tell them anything."

She nodded.

He tightened his hands on her, thinking fast, thinking of what she needed to know. "They won't hurt you. Don't worry about that. Everything changed after the warehouse. They're not desperate now. They've pulled in a lot of the players. They've got you fair and square, and they'll stick to the rules."

She nodded again.

God, she was so beautiful, and he could hear footsteps in the snow behind him, closing in. He pulled her against his chest and pressed his mouth to her cheek, and tried to think of all the thousands of things he wanted to say.

But it was too late.

"You saved me," he whispered. "Thank you."

And it was over.

"Creed." It was Dylan.

He slowly turned around, letting her go.

There were half a dozen people besides Dylan and Skeeter. One man stepped forward and cuffed her. She didn't look at him, and that was for the best, but he didn't take his eyes off her, not until they put her in a car and drove off.

He waited a minute, and then he turned to Dylan. "Call Lieutenant Loretta. You've got a book at the library reserved in your name, and it needs to be picked up now."

Both of Dylan's eyebrows rose.

"She hid the map in the library?"

"Right in the stacks."

"Son of a bitch."

CHAPTER 31

LEAVENWORTH WASN'T such a bad place. As a matter of fact, it was about Creed's favorite place, especially the private visitor's room reserved for special prisoners and their special visitors.

It had taken him eight weeks to get his butt in here the first time, eight weeks of him and Dylan bribing every person they knew and threatening some of the people they wished they didn't know. General Grant had been a big help in the latter department. A general's threats had a way of getting people's attention, and Grant had been glad to throw his weight around. His team had saved the world from rogue nuclear destruction. His stock at the Pentagon was riding higher than a duck in the water. Nobody was saying anything about moving his office over there, but there was hope.

The secretary of defense was happy. General Grant was happy. Dylan was happy, and Creed was happy, or as happy as he could get until he could finagle his way into the extra-special visitor's room—the one with privacy and a bed.

"Conjugal," he said. "I'm lobbying the President."

She blushed, which he loved.

"You are not," she said, but the way she said it sounded like she had just enough doubts to worry her.

"I know you think the job is all about domestic policy and world domination, but the President actually has quite an interest in the conjugal affairs of certain high-security detainees in federal prisons."

He was so ridiculous, she laughed, and that had been the point. Prison wasn't easy. He didn't care how high up the ladder a person's crimes landed them.

She had shackles on her ankles.

He tried not to think about it.

"Dylan says one more month, on the outside." He was holding her hand. That's about all he ever did, and kiss her when he thought he could handle just kissing her, but he was careful with the kisses. They weren't alone, and the way he felt about her wasn't anybody else's business. His life had been irrevocably changed on that cold January night, and it hadn't been a fluke, or some crazed adrenaline junkie sex fixation. Time had proven him out.

She didn't respond to his announcement. She never did. She was careful with her hope, but he always let her know, and he always let her know that he believed she would be released. She'd saved the world. She was one of the good guys. The laws she'd actually broken were minor in comparison to what everyone had thought she'd been doing. In time it was all going to get sorted out. Time just wasn't moving fast enough, no matter what Dylan did. But Creed believed in Dylan, too.

"I took your mom to lunch last Wednesday," he said, saving the best for last, and then just basking in the transformation of her face. There was nothing like taking a woman's mother out to lunch to make her happy. Fortunately, for him, her mother was a really nice lady, and as an added bonus, if he held his head to one side and squeezed his eyes shut just so, she looked quite a bit like Cody. Consequently, her mother seemed to think he had vision problems. She'd asked him once if everything was okay, and he'd tried to be a little more discreet after that.

"Oh," she said, excited. "Where did you go?"

He plunged into the story, trying to remember all the details, which was incredibly difficult. Guys ate lunch. Women expected a whole helluva lot more from the hours between noon and two, especially if they were with a friend.

Cody hadn't been with a friend in a long time, but he was learning to be her friend. She'd told him all about what had happened in Prague, how the visit to find the father she'd never known had turned into the visit to the father she'd wished she'd never known. Life was funny sometimes, difficult, and sometimes really good— like now. Two months without her, and three weeks of twice-weekly visits with a woman he was so hot for he'd had to drain the jungle pool to keep from hurting himself, and he spent their time together chatting.

It wasn't even talk, what women did. They chatted, and it was an art, and he was getting it down, this way of weaving a whole bunch of things together until it didn't even make sense anymore and neither one of them could even remember where they'd started—chatting.

She loved it, and he loved her, but he was keeping that to himself, too. She didn't need his painfully desperate declarations right now. She needed his friendship. She needed to be able to count on him showing up every Monday and Thursday at eleven o'clock without fail.

And she needed to know he and Dylan and General Grant were dealing her an unbeatable hand. She was going to be released. She had to be.

Hell, the job he and Dylan had pulled in Thailand last month should have already gotten her out. Nobody had wanted to touch that gig, with good reason. It had been wet work and politics, and nothing was more dangerous or more likely to backfire on the world stage.

When the guard cleared his throat, Creed knew his time was up. He wanted to throw himself on the floor, but he didn't.

"Hey," he said, leaning down and giving her one brief kiss on her cheek. "I'll see you on Monday."

"Monday," she said, with way more hope in her eyes than he could handle.

So he got up and left, and he walked out without looking back, and he didn't swear when he heard the guard lock the door behind him.

No, he saved that for when he got in the car.

CHAPTER

32

Two months later

IT WAS A SHORT flight from Denver to Leavenworth, Kansas, and he'd done it God knew how many times in the last few weeks, but today was the last time he'd ever have to do it, and Creed was about ready to jump out of his skin.

He had a ring in his pocket.

He didn't know half the stuff Dylan had pulled to make this happen, but Daniel Alden, Director of the CIA, had sent Steele Street a bouquet of flowers that was so frickin' big, it took up one whole desk.

Dylan had done something, all right, and Creed didn't know what it was, and that bugged the hell out of him. He didn't know half of what Dylan was up to anymore, but whatever it was, it was keeping him busy. He hadn't so much as stepped foot inside Steele Street in twelve weeks.

Skeeter sure wasn't happy about it, and an unhappy Skeeter, he'd learned, was a dangerous Skeeter. Nothing worked in Steele Street anymore. The computers crashed, the elevators got stuck, batteries died, organic smoothies went bad in the refrigerator.

"Are you going to be okay while I'm gone?" he asked her.

They were under Mercy's hood, for no special reason, which seemed to describe most of Skeeter's actions lately.

"I'll be fine. *Cripes!*" She jerked her hand back.

"You have to keep your fingers out of the blower, Skeet." He wanted to help her, but if Dylan didn't want to come home, there wasn't a damn thing anybody could do about it.

"I know. I know."

Hawkins was coming home. He and his wife, Kat, had been traveling throughout the South Pacific for the last five months, on the longest honeymoon in the history of mankind, but they were settling back into Steele Street at least through the summer, until the baby came.

Babies. That was a whole other ball game. Creed could dig it, but first he had to get a wife.

He checked his watch and decided that getting to the airport three hours early was probably a smart move and not the sign of an overeager idiot. Visitation today. Release tomorrow. Never-ending paradise after that.

"You know how to get hold of me if you need me, right?" He and Cody were going to be gone for a long time, at least a couple of months, maybe even longer. They'd been planning the trip together. It had been something for her to hold onto, a fantasy to help her sleep, she'd told him.

The marriage idea was all his. He wasn't going to spring it on her all at once. He wanted to win her over first, cover his bases, that sort of thing.

"Homing pigeon. I got it the first time, Creed."

"The guy's name is Javier Bernal, and he won't like you referring to him as a homing pigeon."

"Hey. I saw the photo. That's all I'm saying. He looks like a pigeon."

Crabby, crabby Skeeter. "Your earrings giving you any trouble?"

She smirked, but didn't rise to the bait. The ruby-and-diamond crosses really did look good on her.

"I love you, but I'm not going to miss you," he said.

That finally got him a sincere smile.

She came out from under the hood and threw her arms around him. "Well, I'm going to miss the hell out of you. Say hey to Cody for me."

"I will." With luck, he'd be saying hey to Cody every day for the rest of his life.

CHAPTER

33

H<small>EY.</small>"

"Hey." Cody smiled and rolled over onto her side, not bothering to open her eyes. She wasn't ready to wake up, but she was always ready for him, the jungle boy.

"The sun's coming up."

"Hmmm," she said, snuggling closer, not exactly amazed at his news flash. The sun came up every day in their lost-world paradise, and him with it. The jungles of Quintana Roo on the Yucatan Peninsula were always hot, steaming with humidity, and most days it rained in the afternoon. The weather was wonderfully predictable, day after endless sun-drenched day. They swam in the river, ate fruit off the trees, and lived in a tree house hidden among the overgrown ruins of an ancient civilization.

She felt his mouth on her cheek, the silky weight of his hair brushing her skin, the warmth of his body stretched out along the length of hers.

"You're naked," she murmured.

He smiled against her mouth and slid her leg up over his hip.

"So are you." He pressed against her, and she let her eyes drift open. She loved watching him as he entered her, the way his hair fell down around his face and his lips would part, the dark light that came on in his silvery blue eyes.

"I lost my clothes again last night."

"Hmmm." He moved over her, pressing her back into the soft disarray of sheets and cotton blankets covering the bed.

"I think they fell out of the bedroom."

"Your clothes are always falling out of the bedroom," he murmured against her skin, and then pushed up inside her.

It was the loveliest way to wake up, so hot and sweet, and at the end, so achingly intense. She'd never dreamed she could be so in love.

When she woke up again, the sun had risen well above the horizon. A warm breeze blew across her skin and ruffled through the curtains that were the tree house's only walls. Pink and saffron, each length of cloth lifted in the wind. Every morning she felt like she was waking up inside a flower.

She stretched lazily in the bed, watching the river flow past their small beach. They'd fallen into the most somnolent existence, sleeping, eating, making love. They fished. They explored. They canoed, and they talked, a lot.

He stirred beside her, his hand curving around her waist. "I heard a jaguar last night."

"Close?" She turned to face him.

"Not really. He was about half a mile north of the Achka temple, before the clearing where we saw the tapir."

"And what were you doing half a mile north of the temple in the middle of the night?" He'd been by her side when she'd fallen asleep.

"Hunting," he said, then nuzzled her neck.

He hunted a lot in the middle of the night, just like the big cat.

"What did you get?"

"Breakfast, lunch, and probably dinner." He bit her, once, softly, on the neck, and then she felt him smile.

He'd gotten something big with his blowgun. She would have heard a shot.

"A deer." She hoped.

"Um-hmmm." His smile grew wider.

He still had nightmares about J.T., not so many. Sometimes he went hunting to work them off, sometimes he made love to her, and sometimes he just held her and they watched the stars.

"Where are we exploring today?"

"I think we need to go back to the Altar of the Moon," he said, referring to another of the stone ruins they'd found hidden in the jungle. "I think we missed something, maybe a secret entrance, or a buried stela."

He liked the adventure, and she liked him. It was more than love that bound them, more than the rings they wore on their fingers. Up until Prague, she'd lived her whole life in libraries, reading about what other people had done, all of her adventures coming vicariously. After Prague, and after Leavenworth, it would have been easy to crawl back into the safety of the book stacks and never, ever come out again.

But Creed lived, a hundred percent, every day, out in the world. When duty called, he answered. When things went bad, he survived and kept going, even when it was hard. She'd done the same thing after her father had died and her life had gotten so crazy—and the admiration Creed had for her was as important as his love. He made up adventures just to share them with her. He said it made them all worthwhile.

She felt the same way. Sharing with him, the nature child who never wore shoes, but never went anywhere without his Glock 10mm locked and loaded, had turned her whole life into an adventure.

"So you still think there's treasure there?" she mused aloud.

He grinned at that and let out a short laugh.

"Not really," he said, pulling her closer and kissing her

mouth once, twice, three times. "I just like hanging around the ruins, seeing what comes up, and seeing if I can get you to take your clothes off for me out in the jungle."

"You are so bad." She gave him a little push, and he caught her to him again, pulling her closer.

"One-hundred-percent pure badass to the bone, babe," he agreed, kissing her on the cheek. Then he leaned closer and whispered in her ear, "But you are *so* damn good."

ABOUT THE AUTHOR

Of the mind that love truly is what makes the world go 'round, Tara Janzen can be contacted at *www.tarajanzen.com*.

Happy reading!

Don't miss

CRAZY KISSES

Kid Chronopolous's story

ON SALE MARCH 2006

THE MISSION:
CRAZY KISSES
You can't turn down the heat on a mission this hot....
TARA JANZEN
Author of Crazy Wild

CRAZY KISSES

ON SALE MARCH 2006

Panama City, Panama

THERE WAS A BIKINI bottom in his bathroom.

Curious as hell, Kid picked the tiny scrap of green and purple cotton up off the towel bar and turned it over in his hand.

It wasn't unusual for him to come home and find somebody crashing at his place. He'd known the instant he'd walked in that someone was there. The house in Panama City had belonged to his brother, and J.T. had always had an open-door policy.

But the bikini bottom was unusual.

Combat boots, surfboards, cases of beer—that's what he usually found. Not outrageously green bikini bottoms with purple palm fronds printed on them.

It was enough to make a guy think.

About sex.

And about death.

He swore softly and put the swimsuit back on the towel bar. J.T. had been the kind of guy who took care of people, a lot of people. Some of them had been women, mostly friends, but a couple of ex-lovers had shown up over the last few months. Kid didn't think he could face one of them tonight, and have to be the one to tell her J.T. was dead. He still felt about half dead himself.

Easing himself around, he limped back out to the living room. The house was pure tropical bungalow, with two bedrooms, a bath, kitchen and dining area together, and a living room that opened onto a palm-shaded courtyard. It had lizards darting around outside, a housekeeper named Rosa who held the place together no matter how many unexpected visitors showed up, and neighbors who liked to party—tonight being a case in point. A salsa beat was coming from both sides of the house.

After his and C. Smith's adventure on the Putumayo, two days in a Bogotá hospital, and two days of debriefing with the DEA and the Defense Department guys, he wasn't in the mood to party. All he wanted to do was sleep in a bed he called his own. He hoped the bikini girl had picked the spare bedroom and not the one he usually took.

The thought made him pause.

Geez. No wonder he never got laid anymore.

He shook his head and continued on across to the breezeway and the south bedroom, the one he preferred, and sure enough, it was definitely *ocupado*. There were clothes everywhere, and girl stuff piled up on his dresser and draped over the chair, filmy stuff, bright colorful stuff, bits and pieces. The girl's suitcases were on the floor in a corner, and besides being the most amazing shade of crocodile-patterned hot-pink leather he'd ever seen, they were overflowing with electrical cords, makeup bags, and shoes, like a girl grenade had exploded and sent her clothes flying in every direction.

That thought gave him pause, too, sort of reminded him of something else, but he wasn't going to spend the effort to figure out what. He was too damn tired to sort through anything tonight. All he wanted to do was sleep, and one bed or another didn't really make much difference.

He turned to leave, when a small, torn white T-shirt hanging off the doorknob caught his eye, a plain white T-shirt with a paint smear on it—electric blue paint.

Everything inside him froze, except his heart, which plummeted into the pit of his stomach.

Impossible. It was absolutely impossible—but he knew that T-shirt, knew that paint smear.

His gaze slid to the clothes draped over the chair, and he saw something else he knew, a purple silk robe with a letter "N" painted in pink on the pocket. *Geezus*. He looked around the room at all the stuff. But it wasn't just stuff, and it wasn't just any girl grenade that had gone off in here. It was a Nikki McKinney grenade.

He picked up the robe, brought the silky material to his face—and her scent flooded his senses. Hot sex, warm love, all the memories were there, so close to the surface.

Too close.

Nikki was here, and suddenly, he was in over his head. Way over.

Why in the world would Nikki be in Panama City?

And had she brought the freakin' fiber artist with her?

Geezus. He couldn't take that. No way in hell.

He looked up from the robe and checked the room. No, this was a one-person disaster, from the Panama hat and pink and green striped sunglasses on his dresser to the pile of underwear on the bed. This was all Nikki, every square inch of it.

Underwear. Bed. Nikki.

And suddenly, he was wide awake, every cell in his body.

He dropped the robe back on the chair and headed out the door. In the courtyard, he turned toward the loudest music. Nikki would be at ground zero, which meant the Sandovals' walled garden next door.

Rico and Luis Sandoval were a couple of trust-fund twins whose daddy ran the biggest chain of car dealerships in Panama. They were great guys for a good time, a cold beer, and a Friday night poker game, strip poker if they could talk a girl into playing.

Kid always opted out of any Sandoval-brother scheme that included drunk naked women, but Rico and Luis wouldn't have had to use liquor or talk very fast to get Nikki in the game. There wasn't anything she liked better than naked men. Twins would be an irresistible bonus in her book.

Cripes. Nikki and a couple of Panamanian beach-boy hustlers with a marked deck. The thought had Kid limping at double time. It would serve Rico and Luis right if he just let her have them. They'd never get the drop on her, no matter how much they cheated, and once she pulled her "Gee, can I paint you naked" line on them, they wouldn't have a chance. She'd have them stripped out of their *machismo* faster than they could drop their skivvies. The trust-fund boys would still be looking for their balls come Christmas.

But he didn't want any other guys dropping their shorts for Nikki tonight, or any other night—Panamanian beach boys or fiber-artist fiancés.

A fiancé—how in the hell had he let things get so out of hand? How had he gone seven months without calling her? Without writing her?

He stopped by the gate in the wall—stopped and made himself take a reality check. The truth was, he knew why he hadn't contacted her. He knew exactly why he hadn't gone home at Christmas. And nothing had changed.

He wasn't the man she'd fallen in love with, not anymore, not even close, and there was no coming back from the places he'd been.

But she was here, and he had to see her. He wasn't going to fool himself into thinking she'd come to see him. He was the last person she would have expected to show up in Panama City, despite him owning the house. Skeeter would have given her the key and the official situation report: he was in Colombia, working out of Bogotá.

For the last seven months, no one except the men he was with had ever really known where he was or what he was doing. In the beginning, that had been Hawkins, and later another SDF operator, Creed Rivera. After Creed had finished his mission, he'd gone home, but Kid had stayed.

He'd stayed too long.

Colombia wasn't safe for him anymore. People were looking for him. They didn't know his real name or what he looked like, not yet, but that wasn't going to hold them off forever, not these guys, not if he kept doing what he'd been doing. The airfield on the Putumayo wasn't the first time *el asesino fantasma* had hit Juan Conseco's operation, and the drug lord knew it. News of the "Putumayo bounty" Conseco had put out on the ghost killer had hit Bogotá while he'd still been in the hospital. The cocaine baron wanted him dead or alive, and for half a million dollars, Kid figured Conseco had a pretty good shot at getting him.

It was a helluva lot of money, but Kid had done a helluva lot of damage, including a pair of sniper hits last month contracted for by the Colombian government via the U.S. Department of Defense on two of Conseco's top lieutenants, a mission so black it had been black-on-black. Which all made Nikki's presence even more unnerving, if that was possible—which, honest to God, it wasn't. He was already unnerved all the way down to his gut and his toes by her being here. The situation with Conseco only made it worse.

And wasn't that just perfect? He hadn't been

home five minutes, and the first thing he had to do was literally kick Nikki McKinney out of his bed.

Well, hell. At least now he had something to say that didn't begin and end with "I'm sorry." He'd said that to her so many times, especially when she was crying, and when they'd been together, she'd cried a lot. He had to admit that "Get your butt home" didn't sound much better, though.

He reached for the gate, then had to stand back when a couple stumbled through, their arms wrapped around each other, holding each other up on their way to the Ramones' place on the other side of Kid's yard.

From the looks of the two of them, a little drunk, a little disheveled, and both in drag with half their clothes falling off, the Sandoval party was in full swing—a fact proved when he stepped through the gate.

Every year, four days before Ash Wednesday, Panama City hosted *Carnaval*, a sexually charged, anything goes party leading up to Lent. Every Friday night, the Sandoval brothers did the same.

There were colored lights hanging in the trees, two transvestites crooning on a makeshift stage, well over a hundred other people crammed into the garden, some in costume, plenty of beer, and a bar serving *baja panties*—literally "panty lowerers," which in Panama translated to any drink made with hard liquor.

And there was Nicole Alana McKinney. He spotted her instantly. She was half in costume, with a pink feathered tiara in her black and purple spiked hair, and a blue sequined miniskirt with a matching stole to go with the top half of her green and purple palm-frond bikini. She had a *baja panties* in one hand and five cards in the other. Her back was to him, and she was sitting at a table with four guys, two of them Rico and Luis, one of whom was already down to a pair of tighty-whities and an orange feather boa.

It was like the living incarnation of his worst nightmare—or at least his nightmare before she'd gotten engaged. He'd never imagined that happening.

But this scene. Oh, yeah, he'd imagined it plenty of times—Nikki and a bunch of half-dressed guys well on their way to being un-dressed guys.

It was her work, taking naked guys and putting them through the wringer of her cameras and her paintbrushes until she got what she wanted, which was always more than the guys ever thought they'd have to give.

She was practically famous now, her paintings showing on both coasts and selling in five figures. Three months ago, she'd done an *Esquire* magazine cover of Brad Pitt as one of her fallen angels.

Kid had seen it in Bogotá, and it had been incredible.

Fucking Brad Pitt. Who would have believed? Nikki's mentor, Katya Hawkins, was taking her straight to the top of the art world, exactly where she deserved to be. He'd watched Nikki work once—work a guy over—and it had made him sweat and all but turned him inside out. He hadn't known a girl could be so freakin' fierce.

Yeah. He'd kept up with her career, with her life. He'd been discreet, but he'd kept up, asked a few questions. Her sister was married to another of the Steele Street operators, Quinn Younger, who hadn't gone out on many missions since he and Regan had hooked up.

It was a helluva price to pay for a woman, but under any other circumstances than the ones he'd found himself in last summer, he would have done it for Nikki.

She hadn't come straight out and asked him to quit his job, but he'd seen it in her eyes every time she'd looked at him. He'd known it every time she'd cried because he was going away. So freakin' fierce, and yet so fragile.

Hell, she'd probably made the right choice with the basket-weaver guy, but yeah, sure, he could have done it, left his buddies and turned himself into her boy toy, gone back to school, and become . . . something.

Something other than what he was—a highly

skilled weapon of the United States government. The months he'd spent with Hawkins and Creed, tracking down and taking out his brother's killers, had changed him. Superman and the jungle boy had changed him. They'd taken everything the Marine Corps had taught him and honed it all to a razor sharpness.

He wasn't a bona fide superhero, not like Hawkins, and he wasn't three quarters wild like Creed, but he didn't have to do much more than stand there and look at her to know he was still in love with Nikki McKinney.

God, what lousy news. And it didn't change a damn thing. It only made things harder.

He was going to have to keep his distance. Be professional. Stay cool. Play it smart. Get her back on a plane ASAP—and for God's sake not do anything stupid and spontaneous.

Like kiss her.

Or run his tongue up the side of her neck.

Or put his hand on her ass.

He took a breath, ran through the "don't" list one more time, and was good to go—up until she suddenly turned in her chair, startled like a bird taking flight, feathers flying, sequins shimmering, and looked straight at him. He saw the shock on her face, saw her mouth form his name, and his quickly laid plan started sliding out from under him like beach sand in a riptide.

In combat, "tunneling," focusing on one thing

and losing track of everything else that was going on around you was a good way to get killed.

Apparently, the same rule applied in love, because he was slain. The transvestites went into a butchered rendition of "La Vida Loca," and he could barely hear it. The other hundred people were laughing, talking, singing along, their glasses clinking, their sequins shaking, and all they were was a blur. Loose feathers floated in the air, beer spilled, women squealed—and all he could see was Nikki. All he could hear was his heart beating, slow and steady and strong. He knew what he felt, and there were no words for it. Not this.

Her tiara caught the lights and glittered in her wild, dark hair. Pure bed head, pink feathers, and a couple of purple streaks, strands going every which way. It wasn't an accident. She fixed it like that, moussed it and blow-dried it all into an artful mess. He'd watched her do it, teased her about it, kissed her between the moussing and the blow-drying—and loved every second of it.

She had five earrings in one ear and three in the other, always, and none of them ever matched. She sang in the mornings, and he'd been her first man.

All of that made her his.

He started forward, and she rose from her chair, her cards falling to the table, her hand coming up to her chest—a delicate hand with paint under the nails. There was no Nikki without paint. She painted men. She painted on her photographs. She painted angels and demons. She painted her clothes, and once, for him, she'd painted herself—in chocolate and caramel.

Oh, yeah. He was in way over his head.